RIVER ROGUE

by

BRAINARD CHENEY

MM John Welda BookHouse
2013

Published by permission 2013 by MM John Welda BookHouse

Eastman, Georgia   http://www.lightwood.com

ISBN: 978-0-9892491-0-2 (Hardcover)

LCCN: 2013936899

The Lightwood History Collection: Book 3

First Edition from MM John Welda BookHouse

Cover photograph: Timber rafters on the Oconee River in Laurens County, Georgia circa 1890, courtesy Georgia Archives, Vanishing Georgia Collection

To

ALICE AND BYRON

CAST OF CHARACTERS

In south Georgia, from 1870 through the 1890's, on the rivers Oconee, Ocmulgee and the mighty Altamaha, from the town of Riverton on the Ocmulgee to the port of Darien on the Altamaha, where the mighty river meets the sea, Ratliff "Snake" Sutton voyages out of the river swamps, onto the rivers and into myth

RATLIFF "SNAKE" SUTTON, heroic raftsman, the king of Darien

UNCLE MUNDY SUTTON, former slave, Ratliff's surrogate father
AUNT TISH SUTTON, Uncle Mundy's wife, root doctor, nurturer
POSS SUTTON, best friend of Ratliff, young black man on the run

BUD TRUE, legendary river raftsman and mentor to Ratliff
CHINA SWANN, madam of the Birdcage, true friend to Ratliff
ROBBIE MCGREGOR, society belle of Darien, then Ratliff's wife

GEOFFREY DALE, Oxford, Yale Law School, Ratliff's tavern
EDWARD DALE, father of Geoffrey, timber company owner
OLD MAN MCGREGOR, Darien kingmaker, Robbie's father

DIGGS MACMILLAN, Ratliff's tormentor, then his victim
SEBORN HENRY, China's benefactor, a man from Ratliff's past

ALTAMAHA pronounced ALL'-tuh-muh-HA'
OCMULGEE pronounced OAK'-muhl-gee (with hard g, long e)
OCONEE pronounced OH'-koh-nee

CONTENTS

PART ONE

Poss

CHAPTER

1

THE UNNACCOUNTABLE OCONEE RIVER was at flood stage on a late May day of 1884. A dugout, bearing a boy in its bow and paddled by a negro, moved over the muddy water of its swamp. Out of the woods the boat crept into the opening of an old course, marked only by the trunks of funnel-shaped trees. The woods and stream alike were not a part of the giant Oconee. Moss-trailed boughs still overshadowed their way, giving the water a cream-and-coffee color. Ratliff Sutton, the boy, cocked an ear to listen to the soft, growing roar ahead of him. An inlet from the swollen body to the branch came into view. He tilted his head to gaze through the gap and beyond, across the flat, seemingly still surface of the main stream. Its yellow plain stretched off to a far wood, and disappeared in dim, tree-framed caverns.

He dropped his face in a quick, uncertain manner and adjusted himself in the boat more carefully. After a moment he lifted his eyes again to the distance where the water glinted yellow under the sun. As he looked, a green tree split the hard surface. Boughs nodding, it moved rapidly, as if drawn by some great fish within the depths of the flood. The tree passed out of his view, leaving the motionless exterior unbroken. He continued to gaze fixedly at the river.

His head suddenly shifted to the right as the dugout advanced along the bed of the swamp stream. His bony, boy's shoulders straightened. With a quick motion he raised his arm, pointing at a distant pile of driftwood on a tangle of bushes. The curt hand, the tapering finger focused like a gun muzzle. He did not speak, or look back, but the young negro in the stern of the boat raised his eyes to the driftage and began to paddle rapidly.

When the dugout came alongside the log pile, Ratliff lifted a pike pole that lay across the bow and struck its point into a timber. His narrow face was intent and his big, loose lower lip moved in a mumble as he examined the partly submerged mud-and-trash-covered logs.

He turned back to the negro. 'Yep. Seven. Durn big uns!' His eyes had opened eagerly when he spoke. Now their pale lashes lowered and he looked goatwise down his tilted face. It had an almost nerveless stillness about it.

He stood up, holding the boat steady with the pike pole, and looked the length of the timber. 'Poss, this stuff is bigger than anything we've ever picked up. It'll run sixty foot, durn near it! And big as a bull's belly.' His gaze moved on beyond the logs and he glanced across the inlet to the opposite side. Suddenly he pointed again. 'Say, look!' He sat down quickly.

The nose of the boat swung left as the negro called Poss dug the paddle deep. His snuff-colored arms swung in swift, smooth rhythm, his wide, soft mouth spread in a smile. 'Lawd God!' Poss said.

The ends of the three great hewn timbers struck out from a muddy tangle of bamboo, muscadine, and twisted brush. He ran the boat up on them. Ratliff prodded avidly with his pike pole and brought out two more, making five in the find. Like those in the first pile, they were pine, hewn square and smooth.

2

There had been little talk between Ratliff and Poss throughout their day of log-hunting in the flooded swamp. But now the silence upon them was different. Then there had been no point to talk; now they avoided speaking. Each worked rapidly, getting the timbers out to tow and tying their ends together with hemp rope, though their attention was not on the work. They did not look at each other.

Ratliff's eyes were lowered as usual, but they did not stay on his task: they tarried with a straightening coil of rope, followed the swirling boils of the current, fixed upon the sleeve of his homespun shirt. His lower lip was rigid. Twenty-one ship timbers! twenty-one hewn ship timbers! twenty-one! he kept repeating to himself. And below the soundless chant a more hesitant consciousness was aware that twenty-one would almost make a raft. Nine at the boom, five on the way, and seven more to come! Always he and Poss had sold their occasional pick-ups to raftsmen, but those were twos and threes. This is practically a whole raft, he thought. A good start, anyhow. A good start down the river—a good start to—Darien! The vision made a sweat break out around his mouth, made his insides tremble.

They moved their skiff off down Dead River, the old course. Poss did not speak to him and Ratliff did not look back. He knew he did not need to look. The same vision held him. But they were not yet ready to talk about it.

There was only a lavender strip of sky above the tree-line to the west as Ratliff and Poss got home. Pale light gave a vague opalescent tone to the flood water covering the swamp-hemmed bluff field. From the woods they paddled rapidly toward a house set on piling and standing several feet above the water. It was oblong, with a great brick chimney, erected from the ground, at one end. Built long before the war for a fishing camp, its hewn cypress logs and shingles had weathered silver and gray. To Ratliff, as he gazed across the diminishing sheet of water, it looked like a land turtle trying to ford a pond. He had never seen the bluff covered so deep before.

3

They fastened the chain on their dugout to a post of the veranda fronting the house and got out upon a stairway extending into the water.

An old negro met them at the top of the steps. His insloping cheeks were copperish gray in the reflected light. He removed a battered wool hat from his head and scratched his fingers in his straight white hair. He spat out into the water and wiped the back of his hand across his straggly mustache. 'Look like you boys aimed to spend de night on de river,' he said casually, but without smiling.

The white boy and the young negro both looked up, then out at the gathering dusk in surprise. They did not speak, but stepped on the floor level with the old man. He was taller than either of them and stood as straight. Ratliff was a head lower than Poss and appeared slight beside the negroes.

He glanced sidewise at Poss, then spoke. 'Twenty-one big, hewn logs! Was that sump'n? Dadgummed near enough to make a raft!'

Poss took it up, his mouth spreading and his soft-textured cheeks gathering excitedly. 'Look, we found twelve of 'em right togedder deah at de upper end of Dead River—twelve de biggest uns you ever seen.'

'That's fine,' the old man said, still scratching his head. He paused and looked into their faces sharply.

Ratliff's lower lip tightened. 'Uncle Mundy, we got a big start on a pick-up raft to Darien.'

The old man slapped his hat back on and snorted.

'Listen heah, Unka Mundy,' Poss broke in. 'Dat ain't so alldacious as it sound. You know I done make three raft trips 'foh I come heah. Pullin' a bow oar. All de way to Darien.'

For a moment the old man turned and stared out across the flood water toward the dim fringe of the trees. 'Three,' he said finally. 'What dat! I made it regular for more'n forty year. Long 'foh de war—when de wa'houses backed up on Darien Creek look like Cotton

4

Mountain.' He raised his face toward the sky. 'Rain and sleet, long lonesome river—dey ain't no Sunday! I'm done too ole for timber-runnin', too ole.' He looked back with a jerk of his head. 'I ain't a-gwine on no raft!'

'But we ain't axin' you to go, Unka Mundy—we ain't inspectin' dat.' Poss's voice paused on the inflection. 'Me and Snake kin take down dat raft. Kain't we, Snake?' (Ratliff's hands jerked upward, but he did not try to speak.) 'I'm twenty year old and plumb grown.'

'Humph! A hell of a pair to sell a pick-up raft in Darien: a boy and a runaway nigger! Heah it is slap dark and y'all ain't tended to de stock!' Uncle Mundy had turned away and was walking into the house.

Mutely Ratliff and Poss unchained their boat from the porch and paddled for the tall log barn behind the house. They made haste, the reflected light from the water giving their bodies a floating undulance in the gathering dark. When they had turned the dugout into the breezeway of the barn, Ratliff fastened it to a wide ramp, ribbed with slabs and extending out of the water up to the floor above their heads. In spite of their hurry to do their chores before night, Ratliff held to the ramp a moment, feeling along its edge. 'She's two foot above my high-water notch,' he said, bringing his arm dripping from the water. A chorus of bawling from the calves in a stall on the floor above them drowned out further words and they got out of the boat.

The bawling broke off, then came again with renewed urgency. Poss mocked them with a great bellow that rose above the chorus. He shook his head from side to side so that his lips flopped and gave his voice a hoarse tremolo. There was a sudden and complete cessation of the calf-bawling. He filled in the blank. 'You just makin' that bellyache worse. Hold yoh mouths a minute and I'll give yuh a tit to put in it.'

Ratliff chuckled audibly as he moved across the dim hall toward the feed room. His laughter gave him a relaxed feeling behind the ears and a warmth spread inside him that made him feel close to Poss. You feel more kin to Poss sometimes than anybody, he told himself. Since Poss had come to live with them had been the best time of his four years at Uncle Mundy's. He had always loved Uncle Mundy next to his own brothers and sisters—and mother, he conceded—as far back as he could remember, when Uncle Mundy used to come to their house in Mount Vernon, bringing brown sedge for brush brooms. He saw Uncle Mundy as he had been then, sitting by their kitchen stove, telling him stories—about Ole Master chopping down trees on the Indians for a joke. Ole Master was Richard Perrineau, and Ratliff's great-grandfather.

'You gwine milk Ole Bess, or Lena?' Behind him Poss's voice interrupted his thoughts.

Ratliff chose Lena. Inside the feed room a pile of unshucked corn rose steeply toward the ceiling. It looked like a yellow shadow in the darkness. They sat down on it and began shucking.

'Uncle Mundy sho' talked short to us.' Ratliff broke through the rasping of the shucks. 'He ain't bin that short with me since I shot the heifer in the crabapple thicket.'

' 'Twaun't you, it 'uz me he 'uz gittin' at. He thinkin' 'bout kaze I bin in trouble I kain't leave dis swamp.'

The noise of the shucking went on evenly for a time. Ratliff threw an ear of corn across the room that hit the wall with a slap. 'Poss, we kin git that timber to Darien all right, kain't we?' His voice was high and quivered in the darkness.

'Sho'.'

'We kain't let Uncle Mundy back us down, Poss.' There was a pause, and Ratliff's voice was lowered when he spoke again. 'Ain't nobody ever bin as good to me. I come to him when waun't nobody I could look in the face. He took me in and it didn't make no difference. But he don't know I'm growin' up.'

They both got up off the corn pile and Ratliff spoke again as he moved toward the door with an armful of ears. 'I kain't stay right heah on Dead River, hidin' under a log like a mud puppy for the rest of my life.'

They put the corn for the oxen in their troughs and hurried on to the cows. There was no more conversation, but Ratliff, as he pressed his cheek against Lena's flank and pulled at her teats, muttered vehemently, 'Lena, Goddurnyuh, I'm a-gittin' out on the river—and I ain't a-runnin' from nobody this time!'

When they brought their buckets into the house, the milkers found Aunt Tish, Uncle Mundy's fat black wife, busy over the pots at the fireplace. They poured up their milk and came toward the fire. Uncle Mundy sat near it in a squat chair, his legs stretched out before him. They both took chairs alongside.

Poss spoke to him. 'Forty sticks like us is got 'ud make out a good-size raft.' Uncle Mundy's face did not change expression and he said nothing. Poss went on. 'If us don't pick up nineteen pieces of sump'n twixt heah and Darien it'll be kaze us dodgin' it.'

Uncle Mundy looked on at the fire. He spoke gruffly. 'And git caught by low water, piddlin' along som'ers in de Narrers deah—yo' raft hung up on a sandbar, you out of rations and fo'-mile of strange swamp on both sides.'

'We'd take my shotgun,' Ratliff said, 'and fishin' tackle.' He gazed absently at the misshapen fingers of Uncle Mundy's hands, crossed loosely on his lap. His lashes flickered, then he stared at Uncle Mundy's face with hard eyes. 'We've got to start runnin' the river sometime!'

Uncle Mundy faced them. 'I'm surprised at you, Poss,' he said irritably. 'You ain't got no business mixin' wid people on the river, naer gwine into Darien, nuther. You just as liable to git picked up as not, and you knows it.'

7

Poss raised his hands, holding them out before him in a stiff gesture of measurement. 'I done study 'bout dat—study 'bout it deep. Ole man Peter, who I made dem trips wid, is dead. Don't nobody know me on the river, nor in Darien. And don't nobody hardly know I got sont up yonder to de mines. When de trial wuz deah in Lancaster, de lawyer said dey didn't have no evidence ag'in me, as I done tole yuh. He said kaze I wuz in de crowd deah where dey killed dat white feller, de law would send me along to de gang, too. They had me deah and dey wouldn't break de rule.'

His hands dropped. 'It bin more'n a year since I left up deah and nobody's come lookin' for me. And 'sides, we aim to tend to our own business and not mix around none.'

Uncle Mundy resumed with his voice at the same pitch, as if Poss had not spoken. 'And if Rattler heah do de sellin' of de raft, where he gonna say he git it, who he gonna say it b'long to? No fifteen-year-old boy don't sell no raft in Darien, lessen dey knows whose boy he is. Nobody don't git to sell pick-ups lessen he run de river regular.' He leaned forward and spat a long stream of tobacco juice into the fireplace. 'Soon as dis water drap some we kin dam up de big slough and catch a barrel of fish—a barrel. And 'sides, we got to git some corn in de ground as soon as de field git dry enough.'

'I ain't fifteen: I'm done past sixteen,' Ratliff said, raising his eyes and then lowering them. 'We kain't git nuthin' for fish—even if you take 'em to Longpond. The raft'll bring us a hundred dollars or more. All the fish and corn, too, won't make a part of that. A hundred dollars, Uncle Mundy—maybe more! What's wrong with sayin' the raft's your'n? Everybody knows you got land. Me and Poss done talked all that out.'

Uncle Mundy glanced at Ratliff quickly, then looked away. He got up from his chair and walked toward the fireplace. Putting his hand to his mouth, he dropped his tobacco into it and threw the dry cud into the fire. He turned back. 'And wouldn' you look fine a-settin' out wid a raft on dis river!'

Poss broke in, his voice raised, his manner short and hurried. 'You know we don't aim to drift no logs till de river git down inside its banks—you knows dat. Us got to raft dem logs first, anyhow!'

'Hunh!' Uncle Mundy wiped the back of his hand across his mouth to straighten his spreading lips. 'How we gonna raft any logs wid de handle busted out'n my auger?'

Ratliff's eyes opened wide and the front legs of his chair dropped to the floor. 'Dadgum!' he said. 'Uncle Mundy, you sho' had me scared up.'

CHAPTER

2

RATLIFF stood at the oar of the raft. It moved down a reach below Dead River on an Oconee shrunken within its banks and swift.

Three days had passed since Uncle Mundy gave in to their persuasion, and Ratliff and Poss were now finally and irrevocably adrift. Uncle Mundy had helped them raft the twenty-one logs into a single square-bowed skiff and mount a sweep at the front. He had suggested a bow oar only: the raft was short and, moreover, Poss must break in Ratliff before an oar could be turned over to him. They had brought along axes, an auger, a boat, a gun, rations, coffee-pot and spider, and Aunt Tish had given them a ham already baked and a big pone of sweet-potato bread.

Poss had turned the sweep over to Ratliff to hold on the straight course, and he now stood with his hands upon it. His head was tilted and his eyes lash-hidden, as usual, but there was a sharp tension about his face and in his still grasp of the oar handle. The swamp trees, freshly coated with mud; the rust-red water, shimmering under the sun; the twisting current of the long reach before him, were all as familiar to his eyes as the breakfast table. Yet he looked at them as if they were strange and alien, as if he were measuring the length and strength of an assailant.

He gave the brim of his wool hat a downward yank. 'Them public scalers in Darien—do they root around yuh? Want to know a lot?'

Poss was squatting on the bow of the raft, intently regarding a right-angular turn in the river course ahead. His face was squinted and he did not immediately respond to Ratliff's question. Then, still looking off toward the current, he got up and, crouching a little, walked with measured stride toward the bow oar. 'Not like we got to root if'n us gits around dat damn Devil's Elbow down deah!'

Devil's Elbow! Ratliff hadn't realized it was so near. This crooked trough set the river writhing. He had run it in a dugout, but that was different. It was rough on rafts and raftsmen. He slipped his hands down the handle of the long sweep, pivoted on its bench at the middle of the bow. Poss took hold at the end.

The raft was a hundred yards or more from the bend where the twisting current lashed the low bank when they began their pull. Our first tie-in with the river, Ratliff thought, as he and Poss moved the oar to the edge of the raft for the stroke. They dipped its blade far to the left and walked across the raft, leaning against the handle. By the third step, Ratliff had fallen in with Poss's swinging stride, measured by the sway of the oar in the current. The river ahead had made him fidgety. He was relieved to begin doing something. The stroke complete, they swung the blade free of the water and brought it back to the starting-point. Then they dipped it deep and pushed their way deliberately across the raft again. Ratliff could see now that the raft had begun to turn slowly toward the left bank.

They were angling down on the bend. The rough current seemed to be jumping toward them. He felt the oar almost leave him as Poss bent against it. He had to run to keep out of the way when Poss swung the free blade back. The churn of the current quickened: they were bending the oar faster and faster. Now the lashing, twisting ton-

11

gue of water had them, shooting them toward the bank ahead: Ratliff saw this, though he did not have time now to see, or scarcely to breathe. They ran, their bodies bent like fishhooks, driving the oar pulsing through the current. The swamp bank began to move out of their way, the channel to round again into sight. The raft was almost crosswise the river. The stern was swinging out toward the right bank.

'We gonna slam! Be ready to hold 'er out!' Poss shouted. His mouth stayed drawn open, a black hole between gleaming blades of sweat. Ratliff heard a thud and crackle of limbs behind him. Logs wobbled, lumbered up on each other. The raft shuddered. But they had made the turn.

For a moment he stood with Poss at the left edge, panting. Then they dipped the blade to the right and began pulling the bow steadily in that direction to follow the horseshoe bend of the river. Their breathing spell had been brief. Now they were running with the oar again to make the point, the blade flashing in the sunlight. They glided on around the bend, nosing the bank. Then they reversed their stroke once more and the raft swung sharply around an opposite turn and out of the elbow into straight river. They slowed the oar to a stop.

Ratliff leaned limply on the handle and Poss, dropping down, lay full length on a log. Their mouths were open and their faces creased with hard breathing. 'Didn't bust a thing!' Poss heaved. 'Ole Devil snap he arm at us, but he didn't git nothin'. De water wuz just right.'

They had floated on for almost an hour and were approaching Bell's Ferry, when Poss sighted the first timber adrift: a big scab log, hung in the mouth of a slough. They pulled in toward the ferry landing and tied their raft below it. When they had paddled the dugout back, they found the log was short and had a windshake in one end, but they decided to bring it along. Poss thought it bad luck to leave the first log sighted.

They had meant to fill up their water jugs from the deep spring at Bell's Ferry and swap a little tobacco with Mahlon Huff, the ferryman (it would probably be their last sight of a home face, Poss had said), but when they got back strangers were at the bluff to be ferried across, their wagon piled high with household goods and tallow-faced children. Poss said Mister Mahlon would be busy and it was just as well that he did not run into the strangers, so he stayed on the raft. Ratliff went on up with the jugs, and later he was glad that he went: he had never seen any such folks before. A grown boy, a woman, and a girl were huddled together on the bluff with a patch of cypress-knee children behind them. All of them were staring at the river.

As he circled around them, looking them over, the boy shifted his feet as if they were hard to lift and grinned. 'Thought we'd never come to 'er, but she's plenty durn big when we git heah!' he said. The woman's face was hidden by a sunbonnet and the girl did not look up, neither at him nor at the baby squalling in her arms, but kept staring out at the current.

They had unhitched their oxen and the boy went to help a lanky man, whom Ratliff took to be the pa, pull the wagon down to the landing. As the wagon moved, Ratlifff saw a bare backside come over the tailboard and a little boy drop to the ground with his shirt about his head. A skinny girl followed him down. They squatted there look-ing after the wagon; then their eyes lifted to their ferryboat ahead in the still water, out beyond to the rough current, and on to the far bank that looked like a broken edge of corn pone in the distance. Rat-liff saw their mouths come open. Then they looked at each other and a hard swallow went down the girl's thin neck. He heard her say, 'So this is Comingter Oconee!'

The sunbonneted woman called to them from the ferryboat and they looked back, but they didn't move. They stared at the river with their eyes bugged out. The shirt-tail boy jerked up to his feet and yelled, 'Ma! Ma! Don't git on that!' The grown boy called them, and

13

took off his hat and started running toward them. They looked at each other quickly, then they broke and ran, the girl throwing her arms out and yelling, 'I ain't a-gwine on it!' Ratliff watched until they were out of sight in the swamp, and went on and got his water. It took the grown boy and his pa and the ferryman half an hour to catch them and tote them back.

The flat with its load finally got away, Old Mahlon swinging on his pole and shaking his clabber jowls. 'I'm damn tired of runnin' down young'uns for creek fo'ks,' he said. 'And these durn hoppers don't live more'n fourteen mile away from the river, up theah on Griddle Creek.'

Poss laughed when Ratliff told him about it. He said he would like to have seen the creek folks shy at the river, but it had been safer not to go, there was just a chance that the man might have been in the crowd at the Lancaster courthouse when he was tried.

About an hour's drift below the ferry they saw the longest log they had ever seen, but they had to leave it. It was a big, hewn pine, lying alongside the bank where the freshet had put it. A couple of turns would have dropped it in the river. When they had tied the raft below and came paddling back upstream, a white man was sitting on it, staring at them. His eyes looked like navels in his bulging face and he was as broad as a bale of cotton. He didn't have anything in his hands except a fishing pole, but they didn't slow up. They went on around the bend and waited awhile. He was still there when they passed back by. Afterward Poss said: 'Us sho' couldn't turn de log wid 'im a-settin' on it. And I waun't gonna ast 'im to git up!'

The sun was almost straight overhead as they reached the confluence of the Oconee and the Ocmulgee. Below them in the distance they saw the Altamaha, as broad and shining as the sky, and Poss raised his head and sang:

Look-a-yonder! Look-a-yonder! Yonder!
I see Sunday, I see Sunday—
Sunday, oh Sunday!

He turned the oar loose and cut a step.

Ratliff rested his hands on the handle and watched him, then looked off to the surrounding walls of swamp. There was still an echo of Poss's song. Getting out of the Oconee—with your raft together— was time to sing. Would the Altamaha turn out to be Sunday for them? It looked big as hell!

He glanced to his right up the smooth, gray mouth of the Ocmulgee. He didn't remember that it was so nearly straight. Its banks looked like shedded snakeskins. There was little here at the river forks that seemed familiar to him now, he decided. But on that other trip he had hardly seen it, had avoided looking at the Altamaha. It had been four years ago: that morning when he came around another of the endless bends of the Ocmulgee and saw suddenly before him the terrible spread of water below to his right, and the sharp point of the swamp above, and the Oconee churning in from a direction he hadn't expected it. The sight had addled his head.

But he had been so near gone. He had been on the river four days then, coming from home, from Nine-and-a-Quarter. The name seemed unfamiliar to him now, but it had been home. He thought of his mother's pink-checkered apron, and his older brother, Bob, coming from their stave mill with sawdust on his eyelashes, and little Mona's snaggle teeth, and that red, bald head . . . His face squinted suddenly, as if in pain, and his mind veered off.

He dropped his eyes. His gaze fixed on the current line dividing the muddier waters of the Oconee from the clearer Ocmulgee as they were joined into one river. That line was one thing he remembered. It had scared him. Then the Ocmulgee was the muddier. The Oconee was clear enough to see into for a few feet. As his boat had neared the edge of the muddy water, moving toward the clear, it looked as if he was going over Niagara Falls. The sudden close sight of it was like a falling-off-the-bed dream. But his head had been empty and numb, and his arms had been so raw and his back so broken in two that he couldn't get very scared. He suddenly recovered a sensation of that moment and his face twisted: the sickening, hard lump in the pit of his stomach that drove him on, to get away from it—to get out of the world!

He jerked his gaze loose from the current line, looked down the reach ahead. That ain't me any more, he thought. I don't even have the same name as the boy it happened to. I've grown up since then. There ain't goin' to be any more runnin' away. It's down the river now: down the Altamaha to Darien!

They camped that night at the bluff Poss called Barclay's Landing, passing up one place because other rafts were there. The Altamaha country looked strange to Ratliff, and it grew stranger the farther they drifted into it. The swamps were darker and the banks somehow looked different from any he had ever seen before. If they happened to be close by one and he looked across at the other, it gave him the feeling that he was going to get dizzy before his eyes could settle on it, though of course he never did. But picking up logs went better after they got into the big river. On the second day they found four, and six on the third, all hewn timber, except two round logs. And by the third day the sight of every deep bight ahead didn't give him the fidgets, waiting to begin the pull. They had a scare at a place called Jack's Suck, pulling till their tongues stuck out; and were hung up for most of an afternoon on a snag below Hell's Shoals, but the raft held together. The spread of the river at Beard's Bluff made Ratliff stare. Their raft seemed to shrink up in it. He felt different about the creek folks after that.

On the afternoon of the fourth day they passed a high, yellow-faced bluff with pines growing up it. Poss said it was called Ogle-

16

thorpe's Bluff and that a man by that name, a general, had jumped his horse over it to get away from some Indians—'way back yonder'. He'd never heard how he came out. And Poss caught him on a trick at Lower Bugg's Bluff. He bet Ratliff a dollar of the money they would get for the raft that he couldn't throw his knife up on top of the bluff. It didn't look so hard to do—the bluff was lower than Oglethorpe's— but when they came past, the raft swung right under the top of the bluff. Ratliff lost his knife, and dollar, too. Poss said raftsmen always got a first-timer on that.

They had been on the river almost a week when they got to the settlement of Doctortown. Here they spent a day re-rafting their timber into a two-section float and putting up a stern oar. Poss said they were heading for the Narrows and needed a stout raft under them.

That night, while they were lying in their blankets before the fire, Poss told him about Hannah's Island. He said a bunch of soldiers camping there during the War had a woman. They had all had her and she died. Her name was Hannah and they called the island after her, because her ghost haunted it.

Ratliff craned his neck up and looked closely at Poss.

Old Uncle Cicero Jackson had seen her, Poss told him. He had been fool enough to try to tie up there one night about dusk. There'd been others, but Old Cicero had seen her plain. He said that just as he went to jump ashore with his rope, he looked up and there she was, standing in the edge of the swamp, as white as a scraped hog and smoke pouring out of her belly. She said, "Throw me the rope, raft hand!"

Cicero didn't throw her the rope. He made Darien before he threw anybody that rope.

Ratliff didn't doubt that Poss had heard the story, but he had never seen a ghost and didn't believe in them much. Hannah's Island didn't look ghostly when Poss pointed it out next morning. In the sun

17

and pulling the bow oar by himself now, he was scareder of that damn monkey at his elbow.

Around noon Ratliff treated Rag Point. This was important, Poss told him. His luck as a raftsman for the balance of his life might depend on it. He had never heard of a first-timer who didn't treat Rag Point, so he couldn't say what would happen, but a rafthand needed all the luck he could conjure up and then some. When the raft neared the brush-and-vine-strapped woods of the point, Ratliff saw an array of shirts, hats, shoes, and a variety of torn pieces of garments on the bushes. He stood on the hip of the raft as Poss pulled in close and left his jeans jumper hanging from a crabapple bush in security of his future. Poss hung up an old rag handkerchief, too. They'd had mighty good luck so far, he said, and besides they had to make Old Woman's Pocket next day.

On the following morning, at a crook that was called Kneebuckle Bend and looked like one, a sunken snag dragged two big timbers out of the raft and they ran on almost a mile before they could find a place to tie up. Poss said they had to go back after them and Ratliff got into the boat, but he would have been glad to leave the logs: they had stopped so many times and had been so long in this strange, cow-itch-looking country. He was surprised, but heartened when they got by the pocket without losing any timber. They only slammed the point and roused some wasps in the bushes. He didn't mind the stings.

It was the tide that really wore him out: the tide, after almost two weeks of fighting all sorts of river current. It made him want to quit the raft and walk to Darien. They lost half a day at Swan's Lake and another at Cooper's Bar, waiting for it to change. Poss had stopped talking, except when he asked him a question, and didn't smile at all. It looked as if there wasn't anything ahead but marsh grass and crooked river that ran the wrong way. Uncle Mundy's words, *long, lonesome river,* grinned at his back as he pulled its crooks at the bow oar. And Uncle Mundy's slur, *a boy*, that he had thrown off with quick confidence then, came back to beat at his grip on the handle, at his grip on his doubts and fears. (He had sworn there'd be no more running away.) He began to believe there wasn't any such place as Darien, that it was just a name raftsmen spun yarns around.

Then they rounded the bend at Cathead Creek and he saw ahead a train of rafts tied up. He raised his eyes above the bow oar on his shoulder. Beyond the bend, high above the bluff, were the tall masts of timber schooners, like beckoning fingers.

CHAPTER

3

IT SEEMED to be every flathead for himself, and Ratliff felt relieved. He had observed that men were busy in little groups of three and four over the vast, winding corduroy of logs at the Public Boom. Occasionally someone moved about, but no group seemed interested in another. Ratliff stuck close to the public scaler who inspected and measured their raft, but he gave a fair accounting and asked few questions.

The scaler, followed by his negro log-turner, had just quit the raft when Ratliff noticed the man. He was coming up from the lower end of the Boom and was stopping along to talk to the men at work. He halted Ratliff's scaler on the Boom and had words with him, then the two of them walked across the intervening rafts toward Ratliff. Ratliff glanced at Poss, standing near the bow oar. He didn't like the look of this, either. The man came on directly without lifting his face, his thick body bent forward. His shirt fitted his chest and shoulders as if it had been pulled on wet.

He stopped at the edge of an adjacent raft with the scaler a little behind him. His small, deepset eyes studied Ratliff's logs. His face had the hard-packed look of a hickory nut. He looked up. He examined Poss, then Ratliff, closely, as if they were other logs. His lips twisted and he skeeted a stream of tobacco juice into the water.

'Boy, where do you say you got this raft?'

Ratliff had faced the men as they drew near, and he stood looking down his cheeks at them. Now he turned away without raising his eyes or speaking. His hands were poised at his thighs. He moved toward Poss.

'Where'd you git this raft?' the man barked.

Ratliff's hands grew rigid and he halted. He turned back. 'What's it to you?'

The man was studying the logs again. He turned to the inspector. 'That's my raft—most of it. Those hewn logs: I'd know Nigger Ned's work anywhere.' He spat into the water. 'Couple of green, no-'count raft hands run off and left it up at Hard Bargain.'

Ratliff had had a cold feeling in his marrow ever since the men approached and he hadn't known where to begin to defend himself. Now his lower lip tightened. Hard Bargain! Hard Bargain was on the Ocmulgee; their logs had come off the Oconee, most of them. The fellow's bluffing, he thought.

'Those hewn timbers are mine, boy,' The man looked back. 'Where'd you git hold of 'em?'

Ratliff did not speak. His eyelids and lower lip had a swollen look. His forearms, at his thighs, were lifted a little and he was moving slowly backward toward Poss and their pile of supplies. He wondered if he would have to try—would have to use his shotgun. By God! I can, he thought.

The man was talking to the inspector again. 'I got the word next day, but befoh I could git down theah to save my life, the raft wuz stole. What's this boy's name?'

The inspector said that both the white and the black were named Sutton.

21

The man raised his voice again, not loud, but harder. 'Sutton, you don't' think for a damn minute, do you, that you can bring my timber in heah and sell it under my nose—my own logs that I've put money out to have hewn?'

Ratliff stopped. His eyes were suddenly open without his seeming to have raised the lids. They were fixed on the man, still and unblinking.

'Ain't naer stick of it your'n! This raft belongs to my uncle. Hard Bargain ain't never seen it. It come off'n the Oconee—at his place on Dead River. He didn't come along 'cause he's sick. I aim to sell it for 'im and take the money back to 'im. And I don't aim to be bothered.' Ratliff resumed his slow backing away. 'Not by you, naer nobody else!'

Men coming up from below stopped and looked on. One of them called out, 'Diggs!' Ratliff recognized him: Uncle Mundy had once sold him two pick-up logs. The man laying claim to Ratliff's raft answered to the call, walked back across the logs to meet him. They talked in voices Ratliff could not overhear. Finally Diggs turned away from the newcomer, saying out loud, 'Just what I thought.' He beckoned to the inspector, who had started away. 'Listen at this—I want you to hear it.' He was moving back across the logs toward Ratliff, saying as he came, "I'm gonna git these heah dirt-eaters told!'

He stopped, stuck his thumbs in his belt. 'This uncle you're claimin' so big is an old swamp-rat nigger: Mundy Sutton. Hangs around Dead River, fishin' and stealin' people's hogs. And you are the white-trash, renegade boy that lives with 'im—lives theah in the swamp with niggers, in the house with niggers—in the bed with 'em, too, I reckon.'

He gripped his belt harshly. 'You're nuthin' but a white nigger—livin' with nigger swamp rats that never had a stick of timber they didn't steal in their lives. You kain't name yore pappy, naer yore mammy, and you're just the same as a nigger!'

Ratliff's eyes had wavered when the man said he was a renegade boy, then dropped as he went on. Now his lip trembled. His eyes opened again in a hard squint. 'That's a Goddurn lie!' he said shrilly. He stood still, not saying anything more for a time, then his hands opened and shut. They seemed to jerk him into motion. He turned toward the pile of supplies and Poss. 'Where's my shotgun?' he said hoarsely.

'You kain't run over me like that—just 'cause you're a man and I'm a boy!' He looked at Poss. Poss sat on the gun, trying to cover it with a croker-sack. His face was ashen. 'Gimme my gun, Poss!' Ratliff's voice was labored, spent, as if the wind had been knocked out of him. Poss shook his head and did not move.

The man's hard voice cut in. 'You ain't bluffin' nobody with that gun talk. There ain't gonna be no shootin', naer fightin', neither—not with a white-trash boy. This is my timber, you stole it, and I'm gonna swear out warrants for both of you.' He turned and walked back to the Boom.

Ratliff and Poss stood looking at each other with fixed, drawn faces. Finally Poss's glance dropped to the logs. His lips shook when he tried to speak. He looked off toward the man's disappearing back. 'Us gotta git out'n heah, Snake. Now!'

Ratliff's eyes were still on Poss's face. He was twisting his hands together so hard the fingers were white and purple. He spoke in a measured monotone. 'I'm not gonna leave this raft, Poss—I'm not gonna leave it—I'm not gonna run.'

'You knows I kain't let the law pick me up, Snake,' Poss said softly.

Ratliff broke his hands apart. He choked and spit hard, clearing his throat. 'I know it, Poss—I know it—I know it!' He knotted his fists before him. 'It's git out—ag'in!'

Poss moved about the raft, picking up the coffee-pot, the spider, the auger. He opened the mouth of a croker-sack to put them in. 'I guess us kin paddle de boat back up de river, if us gits away,' he said, without looking up. Ratliff got the axes together. He did not reply. It's Poss, it's Poss's old trouble, he told himself, but he could not stop a feeling of a relief coming over him, like a sweat cooking his body.

The inspector had not left with the man called Diggs, but stood watching them. Now he spoke. 'Bud, it looks like you are in trouble – bad trouble.' He rubbed his flaring nose. 'This may be your raft, but Diggs McMillan's got the advantage of you. He's known around here, got friends, and he'll make out a case against you—he won't stop at anything.'

Ratliff and Poss stood looking at him. He ran his hand into his pocket slowly, hunching a shoulder. 'Got any money?'

Poss shook his head.

The inspector looked at their dugout tied at the edge of the raft. 'It looks like a pretty good boat. I'll tell you, I'll give you five dollars for it. That will get you back home.'

He glanced away down the river. 'The *Sapelo* is at the Magnolia House wharf, getting ready to go upriver now.' He drew a banknote from his pocket and held it toward them. 'You all just leave the bill of measurement heah on the raft. I'll keep my mouth shut about where you've gone.'

Poss took the money. Ratliff continued to stare at the man; it seemed as if he could not look away. Then he swung the axes to his shoulder and turned his back upon the raft. He felt an old nausea coming over him.

The *Sapelo* made Darien River at high tide, crossed Cooper's Bar, and rounded Piney Island and headed up the Altamaha. Ratliff sat in the bow of the lower deck. He sat cross-legged, looking off at the green-topped marsh grass, the blue wild hyacinth, the dim swamp caverns. Poss lay a few feet away with his head on a croker-sack. From the rear of the boat came the sound of the stern-wheel's heavy churning. Ratliff did not see the shore, he did not hear the beat, Poss was not with him.

Before him was the hard-packed face of Diggs McMillan, saying: 'You white nigger! You kain't name yore pappy near yore mammy!' It had stared at him a long time. 'You stole it. . . . Not with a white-trash boy!'

Now another face was superimposed upon it. Ratliff knew the face. His gullet jerked with hard swallowing. Mace Rawlins was looking at him from the main street of Nine-and-a-Quarter: 'What yuh gonna call this heah kid of yuh ma's? What's his last name? Looks like yore pa's lease done run out befoh this un come.'

Again he sensed that first confusion in believing that he had not heard Mace right. The man had never spoken to him before. Then he knew for a second time the feeling that his clothes had suddenly been jerked off him, exposing privates strange and red, like a scorpion's throat—not like those of other boys; that the suspicion about his mother he had not even admitted to himself was true, and the whole town was talking about it.

Then there came that flow of unreal fire from outside him that moved through his whole body, lifted him like a burning piece of paper, and his seeing, in the flash of it, that he must kill his mother, his bastard brother, that he must kill the man who did this to them, that he must kill Mace Rawlins. It had only been a moment, then he was floating cinder; everything had gone black.

Mace, Diggs: the two faces became one. 'You white nigger, what you gonna call this kid?. . . You kain't name yore pappy.'

The *Sapelo* halted at Everett City, roustabouts trucked boxes down the gangplank, the whistle blew, the boat started again. Ratliff did not know it had stopped. There came to him that feeling of weakness he had known when he awoke in his bed at home after the meeting with Mace; that feeling of a body on top of him, smothering him, that he could not, would not strike at, try to throw off. Then the cold, sickening realization that he must slip out from under it, must run away—that he was running away. The feeling of running away, always running away! Ratliff clamped his arms about his middle, his shoulders heaved. He leaned over the side of the boat and vomited.

Night came, but the retching kept up. Finally, he lay on his back in the darkness, shaking with a hard chill.

CHAPTER

4

RATLIFF was hurt dumb, Uncle Mundy said later, and that was the meanest sort of hurt to ever get over. When he and Poss came back from Darien, plodding across the field toward the house, Poss swinging on to his sagging croker-sack and Ratliff toting the axes and gun, Uncle Mundy had called out to them. 'Well, dey did git back—de same two boys!' he yelled. But he had had time to look them over closely before they got to the steps and he had seen trouble. He had seen they weren't the same two boys, not Ratliff, at least. His face looked as if it had been soaked in alum water and wrung dry; it was bloodless and there was a bluish tine around his lowered eyelids and his mouth.

He had not smiled at Uncle Mundy's greeting and had not stopped at the steps, but climbed the long flight at the same plodding gait and disappeared into the house. A few minutes later, Uncle Mundy had seen him going on toward the barn with a milk bucket on his arm. He had brought in the milk, had left the pail on the back porch, and had gone back to the barn. Except to bring in the milk, he had not come out of it for the next two days.

Uncle Mundy did not attempt to approach him and made Aunt Tish stay away from the barn. ' 'Tain't nuthin' kin be said,' he told her when she started to take cold supper down to him. It's like the second time a fellow lets liquor throw him, he thought, studying the tobacco twist in his hand before cutting it.

His memory presented that first time: he saw again a peaked, white-faced boy, limping across the yard—he had seen it was Rattler before he got close, had seen it was trouble, too. That time, Rattler had talked, after he'd got him set down before Tish's washpot fire. Words had come, and the shakes, and crying, too, a little—and the boy had leaned against his knees. Uncle Mundy thought of the limp shock of hair he had laid his hand on. He hadn't seen or heard of him since his folks moved to Nine-and-a-Quarter—hadn't been thinking about him, or about white folks at all. All the white folks who had any claim on him were dead and out of the country, he had believed. It had come to him slowly, he had had difficulty making out what it was all about. And the boy was addled. No wonder: he was worn out and fevered up, and those words were hard for anybody to speak. Uncle Mundy heard again the treble voice, felt it pull at his insides.

He put the chew of tobacco in his mouth. But he had been able to comfort him then. Run away was the only thing to do, he had told him; he could stay as long as he was a mind to. He hadn't foreseen that Rattler would be here four years later, but it wasn't a thing he'd ever felt against. The boy had looked to him as if he were an old sow 'coon; and he reckoned a 'coon had never thought more of her young-gun.

But when a fellow gets thrown like that twice, he thought, there ain't any good talking about the puke on the floor.

On the third morning Uncle Mundy pulled Ratliff out of the hay-loft before daybreak. His manner was impassive, but his words were terse. 'Git up, boy,' he said. 'Work's done crowded down on us heah.' Ratliff obeyed mutely. Uncle Mundy set him to breaking the mud-

28

caked field with a gopher plow. He hitched both oxen to the plow and let Ratliff work alone. Then he went into Longpond early, taking Poss with him, and did not return until nightfall.

Except for the tobacco patch, which he and Aunt Tish had already set out, Uncle Mundy turned the farming over to Ratliff. With supervision and occasional help, he bedded the field, planted the corn, sweet potatoes, sugar cane, and watermelons. Tending the eighteen acres with an ox team was a full task for a grown man, but Uncle Mundy rarely lent a hand, and he kept Poss out of the field until gathering time. From can till can't Ratliff plowed, planted, hoed, fed the stock, moving in an inward-lived silence, not unlike that of the oxen he followed.

When he continued to sleep in the hayloft, Uncle Mundy told him that he would floor one of the stalls in the barn and fix him up a room, fix it up with a bed and a washstand and the piece of looking-glass from the back porch. Ratliff lifted his eyes for a moment and met Uncle Mundy's gaze, then a faint flush came over his face. 'I'm comin' back to my own bed as soon as I git over these nightmares,' he said.

After laying-by time Ratliff took a new hold, it seemed to Uncle Mundy, and joined Poss in setting out trotlines on the rising river. Poss wasn't sure: it looked to him as if Ratliff's lower lip had got bigger and stiffer during the summer, and he still wasn't cracking his mouth hardly. But Poss did see him warm up and talk, too, before fall weather stopped their fishing.

His shouts had waked Poss then, where he nodded on the river bank over their fishing poles. He had found Ratliff walking excitedly this way and that around the edge of the slough near Cypress Spring. Ratliff said he had seen an alligator, lying in wait at the spring, catch a half-grown deer. The fawn had just wagged her tail and put her muzzle down to drink. 'I never seen him move till he had 'er,' Ratliff said, batting his eyes and breathing hard. 'The ole 'gaitor lay there

like a log all afternoon, but come time and he moved like lightnin'!'
He talked on, halting Poss once on their walk home to say, 'I'd never
have believed a 'gaitor could catch a deer if I hadn't seen it.' His excitement kept him going through supper-time. Poss couldn't say that
after that afternoon Ratliff talked so much more, but he was changed
somehow.

It was near Christmas before he heard Ratliff laugh, laugh like a
boy—standing there by the tree with the lightwood torch shaking in
his hands so that it almost dropped, while he tried to get up out of
the brush. Poss had been just under the hole in the tree that he aimed
to ram his pole through to get a 'coon, he said, when the son-of-a-gun
shot his paw out and grabbed him by the hair. He had turned loose.
He was twenty feet up, but underbrush broke his fall. Ratliff hollered
so hard he couldn't' help him to his feet, swore that he, Poss, had
dangled there for a second with the 'coon holding him up by his wool.
Poss said he didn't mind Ratliff laughing at him, he was so glad to
hear the laugh.

But he didn't hear such outbursts often. Ratliff's thoughts were
still too much about himself for mirth. The trees were putting out
leaves when he finally brought his solitary harassment to a head,
closed his mind hard and fast, open to no more of his womanish back
talk. It was a late March morning and he sat on a log looking down
the barrel of his unbreeched gun. Before him lay the young gobbler
he had killed, whose feet he had been examining. The tiny spurs only
backed up what he had already suspected. Twenty feet away lay the
hen the gobbler had been treading when he fired. It had been luck to
catch them treading. Long-chance luck! But he was not cheered: the
heavy feeling of harassment lay just behind his thinking.

He stared off at the sleek feathered bundle. Hens have been responsible in a way for your string of beards this season, he told himself, long beards from old, long-spurred gobblers. They came through
the swamp to his call because they were hen-less. The hens picked

young gobblers, because their treading didn't hurt. It's just like you thought. A girl's, a woman's way! He had never killed a hen before: Uncle Mundy was against killing the hens. He lifted his gaze, the feeling of his violation passing from him.

This is not a turkey you've killed, not a turkey, he told himself, and his hands quivered so that he could scarcely breech the gun. All fall, all winter you've been hiding in Uncle Mundy's swamp, in his house, telling yourself that you were not going to dodge anything. Daring the world to come run over you where you knew it wouldn't come. Picking tenderfooted gobblers, staying clear of those with spurs. Like a hen turkey. By Godamighty, that's done now: shot dead! You're not quitting Uncle Mundy, damn it! And you're not hiding behind him, either!

Ratliff walked out to the hill beyond the edge of the bay and picked up an armful of lightwood knots. He made two trips, bringing the wood back to the log where he had sat. He built a pen of the wood and laid the turkey hen on top—pausing a moment to look at her and fix her wings like folded hands across her breast—then piled other wood around and over the carcass. You're going out on the river, up it and down it: you're going out to tangle with the long-spurred gobblers! The blazing match in his hand caught the splinters in the pen, then spread to the lightwood knots.

But he did not have to go out on the river to meet the spurs of outsiders. Within a week he encountered them no farther away than Uncle Mundy's front porch. Three white strangers were on the steps and Uncle Mundy sat with them, talking. Ratliff took a seat at a distance, on the porch bench beyond Poss. Poss told him in a hurried whisper that they were the Dickerson boys from across the river. He had heard of the Dickerson boys. He wondered what they could be coming to Uncle Mundy about. Their faces looked hard and bright. He had not seen any white people that close in months.

The biggest one stood just below Uncle Mundy, his right foot three steps above his left, resting his forearms across his knee. He was doing the talking. He mopped his forehead and Ratliff thought he had never seen such yellow hair before, nor such a fresh, meaty-looking face. He was telling about their feeding sturgeon stew to their hogs. It had ruined the pork, he said, and his ma had her dander up. He said they couldn't bring any more sturgeon on their place. There had never been such a good run of sturgeon in the river and they were getting two dollar a gallon now for the oil at the market.

Uncle Mundy told them that sounded like a heap of money, that he'd go shares with them to boil out the oil in his big yard kettle. He was gazing down at his knees. He looked up and his face kindled. 'Look-a-heah, dis spearsin' fish is sort of a new trick to me—I'd like to see it done.'

The biggest Dickerson grinned. The other two, sitting on the steps with their backs toward Ratliff, hunched their shoulders. Poss leaned forward, half out of his seat, and spoke excitedly. 'Dat's gittin' like de Injuns—I sho' want to see dat!' The two seated Dickersons twisted their faces around toward the bench where Ratliff and Poss were sitting. But they did not look at Poss, they looked at Ratliff. It was a cold, curious look, he felt, that lasted as long as manners and self-possession would allow. His own mouth and nostrils stiffened. The Dickersons have heard about you, he told himself.

Uncle Mundy smiled. 'I'll go in wid yuh,' he said, 'if you let me and de boys come along and see yuh spearse some of dese sturgeons.'

The biggest Dickerson's lips were still stretched in a grin 'The boys?' he echoed, and looked toward Ratliff and Poss on the bench. His gaze met Ratliff's. The grin on his face slackened. He seemed to be unable to look away for a moment and Ratliff saw a tinge of color at his neck. "Oh-h sho'!' he said finally. 'All y'all can come along. We're going down to the lower shoals right after dinner.' He halted, then added, "Course after today you all will be busy boiling out oil.'

Ratliff looked after the Dickersons as they walked away toward the bluff fence. They were big fellows, except the one with the red hair. The two big ones now grabbed the red-head by each arm and the seat of his pants and pitched him over the fence. Ratliff found an unintended grin on his own face. Something about those fellows took him unawares. But he knew the Dickersons had no use for him. Right off, they don't like my livin' with Uncle Mundy, he thought. He could not keep from feeling astonished at this. They had been respectful toward Uncle Mundy and they like him, Ratliff could see that. During the past year he had told himself many times that Diggs McMillan's abuse in Darien had been just to get his timber, but he knew better now—had known better all along. He rose from the bench and yanked up his jeans breeches. I'm goin' to learn how to gig those sturgeons, he told himself, Dickersons or not.

In the excitement of watching the Dickersons harpoon the fish on the shoals that afternoon, Ratliff forgot their dislike until a late hour. They were already after their prey when he and Poss and Uncle Mundy got there. Bartow, the oldest, stood in the bow of a flat-bottomed punt and threw the 'iron', as they called it. The top fins of the sturgeon stuck out of the shallow water. Bartow aimed his iron above the fin. Peter, the middle brother, paddled the boat. Ratliff couldn't see that red-headed John did anything much, except get in Bartow's way. In two hours they landed three, eight to ten feet long. Ratliff had never seen such wrestling matches: those fish ripped the river wide open when the gig struck them, and pulled the boat after them.

Bartow had put Peter out on a sandbar to take Uncle Mundy for a round and show him how it was done, when the thing happened to remind Ratliff about the Dickersons. Peter picked up one of their irons that had been lying on the bar, got in the bow of Uncle Mundy's batteau and coiled the rope at his feet. Then he nodded to Poss, 'Let's see if you can put me on top of a big un.' He had looked past Ratliff as if he were not there. Ratliff's head tilted backward; he looked down his cheeks and swallowed hard.

Later, as they were leaving the river with the fish loaded in the Dickerson wagon, he almost had hot words with John. Ratliff had picked him out because he didn't seem much older than himself. John was trailing behind his bigger brothers, as they put their irons in the wagon. He had his across his shoulder. Ratliff tried a smile and said, 'You mind a-lettin' me see how it feels in my hand?'

'Hunh?' John stared at Ratliff a moment with a stiff face. 'You speakin' to me?' Then he turned abruptly toward the wagon where Bartow stood and said, 'Le' me put my iron in, too.'

Ratliff's eyelids clapped down and he felt his neck swell. This red-headed snot was too much to stand. I'm goin' to knock hell out of him in a minute, he thought.

But Bartow turned it off. 'You can look at mine, Sutton,' he had said, and Ratliff felt there was reproof for John in his voice. But the next day Bartow was as hard of hearing as John, and when Ratliff asked to be allowed to gig a fish, he walked on by him without a word, looking down at the sturgeon they had just hauled ashore.

It took Ratliff's courage to keep up his face, not to show anything, and that one time with John he hadn't been able to. The Dickersons were using a buggy whip on him, they were cutting him every chance they got. And those lashes hurt worse afterward, at night when he lay awake in his bed thinking about them. They rankled worse then than when the cuts came. But he hadn't run, he hadn't thought once of taking off by himself for the back swamp, he hadn't let himself. I ain't quit, and I ain't goin' to quit! He repeated his resolution silently as he and Poss paddled their batteau toward the lower shoals mid-morning of the third day.

And he had made headway, in spite of the Dickersons. Bartow had tried not to hear him on the afternoon before, but Ratliff hadn't let him get by with that. He had blocked Bartow's way as he walked back to the boat. 'I said, "Let me try it once," Mr. Bartow,' he had repeated. And he had tried it, from the bow of Bartow's boat, and on the third throw he had hit a sturgeon square in the back, two feet above the fin. The iron had held and they had hauled him in, a good big one. It was all the chance he wanted: he had got the balance of the iron from a stance in the bow of the boat. I can hit with it, I knew I could hit with it, hit as good as Bartow even with a little more practice, he thought. I'll show the Dickersons I'm as good as any of them—by durn, better than John!

It was John who put heat into this resolve, kindled Ratliff's insides with an anger that needed no spur of words, even before they had quite reached the shoals. John's voice came across the water. He was speaking to his brothers, though Ratliff suspected that he wanted it to carry to him. 'Here's that albino nigger again with the other one,' said the voice.

He and Poss pulled their boat out upon the sandbar below the shoals and sat in the deep shade of overhanging tupelo trees. The Dickersons went on with the pursuit of sturgeon without taking notice of them. Ratliff had said nothing to Poss when they heard John's voice and he did not talk now. He stared after the Dickersons with a hard, squinted face.

Later, when John told Poss to paddle him awhile and they got into the batteau, leaving Ratliff alone on the bar, he felt no slight. I wouldn't have paddled him if he had asked me, he thought. But he couldn't sit still: he had to get at John somehow. Following the boat's course upstream from the edge of the bank, he watched to see his bad marksmanship. When John missed his first throw, he felt rewarded. Poss paddled hard toward the far bank where the sun shone on the shoals. A big sturgeon was flopping over shallows that made his back shields glisten. John, urging Poss to paddle harder, threw his harpoon too soon. Ratliff knew it when he saw the shaft leave his hand. The iron made the fish's tail , but it tore out when he and Poss leaned

35

back on the rope. 'You bullies too stout!' Ratliff found himself yelling. 'You ought to go whale-fishin'.' This helped him, even though John acted as if he didn't hear. When John gave too much slack on the rope and a fish got away from him, Ratliff told him to get the owl butter off his hands. He had smiled when he said it but it brought fire from John. The boat was not more than ten feet away. 'You dang little albino squirt, I'd like to see you hold one,' he said.

Ratliff paused a moment to get a grip on himself. By God, he had wanted this! He managed a halfway grin. 'Gimme a chance and I'll show you!'

When John pulled into the current near his brothers with Ratliff squatting in the bow of the batteau, he called over to them, 'Says he can hold one by hisself!' Ratliff's lip stuck out and he did not smile. He was coiling the rope carefully between his bare feet. He reached the end of the rope and held a length between his hands studying it. He glanced over his shoulder at John, then slipped the end under his shirt-tail.

A moment later a low roll appeared on the dingy surface of the river a dozen yards ahead of the boat. Ratliff came up quickly, balancing on the balls of his feet. In his right hand he poised the harpoon above his head. Moving toward the rapids, the boat gained on the ripple. The fish was upon the shoals and a fin split the surface. Ratliff stiffened, his shoulders jerked forward like a spring and the iron was in the air. In front of him a geyser rose higher than his head and the rope rasped through his hands, spinning out down the river. He dropped to his knees, braced himself behind a seat, and held onto the rope. Seventy-five feet ahead of the boat the staff of the harpoon stuck up above the foamy water. The sturgeon was pulling the batteau along.

The two elder Dickersons had put their boat into the eddy and were looking on. Poss, sun glare glinting his teeth, watched from the sandbar.

The sturgeon gave up his heavy haul, the rope went suddenly slack. Ratliff came to his feet and grabbed it in arm lengths, trying to bring it taut again. But before he could take up the slack, the harpoon appeared even with the boat and shot off toward the bank. The rope jerked taut again, catching him off balance. He went overboard, his legs spread like a slingshot handle.

The elder Dickersons shouted their laughter. John yelled until he was weak and couldn't paddle the boat. Poss laughed, too, when he saw Ratliff's head appear above the water. It was only chest deep on him. He grinned and pulled on the rope. He looked about for the boat, but before he could move toward it, his body jerked forward, his head split the water like a skittering rock and disappeared in spray.

The big fish shot to the surface above the shoals, raised a spume upstream, and then sank. A moment later Ratliff's head came out of the water twenty yards from where it had gone under. He brought the rope up in his hands and began pulling on it. Bartow yelled, 'Stick with 'im, Sutton, stick with 'im!' And Poss echoed, 'Hold 'im, Snake!'

John paddled up now, but had not covered more than half the distance to Ratliff when his head disappeared again in spray. This time the wait was long. Poss waded into the river toward where he had gone down and the Dickerson boys got quiet. Then Ratliff's head popped up once more. His face was blue. He took a great gasp of air and threw up an arm, but he did not call for help. Poss yelled for him to turn the rope loose, but he was gone again too quick to have heard him.

The sturgeon came to the surface and plowed back down the shoals. Ratliff made the top twice at a running jump, but was pulled under; then the surface stilled.

'That little fool's goin' to drown himself—you better stop 'im!' Bartow yelled to Poss.

'I'm scared o' dese holes: I kain't swim,' Poss said.

37

The surface roiled once more, Ratliff shot up through it like a ram and made great gasps for air. As he went down, he flung both arms above his head. 'Gawd!' Poss said, and waded after him, yelling for John to bring the boat. Thirty feet away, Ratliff's head came to the surface just long enough for him to gag once. Poss was in the batteau now, and before John had covered the distance he dived in and came up with Ratliff and the rope. The water was only chin-deep, but Ratliff couldn't stand. Poss rolled him into the boat. They made it to the sandbar with the sturgeon still fighting at the other end of the rope.

Bartow and Peter helped Poss pull the fish in. He looked almost as long as the boat. Ratliff lay gagging and heaving on its bottom, and couldn't help. Then John found that the end of the rope was tied around his waist. 'Look-a-heah, this pumpkin-head's got the rope tied to 'im!' he shouted, pulling at it.

Ratliff came weakly to his knees, still coughing. He loosed the rope and let it drop.

'You held 'im all right,' John yelled. 'You couldn't turn 'im loose!'

The elder Dickersons laughed and Bartow said, 'But the damn little fool's got nerve.'

John stepped out of the boat and turned away. 'I've always heard albinos didn't have good sense.'

Ratliff did not look up. He remained bent over the gunwale, heaving and coughing.

CHAPTER

5

IT WAS that dose of drowning that brought out Ratliff's spell of ma-
larial fever, Aunt Tish said. He had a pretty tough case, tossing about
on his pole bed in the loft for over two weeks. Aunt Tish's tonics were
slow to take effect. First, she tried mayweed, and later rue, and she
gave him a good dosing of pennyroyal oil all along. The fever slackened in the mornings, but practically every afternoon and evening he
was out of his head. His wits went woolgathering, like they will with
the fever mad. Uncle Mundy knew this, but it troubled him to hear
Ratliff muttering about being an albino nigger, a white nigger, and
calling the Dickersons sons-of-bitches.

'Dis ain't no place for dat boy to live,' Uncle Mundy said to Tish
one night after they had left Ratliff asleep and had come down the
ladder to their room. 'Still I don't know whar is.' He let it go at that
for the time, but he brought it up again a few days later. They could
turn their little old place over to Ratliff—in a way he had a claim to it,
he said. They could stay on and run it for him, in a white folks' way.
But when Ratliff's ma heard about it, she and his older brother would
take it over, and Ratliff would pick up and leave, would run off
somewhere. That time his ma had come, when Captain Henry

stopped the *Asher Ayers* at the mouth of the Dead River to set her and the oldest boy off, Ratliff had run and hid in the swamp. He wouldn't see either one of them. Uncle Mundy rumpled his white hair and stared into the fire on the hearth. 'I thought when us come down heah in de swamp us 'uz through wid white people,' he said.

Ratliff's fever finally burned out, leaving him feeling weak and watery. For days he lay about the house and on the porch bench meddling with his doubts. The moss in the big trees beyond the yard fence was heavy and dark. The odor of fish oil still hung around the place, though the boiling had ceased. It was a rancid smell that seemed to cling in his nostrils. His sturgeon-gigging had made him look like a pretty big fool: tying that rope around his waist. He hadn't used any judgment. Nerve to do things was just plain fool, without the sense to figure them out. It was no joke to pull water into your lungs!

One afternoon, dozing on the bench in the sun, he dreamed that he saw himself a fish-white corpse, being dragged from the muddy water. It woke him up and he shuddered for a moment after he could see the porch shelf in front of him and the white dogwood trees in the crook of the fence. That sturgeon might have drowned me—would have, I guess, if Poss hadn't been there, he thought. You reckon you really would have drowned? he asked himself. Could it have happened to you? He doubted that the Dickerson boys would have done anything about getting him out. They didn't have any use for him. Now they see me for a fool, he thought. I didn't make much headway with them. Hell, I didn't expect to! He pushed himself upright on the bench, fastened his jeans galluses and walked slowly into the house, knowing within himself that he had expected, had hoped for such a thing.

But Ratliff had to doubt his judgment of the Dickerson boys—at least Bartow—and of his own appearance in their eyes, when the oldest Dickerson stopped by the following morning. He wanted Poss to paddle him across the river, but he said he had come by to see how Ratliff was, too. Ratliff was sitting on the steps, pulling ticks out of Ring's ears, and didn't even look up at Bartow at first. As Poss came down the steps with the paddle to go, Bartow said, 'All you got to learn now is how to hold a sturgeon: you don't know how to turn one loose!' He laughed, and finally Ratliff limbered his mouth in a sort of smile. He was so astonished he had been slow to take it in.

Later he decided that he'd got as good as a dogfall out of his wrestling match with the big fish. In September it got him a job cutting logs for Wright Wilton across the river, or so Poss said. Wilton had come to get Poss, but when Poss told him he wouldn't team with anybody except Ratliff, the farmer had agreed: Ratliff was sort of a light weight, but he had heard he wasn't a quitter.

Ratliff said Poss was the cause of his being hired; still he felt heartened. It was headway, even though it took him into another cow-itch thicket. He had to figure on making his way through cow-itch thickets now. But he found work in Wilton's woods unlikely smooth. The only other choppers were four negroes. And he didn't see much of them, except the big one called Jedge who bunked with him and Poss in an old cabin in Wilton's back yard. He found no one to gall him; he was left alone. There was a good stand of timber, hill pine, and he blazed away beside Poss with a stout axe. Poss said he didn't have to slacken up at all for him. Ratliff said there was no 'possum like Poss, but nevertheless he knew that he was good with an axe, and just about a man now. When noon came Saturday, he and Poss had made nine dollars and a half between them.

Waiting about the cabin for Mr. Wilton to get there with the money to pay them off, Ratliff decided that he was a white man to deal with. He seemed always friendly and he had no curiosity for anything but the work he hired a fellow to do. When he did look at him, Ratliff felt, he looked at him just as he looked at everybody else. That was what let Ratliff in for it with the Wilton children, when he saw Mrs.

41

Wilton scrubbing them on the back porch. She was giving the three of them their Saturday wash; however, it was the middle one with the cotton top that put him in mind of himself. The little chap liked playing in the tub, but when Mrs. Wilton gouged into his ear with the washrag, he hollered. She held him by an arm and kept digging with her finger until she was satisfied, as if she didn't hear his squalling at all. Then, when it was over, she laid his head in her lap and leaned down and kissed him while she wrapped a towel around him. It was just the same way it had happened to him. He felt a soft, warm trembling inside him. Sideways, Mrs. Wilton looked like his mother, too. She was fair and plumpish and had a soft mouth.

He broke away from the cabin window quickly and walked out into the yard toward the barn lot. Aw, hell! What brought that up? he asked himself. You don't have anything against Mrs. Wilton: why make out she looks like that woman! It was just he hadn't seen a lady so close since he left Nine-and-a-Quarter.

Still, when the children came out into the yard, dressed in their clean clothes, he was moved to offer the cotton-top an alligator tooth he had in his pocket. He sat in the doorway of the cabin. The bigger boy and the littler girl each wanted a present, too. They gathered about his knees, the girl taking hold of his breeches-leg. He grinned at them and began to search through his pockets. Then he looked up and saw Mrs. Wilton coming across the yard. Her mouth wasn't soft now: it looked like a slice in her face. She snatched the little girl up in her arms without even slackening her lips and shooed the other two before her. They didn't want to go. They asked why they couldn't play with the white boy who lived with colored men. Ratliff, still staring after them with his hand half out of his pocket, caught it full force. 'I'll tell you when I get you in the house,' she said.

When Mr. Wilton handed him and Poss each four dollars and seventy-five cents, under the big oak tree by the gate, and, looking over his spectacles, said, 'We want to git an early start Monday,' Ratliff did not reply. But he knew he wouldn't be there Monday, nor any other day; that he'd never come within sight of Wilton's place again. He was not angry with Mr. Wilton, he felt no anger. He could not have put into words what he felt. He had nothing to say. Going down the road, Poss asked him if the old man had short-changed him, but he couldn't talk to Poss, either, then. Somehow this thing with children seemed to have cut more ground out from under him than anything that had happened.

When Uncle Mundy told him the next morning that he would need him to gather corn, he did not mention the log-cutting. He said he'd be on hand. One afternoon while they were pulling ears an odd memory came to him: his dream of the past spring, the image of his own corpse. He hadn't known that the dream was still in his mind; he wondered about it. He had the sudden thought to leave the swamp, to go away. Where would I go? he asked himself. He could not answer this. Nothing inside him told him to go, or to stay. Once a thing had taken hold of him and shown him what to do, but he had not been able to do it, he had run away. And he had backed down a second time before Diggs McMillan: it had not been all this backing down. Still he had felt sure again last spring; he had believed that he was going to run the river, as soon as he had made a chopper and logger of himself. Now he did not know.

Aunt Tish was taken before they finished gathering corn and the question of leaving, or even of cutting logs, was put out of his mind. She didn't get up one morning and Uncle Mundy said she'd had a stroke. Ratliff went in to see her, she was lying there on the bed as if she were dead, looking smooth and flat and sealed up. When he spoke to her, she didn't make any sign, except one cheek twitched a little bit.

Uncle Mundy cooked up an herb mixture and tried to feed it to her, but she couldn't swallow. Ratliff thought she was dying. He got worked up: it looked as if Uncle Mundy was going to let Aunt Tish lie

43

there and die without doing much about it. He asked him why he didn't go get the white doctor that lived out from Bell's Ferry, and when Uncle Mundy just looked off toward the kettle on the fire, he yanked on his hat and said he was going to get him. Uncle Mundy grabbed Ratliff by the arm and held him steady. Ratliff saw that his mouth cut square behind his mustache.

'Boy, you don't know what you're about!' he said. His eyes remained fixed on Ratliff's face, but there was no look, no light, the gaze was not there. Ratliff stared. 'No white livin' made 'er sick, and no white doctor kin cure 'er,' said Uncle Mundy. Ratliff felt his cheeks tighten, a creeping in his throat. Uncle Mundy loosed his arm, looked down at the kettle. He seemed tall and shadow-marked to Ratliff. He went on: 'I knowed a long time she love deer meat too good: and me, too. 'Tain't nuthin' a white doctor e'er hyearn of. Ma tole me when I 'uz a boy. She 'uz three part Cherokee and knowed all about wild meat, and how to cure its rheumatism.' He looked up. 'If dese yerbs don't cure 'er nuthin' will.'

Ratliff nodded his head slowly. The thought of a white doctor seemed childish now. Later he wondered about Uncle Mundy and his medicine. He got the stuff down Aunt Tish, but she didn't seem to get better, she still couldn't raise her head. He remembered having heard his father speak of 'nigger medicine' and laugh about it. But he left the doctoring to Uncle Mundy. Uncle Mundy stayed close by Aunt Tish's bed. Ratliff and Poss did the cooking, and they went ahead with cutting sugar cane and getting it ground, and killing hogs when the first cold snap came. After a month Aunt Tish began to come around. She was out of bed before Christmas. She kept on dragging one foot, but she got where she could handle the pots on the fireplace all right and took over the cooking again. On New Year's Day she cooked them a big mess of collards and black-eyes peas by herself. Ratliff didn't have anything to keep him around the house now. He was free to go back to log-cutting, or anything else, but he kept waiting.

On a late February afternoon a hard rain overtook him not far from the mouth of Dead River. The leafless trees didn't turn water and he halted at the old steamboat boiler that stood part buried in the mud. He leaned his gun against it, while he squeezed through the door to the firebox where it was dry. He had no more than pulled his arms inside when the half-light became black dark and he heard the clank of the iron latch. The door had swung easy and steady on its hinges and the latch had fastened solidly, as if somebody outside had shut it.

He got a jolt: the dark and that clank of iron. For a moment he couldn't believe what had happened to him; then it came over him in a full clear flash. He went as stiff as a mink in a trap. Without even breathing, he moved his hands to the door carefully, eased their weight against it and pushed. The door gave a little, then stopped, scraping against the catch. It was fastened for fair, locked solid. He was locked in the firebox of the old steamboat boiler, two miles from home, off any road except deer trails, where even hunters rarely passed; walled in close by riveted iron, the only door fastened, locked—and no key! He wasn't saying these things: they were shooting up in his mind like torchlight. Gooseflesh made a ridge down his back. The cheeks of his buttock sucked together, shooting exquisite pain through him, and cramped in a knot. Fright, panic snatched at his self-control. He felt an impulse to yell, to scream.

This all happened in the first ticking of silence. Then he took hold of himself: tightened his chest and belly, clamped his teeth together until his lip hung loose. You can't act like a boy here, he told himself. What the hell? Take it easy! You got to keep calm and think. He remembered his gun outside the door that he hadn't had a chance to draw in after him. Godamighty, if I just had it I could shoot it off through one of the boiler tubes, he thought. But that didn't help him.

The gun might help just as much outside, if Poss or Uncle Mundy ever saw it; might help more than shots in a rainstorm. Yes, sooner or later they would see the gun. Likely they wouldn't get worried or start a hunt before morning. Guess you won't starve before morning, he told himself. His grin came stiffly. You sure got yourself into a hell of a tight squeeze!

Twisting his body half around, he looked behind him. It wasn't quite as dark back there. A vague light came through the tubes. He felt the walls with his hands as far as he could, then kicked the back end with his feet. Solid. Well, he'd known that already: it was just sense to be sure. Of course Uncle Mundy and Poss would find the gun. Seeing the gun, they wouldn't know he was in the boiler, but he could sure let them hear about that. He'd have to keep yelling regular, but no sense in trying to yell against this rain. He wondered if they could hear him through the roar of the downpour, if they happened to be looking for him now. Hell, they won't be looking for you for hours yet, he told himself. Of course they'd find the gun. He kept telling himself this, bringing every uneasy line of thought up short with it.

But time suspended in the roar of rain. The downpour was deafening; sluiced the images of Poss and Uncle Mundy from his mind. The sense of his confinement grew on him. He was alone, buried in an empty swamp, a swamp of deaf trees, mud, water—blind rain beating down on top of his jail. There was no eye, there was no ear to the swamp; there was no God in any of this! Thought did not form: it came to him in a gradual, overspreading feeling that smothered him. He had to shout; he shouted. His voice went off in a long river yell. He heard a flat muffled echo. He hallooed again and again. His voice grew louder, rose higher. It broke, and he dropped his face upon his arms and buried his teeth in the muscle. Hot sweat poured off him and steamed up in the darkness.

Uncle Mundy won't start out before morning, Ratliff repeated to get hold of himself again. Hell, the place is dry, you've spent worse nights. 'Tie up your raft and cook and eat,' he muttered aloud. 'You're acting like a ten-year-old!' Cook and eat: not hungry, but I could sure use a drink of water, he thought. That rain outside didn't help any. He pushed the door against its latch with his chin and felt along the upper edge with his tongue for water.

A recollection came to him like discovery: Make Hawley had sent word to Poss the day before to come to see him about cutting some timber. Poss might have gone during the afternoon, taken the job and stayed at Hawley's. Uncle Mundy may think you're with Poss, he told himself. May not find you in a week! The thought jerked at his ribs, but he controlled his alarm. There won't be any timber-cutting as wet as the woods is; anyhow, Poss wouldn't go off on a job without letting you know. It's just the waiting. You got to quit letting this thing pull at your nerve.

He thought of a dog straining over his business and two boys pulling hard on their little fingers, crooked together, to keep him from ever getting through. His lips were stiff and he licked them. He remembered pulling fingers on Old Lady once with a little hairlipped boy called Fooit. That's what somebody is doing to you now, he told himself. Maybe, the Devil and Aunt Squatty! He lay on his side, feeling the harsh iron-rust particles in his throat.

Hell, you've had to hold out when there seemed to be no end, before! There is that night—just about the time you were pulling fingers with Fooit—when you had these gripes that liked to have killed you. You wouldn't wake ma, because she was sleeping in the bed with pa and he was coming off a drunk. It has never taken daylight longer to come than that night, and getting-up time even longer.

Godamighty, the bends in the river coming from Nine-and-a-Quarter to Uncle Mundy's! You had no more idea than a jaybird how far it was by river when you set out. Coming down the Ocmulgee, you

47

thought several times that you'd run by the mouth of the Oconee and were on the Altamaha. And after you got on the Oconee, you got mixed up enough to almost believe you were on the wrong river. It was just about as bad on your trip to Darien, down in that low, marsh-grass country. The Altamaha meandered around through it pretty nigh to eternity. Dang it, even when you had hold of the sturgeon and couldn't turn him loose—you were dragged through the water when it looked like it was breathe or bust, but you made it to the top—all but that last time. Yeah: that last liked to have been drowning!

Fleetingly, the fish-white corpse of his dream slipped through his mind. Sweat kept trickling into his eyes. He wiped his brow with his shirt-sleeve. A question slipped past his guard, too: Did the dream mean this? He faced it with hard thinking: What are you scared of? Drowning's not so bad. After your first sucking-in of water with the sturgeon, it felt like going to sleep.

His sense of rain washing over the roof in tubfuls became a torture. His mouth was full of cotton and his throat ached. His ears buzzed and his brain got foggy. But I knew what was coming all those other times. This thought grew with the fog. He had known there'd be daylight, that Uncle Mundy lived on Dead River, that there was a Darien—yes, he'd known that he could only drown! This thing might go on forever! Already he couldn't guess how many hours he'd been here: it must be daylight again. And Poss and Uncle Mundy had not come. The firebox was hot, smothering. It may mean perishing for water, or starving to death, he thought—his tongue was swollen—he opened his mouth and panted—or going crazy!

The drumming of the rain gradually slackened. It ceased. Ratliff shook his head. The buzzing cleared out of his ears. Now another sound came to him, a soft roar: the freshet. The river was still rising! He shut his mouth, caught his breath. There was a noise breaking through the roar. It sounded like—by God, it was—voices! He filled his lungs for a shout, then paused. There was the sound of heavy feet, then a voice almost abreast of the boiler: "Ef'n us don't git out'n dis swamp . . .' Ratliff cut loose without waiting! 'Boys! I'm in the boiler! Locked up!'

'Lawd Gawd!' he heard in a swooshing sound that came from the belly. And: 'Jesus!' The beat of feet was faster. He could hear the breaking of underbrush. His pulse receded with the sound. He drowned out the sound: he shouted for them to come back. 'This Snake Sutton! Just Snake, that lives with Uncle Mundy!' He yelled, he pleaded. He lost control of his voice, himself, and he shrieked. Finally he lay limp with exhaustion.

When Ratliff roused from his semi-sleep and stupor, he thought at first that he was in his bed at home, and that the roof above him leaked. There was the roar of rain. His head cleared. The roar was not rain, it was the river! The freshet was pushing into his firebox! He paddled his hands in the watery mud. The action seemed to loosen his muscles; the cold water calmed him. At the rate the river had been rising, the freshet would probably cover the firebox before day-light. Damn it! Why go crazy about it? You have only drowning to face! The thought was a relief. He wondered why God, or whoever it was, wanted him drowned. That wouldn't make any difference when the water came over him, he guessed. Still he couldn't help feeling incredulous. Once he had believed there were things he had to do before he died. The iron taste hurt his throat.

At first he thought it was the chill of the water. Then he knew that a strange current, at once fire and ice, was spreading upward through him from his belly—into his legs, his arms, his neck, his face. He found it familiar: he had felt it before, long before, on Main Street in Nine-and-a-Quarter. There was numbness, then he was floating. Now he saw the firebox at a distance, in a pale blue light, and himself hunched before its door. He was digging with his knife in the mud. But he saw that he was calm: he was singing, 'I see Sunday.'

49

Suddenly the door to the firebox swung open, and there was a black oblong of night. 'Come outside!' a voice said. At first he took it to be Poss's, then Uncle Mundy's, but there was a tone he remembered as his father's—yet it was not his father's voice either.

Then Ratliff knew that the cold creeping up his arms was real, that it was muddy river water, and that he was again in the darkness of the boiler. He had never been out of it. The freshet was still coming. This did not disturb him. He felt a hard-ribbed assurance, for now he knew, he had been told: it was not his time to die.

At three o'clock in the morning, when Poss opened the door of the old boiler and Uncle Mundy bent down with his lightwood pan to give light, they found Ratliff squatting inside on his all-fours, the freshet up to his armpits. Poss said, "Kin you git out, Snake?' And Ratliff squirmed silently through the door. He straightened up, but without looking at either of them, or speaking, he took the axe from Poss's shoulder and turned back to the boiler. Uncle Mundy had waited for Ratliff's answer; now he sloshed about to bring the light on him. Ratliff raised the axe high and swung it against the firebox. He had broken off the iron catch.

CHAPTER

6

RATLIFF FOLLOWED POSS though the sparkleberry bushes that fringed the low bluff, holding a forearm before his face to break their fly-back. He heard a voice above the pounding of logs, being dropped on the river bank beyond the bushes. It was a big voice that came without effort. 'I don't give a damn 'bout his livin' with niggers. He could live with 'gaitors, if he was just a bowhand!' Ratliff heard an indistinct response, then: 'I won't have a real hand in the whole assortmint, and this river's fallin'. The nigger's green, and yo' ambition gits weak on the hard pulls.' That's Bud True, Ratliff thought. The voice fitted his idea of Bud True. It sounded like the old copper bugle his father used to call dogs with. Looks like Bud's talking about you, he told himself. Well, by now you ought to be tough enough not to give a damn one ways or the other—about what anybody says. Still the sense of True's words rang in his ears as clearly as their copper tone.

They were out of the bushes. He stepped up beside Poss quickly and they walked toward the corduroy of pine logs on top of the bluff. He had no trouble picking Bud True out of the two men standing by the logs: he had heard of his size. It astonished him, however, now that he was confronted by the man. He looked like a bull put in with the calves. He wasn't a high-pockets, just big; like two men poured into one. True looked toward the two boys, released the pole with which he was prizing at a log, and took off his wool hat to fan. Ratliff was taken aback by his fierce looks. His eyes shone out between his cheekbones and brows like a bobcat's in a hollow. He had a rocky-looking nose and chin and pump-handle mustaches. He had always heard tell of Bud True's sayings and jokes: this bull-ox didn't look like any jokester!

They were still a little way off when Poss spoke. 'Mist' True, dis de feller I bin tellin' yuh 'bout.'

True folded his hands on top of the pole and looked Ratliff up and down. 'This boy heah says all you lack of bein' a bowhand is the chance to pull an oar.'

Ratliff raised his eyes and met True's gaze. His lips barely moved as he spoke. 'I reckon I couldn't prove it 'thout an oar to pull.'

'You ain't none too big, but then it don't take so much size.' Bud wiped his mouth with the back of his hand, pulling a mustache through his fingers. 'You look like one of these heah pignut fellers: don't grow no bigger, just gits harder. How's yo' wind?'

'Ain't never troubled me none.'

'Reason I ask is Mister Ballantine over heah.' Bud jerked his head toward the sallow-faced man on a log behind him. 'He's as purty an oar-puller as you're likely to see, knows the river, but these elbows and sucks and double p'ints gives 'im bad breath just to look at 'em. This raft don't really need another hand, kain't pay one, but you could help out Mister Ballatine's wind.'

Ratliff nodded without smiling. 'I could help out.'

Bud went on. 'Yuh chum said thought you'd be willin' to make the trip for expairience.'

'I'll do it for my rations and my way back. 'Bout fo' year ago I made a trip and didn't run into nuthin' on the river too much for me.'

52

The sallow-faced man, whose jeans breeches were stuffed into new woods boots, got up off his log and came forward. As owner of the timber, he assumed the final word as his right. 'Can yuh cook raft rations?'

Ratliff shifted only his glance to confront his questioner. 'I have done it. Bin-a camp cookin' most of my life.'

The man went on: 'As long as Poss don't want to go without yuh. I don't mind yuh goin' along. They'll be plenty of rations and we'll git yuh back. And if it's expairience you want, they ain't none better'n Bud True to give it to you. He'll make you do all the pullin', if he can.' His long lips, which had the drawn look of the toothless, curved in an uncertain smile. 'That's why he hollers about my wind: I make 'im keep his stern up—I don't hit no licks for 'im.'

Bud jammed the end of his pole under a log and began to pull up. 'Wanna start raftin' this in the mornin': y'all be heah by first sun. And day after tomorrow we oughta be ready to cut loose, if the water holds.'

After they had quit the bluff, Ratliff and Poss crossed the river at Bell's Ferry in the ferryman's batteau. They started up the road toward home in silence. Poss was the first to break the sandy sound of their walking. 'Dat Mister Bud True de man fur us to tie onto, if us kin.' The low hiss of their feet intervened for a moment. Poss's teeth showed in a slow grin and he went on. 'Mister Bud run de river all de time dey's water enough to drift logs, and sometime when dey ain't,'ceptin' fur him. He bin at it twenty-five-thirty year. Us might git to gwine regular wid 'im.'

Ratliff gazed on at the sandy ruts of the road. After a time he raised his eyes to a clump of palmetto shoots at his right, to the crooked rail fence and young corn beyond. He looked across at Poss. ' 'Member I told yuh to git ready to go down the Altamaha: we 'uz gointa run timber ag'in, that mornin' at the shad nets—the day after I got out of the old steamboat boiler?' They walked on in silence, then

53

Ratliff spoke again. 'That's bin a year and two months. I knew the right time would turn up: I waun't in no hurry.' He hadn't been ready for timber-running then, he reflected. He had needed the six months of log-chopping for Make Hawley, and his winter snaking logs out of the Sumner swamp. He aimed to stay with the river when he started again.

Poss broke into his thoughts. 'Yuh reckon them Hawleys'll say anything to Mister Ballantine 'bout us?'

'Hawleys? Hell, naw!'

Poss looked over his shoulder, then at Ratliff. 'Snake, you oughten not done whut yuh done down deah. You kin take care yuhse'f, but I'se a nigger—dey like as not take it out on me.'

Ratliff looked at Poss sharply. 'I oughten to done what?'

'Oh, I ain't a-sayin' yuh done a thing, but Mist' Jake, he know. He made his brudder git shet of us, didn't 'e?'

Ratliff reflected that he had needed the run-in with Jake Hawley, too; he had proved what keeping his head and biding his time could do. He said, 'Don't call that self-made son-of-a-bitch Mister to me! And all his brother, Make, ever said wuz they had more choppers'n they needed, didn't he? Poss, Jake knows if he ever said what you're hintin' at, people'd laugh at 'im—they did a little at the camp, like it was. And he won't let Make tell it, either.'

Poss shook his head dubiously.

'Look heah, Poss, Bud True may not like us—'specially me—but it won't be on account of what the Hawleys tell 'im, 'bout that thing.'

Poss turned his face quickly toward Ratliff, tightening the corners of his mouth. ' 'Specially you! Whut yuh meant: 'specially you? You'se a cleaner axeman and faster logger'n I is now. You'll show up on a raft, too. It ain't no different.'

Ratliff knew he would: he had to. He'd show Bud True and everybody else that he had river-running in him. The sound of the sand enveloped his thoughts. He hadn't got along with white men, they looked down on him; he believed maybe he could with Bud True. But like it or not, he thought, I am going to show them all I am a river-runner. He'd made up his mind to that fourteen months ago: the word was, 'Come outside!' and he was coming.

The care with which Bud True rafted his timber impressed Ratliff mightily the next day. He watched Bud chop out his pins from picked white oak, then round them down with an axe, a little bigger at the top and bottom than in the middle, and score-hack them. He couldn't have been any more careful if he'd been carving a leg for the parlor table. Bud let him cut some of the binders—after Bud had picked them out, all black elm. But Bud himself fastened them across the logs: they had to be pinned solid, he said. 'Raft yuh logs right and you'll git there with 'em,' was the way he put it. Ratliff didn't mind his watching and asking questions.

He thought about it while they made camp for the night on the bluff, after the raft had been finished. He and Poss weren't half-raftsmen alongside Bud; though he had found plenty to do, rolling in logs, cutting binders, and building the lean-to. After the others snored, Ratliff lay in his blanket watching little gray-tailed clouds pocketing the stars and thought about the morrow. If Jerry Ballantine doesn't want to work any more than he did today, he'll probably hunt the lean-to when we get to Devil's Elbow, he told himself. You and Poss can pull 'er! He saw them again, as they had been before, running with the oar, driving it through the rough current. This time we'll swing around the turns without even slamming. He could see old double-jointed Bud crack his teeth together and say, 'Durn if we didn't make it!'

The next morning, however, Ballantine showed no signs of wea-kening at the sight of Devil's Elbow. He held his place at the oar. "Heah come a mean-pull!" Ratliff yelled out, but it took no visible effect on Ballantine. Later Ratliff doubted the wisdom of his speaking out about it. 'Stoopin' Jerry' held on to the handle like it was drown if he didn't.

The first chance Ratliff got to take the oar was at dinnertime, to let the bowhands eat. He had cooked the meal, then he had to hold his appetite until they'd filled their bellies. He had heard of this custom among regular raftsmen: the bowhand cooked the meal and the pilot ate first. But he wasn't even on a footing with the bowhands. The next chance he got at the bow oar was on Nayle's Ferry Reach: a half hour's straight drifting, without even a single crossing. He scarcely moved the oar.

When the raft was secured for the night at Gray's Landing, at the end of the first day's run, he carried a tight, stiff ache in his chest. He got up off the butting binder, where he had been gazing at ripples on the yellow-green river for the last two hours, and slowly followed the others off the logs and up the bank. Expairence! Whatever that is, I didn't look for this, he thought. By God, all I've done all day is count 'gaitors and rub my butt raw on the binders! Bud hadn't even called on him to help tie the raft: Poss had jumped ashore and caught the rope.

After supper, Ratliff sat in silence at the campfire. He hadn't minded doing the cooking, or waiting on the others to eat first on the raft, he told himself. He hadn't minded Bud's saying 'Poss and Possum: Sut and Sutton,' or Ballantine's calling him 'coonshine.' He knew he had to look for that. It was holding his hands all day!

He did not look up when Ballantine quit the circle and walked toward the woods, with Bud's injunction to go a long way off. Ballantine turned back at the edge of the firelight and gave his warped smile. 'We got a black 'possum with us. What's this other un: a white coon? Aer a polecat?'

Ratliff held his gaze to the fire. He felt the lump in his chest swell into his throat, blood come into his face. Bud and Poss were looking

56

at him. He spit between his feet and clamped his teeth together. He looked up 'Might be a rattlesnake,' he said.

On the second day he brought himself to ask Ballantine twice if he couldn't rest him around the next bend, and Ballantine had said shortly, 'Bad river ahead.' Then Ratliff turned his thoughts to another plan. He couldn't work it out cooking supper that night, nor cooking breakfast, but he made his chance at midday. Ballantine sat on a binder in the shade of the lean-to, his arms out beside him, and he didn't notice when Ratliff set the hot can of grease by his hand. But luck didn't hold. Just as Ratliff tipped the can (by conspicuous accident), trying to pour grease from his spider into it, Ballantine reached toward his hip-pocket for his chewing tobacco. The hot liquid only spattered on his pants and the logs. He gave Ratliff a hard look.

But Ratliff hadn't quit. He tried another long shot that night, calling on Poss for help. He stayed away from camp, fishing a trotline to give him plenty of time. Ballantine and Bud were lying around the fire, smoking and chewing, when Poss began. He said Ratliff worked with him at a bow oar better than anybody he'd ever tried, and had a sleight to throwing his weight behind it. He said the boy had been waiting more than a year for a chance to pull an oar; he'd never seen anybody that wanted to be a bowhand as bad. He wondered if they couldn't use him a little more. Poss watched Ballantine's face. It did not loosen up and he made no response.

Then Poss talked around as if he were just talking and pretty soon he was into Ratliff's trouble with Jake Hawley. He told how Mister Jake (almost as big as Mister Bud) had taken out after Snake and bullyragged him in a rough, mean way, just keeping it up after there wasn't any sense to it. Snake hadn't named a word to him: had just shut his eyes, like, and gone on about his business.

Then he told how Snake had slicked Mister Jake into letting him guide the hind wheels of the rule cart, while he, Jake, got off to pick up something; how Mister Jake got back on behind the wheels, looking at this whatever-it-was, and didn't notice when they came to a turn in the road; and how Snake tried to handle the hind end around the turn.

'Snake fed de chain out fast to give de tongue slack,' Poss said: 'It jump up in de air and de hind wheels start to turn to de right, lack dey oughta. Den, wham! De back end of de log hit de ground. De chain was out'n Snake's hands and de truck tongue had done swung clean over back and fram Mist' Jake on de head and shoulder. He 'uz a-layin' in de road, cold's a cucumber!'

Poss stopped, borrowed Ballantine's tobacco and cut a chew. 'It happen like Snake 'uz just too green wid handlin' de chain,' he said, handing it back. 'Dey all took it to be a acksadent. At fust.'

'Too green and not green enough!' said Ballantine. His drawn lips twisted as he stuffed the plug back in his hip-pocket.

The next afternoon, as they were rounding Mad Dog, Bud railed at Ratliff for throwing away their lightwood at an alligator that floated close to the raft. 'Hell, I got to do somethin'! he replied. 'Looks like I ain't gonna git a chance to help out Mister Ballantine's wind.'

Bud grunted from the stern oar that bent under his weight. 'Son, you done improved it 'thout turnin' a hand.'

Ratliff looked toward the bow where Ballantine and Poss were still running with the oar to keep the raft out of the bight. They made the point and Ballantine sat down to wipe sweat off his face.

Ratliff turned back toward Bud. 'Yeah, he's bin a-runnin' like a snake was after 'im!'

Bud snorted, and even Poss's mouth twitched. Ballantine paused a moment, then went on mopping sweat. Ratliff felt eased: Stooping Jerry didn't even have a come-back.

But Ratliff was wrong. An hour later, as he as holding the oar on a reach, Ballantine looked up at him from his seat on a binder. 'You know, I've seen a lot of niggers that wanted to be like white people, but you're the first man with a white skin I ever seen that wanted to be like niggers.' He warped his mouth in a smile.

Ratliff's head tilted back and the oar slipped out of his hand. He blurted, 'Maybe I ain't never seen any white people I wanted to be like—none 'round heah, anyhow!'

Ballantine's voice sweetened. 'Did yuh ever have any white fo'ks?'

Ratliff whirled halfaway from the oar. His eyes set in a hard squint. By God, he'd axe the son-of-a-bitch!

'Hell, naw!' Bud blared from the stern of the raft before he could retort. Ratliff looked up and Ballantine twisted his head around. Bud walked on across the logs at his oar before he spoke again. 'Uncle Mundy found 'im in a 'gaitor hole. I hyearn he hatched 'im from an egg.'

He had restored good humor to the bullyragging, but it went on after they had tied up the raft for the night at Steamboat Cut. Ballantine took to calling Ratliff 'gaitor bait and said that he might not look like 'gaitor bait, but he smelled like it. Ratliff retorted that at any rate he wasn't a dirt-eater, but nobody laughed. And Bud was short with him: wouldn't let him fry the fish Poss had caught, because he'd dipped the spider in the river. If he didn't' know that was bad luck, he couldn't be trusted with a frying-pan, Bud said.

Next morning as the raft approached Rag point, Bud told Ratliff here was his chance to change his luck. Ratliff said he wasn't a first-timer: he had treated Rag Point on his other trip. He was sitting on the middle binder, looking off at the dark, grayish water that now ran level with the roots of the swamp trees. He felt sore and tense.

Ballantine turned loose the bow oar and looked at Bud. 'Hell, 'Gaitor Bait ought to leave all of his clothes on the bushes.' He grinned. Bud had left the stern and was easing his way up a log behind Ratliff. Ballantine came on from in front. 'Le's holp 'im,' he said.

As Bud plunged for him, Ratliff sprung to his feet and whirled around. Bud had missed him, got only his hat. He snorted. 'Looks like our cook aims to be chinchie with Old Rag Point!'

Ratliff managed a laugh. 'Goddamn you, Mister Bud, gimme back my hat!'

Ballantine was now at him and jerked out his shirt-tail, shouting, 'Come on. Le's make 'im loosen up!' But Bud had retreated with the hat under his arm. Ratliff lowered his head and ran at Ballantine, who scrambled to the safety of a binder as the log they were on started turning. Ratliff had to jump for another log to keep from being turned under.

Poss had brought the bow of the raft toward the left bank, at Bud's order to 'pull to the white,' and it now swung down upon Rag's Point. Ratliff glanced over his shoulder at the approaching woods, started to run toward the stern, then stopped. ' 'Tis only hat I got, Bud!' he said, throwing up his arm, his hand outstretched.

Bud's big mustaches spread outward over an invisible grin that only made his face look fiercer. 'Hell, boy, we got to git this raft to Darien—and you on it!' He tossed the hat toward a bush.

Ballantine's voice came from the other end of the raft. 'Yeah, a 'gaitor might 'git 'im.' Ratliff looked back to see Ballantine throwing one of his shoes, which he hadn't worn on the raft, at the bank.

That afternoon, as they were passing the lake called Alligator Congress, Bud thought they might have some more fun out of Ratliff. He saw ahead a rusty rubble of alligators sleeping along the edge of the right bank. He ordered the raft pulled to the 'Indian,' and when Ballantine looked back, knowing that this was off course, he motioned to him to turn the oar over to Ratliff.

Ratliff was sitting on a binder with his back to Bud. He glanced around: he hadn't expected to get the oar. But he came up quickly and took Ballantine's place. He and Poss stood waiting for the order to pull out, as the raft kept swinging shoreward. Instead, Bud pulled the stern sharply to the left and threw a corner of the bow into the bank. An inert, black bulk bounced onto the raft. The 'gaitor bellowed, flipped himself to his feet and started lumbering across the logs. Poss stood rigid for an instant, facing him, his eyes glazed with shock. Then he made a noise like the suction of a pump, and gave him a sidewise leap. Ratliff had jerked his head around when the raft bumped. Now he stood quite still in his place at the end of the oar. He heard shouts, laughter behind him. The 'gaitor came swiftly, clacking his jaws together. Ratliff's hands drew slowly back from the oar handle, his eyes fixed on the long, lunging head. Imperceptibly, he drew into a crouch as the head came on. It was at his side, in front. On his toes, hands out before him like cat's claws, he plunged.

The 'gaitor's stubby legs shot outward and he grunted. Ratliff was on his back, knees clamped to his belly, hands about his neck. In the fragment of time while the 'gaitor lay still, sprawled upon the logs, Ratliff's hands slid swiftly along his throat. Fingers went under his jaws, over his eyes. The big reptile bellowed and bowed upward, then left the logs in a spasm of flapping that made his tail a black blaze of motion. He landed with a bellow, rose up on his hind legs and leaped, bucked like a horse. Ratliff was still on him, riding behind his forelegs.

The 'gaitor's head bent upward toward Ratliff's face. The wide mouth rounded into a barrel. Foam and a bellowing scream shot from it. The long jaws clamped shut like a bear trap and he rose up on his hind legs and tail. With a whirling motion, he lunged forward into the air, off the raft, Ratliff still leeched to his back.

The river's surface split in butter-colored waves, spume rising. It crumpled into a whirlpool with a dark, dizzily spinning core. The men on the raft could see the hump of Ratliff's shoulders. The vortex spun a zigzag course out into the river and disappeared. Water boiled, foam, mud, bubbles rose to the surface. They kept rising for what seemed a long time to the men who stood watching.

Suddenly Ratliff's head appeared near the boom log, he swam in and pulled himself up on it. He leaned over on his knees and gave himself up to breathing. His face was blue and he sucked the air in in great gasps.

Bud came close to him and bent down. 'Jesus Christ!' he said. Then he lapsed into silence with the others and watched Ratliff breathe.

After a time Bud asked, 'Yuh hurt anywhere?'

Ratliff shook his head. In the same motion, he threw wet hair back from his face and braced himself on the log with his hands.

Bud looked at them. 'What's that on your fingers?'

"I gouged his eyes out,' Ratliff said.

CHAPTER

7

THE FILMY-EYED barkeeper was talking and wiping off the bar when Bud True and Ratliff entered the Timber Tavern in Darien the next morning. He greeted Bud and paused to stare at Ratliff as they crossed the room toward the fireplace. Ratliff was barefoot and hatless and his hair stood out like cattail down. His mud-packed jeans breeches had rents at each knee. He had been reluctant to visit the barroom, but now he moved behind Bud in an even, pigeon-toed walk, stepping neither lighter nor heavier than usual. He kept his face to the front, regarding the bartender and the half-dozen loafers in the place with watchful, sidewise glances. He did not avoid their gaze, he ignored it. When Bud stopped by the cold hearth, he halted, too, remaining in the position in which he had ceased walking, as if he might move on in a moment. He wondered why Bud did not go on, get their drinks and get it over with. Bud had not been able to wait for Ballantine to sell his raft before he got a drink. Ratliff heard the bartender's voice, but he didn't listen: the bartender was not talking to him. He was surprised when Bud spoke up.

'What did Bartow kill 'im with?' he asked.

The barkeeper had been talking about a catamount, the biggest one ever killed around Darien, four feet, seven and three-quarters inches from front foot to hind. Now he looked up in surprise. 'Kill 'im with? Huh-ah, shotgun, I reckon.'

Bud moved toward the bar and Ratliff followed him. 'Aw, hell, I thought there 'uz sump'n to it!' he said. 'Two whiskies, barfoot.' Bud gulped his down, looked at the barkeeper as if he did not see him but was reflecting upon his drink, then glanced around the room. His eyes came to rest upon Ratliff. 'See this clabber-faced boy heah? He don't even tote a light'ood knot.'

Ratliff was bringing his drink to his mouth when Bud spoke; his lips had formed to swallow. He jerked it away, spilling part of it. What, in the name of God, was Bud doing to him! His mouth closed tightly and he stared up at him. He hadn't looked for such a thing from Bud. A vague nausea stirred inside him.

Bud looked over Ratliff's head. 'Grapples 'gaitors bar-handed: catch-as-catch-can. He put on a wrasslin' match with one on the raft yestiddy, just to jog things up a leetle.'

'You mean jug 'em up, don't yuh, Bud?' A voice came from the fireplace. Ratliff shifted his gaze from Bud to the man. He had a purple birthmark on his face, he grinned. 'What 'uz y'all a-juggin' on?' Ratliff saw that all of the faces at the fireplace were turned toward him He backed up against the bar. Fleetingly he wondered if all of this could have been worked out ahead of time. He had let Bud take him into a trap: to be bullyragged by strangers!

'Yeah, I know. Y'all kill stray house cats, usin' a shotgun— buckshot—a-pullin' both barrels.' Bud threw up his head, jerked at his mustache. 'I stood theah and seen this half-a-peck of gall 'n' giz- zard throw a twelve-foot 'gaitor. I mean, crawl on top of 'im and stay theah . . .' His voice went on. It seemed to Ratliff to have grown se- rious. The men at the fireplace stopped grinning. 'Hold on, hold on, don't whistle yet: this boy wuz still on the 'gaitor!' Ratliff felt as if the floor beneath him was beginning to sway, as if his head were turning a handspring. Bud wasn't making fun of him! He blinked tight eyes at the men across the room. They were looking at him with new faces. The birthmarked man's lips had parted. A thrill so sharp shot through him, Ratliff did not know whether it was pain or pleasure. Godamighty, Bud was making big of him! The strangers were goggle-eyed! His gaze dropped to the bar. He picked up his half-filled liquor glass and drained it.

Bud's voice went on. 'But after 'bout half'n hour, heah 'e come swimmin' back with one hand.' Ratliff was finding it hard to breathe: he had a sweet, bubbly feeling in his stomach. 'I thought the 'gaitor had got the other un, but, hell naw, he 'uz a-holdin' the gaitor's eye-balls in it.' Ratliff began to feel light and giddy. He couldn't stand any more of this. He picked up his empty liquor glass and drained it over his lips again, never knowing that it was empty.

'We gotta go, Bud,' he said, turning away from the bar; then he felt a hand on his elbow and looked back. The barkeeper's eyes were soft and bright now, the frog film was gone. He was filling Ratliff's glass. 'On the house,' he said. Ratliff gulped it down and batted his eyes at the barman. 'Got to see a feller a-sellin' a raft,' he said.

He walked fast, unmindful of the deep sand in the streets. He did not stop until he came in sight of the Public Boom. Pausing under the live-oaks on the bluff, he looked off across Darien River at the green gulf of marsh grass beyond. From the shimmering distance the faces of the barroom loafers were still looking at him. Strangers' faces, blinking, staring: he had never seen that look before. Blood contin-ued to pump in his neck, press against the skin of his forehead and cheeks. 'Gall 'n' gizzard!'—' 'Gaitor-grappler!'—'Wrassles 'em bar-handed!'—' A-holdin' 'em eyeballs!' The words, the fragments kept popping in his mind like hot grease, bubbling like beer. He stared across the marsh until his insides began to quiet. I reckon they know who I am now, anyhow, he thought—finally thinking.

His head felt clearer. They looked at me like I'd just bought the Tavern and paid for it in Spanish gold, he thought, and laughed. The

65

laughter made him feel at ease and warm and his shoulders shook a second time in silent mirth. People, nobody had ever looked at him like that before. I reckon they know about the white nigger, the swamp trash, the son-of-a-bitch, now! he thought. I wasn't mindful of Darien and barrooms when I jumped on that 'gaitor's back—I just knew those bastards, Ballantine and Bud True, weren't goin' to make a laughing-stock out of me—but I reckon that crowd heard an earful.

He had not studied about riding a 'gaitor: it had just come to him that he could do it when he saw the thing running toward him. It had come to him that he could take the laugh off his tormentors' faces, too, Goddamnit! He had: they had been quiet for the rest of the day. The fight had worn him out, but he hadn't been too whipped to see that.

I wasn't ridin' that 'gaitor to be a circus show for Darien, he thought. I knew I'd opened Bud's eyes, but I didn't know he was goin' to put on a show over it, there befoh a lot of strangers. He saw again the bartenders' eyes as he poured him the drink on the house. A loose smile overspread his face.

Later he heard a negro version of his fight. Poss had picked it up at Hammersmith's place for colored rafthands. That was on their second trip with Bud True. Bud had taken a contract with Make Hawley to get six rafts to Darien before summer low water, and he had hired them for bowhands. Ratliff thought about the account and laughed as they swung along the sandy road to Everett City, to take the train back home. 'Dis feller say 'e hyearn you plowed a team of 'em on yo' Dead River farm,' Poss had said. Takes a nigger to put the master lie to it, Ratliff thought. Nuthin' you can do about it, they're goin' to have it their own way. Poss must have been tellin' about my 'gaitor fight everywhere fur it to get back in that shape so quick. Of course Poss told it just like it happened. Old Poss! His thinking about Poss gave him a warm, snug-fit feeling beneath his ribs. It was more

66

feeling than thinking. He glanced back at him now. Close at his heels, Poss was wiping sweat off his face with a swipe of his shirt-sleeve.

' 'Nother un said yuh toted a 'gaitor's eyeball in yo' pocket fur a charm,' he had said. 'Gaitor-eye 'stead of buckeye, Ratliff thought. That's an idea. He smiled. Have these niggers wantin' to borrow it to put the eye on each other. But nobody except me and Poss will have one.

Bud says a nigger couldn't tell the straight of a thing, if he had to, not a nigger rafthand. Bud's somebody to talk about stretchin' a story! Wish he'd stick to what happened—he didn't tell it right today at the Blue Goose. Left out the part about waitin' so long to see me come up and then thinkin' I'd had my hand bit off. Didn't even mention the eyeballs. Ratliff wondered what he had done with the eyeballs; then he remembered that there had never really been any eyeballs, not whole ones. He smiled, and felt his cheeks move with the swing of his step in the soft sand.

Early in June he offered to prove he was a 'gaitor-fighter. It was at Cooper's Bar while he and Bud and Poss waited with the other raftsmen of the tide. They had seen the faded light of a campfire in the level distance of marsh grass ahead when they rounded Piney Island, still in the shadow of the cavernous swamps. They had found four rafts sanded on the bar. Raftsmen stood about a fire that boiled a coffee-pot. Behind them morning sun cleaned the two-mile stretch of sand. Bud lifted his hand in salute when they grounded and several from the crowd called, 'Hiyuh, True!'

Bunched in a quiet group, the men looked as if they hadn't come out of their shells yet. There were nods for Raftliff and Poss, but no one called their names. Ratliff noticed this. He knew three of the men, had talked to them. Some time passed before a rib-shaped fellow with a cast in one eye said finally, 'Yuh ain't rid no moh 'gaitors lately?'

67

Ratliff felt eased. His lower lip loosened imperceptibly before he spoke. 'Not lately.'

A short man with a long, yellow-stained beard looked at him. His drawl was uncommonly slow. 'This the feller fit the 'gaitor?' he said. Nobody spoke and he turned his back to the fire. 'I hyearn 'twuz an ole 'gaitor, a-done lost his teeth, aer eyes, aer sump'n.' Ratliff felt annoyed, but there didn't seem to be anything he could say, or do. After a while a man behind him volunteered, 'Bud True, heah, said 'twuz a fourteen-footer.'

'Well now, I'd a-split that fo' ways to find the fact, if 'twuz one of True's yarns,' the old man said. Several laughed, including Bud, who made sort of a clucking noise. Ratliff's face went wooden. Things moved quickly. Somebody thought it was too bad there wasn't a 'gaitor around for Ratliff to fight; somebody else wondered if they couldn't' scare him up one.

'I ain't pertickler about the sort, I'll take on any kind,' he said sharply. He stretched his arms upward, then hit himself on the chest. 'If they's anybody in the crowd a-wantin' to play 'gaitor fur me?'

A young man, taller than Ratliff, with blue eyes that looked like glass, stepped out of the bunch. 'I ain't got no tail, but I'll tussle yuh— throw yuh two out'n three times: wrasslin'.' His pointed Adam's apple shuttled as he spoke.

The group spread out and the pair locked arms. They capered about. Their bare feet made a barking sound in the sand. They were oblivious to the men circled around them and to the sound of the tide: the dry whistle of the rising rill of water on the bar. Once the taller man lifted Ratliff off his feet, but he regained them. Then they came down in a dog-fall. Ratliff, ducking quickly, got his man by the legs and finally threw him, but there was no one left to see it. The tide had floated the rafts and the men had hurried to them. They yelled back, but the wrestlers still floundered in the sand. Bud told Poss to get Ratliff. Poss couldn't make him hear.

Bud ran back to the campfire, kicked him (his backside was up-permost), then yanked the long fellow loose by his neck. 'You dang boys quit this tusslin'!' he bellowed. He dragged Ratliff off with him. 'The tide's done riz and my Goddamn timber's a-goin' down the river. If you aim to make a bowhand, git on this raft!'

Bud didn't speak again until they were at the Boom in Darien. Then he talked to Ratliff in a straight-faced way. 'It ain't fightin', be it 'gaitors aer men, that makes a raftsman. It's a-puttin' yo' timber to this boom,' he said.

Ratliff was sitting on the binder in front of the lean-to, putting on his shoes. He didn't make any answer and he stared at Bud's back after Bud had turned away to leave the raft. His hands still held to his shoelace. Bud's tone of voice had been like a slap in the face. Not fighting, eh, he thought. Not fighting! He lowered his eyes and spat tobacco juice into the water between the squared logs. The lipless mouth, the hard-packed face of Diggs McMillan rose before him. There's one man on this river I'm goin' to mop up with, if I never make a rafthand. And I'll keep fist-and-skulling till I'm grown up to the job. He hadn't liked the way Bud yanked him out of his scuffle at Cooper's Bar, but the raft was going on down the river. A sense of guiltiness came over him. I reckon being known just as a scrapper might not help a fellow any, he thought. But Bud don't know about Diggs McMillan. Now he was lacing his shoes again. I ain't lookin' for him yet, but the time'll come!

He got up and crossed the intervening rafts to the Boom and fol-lowed along the course Bud and Poss had taken. You been thinking too much about this 'gaitor fight, without knowing it, he told himself. Still he didn't aim to let a crowd like those dirt-eaters at Cooper's Bar pick at him. After he had crossed the rice-field dyke that lay between the Boom and the bluff and had started into the town, he wondered suddenly if they had set out to get him into a fight. Hell, that glass-eyed hopper didn't really want a fight! But he resolved to keep his mind on timbering. He surely didn't want Bud bringing it up to him again. That wouldn't do.

The second week after they had returned to the Oconee country and were rafting more of the Hawley timber below Bell's Ferry, Bud showed him a bow oar he had hewn out. The long blade was as smoothly shaped as a fish's tail. The handle, cut smaller than the blade, was hewn square and slick as a cedar bucket. 'When yuh kin do that, you'll be a raftsman,' Bud said.

Ratliff looked the oar up and down, turned it over. He saw it was fine work. He knew good hewing: he was almost as good with a broadaxe as Bud. 'She's a beaut, Mister Bud,' he said. He thought: she is a beaut. But somehow the sight of another bow oar did not stir him. He believed he could turn out one just as good, with a little more practice in picking the right stick of timber for it.

Later, after it was mounted on its bench at the bow of the raft, he looked at the oar again. It's a perfect job, he thought. He pushed the handle down to the logs to test the oar's balance. It works fine, but I've seen others just as smooth and well set. There're plenty of good axemen, though Bud don't think it. He remembered a heart-pine oar with a crinkly grain to it that had caught his eye in Darien. Bud said then, "it's a good oar, yep, it's good work, but I've seen a thousand like it.' If you turned one out like this, he told himself, holding the handle of Bud's oar, he'd still think it wasn't quite as good as he could have done. And it'll be just another good oar to be thrown away when you get to Darien. At Darien it wouldn't even be noticed. A feeling of futility weighed upon him. Raftsmen put a lot of work into an oar, just to throw it away.

After they were adrift the next day, while he and Poss were idle on the reaches, he got to thinking about a bow oar, even forgetting to watch the river. He wondered why it had to be hewn square: it hurt a fellow's shoulder more than if it were round. Still he didn't know how one could be hewn round. Of course the tree was round, but its size had to be cut down for the handle. He studied over the matter off and on all the way down.

A week later, when he bore a long, peeled cypress sapling to the log-littered bluff where they were rafting the Hawley timber, Bud asked him what the hell he had there. The butt end of the tree was hewn smooth into a blade, but the upper portion had been left round. It tapered off to the right size for a handle.

Ratliff walked around it, where he had thrown it down on the bluff, smiling and staring at it. He looked up at Bud excitedly. 'Here's your bow oar, Mister Bud.'

Bud looked at the oar, then squinted his eyes. He did not approach it. His shaggy eyebrows came down and his cheeks flattened and drew up. Blood came into his face. 'That ain't no bow oar!' he almost roared. 'What the hell you mean, bringin' that saplin' in heah?'

'Don't yuh see, Mister Bud?' Ratliff said. 'It'll make an oar.' He went to it and picked up the rounded end.

'I see! I see! I see you're too damn lazy to cut a decent oar for this raft. You don't think for a minute I'm a-goin' out on the river with a saplin' like that on the front of my raft. What in hell you tryin' to pull off heah?'

'This un'll lie on yo' shoulder a lot easier than one of them square-cut ones.'

'Yeah, and it'll lie on the logs, and t'other end'll be a-saggin' under the water afore you git halfway to Darien!'

'It's red cypress. I don't think—'

'You don't think! Listen, bow oars was hewn out on this river afore you 'uz borned—since the days of my grandpappy, to my own knowin'. And they're still a-goin' a-be hewn out on any raft I drift. What do you think the raftsmen on this river, the regular raftsmen, would say if they seen us a-tryin' to make a bight with that cypress switch on the bow of the raft?'

71

Ratliff dropped the oar and looked at the ground. 'We ain't tried it,' he said without raising his eyes.

'And we ain't a-goin' to. I'd ruther face a woman with a limber root!'

Ratliff laughed and looked up.

Bud's face loosened. 'Aer just as soon, anyhow. We done lost an hour heah. Now, am I a-goin' to have to go git that oar?'

Ratliff picked up his axes and turned back into the swamp.

CHAPTER

8

IN BUD TRUE'S thirty-two years on the river (twenty-six at a stern oar) he had broken in a slew of rafthands and some had made good pilots, but Snake was the strangest recruit he'd ever come across. He reflected about it as he watched him handle the bow oar one October afternoon. They were in the Altamaha, below Dick Swift, with a heavy raft of hewn pine. Bud's gaze moved on after a moment to the swamp jungle of the bank beyond. I've seen reckless nerve to match his, he thought. There had been the Dickerson boys: Bartow wasn't scared of hell in a morning fog. And Lit Corn from up on the Ocmulgee: he'd rather take a raft through a suck than around a bend. And Peter Snell from Dublin: he'd throw an axe thirty feet in the air and catch it by the handle. I've seen one other fellow as good with his hands, as fast and just about as true, he thought—club axe, broadaxe, or gun. That gray-haired nigger, Ginger Jim, from English Eddy. I broke Jim in. But Snake's got more different things about him. And he's the curiousest scaper I ever saw.

Bud had finally got Snake into a barber's chair. He thought of the morning he had first tried to persuade him to let a barber shave him. Snake had wanted to know how he, Bud, got his jaws scraped off so clean and he had led him to the shop. But when Snake saw that barber flourish his razor around, he wouldn't even go in the door. Bud thought he'd have some fun: he tried to drag Snake in, but Snake bit him and slipped his hold. He said he wasn't going to let a man he'd never seen before get that close to his neck with a razor. It wasn't till a month ago that Snake took his first barber shave. Growing up in a nest of swamp niggers, the way he had, made him curious about a lot of things.

Bud paused to watch him as he began to pull at the end of the reach. He made Poss stand back while he shoved the oar handle down to the logs, so that it bounced high when he released it. Bud drew his lips in dryly and turned away to dip his own oar in the water. By God! There the son-of-an-eel-worm goes again, he thought. He's got turpentine up his butt, or something. Snake had worried him to a frazzle with questions all last spring: thought he had to know it all at once. And here lately he couldn't take time to learn drifting and the river for studying how to do something different from everybody else. Bud thought women explained part of it: for some reason he was scared of women. He never talked about them and didn't listen much to anybody else. I reckon that's enough to keep him restless, Bud thought.

As he pushed his oar across the raft, he looked at Ratliff from the tail of his eye. When he had swung the bow sweep back, free of the water, to the raft's edge, he slammed the handle to the logs again and it bounced up just high enough for him to catch it on his shoulder. Bud stopped pulling to watch. He'll break the oar bench down if he keeps that up, he thought. Though he knew he'd never seen an oar bench broken in that way. Slowly he spat off into the river and resumed his pushing.

But before they reached Darien, Ratliff and Poss had perfected their teamwork on the stroke and Bud couldn't deny that it was a pretty solid lick: it brought the river with it.

The elliptical–shaped Public Boom was full when they got there and they had to drift on around the bend to the lower end. As they skirted the long line of rafts, crawling with busy and idle raftsmen, Ratliff and Poss swung the oar in their fancy lick. Like a pair of circus horses, they slammed it down, caught it on their shoulders, and turned for the pull, as one. The idlers watched them, and some who were occupied looked up to see what was drawing attention. Bud conceded the thing did have style.

Before Ratliff and Poss had gathered their tools to leave (they weren't going to stay for the inspection), a white bowhand, a stranger, with a face as long as a broadaxe blade, yelled to them from a raft above. 'Y'all 'uz sho' a-promenadin' with that oar! Whut yuh call that?' Poss let out a sort of grunting laugh and went on stuffing the spider into a croker-sack, but Ratliff called back in a sharp voice, 'That's Sutton's Lick!'

When they had moved along the Boom a short way, two bright-skinned negroes stopped them. 'That thing didn't just look good,' one of them said. 'It 'ud save a feller's back!'

Ratliff half-smiled, then straightened his mouth. 'Would? It did. You're a-lookin' at the man that oughta know.'

The mulattoes wanted him to go back and show them how the lick was made. 'Mhii!' He uttered a mock laugh. 'I'll learn yuh for a dollar a lick.' He stepped past them and walked on. They took Poss by the arm, but he said it was Snake's lick and he'd have to show them.

As he passed the Blue Goose on the riverfront street (Poss had left him at Hammersmith's), he met a man he knew as Son and the fellow with eyes like glass whom he had wrestled at Cooper's Bar. 'Hi theah, Snake!' the latter called out. 'I seen yuh comin' into the Boom—you and yuh nigger a-doin' that fancy lick.' His mouth spread in a grin, in which his eyes took no part.

75

Ratliff looked around and his face tilted. He wondered hurriedly if the fellow aimed to start trouble. He seemed friendly. 'Yep,' said Ratliff.

'That's the slickest trick I've seen on this heah river.' Still grinning, the man leaned toward Ratliff and extended his hand familiarly toward his shoulder. He turned to Son. 'Yuh know it 'uz me and ole Snake had that tusslin' up at Cooper's Bar when the tide riz and y'all like to left us.'

Ratliff kept his gaze on the man and his shoulder drew away imperceptibly. There was a subconscious hostility in him to the touch of this stranger. He wondered what Glass-Eyes was headed for.

'The tide wuz all to the good for me, 'cause he 'uz a-beatin' my tail!'

Suddenly, Ratliff's sense of aversion melted. He did not move from the uplifted hand, he let it come down on his shoulder. It became a bond: he felt a bond with this glass-eyed fellow whom he'd thrown and who liked it. He smiled. ''Tain't just looks: my lick'll save yo' back.'

'I could see that. Listen, I want to celebrate on that lick: it's sump'n to celebrate! Come on, I'll buy yuh a drink.' The glass-eyed fellow swept his free hand toward the entrance of the Blue Goose. 'You, too, Son.'

Walking between them, Ratliff went into the saloon.

Two hours later a man pushed open the swinging doors to the barroom and stood just inside them looking on. Ratliff and the glass-eyed fellow, whom by this time he called Boze, were again demonstrating Sutton's Lick. They held in their hands (not too accurately now) an imaginary bow oar. They slammed it down upon an unseen raft, caught it upon their shoulders with an exaggerated grasp, and heaved their way across the space cleared for them in the room.

Finally Ratliff looked up at the man. He had just caught his invisible oar on his shoulder. He halted in the act of turning. The face he saw became quickly familiar. Diggs McMillan was gazing at him with a thin smile on his face. The sight tightened him like a live coal. The liquor haze was gone. He knew that he was alone in a barroom full of strangers, that he did not know where Bud was, or even where Poss was. He saw the bulge of a pistol in McMillan's pocket. He kept his eyes on the man and the crowd's gaze followed his.

'So, it's you!' McMillan said. He looked at the faces around the room, still wearing his smile. 'I seen yuh come in down at the Boom with Bud True and I didn't have no idee it wuz my ole borrowin' friend.' He paused for a moment, but no one spoke. Ratliff's face had become wooden. McMillan went on, 'I seen yo' monkey motions. Look like a gal in her Sunday dress, a-tryin' to pump a drink for her feller.' There were a few halting laughs. He looked around the room casually. He faced about and pushed through the exit.

Ratliff stared at the swinging doors until they had stilled. Then he glanced at Boze, at Son, at faces about the bar. There was a look of unrecognition in his eyes. Without a word he left the saloon.

During the winter, he saw the bouncing flip of oar handles of rafts adrift more and more often: especially with regulars, like the niggers who drifted for the big Yankee sawmillers, Coventry and Company. The first time he saw a strange pair of bowhands giving an oar his lick (on the Altamaha, just below the forks), it gave his insides a hoist. But this was momentary. The popularity of his stroke left no good taste in his mouth, for the flavor of intervention had been spoiled for him. And damned if Bud hadn't come along and said almost the same thing that Diggs McMillan had said: while they were on their way back to the Oconee from Darien the same day. It reminded him of a woman in her good clothes, trying to pump, Bud had said. Bud swore he hadn't heard anybody make the comparison: it just looked like that to him. Some had taken to calling it the 'Sunday Lick,' or the 'Sunday-Dress Lick.' McMillan's words kept him thinking more about the man than about his lick, though. Ratliff had known it before, it had been with him a long time, but now the gnaw-ing never left him: he had to square the deal with Diggs. And he would at a time of his own choosing.

Twice in February he thought of quitting Bud. Bud kept complain-ing about Ratliff's sullenness and jumping him about old river signs, saying that he didn't pay any attention to them. And he kept harking back to the 'Sunday-Clothes Lick,' saying Ratliff wasted time putting on a show when he didn't know the points of the river from the forks to Darien. To hell with the lick, Ratliff said finally. Bud said it wasn't an oar, it was a whore at the bottom of Ratliff's trouble: he needed to get him one. In April Ratliff agree to try this remedy, but he never did get to the bawdyhouse, he got too drunk to go.

They were three days out of Willcox's old boatyard up on the Oc-mulgee with a raft of cypress, almost a week afterward, when Bud brought it up. They had tied up for the night at Hard Bargain, and Ratliff was frying the sowbelly.

'If liquor is a-goin' to down yuh like that, son, you ought to stick to beer, aer river water,' Bud said.

Ratliff hadn't spoken since Bud started talking, he had hardly spoken since they left the boatyard. Now he turned the bacon over in the spider without looking up.

'If you'd a-bedded with that gal I had picked out for you, you'd a-got some of that pizen out'n yo' system.' Bud leaned down, kindled a splinter at the fire, then put it to his short-stemmed pipe. He let out gun-bursts of smoke and looked down at Ratliff, whose eyes were on the cooking. 'Fust, you had to liquor up so yuh wouldn't feel so green—hell, I doubt if you've ever even crawled a nigger-gal: and you twenty year old! Then yuh drunk so much, just to be damn-good-'n-sho', yuh got sick and puked all over the place!'

Ratliff jerked his head up. 'Take your whores and jump to hell, Mister Bud! I wouldn't-a tetched that crab-nest of your'n. I got sump'n on my mind.'

78

'God, a ground mole could see that!'

Ratliff set the spider down. He took out his tobacco quid and threw it in the fire. 'I've figgered out whut's wrong 'ith my lick, but I don't know whut to do about it.' He spat in the ashes and stared at the embers. 'It shows yuh up too much slammin' that oar to the logs. 'Course, it's not as slow as the old way. But yuh got to bend down a little to slam it.' He cupped his hands together and threw down an imaginary oar between his feet. ''Tain't much, but any bendin' off yo' stride tires a feller.' He put the pan of meat on a log and sat beside it.

'Damn'f you don't work harder to git out'n work'n any man I ever seed,' said Bud.

Ratliff slept soundly early in the night, but before day he was suddenly and completely awake. It was as if someone had shaken him. He raised up on an elbow and saw that the dim blanketed forms of Poss and Bud were still. After he had lain back down, he knew that he could not sleep again. He got up and walked over to the edge of the low bluff. Across the river, the tall swamp trees made a black silhouette against the paler sky. Momentarily this ebony screen was touched with a million tiny sparks: the glow of lightning bugs. The sparks went off and on, whirled and shifted through the tree-blackness as if in some silent rhythm. Ratliff stared at the swamp. The silence of it strained his ears. In and out, now here, now there, the tiny glow-spots moved through the seemingly solid mass. Yet they did not move, either—he could not see them move—off here, on yonder. Ever they shifted, but there was no sound, no motion: a million glowed at once, yet they gave no light. When they went off, it was as if he had never seen them, yet almost instantly they were on again. The whole thing seemed an illusion, a make-believe.

Like the glimmering of his own mind: at one moment he saw a solution; then, when he tried to look at it, it was gone. Ratliff moved closer to the edge of the bluff, stood with his legs apart. The vague ghost glow of coming dawn touched the surface of the river. As he gazed at the water, a mist above it became visible to him and there was sound in his ears, sound so fine, so tiny he could hardly be sure it was there. He stuck his fingers in their openings and cleared them out. Yes, it was sound: sand gnats, swarming over the river surface. Sound like the ghost of a bumblebee boring in his ear, he thought, like an auger, like augers boring in his brain.

He moved away from the edge of the bluff and walked down to the landing where their raft was tied and boarded it. He hardly knew that he walked: he felt as if he were floating in a drone, a mist of sand gnats. The air on the river was warm and heavy and soft, like the feeling of going to sleep. His head seemed alive with glowing images, thoughts that went on and off before he could see them, know what they were. Ratliff wondered if he were really awake.

He put his fingers to the end of the bow oar. It was solid, hard, cold. The touch of it went up his arm. He laid his fist on top of the oar, loosed his fingers. Suddenly it was there, in his clenched hand, sticking straight up from the handle! Godamighty! There it was complete, the whole thing! Without your thinking about it, or even trying to think about it, he told himself.

Sweat broke out on his face, though a chill shook his back. He got coals from the campfire and built up a blaze on the raft. He tied the oar handle to a binder so that its end was solid against a log and set to work with Bud's auger, boring a hole in it. When the hole was almost through the handle, he stopped and cleaned it out. Then he got an axe and went out into the swamp to look for an oak sapling, though it was still too dark to see clearly. He felt the oak clumps with his hands, till he found what he wanted. He cut off a length of it, a little more than a foot long, which he barked and trimmed with his axe and finally smoothed with his pocketknife. Then he drove the oak pin into the auger hole at the end of the oar, joining it to the handle at a right angle, and drove it in full and solid. When he was satisfied with his job, he untied the handle and let the oar blade drop back into the river. The clean pin thrust upward in the sunrise glow. He sat on a binder looking at it.

'A handle on a handle!' The voice had a hushed sound. Ratliff looked up and saw Bud True standing on the edge of the bluff, staring at the bow oar. He climbed down and came aboard the raft, took hold of the upright pin in the handle. He depressed it and released it, the oar handle flew up. He depressed the pin again until the handle touched the floor and let it go. Then he lowered the handle to bring the oar blade free of the water and walked it across the raft. With a flip of his hand on the end of the pin, he slammed the oar handle against the logs. It bounced high in the air and he caught it on his shoulder. 'Well, I'll be Goddamn!' he said. 'Snake, you've whittled yourself a play-purty—yes, suh—a play-purty that's a-goin' to git more playin'-with on this heah river than all the whores in Darien!'

The first rays of the sun came up the reach below them and gleamed in Ratliff's face. 'Yeah. I'm a-callin' it the lazy-pin. Just another trick to git out of work.'

CHAPTER

9

WHEN DIGGS MCMILLAN came down China Swann's front steps, Ratliff rose from his lookout at the forks of the Darien road and began to move slowly along the branch that led toward the whorehouse. McMillan paused at the corner of the picket fence and raised his head. His face was flushed with liquor. Within the shadow of the wistaria vines that screened the porch of the brothel, China Swann watched him. She had got him out of the house by a ruse, but he seemed still suspicious and combative.

He looked toward the road where Ratliff was approaching some thirty yards away. His head thrust forward. 'Sutton! By God, I want-a see you!' Ratliff stopped slowly and turned an expressionless face toward him. He had started walking rapidly across the sandy ground that lay between them.

China was not interested in McMillan's fights beyond her fences, but her gaze followed him to be sure he was quitting the premises. Regardless of what his condition was when he was let into her house, he was always quarrelsome drunk before he left. She had been able to get rid of him this time only by making him believe the supply of liquor was out. He was worse than a rowdy.

She gathered her green wrapper more closely about her and leaned near the vines to see better. Diggs was picking on a boy! The sight of it somehow stirred again the annoyance she had felt while Diggs was in the house. To China Swann all men were contemptible, but there was something in Digg's nasty, harsh manner with her girls that had several times moved her to anger.

Now he had come upon that boy. He stood a half-head taller and fifty pounds heavier, China judged. She could hear his brassy voice. Her eyes opened wide. The boy had spit in his face, a mouthful of tobacco juice! Diggs lunged at him and the boy was running backward. She felt her heart change its beat. There was something in the still-faced impudence of the boy that touched her. Maybe he can put up a scrap, she thought. She leaned nearer the vines, then glanced over her shoulder. It isn't sundown yet: you can't be standing out on your porch like this, she told herself. She straightened up and turned away. Anyhow, somebody might come. And catch the madam of the Birdcage, Captain Seborn Henry's woman, standing here watching a rafthands' fist-and-skull brawl!

China walked toward the doorway. As she moved, looking off meditatively, her mass of sorrel hair and white skin made her deceptively ornamental. Temper threatened in her sharp-cut forehead and mobile eyebrows. Her eyes were yellow. The skin beneath them was a seamless buff, like fire-seasoned leather.

Inside the reception room, she met a weazened negro woman, wearing a white apron. China's face softened. 'Now he's got up a fight out on the road, Delia. Keep the girls quiet. I'm going upstairs to watch,' she said, moving off.

When she looked out the front side window she blinked. The boy astride Diggs, beating him on the back of the head with a shoe. She smiled. They were only a few yards beyond her fence and she could see here better than from the porch. The boy didn't seem so much of a boy now. Hell, I hope there'll be no killing this close to my house!

she thought. Wonder if I oughtn't to send Eef to the sheriff and let him know?

Diggs was rolling over, coming up with a bellow. Now they were standing on each side of the strip of ground between the fence and the road. The boy was facing in her direction. His cheeks looked soft and beardless. For an instant she thought he was a half-wit, the way he held his head back, with his eyes down and his big lip. But he moved like a cat. As Diggs eyed him, he kicked off his other shoe and stood barefoot in the sand. Diggs circled, rushed in from his side. He ducked the right swing, but Diggs caught him on the jaw with a left. He went down to a knee and scrambled out of reach. Diggs charged him and he broke. Now Diggs was running him around and around the sand plot. She got up and walked to the bureau that stood across the room and dusted her nose with powder.

Circling, she came upon the window just in time to see the boy butt Diggs in the stomach like a goat. Diggs went down. She hadn't realized how broad the boy's shoulders were: he had little wrists and ankles. He straddled Diggs quick as a cat squirrel, grabbed his throat. She sucked in a sharp breath, grasped her wrist with the other hand. Diggs struggled to get up, but the boy held on, choking. She found that she was squeezing her wrist harshly, shaking it. She hadn't suspected that she despised Diggs so much: now that he was on his back and his face purpling, she could choke him, too! There's something in his Goddamn eyes like pa's, she thought. Yes, I'd seen it, but I hadn't figured it out before.

She broke her hands apart: Diggs had rolled the boy over, was on top, pounding him in the face. She licked her lips and started to get up. Oh, it's not your fight, she told herself. Hannah's Hole! He had thrown sand in Digg's eyes, a double handful. He locked his bare legs around Digg's head in a flash, was pulling him backward, coming up from there! This boy fights my style of fighting, by God! she thought.

84

Diggs went on his hands and knees, clambering to get up, with the boy on his back, trying to get a Nelson on his neck. Diggs rolled over, but the boy jumped to safety; then he whirled and kicked Diggs in the crotch. Her lips loosened over her clamped teeth, but before the smile had formed, Diggs had hold of the boy's foot and her lips straightened. Then the boy was running backward again, Diggs reaching for him. Unh! The boy's face! His mouth open, his eyes bugged out, staring at Diggs. Diggs was almost touching him every jump. 'Look out!' Her voice became audible. My God, the boy jumped the log backward: how did he know it was there? And Diggs saw it, but was following so fast that he fell over it anyhow when the boy jumped. She laughed softly. That face! He was fooling Diggs with it, while he read his, she thought. I'd be proud of that trick myself. Who the hell is this boy? She noticed a snuff-colored negro man standing at a distance, grinning.

The boy had jerked Diggs across the log by his feet, now he was dragging him back over it. That lick on the back of his head ought to have just about knocked him cold, she thought. But it didn't. Diggs had hold of a bush. The boy couldn't budge him. Humph, the boy went backward with Digg's breeches in his hands. Diggs looks like a peeled banana in those long drawers, she thought. That shock-headed boy looks at them like he's never seen drawers before. She had an impulse to smooth the hair out of his face. His eyes, when he did open them, were like a cat's—no, a gray-eyed nigger's in the dark! His shirt was gone now. She hadn't even seen him lose that, but it had been hanging in shreds. Perspiration streaked the paint on her face and she dabbed carelessly with her handkerchief.

Suddenly Diggs and the boy were running at each other from opposite sides of the sand plot. The boy moved much the swifter now. They were hitting head on—no, the boy dropped down on one knee and got under Diggs. My God, he was coming up, he was up! With that tub of guts above his head, a hand at the throat and the crotch!

Her face went perfectly still, her breathing stopped, her shoulders shook slightly from her heart-beat. For an instant she felt dizzy, as if she were swaying in the air. Then she looked and saw that Diggs was on the ground, lying still. The boy's back had been like a hawk swooping!

She concluded the fight was over and stood up, but before she had quit the window, Diggs was on his feet and the boy pressed him to the plot. Now they were down on the ground, rolling over and over. The rolling stopped with Diggs on top. He reached toward his hind pocket, but he had no hind pocket now. The son-of-a-bitch! She was back with her hands on the window-sill. Diggs pounded the boy's face and she felt her own twitch. God, he was trying to gouge the boy's eyes out! The boy jerked his head from side to side. Her head jerked, too. Hah, he had Digg's thumb in his mouth! Diggs was doing the jerking now. He yelled, he came up on his feet, bringing the boy, clamped to that thumb like a cooter. He jerked his hand loose. Loose hell! That thumb's a stump! The knuckle's gone. The boy is spitting it out. Diggs stood staring at his bleeding hand. Then he picked the knuckle up out of the sand, got on his trousers and started walking toward Darien, reeling a little in his steps.

China slumped back in her chair, but her face was sharp with the fight, the fight that had gone her way. She gazed after him. His head swayed to one side. His back was growing vaguer in the dusk. Like pa's back—going—afterward, she thought. But the son-of-a-bitch don't have no thumb! Just a nub. Goddamnit, I'd like to brand 'em all like that!

She sat with her legs sprawled before her, trembling, feeling too weak to get up. An hour ago nobody could have made her believe that she could get so worked up over a raftsmen's brawl.

A knock sounded on her door. It was repeated. China cleared her throat. 'What you want, Delia?' she called.

'Deys-a collud feller out back want-a borrer a pan of water fur one-a dem mens in de fight.'

China came out of her chair quickly and moved toward the doorway. 'Tell 'em to come on in. He can wash up inside.'

She went to her own room and tore up an old petticoat for bandages, found a bottle of turpentine and one of brandy. When she got downstairs, she found them on the back porch. She met the big raftsman, Bud True (she hadn't seen him at the fight), as she reached the door.

The boy, still naked at the waist, was bending over a pan of water, while the snuff-colored negro helped him wash. As she came onto the porch, he jerked up and turned his back. She looked at Bud. 'Hell, tell 'im to furget that. I want-a doctor 'im.' She moved toward the boy, but hesitated as she drew near. She handed a glass of brandy to the negro, who gave it to him. He turned back and nodded his head, before he swallowed the liquor.

'Lemme put some turpentine on those gashes,' she said, holding out a length of bandages between her hands. He set the liquor glass on the wash-shelf, put on a cotton jacket, and walked down the back steps without replying to her.

Bud laughed, but China did not join in. She stood looking after Ratliff with the bandage still held between her hands.

'Used to lickin' 'is own cuts,' Bud said. His teeth showed briefly under his spreading moustache. 'And a leetle gal-shy.'

She didn't look up. 'What's his name, Bud?'

'Sutton.'

'Bring 'im around to see me.'

'Snake don't throw 'is money away on—on gals.'

'I said, "Me"!'

Bud whistled. He walked heavily across the porch and out the gate by which Ratliff and Poss had gone.

'Snake,' she repeated for her own ears. What in the name of common sense do you mean, telling Bud True to send him to see you? she asked herself. She hadn't been to bed with a man—except Seborn—since soon after she started running the Birdcage, nearly two years ago. She rolled up the bandage and put it in the pocket of her dressing-gown. It's not going to bed with him that I want, she thought. What the hell's that! She had wanted to bandage up those cuts. Dark was gathering, but she continued to stand staring off toward the gate. I want to be there, ringside, the next time he starts a ruckus, she thought. Again she saw the running muscles of his back set like cut stone, and felt herself lifted into the air, struggling helplessly.

In her room she took a drink from the brandy bottle before she put it up. Then she sat down at a high carved dressing-table and began to arrange her hair. Her forehead shone in the lamplight. The little white scar in the edge of her hair where pa had hit her with his gun barrel, used to be right above her eyebrow. That was the first time she had ever really tried to stand him off. You hadn't thought of that piece-of-scum in a year, before today, she told herself, and remembered the slight froth that was always on his lips, and the harsh smell of whiskey when he used to come to her bed. If you could call that box of straw a bed! she thought. She could hear the loose boards of the shed room, on the back of their old log house on Buzzard Ridge, flap, as they always did of a windy night. The first time he had come to her bed was soon after her half-brother, Robert, ran away—pa had run him off. Bobbie had shared the straw box with her, but they were only children.

That look in pa's eyes, mean as hell, and drunk, and coaxing, but somehow that of a dog who'd just been caught sucking eggs! Something like it in Diggs's face. She felt a touch of nausea.

Her hand, holding a hairbrush, lay on the dressing-table, and she stared into the mirror without seeing it. She was just past twelve years old the first time she had known, had felt sure of the harm. Ma, poor zany, had already put pa in the wrong, in her crying and singing, and rocking before the fireplace, when he wasn't there. And she had noticed the niggers on the place: Sulie Bivins, who worked at the house sometimes, looked at her in such a funny way. The roar of the rain that night had grown louder and louder overhead, until it was paralyzing. Afterward, after everything had stopped, even the rain, she was so scared and weak her heart could scarcely beat. And she had known! Later it had come to the point where, when it was all over, she would feel lower than the hogs wallowing in the pen. She had believed then that pa had abused ma until she was like she was— she still believed it—and she had imagined that in the same way the disease was eating on her.

She tasted the salt of sweat and rain. It had rained the night she ran away, too. She could feel the drizzle dripping down her face and her back now. That night she hadn't been able to see it, just a vague gray between the pine trees. That was a long, cold, hungry walk for a fourteen-year-old girl, four miles through the woods to the railroad, then twenty miles down the tracks to the first way station! she thought. Pa's shotgun and a pone of corn bread! You ate the corn bread pretty soon and got rid of it, but that gun! You ought to have just left it along the tracks, you couldn't have hit the side of a cow with it. But you toted it on. Your legs were numb and your toes busted open when you stopped at that first farmhouse in the morning, that log house with chinaberry trees in the yard.

She remembered how far away she could see the tops of those chinaberry trees, and how long it took to get to them. They were the tallest chinaberry trees you'd ever seen, or ever will see, she told herself. Not any kin to the umbrella chinas in old man Rowe Lilly's yard in Pineville. I wish you had known as much about men when old man Rowe started pestering you as you do now: he'd have been easy to handle—there was nothing to be afraid of. That was the only chance you ever had at living in a decent home! You thought the Lillys' house was the cleanest place you'd ever seen that morning they hired you—took you in, was what they did: sent you to school, tried to make a Christian out of you. Mrs. Lilly was a good woman, in spite of her funny Canadian ways!

She saw now the white-uniformed figure of Miss King, bending over Rowe Lilly's bed, as she had that first afternoon, and a sense of her awe returned. Miss King was the first trained nurse you ever heard of, she told herself, a high-class English lady who made even the Lillys look common. It was just a happen-so that the company got her to nurse old man Rowe when the broken saw cut him at the saw-mill: She was in Pineville visiting her sister. And she told you that if you finished the academy at Pineville—and you only had two more years—and got the Lillys to send you down to the hospital in Savannah where she worked—oh, hell, why go into that! she asked herself. It wasn't three months after Miss King left Pineville that you left, and not headed for any Savannah hospital. If your bosoms just hadn't swelled up so about that time to make old man Rowe want to pinch 'em! The Lillys thought a lot of you.

Hell, you could have got the money out of that Goddamn Greek, Joe, in Brunswick: if you'd have slept with him! Jesus, how many have you slept with since for two dollars! China's eyes focused on her image in the mirror. But you had to come to it, whore! It's hard for you to understand, I know, but even when you started off at Miss Nona's in Savannah, you thought it was meaner work than waiting tables at Greek Joe's. At first it was just like a spell coming back on you to get in bed with a man . . . . Remember the night that the bald-headed farmer from Hazlehurst kicked you out of bed, called you a 'Goddamn bag of mean!'

If Miss Nona hadn't taken you in hand, and if I hadn't done something about you, you'd never even have made a good girl. You learned a lot from Miss Nona, but most of it, I taught you. I had to, you weren't made up like the rest of them. And I did a good job. Hustling never got you like it did some of the girls, though sometimes you did get drunk and let yourself go. Yes, that was bad business: every time. You never failed to have a touch of the old trouble the next day, like it had been when pa came to your bed: when you got drunk. Still it was one of the reasons that kept you working to be a madam, to have girls of your own to take the trade. You knew you couldn't make a business of just being a girl in a house, whether you were the best, or the worst.

She picked up the brush and brushed her hair vigorously for a while. Then she stopped. The figure of Snake Sutton was before her: his face—swollen, cheek split, but a sort of hard cocksureness sticking through—when he nodded to her and swallowed the brandy, and turned his back on her, and walked out! She dropped the brush. It clattered to the floor and lay there. She got up and went to the wardrobe where she kept the brandy bottle, hesitated a moment, then took it out and poured herself a small drink. Sure as hell, you're not going to act like a simple, bat-brained whore! she told herself. What in the name of common sense is trying to happen to me? she thought.

She had a good thing in Seborn Henry; he was better than most girls ever got hold of, or would know how to handle if they did. He isn't the Savannah chief of police, or a millionaire, she told herself, but he totes his end of a bargain. You are getting along with him better, more agreeably, than with any man you've ever known: he's a man, like every other man, but at least he's dependable. Standing with the glass of brandy still in her hand, she picked up the bottle and carefully poured the liquor back. You sure can't look for anything out of this rag-tailed rafthand. Then what do you want to fool with him for? He isn't anything but a boy. She started across the room toward her dressing-table. Not that you're old by a damn sight: twenty-one is young, damn young to have a house of your own. He's likely just about your age.

Midway of the room she shifted her direction and sat down in a rocking-chair by the fireplace. She stared at the soot in the back of the chimney. He isn't a good thing, she told herself after a time; he isn't even a man! He's a wildcat, a wildcat that don't give a damn for you, or anybody else in the world! She rocked back and forth in the chair.

CHAPTER

10

RATLIFF AND BUD reached Darien's riverfront thoroughfare as the lamps were being lit in the stores. Their windows threw pale, fanwise paths of light across the shell sidewalk and the broad, sandy street. The mast tips of schooners, on the river below the bluff, caught the last ghostly light of an opalescent horizon. Gray darkness obscured their hulls, and the wharves, and the tabby ruins of Old Darien's warehouses, burnt during the War. Two-story stucco, brick, and wooden buildings above the bluff fretted the way in uncertain light and shadow. Ratliff walked a half-step behind Bud, his feet shuffling in the loose shell fragments.

As they turned into North Way, Bud was accosted by a bearded Jew, who took hold of his elbow. He had just the suit, a suit of clothes he had been saving for 'Bik Bud.' Bud grinned. 'You Jews kin tell when I got money better'n I kin!' They walked on by the dim-lighted shop and past a Sicilian fruit-vendor who stood on the sidewalk holding a bunch of bananas up to them. Then a young Jewish woman stood in thier way. Her oval face had a polished look in the doorway light and her breasts made a pointed shadow. She took hold of Bud. Ratliff was conscious of the fact that she did not even glance in his direction. They know to a penny what Bud got for that raft, he thought. The woman had hold of Bud's shirt-front. She was fingering his huge biceps. Bud was looking down at her, his mustache spread in a smile.

'Come in,' she said. 'I sell you enything in the store. Cheap.' Her fingers took hold at the opening of Bud's shirt. She looked up at him with glistening eyes.

'You ain't got but one thing I want and it ain't in the store, right now.'

Ratliff looked up at Bud. The damn fool! He began to feel fidgety, and wanted to go on.

The woman did not shift her gaze. 'Come on,' she said, jerking at the shirt. 'We ged it. We sell you enything.'

Ratliff moved on two steps and looked back. Bud was saying, 'I'll give yuh twenty-five cartwheels to sleep with me tonight.' Ratliff heard her laugh. She had not turned Bud loose.

She called back into the shop. 'You hear dod, Horry? He want to pay twenty-five dollar to sleep wed me!'

Ratliff saw a man's bushy head emerge in the dimness of the doorway. The man repeated her words and laughed. Then he said: 'Tell 'im, fifty dollars. You sleep wed him for fifty dollars. Go on—tell him!'

Ratliff squinted so that his swollen eyes pained him. He tried to see the man's face in the shadow. 'The self-made son-of-a-bitch!' He moved on painfully, slowly, waiting for Bud to catch up with him.

Bud had done extra washing when he came back into the big dormitory room above the Timber Tavern, where he and Ratliff had beds for the night. His jaws were blue and shiny from a shave and his hair was parted and wetted down.

Sitting on the edge of his bed, picking his teeth with a quill toothpick, Ratliff looked at him. 'I bet she don't wash up like that for you.'

'Oh, well, I reckon I 'uz a leetle dirtier: she ain't bin a-pullin' an oar.' He started off toward the stair landing, then turned back. 'Ain't yuh gonna eat no supper?'

Ratliff was silent a moment, then shook his head. 'Looks like that hunk of Diggs' thumb's gonna do me.'

'Git yuh another slug of liquor and come on. You git yo' belly full and you'll feel like wrasslin' that yaller-eyed wench of Seborn Henry's.'

Ratliff took the pick from his mouth and spat. He shook his head slowly.

'Hell, they ain't a rafthand in Darien wouldn't give yuh five dollars to fill yo' place. If I hadn't bin lookin' at this other thing for two years and a-wantin' it, I mought talk to yuh.'

Ratliff gazed after Bud True's big bulk as it disappeared down the stairway. The image of China Swann in the green wrapper came to him: the white neck, the long yellow eyes, the loose red hair. Sending you word on sight! he thought. He laughed so that he heard his own voice. The weight of his shoulders seemed to lighten, his backbone to stiffen. Bud said he had seen a raftsman offer her ten dollars, there in her own house, and she wouldn't. And she had sent *him* word!

He wondered what it was. The damn bitch! She would take you in through the back door while Captain Henry is up the river, he told himself. He felt anger rising in him. If you'd come. Well, by God, you won't! The captain ought to know to expect such a thing: keepin' up a woman like that. But most of them are like that. Captain Henry was one man he'd known in Nine-and-a-Quarter that he still had something for. You hadn't thought of him in a long time, but you damn sure ain't goin' to take his woman, he told himself. The captain was the one that saved us after pa died, saved the stave mill. And it didn't mean a thing to him except the few stave bolts he hauled on his boat. He remembered Captain Henry's handing him the fine, two-bladed barlow knife with a chain on it and saying, 'Came from Savannah,

95

son.' The first knife I ever had, he thought. Ratliff took a pint flask out from under his bed and swallowed the liquor in it, then he got up and began to take off his clothes.

'She knows a good man when she sees one!' He repeated the boast to himself and laughed. He wondered what in particular it was about him that had got China Swann. He saw himself naked, about to get into bed with her. A sense of embarrassment came to him. He might give it away that he had never been on a woman before. Something might give him away. Well, there's got to be a first time for everything, he thought. It's a hell of a sort of business—damn low way that we come into this world, anyhow!

The thing hadn't bothered him until he started coming to Darien. Women are something to let alone, especially the white whores in Darien: they take your money and give you the clap, he told himself. Once he had thought of getting him a yellow girl: one of those Hall niggers in the forks of the rivers. Poss used to go down there. That afternoon below the field—they had been calling up the hogs to feed—when Poss had said he believed he'd go over to Sodom and make a yellow girl happy that night, he had almost said to take him along. He had known there wasn't anything he couldn't ask Poss, or Poss say to him. But he hadn't. There was something. Something had told him that Poss wouldn't have felt right about it. They couldn't climb white women together, or black ones.

Ratliff crawled into the bed and sprawled on his back. With the relaxation, a cool, sweet, bubbly feeling bore him upward. Hell, you've beat Diggs McMillan, he thought. And there's plenty of women, plenty, who would go to bed with you!

Bud got in at three o'clock. Ratliff awoke. After his first hours of dead slumber, he had grown restless. He told Bud he hadn't looked for him back before daylight. Bud didn't answer and Ratliff sat up in bed and struck a match. He wanted to know what was the matter. Bud was putting a long-barreled pistol under his pillow. 'Well, I got her Goddamn gun, anyhow!' he said. Ratliff wanted to know what had happened, but Bud, wabbling a little, got under the cover.

Then he sat up, swung his feet to the floor and blurted, 'The Goddamn bitch put a gun on me!' He went on, whispering harsh and fast. 'When I started toward 'er in the room, she threw that thing in my face.' He jerked his head toward the pillow. 'She said, "I trade to sleep with you. I do it. You stay on yo' side o' that bed." She meant it, the hell-fired bitch!

'I had to lay there a couple of hours and snore to ever git a chance at her gun, and her a-layin' alongsider me. But I snatched it, finally. Damn 'er soul to hell!

'And I cold-cocked that yellow-bellied Jew pimp of a husband as I come by 'im.' Bud went off into a hot, thick-tongued stream of obscenity.

Ratliff laughed. 'D'ju git yuh money back?'

'To hell with the money!' Bud continued to mutter to himself as he straightened out in bed for sleep.

Ratliff lay on his back and shook with laughter. Bud had begun to find out about women, find out what he had learned early.

Next morning aboard the *Hessie,* as he and Bud were on their way to Brunswick to take the cars back home, he looked through a window to the captain's cabin and saw a thing that galled him. There sat China Swann, done out like Pharaoh's daughter, or one of Darien's big rich. A black-headed wench was with her, all done out, too: one of her girls, probably. At the jump-up, he thought the hussy was trailing him. He could have sworn she was staring at him just before he looked in the window, but she never did give any sign of it while he stood there. She's propositionin' the captain now, likely, he thought. She stayed in the cabin most of the way, coming out on deck just one time. She spoke to Bud. He was up toward the front. But Bud paid her no mind; that was one time in his life he wasn't in the humor. She didn't go any further with it. Ratliff kept to the stern, talking to the other rafthands. He told them about Bud and the Jew woman. He had to talk loud on account of the racket of the engines, but he didn't care if she heard. He didn't even tell the boys he could have slept with her the night before if he'd a-wanted to.

When he and Poss got back to Uncle Mundy's, he learned that his mother had died at Nine-and-a-Quarter. She had died suddenly with heart trouble, according to a letter from Mona, written two weeks before. The news made him glum. Once, he had wanted to kill her and hadn't: couldn't—he wasn't sorry for it now. That seemed far back, in another time. Still, he hadn't looked for her dying to make him feel like it did. He had cursed her many a time, and hadn't thought of her to give a damn, since he left there. Somehow, though, it was like shutting the big, black book the last time and for all—the way the preacher did it at pa's funeral.

He got to thinking about Mona the next day. He wondered what ever happened to that playhouse they built out of stave backs, just before he left. It probably went up the chimney in smoke a hundred years ago. He kept hankering so to see her that he told Bud he wouldn't be able to make the next trip with them. He even started to Nine-and-a-Quarter and got as far as Longpond. Waiting for the train, he decided he was a fool for ever thinking of it: he'd been as good as dead to Mona and Bob for eight years!

When he got back to Uncle Mundy's, danged if Poss and Bud and some strange nigger hadn't gone on with the raft. It looked like Bud didn't mind at all filling his place at the bow oar with a nigger, nor Poss mind going off with him—a strange nigger he'd never seen before!

A month had passed before Ratliff drifted logs again into Darien, but he was still sulking when the trip started and he quarreled seriously with Bud before they reached the Public Boom. It was well after dark when they tied up. An inspector, however, had heard Bud's approaching hallo and was waiting for them. Ratliff did not remain

98

for the measurement of the timber, but walked into town alone. As he passed the lights of Hammersmith's saloon and restaurant on the riverfront street, a voice called to him: 'Snake Sutton!'

He halted and looked back. A woman was poised on the doorstep, facing him. It was China Swann. He started, but he remained standing where he had paused. She was coming toward him. She looked like a sycamore after a rain, in her white dress and red mantilla. She moved rapidly until she was almost to him, then she slowed her step, hesitated.

'Where's Bud True?' Her voice sounded as if she were asking just to have something to say.

Ratliff's head jerked backward. 'At the Boom.'

'At the Boom,' she said. The pupils of her eyes seemed as big as nail-heads. She looked away. 'Oh, I just heard his holler.

Ratliff shifted his rifle to his shoulder and glanced behind him down the street. As the pause widened, he started to move on.

Her voice was raised to arrest him. 'I saw you frail hell out of McMillan that day. I just wanted to make my thanks.'

He looked at her as if he smelled a bad odor. 'No cause for thanks.' One side of his mouth twisted up as he paused. 'I'd bin a-layin' for 'im.'

'I didn't have any more use for him than you did.' The black holes in her eyes were focused on his face.

'You?' He looked her over warily, then his gaze rested on hers. 'He took a raft away from me once.' She did not speak, but her eyebrows gathered swiftly in an expression of sympathy. 'When I wuz nuthin' but a boy! The self-made son-of-a-bitch!'

'He's that, all right!'

'My first trip to Darien—I was just sixteen—he wuz twice my size—said I stole it at Hard Bargain—ever' stick come off the Oconee!'

She was closer to him now. 'Proud he ain't been back around to my house any more.'

'Ain't?'

'Guess he thinks I had something to do with it, and I don't care if he does.'

Ratliff smiled.

She twisted a red fan in her hands, as her gaze held on to his. 'Had to say my thanks. Didn't want to bother you. Not when you were washing up on the porch that evening.

'I reckon I ought to be a-thankin' you.' He cleared his throat. 'Using yo' porch, and that drink.'

Her lips had parted and she closed them and swallowed before she spoke. 'Oh, nottall!'

'It 'uz a big help!' His eyes dropped awkwardly.

The fan came open in her hands. It fluttered against her bosom. 'The man that bites Diggs McMillan's thumb off can use my back porch, or front either—any time.'

He looked up. As he stared at her, his mouth set and his head tilted. He turned around without a word and walked away.

Before he reached the Timber Tavern he was pleased that he had met China. It perked him up. She's a shiny-lookin' bitch and just as slick as she looks, he thought. His step livened as he passed by the Jew stores and fruit stands of North Way, and he smiled. She took Captain Henry in, but she can't trick me. Her face formed before him: the pupils in her eyes growing bigger, her cheeks seeming to draw in and her white skin to glow in the shadows. It looked like she was feelin' it, like it meant a lot to her, he thought. And that jerk that came into her voice. She damn near fooled me for a minute. But she ain't sharp enough for that.

He had been low in his mind when he met her. Now the thing he had been thinking of doing didn't seem so hell-fired terrible. It just seemed necessary. My quittin' Bud True wouldn't be as bad as tryin' to stay on with him, looks like, he thought. I'm not sayin' for good an' all yet—I'm just tryin' to get on to the Tavern and get good an' drunk.

He had supposed that his row began yesterday about the 'gaitors and the weather. He saw now that that was not the beginning. Bud's been different toward me ever since I made up the lazy-pin, or as soon as everybody got to usin' it, he thought. I wonder if it wasn't really before that: as far back as when I worked up my lick. There's always been only one way to do a thing with Bud, he says the right way: his way. He believes everything about the river just like it was handed down to him, because of his pa and his grandpa, because they were pole-boat captains. He says it's bad luck to set out on a black-water freshet, to mock an owl in the daytime, to kill a water spider, and a lot more things. On account of it's always been said. He's never tried them out to see. He thought there wasn't but one way to build a bow oar, too!

Bud had reared up right now when he had tried to joke him about the 'gaitors. And it's a fact: Bud didn't say anything about it yesterday morning when they were growlin', he thought. Just after he tied up there at Sister Pine Round in the afternoon—in broad daylight— sayin' that the 'gaitors had told him, Bud, that there was goin' to be a storm, like he and the 'gaitors had a special language between them. It wasn't a damn thing but luck—good, or bad, as you look at it—that it did rain and blow some. We could have made another ten miles before dark if we'd gone on and we'd have hit the tide right today. Ratliff looked up and saw the oblong of light from the door of the Tavern.

There had been no excuse for Bud's saying what he had that day. He was just mad and contentious because he'd been shown up. Ratliff saw his face now: eyebrows and cheekbones almost meeting and his short-stemmed pipe smoking in his whiskers like a brush fire. He heard the words:

'Even if I hadn't told yuh better, looks like anybody with good sense wouldn't put a sinkin' gum raft, a raft we didn't put together and don't know what it'll take, into a tight place like that . . . Just

'cause yuh got through 'thout tearin' up don't make it right. . . You
didn't have no business a-puttin' a raft into Sansavilla Cut at this
stage of water . . .You didn't know that bar at the lower end had
washed out. . . Just fool's luck! Fool's luck don't make a raftsman . . .
Yo' trouble is, young man, you done got too damn big for yo'
britches!'

Ratliff felt warmth creep up his neck, into his ears. Fool's luck!
Fool is right! I'd be a fool to stay on under a man like Bud, he
thought. He pushed open the swinging doors to the Tavern, walked
up to the bar. I know enough to be my own pilot. The bartender with
the filmy eyes looked at him. I'd be a fool to stay on as anybody's
bowhand. 'Whiskey, barfoot,' he said.

He had downed two drinks in silence when a group of raftsmen
thudded across the sawdusty floor of the barroom. There were three:
one a young fellow, limping on a shortened leg, who spoke: 'How's
the ole rattler this e'nin'? Chokin' any more 'gaitors' lights out?'

Ratliff smiled with dignity. The intruders, who looked washed-up
and well-fed, had money on them and wanted liquor. They urged
Ratliff and he drank with them. By the time the treating had gone
around the group to him, his state of mind had considerably brightened. And the group had gone from first names to more familiar
terms. The cripple, Ike Pippin, devoted himself to drawing Ratliff
out. He told a funny story about Sutton's Lick, involving a raft race
between two Coventry niggers, one of whom had used the lick. He
talked about the lazy-pin and asked Ratliff if he had any new tricks
with a raft. Ratliff's eyes had grown bright and his lips loose and he
felt inordinately excited without knowing why. Yeah, he'd been workin' on a device, he couldn't tell the particulars, that would make a
raft steer itself: so the hands could drink and play skin all the way
down. The crowd had another drink on this.

When they had downed it, he turned from the bar and looked at them solemnly. 'I come by way of Sansavilla Cut today. That's why I 'uz feelin' so low this e'nin'.'

A fat, clean-shaven fellow leaning against the bar spoke, in a barking voice: 'Sansavilla Cut! How'd yuh git down heah? Walk?'

Still solemn, Ratliff looked steadily at him for a moment, then shifted his gaze. 'Drifted. Made the Cut all right. It's left me feelin' powerfully low, though.'

'Made the Cut, hell!' said the fat man. 'You might-a made it, but not on no raft.'

Ike Pippin asked, 'How come you so low?'

For a moment Ratliff looked above their heads, saw Bud's beetling face again. 'Looks like it's about broke me and ole Bud True up. And there waun't a thing to it. I didn't mean a thing.' His voice, somehow, sounded to him like Bud's. ''Twaun't the raft: we come through 'thout a-loosenin' a binder, aer losin' a pin.' Fleetingly, tangentially, he promised himself it would not be Bud's voice when he got through. 'It 'uz that ole pair of baggy-butted jeans of Bud's. You know the ole pair he's wore so long: looks like he's a-totin' a bushel of meal in the bottom of?'

The raftsmen laughed. 'How in hell did yuh git by that bar at the lower mouth?' asked the fat man.

'I 'uz a-comin' to that.' Ratliff looked off toward the fireplace where a stuffed catamount stood on the mantel. 'Right smart current in the Cut today, and a gusty breeze—you know, one of them kind that smacks the water and bounces up ag'in. Well, I'd bin thinkin' about helpin' git rid of them ole baggy britches a long time and it come to me, as we 'uz just above the Cut. He had turned the stern over to me, a-sayin' I'd better stick to the river: we couldn't make the Cut. And he'd done gone to sawin' gourds in the lean-to.

'Just 'foh we turned in the Cut, Poss and me rigged us up a pike pole with a cross-arm on it, so we could stand 'er up right 'hind the second binder. Then I slipt up to where Bud 'uz a-sleepin'.' Ratliff paused a moment and his eyes shone brighter. 'I loosened his jeans. I got hold of his pants-legs and when I started easin' 'em off, he turned over and muttered sump'n in his sleep.'

Ratliff paused with a suppressed smile on his face.

The fat man grinned. 'Whut'd 'e say?'

'I couldn't be sure—didn't make sense to me—sump'n about, "I'll git over, Jew lady—please, be keerful of that gun!"'

The raftsmen whooped. Ratliff waited straight-faced and patient. He went on. 'We got set. Come down the Cut at a purty fast clip. We had them britches fastened on our pike pole mast and just above the bar we raised our sail. The wind caught 'em and bellowsed out the butt like a big hornets' nest. We had ropes tied on the end of the legs and Poss had hold of 'em. Just as we got to the bar, he pulled them pant-legs down, and I'll be a son-of-a-bitch if the wind didn't pick up the front end of that raft like you'd snatch up a youngun. The dang raft jumped the bar, jumped it like a hound over a rail fence.' He stared with serious eyes, glanced toward the bartender. 'Goddamn thing set us down on t'other side, as neat 'n' smooth as ole Joe, heah, kin set down a glassful of whiskey.'

'The trouble started when we slapped down on the water ag'in. It disturbed Mister True's slumberin'. He got up, he seen his britches 'uz gone, and started a-cussin' and a-rearin'. They waun't plum gone, neither. The wind had just frazzled out the legs. But you know how he is about them britches. He's madder'n hell right now: I don't know whether it's more his britches, aer me a-goin' through the Cut.'

Everybody but the bartender laughed and the drinking was renewed. The talk turned to fighting (Ratliff was asked about the flavor of Diggs McMillan's thumb), and then to women. Ike Pippin and a dark, wiry man called Jack wanted Ratliff to go with them to Miss Pearl's: the girls there had asked Jack to bring him around. Ratliff said he had no time for those bags as Miss Pearl's; his voice was thick and gruff. Three there were good-lookers, Jack said.

Ratliff felt like having a woman. He wondered if this wasn't the time to go. He looked at the faces before him. But, are you going to let these country hoppers take you to a whorehouse? he asked himself. 'Hell, I don't spend no money on it,' he said. ' 'Sides, I got more stuff'n I kin git around to nohow. I got a date with the best un in Darien—the only un I'd tetch—and I don't aim to pay for that.' Jack's thin face turned away. Ratliff saw disbelief in it. 'She stopped me as I 'uz comin' up heah. Don't know yit whether I'll go.'

'Hell!' the fat man said. 'You don't aim—I saw you talkin' with a pertickler woman in front of Hammersmith' early this e'nin'. Don't try to make out you gittin' that!'

Ratliff turned toward the bartender. 'My whistle's dry. Le's have another un.' The three men were looking at him. Captain Henry's woman, he thought. Why not go? It's not doing him any good for you to stay away. The sooner he knows she's crooking him, the better off he'll be. 'Like as not, if she had on a white dress and a red head rag,' he said.

'That smells like manure to me,' said the fat man.

'I'll tell yuh, le's just escort 'im 'round to the Birdcage,' said Jack. 'See that he gits theah safe.'

Ratliff stared at the man. His face grew more flushed. 'All right, Goddamnit, we'll just go,' he said. 'I'll make you acquainted with some gals—I'll let you watch me go to bed with her—at least as far as the door!'

Ratliff and the three others gathered up their hats and strode unsteadily toward the barroom door.

CHAPTER

11

AS CHINA STARED at Ratliff's retreating back after their conversation on the riverfront street, she dropped her fan. Her breathing stopped, her face grew twisted. She felt an impulse to run, to run after him and grab his arm: to take it back; that last she didn't mean to say! But he did not waver, he walked steadily on. She picked up the fan. Then she inhaled in heaving gulps. The dirty rat! The stinking rafthand! Hoghead! Idiot! The Goddamned—her silent expletives grew more and more violent and obscene.

After a while she looked around her in the empty street: gray, uncertain ruts of sand, daubs of yellow light at the windows, the blank hollow of the worn path in the sidewalk. She felt weak and suddenly tired. She put her fingers to the little white scar at the edge of her hair and turned slowly around. Her feet moved along the path toward home. She walked faster. You ought to have been there long ago, she told herself: with sailors in town tonight. Lou and Delia won't know what to do if anything happens. She turned off the sidewalk into a sandy path. What the hell, anyhow! Out in the night like a streetwalker! Playing for a penniless rafthand, chancing yourself and your business—a good business, with a house and lot almost in your hands. Seborn'll deed the place to you if you work it right. He's just about as straight a man as you'll ever lay hand on, big-hearted really. What the hell do you think you're looking for? Yes, what the hell! The routine of this argument was familiar, wearied her. She walked on, entered her gate, and climbed the steps in the soft, varicolored glow from her front door.

When she was in her bedroom, she changed her dress for a silk wrapper and rang for the black maid. Delia reported that seven customers had come while she was gone; five were in the house, mostly sailors: no racket yet, and China smiled attentively. After she had gone, China swallowed down a quarter-glassful of brandy, but it did not burn beyond her throat. Like water tonight; you'd better leave it alone, she told herself, and stood staring at the open wardrobe. Snake's grim, muddy face, with its look of astonishment, has slipped into her mind. She closed the door. You didn't go about it like you planned, she thought. She had expected Bud True to be there, to give her help. When you saw that face you forgot your tricks, she told herself. You didn't know what you were going to say next when you started. But the hunch you had was right: right up to that last chirp of yours, when you tried to draw him in. Chirping! She went downstairs.

Downstairs, she put on her manner for trade: she walked with a loitering step, posturing and smiling as she paused to speak to her girls and their men. But she did not stop. She moved through the long parlor, weaving past sofas and taborets, through the back parlor and the taproom. For a while she waited with Delia in the reception room and answered the door. Later she sat with the black-haired girl, Lou, in the back parlor and listened to a big German sailor blow a piccolo. She held her gaze on the fat fingers and the long hooked lip, but she could not hold her ears, her mind. Chirping: could use her back porch, or her front! You ought to have known better than to pull a used trick on him, an old game, she told herself. You threw away the chance you've been waiting a month for. And a hell of a month! At first, she had tried to laugh it off like a drunk; then she had tried to make sense of it; then she had tried to buy her way out: white satin dress, beaded slippers, red mantilla. But finally, two weeks ago it had come to her that she had been fumbling and losing the deal for lack of nerve and sense. This was a master, a master of the breed. And you've never met a master before, she told herself. She no longer saw the sailor's fingers.

At midnight, as she played solitaire in her bedroom, her mind was back at it: she had pitched away her chance! What did you think he was going to do, follow you like a puppy? she asked herself. She dealt cards upon the piles on the table before her with tense care. Hell, this isn't any three-dollar job, or ten-dollar night! He isn't any pilothouse sport, any gold bed-brick, any jack of diamonds! Snake Sutton uses a different kind of money. Her gaze strayed. She saw his back swoop up; a paunchy body floated before her in the distance of the room. Swoop like a hawk swoops! Quicker. She had not seen it then: she had only remembered seeing it afterward: afterward, a hundred times. Her hands rested on the table-top, spilling cards.

Ratliff and his companions had stopped on the way to eat after they left the Tavern and it was one o'clock when they got to the Bird-cage. The place was quiet. The parlors had cleared. The German sailor's piping had ceased and he had gone to bed with the black-haired girl.

As Ratliff strode into the reception room, followed by Jack Jolley; Willard, the fat man; and the cripple, Ike Pippin, Delia scuttled away from the door to get in front of them. She stopped in the double entrance to the long parlor to head off their advance. Their faces were still heavy with the liquor they had drunk and the fat man's neck seemed too big for his collar. Ratliff looked around him. He felt astonishment. Even with the dim lights, he could see it was a mighty dressed-up place.

'Any pertickler guls y'all wanted to see?' Delia's tone was professionally polite, but her black face was impassive.

The fat man pulled at his collar and grunted. 'Run 'em all out and let us look at 'em.'

Ratliff glanced down at her. 'Yeah, run 'em all out.'

Jack Jolley stepped forward. 'This heah's Mister Jones. I think he—'

'Hup. Hold it!' Ratliff interrupted. He looked at Jolley and smiled loosely, then shifted his glance to the maid. "I want—you know who I want! Where is she: where's China?' His head weaved a little as he looked out from under his lashes.

'Miss China?' Delia's manner stiffened. 'Miss China's gone to bed.'

'Well, git 'er up!' Ratliff said.

'I kain't wake 'er. You don't' need Miss China heah. Just tell me what gurl yuh wants.'

Ratliff wagged his head. 'I said China. Go wake 'er up. Tell 'er I'm heah.'

Delia did not move. 'Miss China don't' go to bed wid nobody. Y'all knows that: y'ought-a know it.'

'That's what you think.' Ratliff turned half around to glance at the men with him. 'I got a date with her. Go tell 'er I'm heah.' He took a step toward Delia. 'Don't stand theah with yo' teeth in yuh mouth. Go tell 'er 'fore you make both of us mad.'

Delia moved up the stairway, a step at a time. After she had reached the landing, Ratliff followed her with the others behind him. When they got into the upper hallway the maid was out of sight and they stood looking about at the pink wallpaper and dark closed doors. The door at which Ratliff was gazing opened and China stood in it, dressed in a purple wrapper. Her eyes widened when she recognized him. She turned loose the doorknob. He was drunk, pretty drunk. Her eyes narrowed, then their gaze moved on to the others, gathering close to him. What the hell are they doing here? she thought. She swallowed. Why, the drunken son-of-a-bitch has brought along his bodyguard! To go to bed with me? To watch?

Her voice was cold when she spoke. 'What's this all about? What are y'all doing up here? Why didn't you wait downstairs?'

The chill of her words laid Ratliff's inner fog, brought feeling to the numbness. Her forehead below the red pompadour looked sharp as flint. He put his hand to his neck and dropped his glance. 'Hell!' he said, in a raised tone of voice, then he grinned. 'I didn't like the front porch, aer the back porch, so I just came inside.'

China's mouth crooked briefly. Oh, the drunken dog, hog—no, man! she thought. She wondered fleetingly if he could be got away from them, got soberer. 'You came a long way inside,' she said. 'Did you find those fellows on the porch?' She stepped aside to let the maid pass. 'Delia, see the gent'-man downstairs.' Ratliff's loosened face twitched. She saw stage-fright on it, followed by disappointment, supplanted by wounded pride. It was more than she had ever been permitted to see on that face before.

'We ain't a-goin' downstairs,' he blurted, and his head tilted back. The crippled Pippin sidled along the banisters toward the landing. 'Hup, theah, Ike! Hold it.' He rocked on his feet. His eyelids and lips seemed to swell. 'I—I got invited heah. And I want to prove it to my frien's—tha's all!'

The buff-colored skin beneath China's eyes hardened. 'Get out, you drunken river rat!' she said.

He took a step toward her. 'Was all! Was all! But since you a-tryin' to gimme the lie, it's not, you slut!' He raised his fist. 'You're goin' to bed with me, aer I'm a-gonna—'

Her lips had moved while he was still speaking, 'Send Eef for the man,' she had said to Delia. The maid had sidled down the hall and around the corner. Jack Jolley, who had seen this, moved toward the landing. Now she cut Ratliff off. 'I may be a whore, but I've got some rights in my own house.' She glanced quickly at the other men.

110

'I'm gittin' out 'fore this fool gits us in trouble,' Jolley called to Pippin. Willard grabbed Ratliff by the arm and pulled him toward the stairway. Pippin gave help as Ratliff struggled. Seesawing, they drew away to the landing.

China looked after them. Her face grew distorted and purplish. She leaned forward, followed them up. 'Get out! Get out, you son-of-a-bitch!' she yelled at Ratliff.

He heaved his shoulders, broke loose from Pippin and Willard, sending the fat man backward down the stairs. He seized China by the forearm. Delia (who had returned unseen) came up behind him and struck him on the shoulder with a club. He whirled swiftly, grabbed the front of Delia's dress with a lunge and slammed her against the wall, so that her head popped. 'Come on back!' he yelled to the men below. 'This just started!' Still holding China's forearm, he yanked her toward him, forced her toward her knees.

She went limp and stared up into his face. "Let 'em go, you drunk fool! Let 'em go!' she said.

Ratliff stood over her, gazing into the big pupils of her yellow eyes, and listened to the front door slam.

CHAPTER

12

'NOW THAT WE'RE OUT for ourse'f, I'm goin' to show yuh how to make us some money.' Ratliff spoke to Poss, as they waited on the wharf at Darien for the early morning boat to Brunswick. He stood with his legs apart, bouncing his back against a piling that extended above the edge of the platform. The marsh grass across the river, the hull of the overturned boat beyond the quay, the barnacles on it, even, looked clean-washed in the slant sunlight.

'I all 'uz hyearn it take money to make money.' Poss did not look up from where he sat on the wide planks, tying a broken shoestring. He sniffled and hawked to clear his throat.

'I've got sump'n figgered out,' Ratliff said, shifting his gaze from Poss to the gray-green river. The tide was coming in and dead grass and other driftage moved slowly on the surface. Two hours before he had gone swimming in it. But the river had been clean enough then: what he could see of it. He had come to the wharf after he left the Birdcage and had caught him an hour-and-a-half nap on the boards, before he took his wash. He looked back at Poss. "While I 'uz walkin' 'round waitin' for it to git time to pull you out, I run into ole man Jackson—you know, buys for Schardt and Schiewitz—on the street a-goin' some'ers—God knows where! He said they had an order for a limited amount of ash and would pay twelve dollars a thousand for it, six-hundred-foot average. We're a-goin' into the ash business and git rich.'

Poss sniffled again. 'I'd be satisfied if'n us could git another job on a bow oar. I sho' need a chew: you got any 'backer?'

'A bowhand's never made more'n his rations, and damn hard rations to boot. Even Bud True admitted to that. We know better'n to try to make money pullin' a bow oar, Poss.'

Poss raised his head. 'Seems sort-a funny not to be wid him no moah!' He looked at Ratliff. 'Ain't yuh got no 'backer?'

Ratliff ran his hand into his hip-pocket. 'Damn good fun to me!' His eyebrows puckered as he looked down at Poss, handing him a tobaco plug.

'Sho', us'll git along.' Poss turned the chew over in his mouth. 'Us all 'uz has.' He grinned. 'How us gonna make dis money?'

Ratliff looked at the plug he held again in his hand, but slipped it into his pocket without cutting a chew. 'Goin' to buy stumpage and operate for ourse'f.'

'Where us gonna git money to buy stumpage? Mister Bud didn't even have money to do dat.'

'Maybe it waun't just money he needed. 'Tain't all money. Sho' it takes some. But maybe it won't take so much if we work it right. And that may not be so hard.' Ratliff started bouncing against the piling again. 'I feel lucky today: luckier than I ever felt in my life.'

'You mean lucky wid cyards?'

'Yep. I feel like I could take 'em today.'

'You ain't never played so much cyards, Snake. How much money yuh got lef' on yuh?'

'I'll have five dollars left when I git my ticket home. How much kin you let me have to git in the game on the cars going back to Lumber City?'

113

Poss looked off at four axe-toting raftsmen coming toward the wharf. 'I reckon I'll have 'bout eight dollars over. S'pose you lose: where us be den wid our money-makin'?'

'Not much worse off—not enough to make much difference. And I'll still figger out sump'n. Maybe I kin git Uncle Mundy to let us cut the ash on the place.'

'Unka Mundy ain't gwine do dat. 'Sides, dat ain't enough to make up no raft.'

The soft, vibrating whistle of the boat came to them from the river below. The talking stopped for a moment, then Ratliff went on. 'It'll be a good start. You kin git a long way on a good start.' He began his bouncing again. 'But you forgettin' I'm feelin' lucky today: luckier than I ever felt 'fore in my life.'

Poss grinned at him. They both stepped to the edge of the platform to watch the small, stubby-looking boat pull up to the wharf.

But when they quit the train at Lumber City to walk the ten miles home, Ratliff's luck had added only eight dollars to their joint capital. Their twenty-one dollars would not even pay half of the haul bill, not to mention stumpage. Still he paused on top of a hill, as they crossed the sand ridges east of the town, and gave his river holler. And he shouted at Poss, 'A big ash raft!'

During the next two days he talked Uncle Mundy into selling them his forty-three trees at three dollars a thousand feet, to be paid after the raft was sold. With the old man going along to back him up, he extended this credit to cover fifty more from a swamp-owner above them, at three dollars and a quarter a thousand feet; and he hired an ox team for the hauling. This last he effected by paying fifteen dollars on the feed bill and helper's wages and promising to pay a dollar a thousand for the logs hauled. He borrowed Uncle Mundy's yoke of oxen to fill out the rule cart team. At daybreak Monday morning his and Poss's axes were chucking among the big trees below the bluff field. He said they couldn't afford to lose a minute: it was July and low water was at hand; if the river fell another foot they couldn't get through.

On the following Sunday morning he thought about the contrariness and general cussedness of things as he and Poss put logs into the water at the upper swamp. They were 'skiffing' these logs down to Dead River to raft them along with those from Uncle Mundy's place. But Uncle Mundy's logs were still in the woods; the teamster hadn't touched them. He cursed silently as he guided a ten-log skiff along the river channel with a pike pole, his wet shirt-tail slapping bare legs. He had counted on having the logs rafted and ready to go Saturday, but it was black dark when he and Poss had dropped the last tree. He had been surprised that the river had stayed up as well as it had. And on top of everything else, Uncle Mundy had to rear up about their getting the timber out on Sunday, as he and Poss were leaving home this morning. It tried a fellow's patience.

He looked down at his pole as it stood perpendicular in the water for a moment. It seemed that the river was rising instead of falling: up a couple of inches since they had started. They might have plenty of water, might be better off for havin' lost two days. He hadn't figured the river to rise any in the middle of July. It was beginnin' to look like he might be in too big a hurry. He guessed the market would still be there when they tied up at the Boom. Suspicion rose in his mind. Has all your hurry been gettin' to market? he asked himself. Haven't you been thinkin' about that whore too much? To be sure, he had remembered China since he got back home. Hell, he wasn't a no-mind! He had thought about the let-down feeling that came over him as he got out of the bed that night. And his desire to get away from the place. Reckon you oughtn't to have hit her, but she looked like a dyin' calf when she caught hold of your wrist, he told himself. A whore had no cause to look like that. And it was only a smack with the back of his hand.

But since then you've turned around in your mind and started back-trackin', he told himself. Queer thing: looks like your through-with-it feelin' got less the farther away you came, and your ready-to-go-back feelin' gits bigger the longer you stay away. He had heard men say they'd got enough—for one bedding! He turned the skiff into the mouth of Dead River.

The flat echo of wooden mauls continued to fill the swamp after night came Monday. From either end of their raft, Ratliff and Poss cast tall, swaying shadows in the wavering light of a small fire. About them in every direction was a dark, level surface of water: it issued from the blackness of the trees to the left, from the trees above and below; to the right (on the open course of Dead River) it caught a pallor, like blue milk, and became invisible again in the woods beyond. The flood water made shallow concave circles about the fun-nel-shaped trunks. At the raft stern, Ratliff's mauling ceased and he passed by the fire, walking toward the bow. He wore only a pair of muddy pants, rolled up above his knees. His shoulders and back glis-tened with sweat. Then his maul sounded alternately with Poss's as they drove the last pins into a forward binder.

When they had finished, he stood leaning upon the mallet handle. His face was drawn and the stubble on it stood out like hog bristles. There were pallid bulges beneath his eyes and a gray-brown ring stained his lips. 'Jesus, dark comes quick in this damn swamp!' he said.

The points of Poss's jaws and cheekbones caught the light as he looked up from the binder where he sat. He breathed with a heavy soughing. 'Dis fresh come quick, too.'

'Yeah. If that Goddurned Terry knew how to handle an ox team in the mud, we'd 'ave had our oars up by now and be ready to go.'

Poss wagged a heavy head on a limber neck.

'Well, come on.' Ratliff loosed the maul and picked up an axe. 'I know where's some black-cypress saplin's that'll make oars—not so far from heah. Reckon this'll gimme a chance to try out my saplin' idea that made Bud True so mad. Git the boat paddle.'

Poss had been sitting with his legs flat on the logs, his knees turned in. Now he pulled his knees up under his chin, but did not rise. 'You don't aim to git 'em tonight? You kain't see to cut no oars!'

'Christ, yes! We got to git away from heah.'

The whites of Poss's eyes caught in the firelight. 'Gret Gawd, Snake! You don't aim to turn loose tonight?'

'To hell I don't!'

'Yestidy you say us had plenty time—wid the river a-risin'.'

Ratliff let the axe slide from his shoulder to the log on which he stood. 'Yeah, Goddamnit! That 'uz yestidy. How'd I know the river 'uz a-goin' to break loose like the bottom of hell? And she's goin' higher still: we gotta git out'n heah now to have a chance to run off'n this fresh.'

'I don't believe us kin keep out'n de swamp on dis much water.' Poss looked off toward the river.

The bulges beneath Ratliff's eyes twitched as he looked at Poss. 'Kin if we start in time and keep in the middle of the stream.'

' 'E's a rough ole river, lak dis.'

Staring at Poss, Ratliff's eyes widened and his right cheek trembled. 'Hell, Poss.' He paused. 'Yuh ain't losin' confidence in us?' His gaze shifted to the water pushing against the trees, carrying away bits of moss and bark on it's flat surface.

'Naw, sho' not.' Poss cleared his throat. 'If'n us waun't so wo' out already.'

Ratliff squinted like a man in pain. He struck the log with the end of his axe sharply. 'This Goddamn son-of-a-bitch kain't lick me!' His voice sounded strained. 'I don't git tired.' He spoke louder. 'I'm a rattlesnake! Just makes me mad and lets out my poison. I'm full of poison and rearin' to go right now!'

'Sho'!' Poss grinned. He slapped a mosquito on his forearm and got up and followed Ratliff to the batteau.

When they got back with the timbers for the oars, Poss said his backbone was making his belly look like a crosscut saw. Ratliff said Uncle Mundy would be sure to bring them some supper when he brought rations for the trip. It was time he was coming. But it seemed a long while before Uncle Mundy got there, and he brought no supper. He paddled the end of his boat up on the logs and remained seated in it. He had brought neither supper nor rations for the trip. He wanted to know when in damnation they were coming to the house!

Ratliff felt harassed, frazzled out. Damn if Uncle Mundy wasn't gettin' plumb childish. He laid down the oar he was peeling and came to the edge of the raft. How, in the name of common sense, did Uncle Mundy think they'd ever get off tonight without everybody helping some? he said. Tonight! In this freshet? Uncle Mundy caught hold of the sides of the boat and crawled out. He straightened up before he spoke again. "You talk lak you ain't got much respeck for dis river, not like no raftsman!'

Ratliff frowned and jerked up his chin. 'Do? Well, I got respeck enough to know if we don't go pretty quick, we may not be able to in another week.' He went on to say that then everybody between Dublin and Darien would be floating ash out of the swamps and drifting it down the river to put a freshet on the market.

'Dat's a thing yuh got to git used to if'n you run de river,' Uncle Mundy said.

Sure, if you trifled around and let it happen, Ratliff told him. Uncle Mundy spoke to Poss, too: he urged them both to stop and come on to the house, but when Ratliff said angrily that he would eat supper in Darien three nights hence, he went back to his boat. He stopped beside it and turned again. He looked gaunt and bent in the firelight, but he brought his shoulders up straight. 'Dis river a big man! You ack like you don't know dat.' He left and he did not return.

The old man had grown fractious as hell, Ratliff thought. Since yesterday morning he had deliberately gone about making trouble for them. Ratliff had to take off time to paddle to the house and get the rations. It was midnight before they finally untied the ropes that moored the raft among the swamp trees and pushed it out into the open course of Dead River.

As pilot, he worked the bow oar at night to see ahead better, and left the stern to Poss. Now the current (usually slight in Dead River) moved their raft like shoal water, carrying them, when they came out of the mouth, beyond the middle of the main stream. Slowly the raft responded to Ratliff's deep, short pulls and straightened out on the back of the big Oconee. He stood still for a moment, mid-raft, with his oar motionless. The pulse of the current was like a drink of liquor to him. Blood stirred in his head, the heaviness behind his eyes, on his shoulders, dissolved.

He turned his face slowly about, staring into the vagueness of the dark. The heavy overcast of clouds was now dimly translucent with moonlight. Beyond the circle of their raft fire, it sifted a thin, shadowy, gray dust upon the scene. The river's spread, invisible in extent, made it look unfamiliar. Near-by its surface took shape and was touched with evanescent glints, but he could not make out the edge of the swamp, only its indefinite outline against he sky. The raft moved on and he discerned a formless, darker gray to his left, which he knew to be the willow piles at the end of the reach.

He felt the tug of a cross-current toward the willows and dipped his oar to the right. 'Half-a-lick to Injun!' He called to Poss in a low voice, as a driver reassures a horse. Far in the swamp to his left, he heard the flapping of an owl's wings. He'll have to get out of there to find supper, he thought. Now he felt a pull beneath the raft to his right. Her back's damn slippery tonight! He stood still and squinted his eyes at the dark. Then he shut them for a moment and stopped breathing. That's it! The rattle of the water at Devil's Elbow: he could hear it above the soft swell of sound on the surface around him. He had told Poss before they left that they'd know pretty quick whether they were going to get to Darien, they'd know as soon as they hit the Elbow. If they got by that, there wasn't anything else could stop them.

Now he tried to estimate the distance of that indistinct rattling. 'Heah 'er, Poss? 'Sa half-a-mile.'

' 'Bout dat.' Poss's voice sounded distant.

Ratliff began his pull by the sound in his ears. He moved his oar with deliberate care, calling the licks to Poss in a low voice. As the rattle grew louder, he moved faster. Then suddenly he was on it: the swarming hiss and slap of sound was in his head; glints of light, flecks of foam, slats of shadow danced at the corners of his eyes. His oar bent like a rib under his driving. He ran and sweat rained down his body. The logs under him rocked on the flood, sweeping down upon the swamp. There was a crushing jerk and a shadow became solid: the right corner of the bow had hung on a tree. The stern was swinging fast into the suck. He strained at his oar. Then a wooden pin popped up in to the darkness, the boom log and butting binder pushed upward and skidded past the black trunk, leaving a white scar. The raft moved again; momentum carried it onward down the river, past the suck.

Now it was in the grip of another unseen current, that dragged it toward the opposite swamp, and Ratliff bent his oar again. 'Strap 'er to the point!' he shouted at Poss. From both ends of the raft they pulled against the drift. The dark, rumpling river swept across the logs. Water sluiced about his ankles. The raft was sinking. Slowly the logs rose above the surface again, and they were around the bend. They continued to pull at the oars for a time, then the pulling slowed, stopped. They were in the reach: Devil's Elbow was behind them.

Ratliff leaned against his oar and panted, looking back at Poss's crooked, shadowy form beyond the firelight. His gaze shifted to the water lapping at the edge of the raft. Plenty of current in the reaches, all right, he thought. Then he clasped the lazy-pin on the oar handle and leaned backward. He lifted his face to the sky. He yelled, starting low and gathering volume and pitch in a prolonged hallo. He listened to the echo rocking down the river. 'Catch 'im, rabbit dog!' he called. Poss laughed. He yelled again. 'Red-headed woman!'

The raft drifted out of the reach and around a bend, and another, and another bend. Sometimes he could recognize the shoreline, sometimes he could not make it out. The night wore on in even darkness. The shadow swamps, the invisible currents, the wabbling shapes of his oar blade and the water before him, grew unreal. They lulled his senses. Standing still on a reach, he could feel his feet growing numb, his shoulders sagging under their weight. The Elbow was back there, but—a feeling of steep sliding took hold of him. Some new, unknown current sucking them into an unknown swamp! His throat tightened and his insides jerked. He shook his shoulders. 'Cut it out!' he said.

He turned and looked behind him. Beyond the flickering embers was Poss's pale figure sagging against his oar handle. 'Wake up, back theah, Possum!' he yelled.

Poss grunted. 'Wish I had me a block to sit on,' he said.

'If'n you did you'd topple over in that river in five minutes.' Ratliff cut a step on his plank walk. They drifted on.

He began thinking of his experimental bow oar. Bud True raised hell with you for bringing that cypress sapling to the bluff that day, he told himself. He recalled Bud's oaths. Old Bud's eyes would bug out if he could have seen the way this cypress sapling worked at the Elbow, he told himself. He tried to conjure up the astonished face. But the face that suddenly formed in his mind was not True's: it was Mona's, sharp and greasy-eyed. He started from fright. He did not know why. Then a wave of embarrassment and shame came over him, making the nerves jerk in his arms. Name of Christmas! he thought and astonished himself. The phrase gave him almost as strange a turn as the face. He had not used it since he ran away from home. What in hell is it all about? He asked himself. He did not try to find out.

'Poss?' he called and Poss grunted. 'Yuh still back theah?' He grunted again. 'Ole Debil snap 'e elbow on us,' Ratliff said imitating Poss's voice, 'but us ez slip tru!' He gave a hacking laugh. Then he lifted his face and yelled:

> Run, Mister Bug, your bee gum's gone!
> Run, Mister Bug, the raftman's horn!

He yelled it again and again.

The raft picked up speed. He saw the gray fog of willow piles to his left, close at hand. He made out the shallow bend in the river. They were just above the mouth: the Altamaha was beyond. Then we will be out of trouble, he told himself. The raft seemed to be sliding down a rapids. He stood rigid and staring. Now it seemed to be slowing up: they must be in the bight below the mouth. He pulled at his oar, called for strokes to the white side. When they were in the reach, he yelled again:

> Look-a, look-a heah –
> We got Sunday, we got Sunday!

He walked back and put lightwood on the embers of their fire. His eyes looked like a startled deer's in the fresh blaze.

At his oar again, he could see no shoreline. Then he made out a gray-black silhouette to his left. That must be Town Bluff, he thought, or was. He felt the tremor of a cross-current, but did not move. The face in his mind now was his mother's. It stood out like a stereopticon picture. There were reddening patches on her cheeks below her temples and she stared at him. There was another face beside it: the young doctor's, Watson's. The faces brought him a feeling of confused suspicion. They were standing at her bedroom door, where they had started up from their seats as he opened it. What the hell! What the hell! he thought.

He turned back. The fire still sent up flame and he could see Poss's glazed eyelids. He looked like he was asleep, standing there with the oar in his hand. 'Cheer up, Possum,' he called. 'I'm a-goin' to fix you so yuh kin stay awake.' He went back to the fire and picked up the coffee-pot. He shook it, then dipped it in a jog hole and caught river water in it.

Poss stirred at his oar. 'Snake, you better not stay 'way from de bow so long,' he said. 'I'll fix dat coffee.'

'Aw, to hell with the bow!' His voice had a sharp, unsteady inflection in it. 'I got eyes in the back of my head.' But Poss sidled along the boom log toward the fire and Ratliff went back to his oar. 'Cook us sump'n t'eat while yuh at it, Poss. Ain't you hungry?' Poss was getting out the frying-pan and did not reply, and he went on in his heightened tone, 'Danged if I couldn't eat a billygoat, horns and all!'

The surface of the river was losing its form, growing misty. The moon must be down, he thought. Day is coming. He spoke to Poss over his shoulder. 'Warehouse Landing's ahead of us yonder. We're a long way from the bight.' He mocked the hooting of an owl shrilly, then he turned toward the fire. 'Put some taters in those ashes to roast, Poss. That's fine ashes. And hell, cook us up a pile of that sowbelly We still got some of Aunt Tish's cold biscuit. 'Le's celebrate!'

He looked back. He had felt something behind him. It couldn't have been a shadow, he thought as he stared into the misty darkness. Cross-current? He saw a gray pillow loom in the haze. It took shape. 'Great God, a texas, a steamboat!' he said. It was standing nearer the Indian side. He thrust his oar to the left. 'Run to the stern!' he shouted at Poss. Behind him Poss set down the spider, and stared. Ratliff could hear the rattle of water around the boat's hull. He looked ahead over his shoulder at the end of his pull. No, the damn thing had moved toward the white! He ran the other way with his oar, yelling at Poss, who had moved only a few feet and stood staring. "Sa steamboat! Git the hell back, theah!' He did not hear the long, quivering moan that came from Poss. He kept pulling, looking over his shoulder. No noise from the stern wheel, but the damn thing was coming: the deck, now the green window blinds in the pilothouse— plain as midday. He paused. Great God, the thing was still in front of them! 'Pull white! Pull like hell!' he yelled. He halted. 'Goddamn! We're gonna bull 'er!' He shoved his oar handle upward to bury the blade.

Suddenly the boat faded, and a piercing belly cry broke from him. It had become trees rushing toward the bow of the raft. The oar jumped out of his hands, caught on a tree-trunk. Its blade bent like a hoop and snapped. There were more trees: crunching, crackling noise. The butting binder jumped into the air. Logs reared up. He felt himself going upward, and leaped.

Warm, thick water closed over him, piled on top. He was rushed along, bumping into things. He tried to pull up to the surface and his head hit a log. He pushed downward and was swept on. He bumped a tree, caught it, and was swung around to the lower side. He made the surface and held to the trunk, panting. He could not see anything, but he could still hear limbs crackling and breaking. Gone to hell! he thought—the whole caboodle!

He got his wind and yelled, 'Where yuh, Poss?' He could hear his echo above the rattling current. He called again. It brought only an echo. 'Goddamnit, Poss! Answer me!' He kept yelling.

Day came. The surface of the water cleared. It was a milky rust-color and spread about him in thick rumples. Around the tree trunks, it spun in tight whirls. He saw one of his logs hung crosswise between two cottonwoods. Ahead through the trees, he could see the river. It bent out of sight in the distance. He looked behind him in the swamp. There were the ends of other logs along the suck, wabbling up and down. He did not call. Poss was not there.

PART TWO

China

CHAPTER

13

WHEN RATLIFF REACHED Ochwalkee that brisk February morning in 1890, his shirt was gray with sweat-wet dust—that morning that he was to drift timber again, again with Bud True. He did not pause on the threshold of the settlement. Glancing over the clump of wooden buildings at either side of the big road, he turned toward one with a painted sign above the roof of the porch. His shoulders bobbed on and his heels hit the ground in unslackened rhythm as he crossed the dirt side-walk before the store's entrance. A light dust on the road behind him settled slowly.

His eyes lowered after the momentary look and he did not lift them again, as he clomped up the steps, swung the door inward and moved toward the rear of the long, counter-lined room. The beat of his feet was loud, and the four men about the stove looked up in surprise. When he reached the big-bellied, hatless man, leaning against a counter, he stopped suddenly—as if he had halted with a company of marching men. He stood, holding to the leather jacket slung over his shoulder, and let sweat from his hatband run down his gaunt cheeks without wiping them. His face was tilted back and his eyes and mouth cut downward, as if against pain; but it was the set expression from feeling that had long since passed into numbness.

'You Grizzard?' He gave the fat man a brief look. 'I came by to pick up rations for True's raft.' Then his gaze moved past him, not fixing on anything at hand. It was as if he were looking on down the road ahead, intent upon his journey.

Grizzard wiped his owl-beak nose—it looked oddly thin in his broad face—on the back of his hand and cocked his head to one side. 'You the other bowhand True said he had to have?' It was more of a statement of confirmation for himself than a question. With half a turn, he rolled his fat back away from the counter and went around behind it.

The other men about the stove looked up at Ratliff over their outstretched hands. He appeared unconscious of their gaze.

Grizzard swung a half-filled croker-sack, the neck of which had been tied in a knot, up on top of the counter. His palm spread upward for an instant after he loosed his hold. "There she is. All ready to go.'

Ratliff picked up the sack as if to bring it to his shoulder, and then set it down.

Grizzard's fat lip parted. He batted his eyes, looked closely at Ratliff, and began talking. 'I'm new in the timber business. Looks like it takes a lot of rations to get a raft to Darien. But I fixed it up, just like True said.'

Ratliff's attention was on the bag of supplies. He began pulling at the knot that closed the mouth.

Grizzard cocked his head and went on without pausing.

' 'Sall there: fifteen pounds of lean sidemeat, a peck—no, a peck and a half of meal, a quart of coffee beans—' He turned away from the counter with a sudden show of indifference. 'Say, ain't your name Sutton?' Ratliff continued pulling at the knot, as if he had not heard him. 'Ain't you Snake Sutton?'

130

Ratliff looked up quickly, his eyes widening. Snake: he hadn't heard the name since he quit the river. He wondered fleetingly if it still belonged to him. 'Used to call me that,' he said. He put his hands on the sack again and began to feel of its contents.

Grizzard, who had come from behind the counter, turned to the men at the stove. 'This the feller who invented that pin on an oar you were talking about awhile back, Zeb—that lazy-pin.'

Ratliff spoke without looking up from the croker-sack. 'I don't feel no taters in here, Mister Grizzard.'

Grizzard shifted his gaze toward Ratliff, but went on. 'They tell me he's one of the smartest raftsmen ever run the river.'

'What about the taters?'

'About the taters?' Grizzard's voice was testy. 'Taters? I didn't know you all was supposed to git taters, too. 'Twaun't said. Not that I don't want you to have 'em and everything else needed to get that raft there. I sho' wouldn't hold out a few taters on yuh—as cheap as they are. Bud True didn't mention taters, 'cause I'd-a had 'im a bushel.' His voice became tinged with disappointment. 'And damn if I got a single tater in the whole store right now. Melissie is bringin' some more down from home this mornin', but they won't git heah for a while yet.' Now it grew hearty. 'Zeb Tompkins heah is interested to know how come you think of that lazy-pin.'

A sickle-shaped man spat at the stove and tilted his chair back. 'You one feller I bin a-wantin' to lay my eyes on,' he said. 'That lazy-pin's saved my back more'n anything ever come along.'

Ratliff blinked, stared at the man. Then he took his hands off the sack and his gaze moved past the unfamiliar face. Lazy-pin! The word was sweet, like new syrup after a summer of dry corn pone. Deep-buried images tumbled into his mind: Bud True's big back, pumping up and down, as he played with that first lazy-pin on the bow-oar handle; the fast-talking inspector at the Boom, who made the joke about it. Wrinkles gathered at Ratliff's eyes and his mouth loosened.

'Yeah?' He looked quickly at the man. 'Proud to know that—saved mine a lot, too.' The man resumed talking and he moved nearer the stove to listen, but after a few minutes his hands jerked upward from his sides and he went back to the croker-sack. 'I'd seen the need of it a long time,' he said, pausing and fingering with the knot again mechanically, 'but it just come to me one night.'

Grizzard glanced at Ratliff's hands, then spoke sharply. 'You been off the river for some time, ain't yuh?'

The hands were suddenly still. Ratliff looked up at him.

'I heard you quit it altogether—'

Ratliff's gaze dropped. He felt a threat impending in the man's words, a black shadow behind the pause. His hands gripped the sack reflexively, as if in pain. He did not think what the threat, the pain was: he did not pause to think. He was swept by an urge to hurry, to hurry away before the thing could be said—the threat made good.

He shouldered his baggage and swallowed stiffly. 'How long would I have to wait for the taters?'

' 'Tain't no tellin'. And I want you to have 'em too!' As Ratliff turned away, Grizzard continued, 'Tell you what I'll do: as soon as Melisse gits heah with 'em, I'll git her to drive on down to the river with a bushel.'

Ratliff looked back and nodded then he moved rapidly toward the door. As he walked, he felt an encroaching darkness near him, a darkness that he knew—coming back. For a long time he had been getting away from it, leaving it behind. Grizzard's look, words, had loosed it, let it at him: the brown haze, numb, dried-tobacco-cud monotony, weak with biliousness, puncture by raw-bellied ague, dull aching; and only broken, timed by flashes of fright. The sound of his feet was suddenly muffled in the sandy road. He felt the sharpness of the February air on his face and sucked it deep into his lungs. Though it came near, the darkness did not envelop him now: he found that he was looking upon it, not living in it again.

Lazy-pin! he said to himself, and he felt his cold cheeks limber. How long ago it was! It seemed if he were seeing daylight through a hollow log. He remembered now the big cypress in the Altamaha swamp that he had crawled into out of a windstorm and suddenly the sun had broken through and he had seen the glint of the river in the distance beyond its black barrel. It was like that. But he was not in the log now, only looking back through it. I am out of the log, he thought.

He had come out of it three days ago, when he stood on the willow-oak knoll behind the old log house on Dead River, the black-faced, black-coated preacher dropping spadefuls of dirt on Uncle Mundy's coffin. He, Ratliff, had dug the grave, he and the bullet-headed boy who was some of Aunt Tish's kin. And Aunt Tish's mound was next. Beyond was that other grave he had made so long ago.

As he dug the hole to put Uncle Mundy in, it had been like digging Poss's over again: the same feeling had come back to him—the waves of numb, reeling dread. It had come back, but in a different way: as something gone by and now almost harmless. And there had been the clear image of Uncle Mundy standing at the head of Poss's grave after the coffin was sunk in it, saying—But Ratliff could not recall those words: he had only half-heard them then, for that was when he had left, had walked away—headed for nowhere.

He had wound up in Dublin and later in Mount Vernon. And he had not come back until the bullet-headed boy had found him trucking cotton in McFerrin's warehouse and brought him the word to come. He hadn't made it in time to hear quittance from Uncle Mundy's mouth, but Bartow Dickerson had told him: Bartow, now a big lawyer in Mount Vernon, though Ratliff had not known he was there, had hardly thought of him since sturgeon-fishing days. Bartow had shown him Uncle Mundy's will, drawn up according to law on a long sheet of paper, that left the place, the Dead River patch, to him. Uncle Mundy had shown him what he meant in that way—had said: *You have bought and paid for your experience: you can come back to the river now.*

It had been pretty hard to go through with the to-do over Uncle Mundy's burying: there had been singing, and preachers, and a crowd of people. There had been a lot of Aunt Tish's kin, and white folks, too. But after it was over, he had got together with Bud True, and that was worth it all. Bud had been quiet; quieter than he had ever seen him before. He seemed to agree with Uncle Mundy, though nothing behind the funeral was talked about.

Ratliff felt the slant of the hill beneath his feet and his step quickened. Uncle Mundy told you the river was a big man, he said to himself. And before him, Bud: *too big for your britches*. But it took the river—it took God Himself to beat it in to your swelled-up head. And all the time you thought the river would take anything off of you. Maybe you've got your experience, but you can't be too sure. There's a lot Uncle Mundy would have learned you if you hadn't been a fool. Don't mess up your chances with Bud True!

He noticed mud-stain high on the trunks of trees about him: he was in the low swamp. He felt an impulse to hurry. The raft, the new-type raft! They call it a sharpshooter! By damn, it's been on the river nearly two years now and I've never seen it, he thought. That's the first thing I aim for Bud to show me. He moved out of the road, pushing leafless branches aside, to take a short cut to the river bluff.

When he reached the raft, moored under the bluff, he called a greeting to Bud True and the negro bowhand and cat-walked a log to the front end without pausing. He dropped the bag of provisions in passing the lean-to and moved on to a hip of the raft to stare at its pointed bow. He bent down and examined the fastenings of the near boom log to one of two short logs that extended from either side of the raft to a point in front. He stood up. 'I'll be goldurn! I reckon I'd-a never thought of that in a hundred years, but it's plain simple—after

134

you see how she works.' He glanced over his shoulder. 'That nose binder the only thing holding them bow logs together?'

'Chute logs,' Bud True corrected, standing behind him in a haze of smoke from his short-stemmed pipe. 'The nose binder and that hold-up binder on this side. But she holds together: you can slam a rock pile with that p'inted bow. It's made a different thing out of timber-driftin'.'

Ratliff moved to the oar bench to examine its supports. He continued to ask questions until Bud halted him. 'Josh, untie us.' Bud spoke to the negro, who was tar-black and had a Roman nose. 'Hell, we got to git away from heah!'

'Wait! Ole man Grizzard's sendin' us down some taters.' Ratliff turned back from the bow.

Bud looked at him sharply and his face clouded. 'You mean you come off 'thout the taters?'

'He'd run out. Said he'd send some down soon's more come.'

'Hell, that chinchie skinflint just talked you out'n our taters: he ain't a-goin' to send none down heah.'

Ratliff looked fixedly at Bud a moment, then dropped his gaze. 'He made out 'twaun't nothin' said about 'em, and he 'uz fresh out.'

Bud jerked his head up. 'He's a damn lie!' His eyes leveled on Ratliff again. 'And crappin' you along all the time 'bout bein' a smart rafthand, I reckon?'

Ratliff turned away. 'He run off at the mouth, all right.' His voice grew muffled. 'He asked me if I didn't quit the river.'

'Git a pole theah and help Josh push us off.'

Ratliff moved toward the edge of the raft. 'All right, Mister Bud,' he said.

They had drifted for more than three hours and were nearing Buzzard's Bar, when Josh put the spider on the fire and got the meal and meat out of the croker-sack. He held the slab of salt pork between his knees and began sawing off a cut with his jackknife. Midway, his sawing ceased and he looked closely at the meat, brought it up to his nose.

From his post at the stern oar, Bud glanced at him. Josh was gazing into the fresh cut he had made and shaking his head.

'What's the trouble?' Bud called.

'Dis meat don't smell right—Lawd Gawd, heah's a skipper!'

Bringing the bow oar to a halt, Ratliff looked back at the negro. Bud was moving rapidly along the boom log to the front of the raft. He took the pork from Josh's hand and examined it. 'Well, that son-of-a-bitch!' he said, and stared at the wormy meat.

Ratliff looked on, blinking, his face tightening. Bud glanced toward him. 'Pete sho' slicked you! Did you git away with yo' pants on?' He looked down, as if to see.

Red streaks crept slowly up Ratliff's neck. That Goddamned polecat! he thought. But a sudden sense of his own vulnerability overshadowed his resentment. It was strange and poignantly painful. He had never seen himself in this light before: as a crazy fool, surely; but in his own eyes—not as a weakling, a cripple to be preyed on by others. Yet it was his hell-born, hell-bent folly that had laid him open, made him a goat for Grizzard's shoddy crookedness. It wasn't that Grizzard was so good at it: somehow he had known about his sore place.

Absorbed in his own emotions, Ratliff stared at the two men beside that lean-to. Finally he became conscious of Bud's gaze. He had set out to reinstate himself with Bud, and Bud would think him a clumsy clodhopper. 'He slicked me,' Ratliff said simply.

Bud's eyebrows had drawn down. Now a dull red came into his flattened cheeks. 'You had no cause to be lookin' for tainted meat,' he said. 'Pete Grizzard knows better than to put off rotten rations on a rafthand, regardless who he is.' He paused and stared grimly into space.

Josh spoke. 'He a lowdown son-of-a-bitch!' Ratliff looked at him and saw that his face and neck were swollen with anger.

136

'But he thought,' Bud resumed, fixing his gaze on Ratliff, 'he thought he seen a chance to put if off on you. Yep, that's why he tried it. The Old Marster dealt with you, Goddamnit: you ain't payin' for nothin' to Pete Grizzard, the lowdown, lily-livered louse!' Bud jerked his hand outward, spoke in a deep, swelling growl: 'Pull the bow to the Injun! This is a thing that's got to be settled now.'

When Ratliff had tied the raft and Bud had jumped ashore to join him, Josh hung back. Bud turned and called to him: 'Leave the damn raft and come on. This was part yo' meat, too!' Bud carried the bacon in a croker-sack, slung over his shoulder. They headed through the swamp to walk the seven land miles back to Ochwalkee.

The raftsmen sounded like a mule team crossing a plank bridge when they clomped down the aisle of Pete Grizzard's store. He paused with a stick of wood in his hands and looked around the big belly of the store. Then he pushed the wood through the open door and straightened up. His face spread in a feeble smile, one side of his mouth twisting downward. 'I'd a sent those taters, but it was so late when Melissie got heah—'

Bud, leading the way, did not pause in his enormous stride. His eyes were gleaming fiercely between bushy brows and cheek bones, his mustaches struck forward, like brush brooms. 'Taters, my butt!' He towered over Grizzard, who now lifted his fat face, lips parted and eyes walled open. Bud seized him by an arm, then grasped the other, holding him from behind. 'You buzzard-nosed, pussley-gutted bastard!' he barked. 'Don't talk to me about taters!' He shook Grizzard as if he were shaking a child, almost lifting him off his feet, and bellowed a stream of obscene epithets. 'Thought you could put off rotten meat on this boy, kaze he tore up a raft and drowned a man, eh? Treat 'im like a dog—no, a hog—no, by God, yuh wouldn't feed such meat to yo' hogs! And what 'uz you thinkin' about me and Josh, heah?'

He nodded at Ratliff, who faced them with a set mouth. 'Git that sowbelly out'n the sack.' Josh, his big nose spread, stood a little way behind, looking on. Ratliff shook the meat out of the croker-sack with a single jerk. When he came up with it in his hands, his eyes were dark and hard-staring. Anger had made him whole: he felt strong, impervious, sure of himself.

Grizzard began blabbering, and he jerked his face from side to side as the slab of pork in Ratliff's hands approached it.

'Git yo' buzzard bill in theah with the skippers,' said Bud.

Ratliff seized Grizzard by the back of the head with one hand and rubbed his face in the spoilt meat. He spat and heaved, but Ratliff kept rubbing.

When they loosed Grizzard, his face was the blue of a blood blister and puffy. He retched and trembled and caught hold of the counter for support. Going shakily behind it, as if for protection, he leaned his paunch against it and wiped his face with a flour-sack handkerchief. Finally he brought the cloth down and spoke to the men across the counter. 'Think you can git by with a thing like this! I'm goin' to—'

Ratliff grinned. 'You're goin' to which?' He still held the meat in his hand. His eyes shone. He felt a sudden, overwhelming uplift: joy. He laughed. Here's one son-of-a-bitch won't ever throw it up to me again, he thought. He dropped the meat in a woodbox and walked around to where Josh stood before the stove. 'Let's go git a drink. We ought to celebrate this.'

Josh looked away. Two sunbonneted women had entered the store and Grizzard moved behind the counter toward them, a pallid semblance of his professional smile on his face.

'Let's go git us a jug!' Ratliff repeated.

'Jug, hell!' Bud spoke from the counter where he was cutting a piece from a slab of pork Grizzard had laid on it. 'We got to git back to Frying-Pan Cut before sump'n happens to our raft.'

'Raft?' said Ratliff.

138

'Look heah, boy, you've played hell enough already. Don't you start hintin' at quittin' a raft you done turned loose on the river with!'

Ratliff picked the croker-sack up off the floor and carefully folded it in a square. 'Sho,' Mister Bud. I hadn't seen it that way.'

CHAPTER

14

SILENTLY, VIOLENTLY—as they drifted the Grizzard raft on toward Darien—Ratliff resolved that he was not going to mess up this second chance God and the river had seen fit to give him. He had let his mouth get away from him there in the store and he was ashamed. He would strap a horse collar on his fool-headedness: watch Bud and do what he does, or says do. He didn't aim for Bud to have to call him down again.

As the raft moved on, Bud used Josh to relieve him at the pilot oar and to tie up. Most of his talk was with Josh, and when he spoke to Ratliff he called him Sutton, instead of Snake. Bud's attitude was salt in Ratliff's welts, but he knew he had it coming to him, that he had to take it: it was the right sort of thing, until he could prove himself. His part was to keep his fly-trap shut and his eyes skinned: to see if he couldn't learn a little sense.

He was silent to the point of glumness, yet beneath his chagrin a measure of the buoyance that had come to him in his wrathful moment of vengeance remained. He felt stouter, more assured. And the way in which Bud had punished Pete Grizzard and then had gone on with Grizzard's raft gave him a new slant on Bud and on rafting, too.

Already he was seeing into things he'd been too hell-bent and big-headed to notice when he was on the river before.

There was a lot more to rafting, he reflected, with the feeling of having come into a new power of perception—a lot more than just a sleight at handling logs—and a lot more to Bud, too. A sense of the importance of his discovery lingered with him as the river's broad yellow back carried him on between the familiar gray-brown swamps.

On their second trip down, he was permitted to see still farther into rafting and, thankful for his resolve to keep his mouth shut, into the hazards of loose talk. It may have been Bud's free way of taking in a stranger on the river, Ratliff thought, or his saying, 'I run timber some,' when the old man had asked who they were, but it was plain the old man got the idea they were sawmill hands, or farmers. They were at supper at the Piney Bluff sawmill and he made himself acquainted like a sheriff crying a sale: 'Maybe ye ain't heard of me? I'm known from Dublin to Darien as Driftin' Dick Sampson.' He looked like nothing so much as a grandpappy crawfish as he stood there with his long sidewhiskers, red crusty face and dangling, bent arms.

His being by himself, Bud asked him if he was drifting a skiff. He admitted—and a little slow to do it—that his raft wasn't much more than that, but said he never used any help: 'Big uns is like little uns to me,' he bragged, and told about taking down ninety thousand feet of sawn timber once without even hanging up. Had to take off the hips to get by the railroad bridge, he said.

'I'd-a swo' it couldn't be done!' said Bud, like he swallowed the whole thing. Bud and Josh kept the hocus going through supper, there on that slab hog bench, but Bud had had enough of Drifting Dick by that time and began to get ready to pull out: aiming, since the old man had claimed he was against night drifting, to leave him behind.

Then the old cuss said, 'Think I'll break my rule and go long with you fellows: I like yo' company.' He was standing there at the end of the bench, belching and pulling a whisker, as they started down the bluff with their croker-sacks and tools. 'After all—night aer day—it don't make me no difference. I could drift 'er blindfolded.'

'Blindfolded!' Bud opened his mouth and let his sack plop to the ground.

'Yessuh.' Drifting Dick waggled his head so that his whiskers waved. 'I kin drink a teacup full of water runnin' past and tell ye whur 'tis. I kin tell you any point on the river by the taste of the water.'

After they had turned loose and were in the reach below, Bud spewed and cursed like a bull 'gaitor. He got quiet for a while, then he called Josh to him and they shifted their fire onto the end of a long scantling, which they began easing out over the water to the left of the raft. They were in a horseshoe bend below Golden Grove Bar and could see Drifting Dick's raft fire a quarter of a mile behind them. By the time they had got to the bottom of the horseshoe, where a dead river made off in the same direction as the main stream, they had pushed the end of the plank out so that the fire was over the mouth of the old course. Then they doused the fire and pulled the plank in while their drifted on around the bend.

A few minutes later, Drifting Dick's skiff came into the horseshoe and put into the mouth of the old course, where their light had last shown. His fire went out of sight behind the trees, but before long they heard a crackling and the muffled ring of bouncing logs, then Drifting Dick's hoarse Goddamning: he had broken up in the swamp.

Bud set it off with a roar and they all laughed. 'I reckon he forgot his teacup,' Bud said.

But as they drifted on and the night began to grow gray, Ratliff could see the old crawfish's whiskers wave and hear his hoarse bellowing again, alone there, in the swamp, in the night, and the river rising. He could see beyond the joke. This river ain't no place for a jarhead to try to act like a stud, he thought. Once or twice he himself had talked taller than he could stand up to.

Bud had not drawn Ratliff into his joke on Drifting Dick and Ratliff had felt it keenly, felt it like a snub. He had to lace on his horse collar hard to keep his fool-headedness in hand, to admit he had it coming to him, to keep on feeling right toward Bud. And in Darien, at the end of the trip, after they had gone to the Birdcage and Ratliff had run out on Bud, quit the place in anger, he found Bud's schooling even harder to take—he found it confusing, too.

Ratliff had not wanted to go to China's place, but somehow he could not tell Bud why and they had gone anyhow. And when Ratliff, sneering inwardly at his own unwillingness, had called for China and she had not come, but had sent down one of her girls, a round, black-haired girl with a tiny fat mouth, who had asked, 'Don't you like my looks?'—when that had happened, he had blurted, 'Hell, naw—not your'n, naer nobody else's around heah!' and had stalked out of the house.

Ratliff wasn't altogether sure why he had left: he had got mad, mad with China and, maybe, with himself, too. He couldn't make himself feel right about being there; somehow China was tied up in the hell-bending that had sent him out onto the river on the freshet to drown Poss.

Bud had told him later, as they took a nightcap in Hammersmith's, that he was too damned old to act coltish about women. He had been able to reply only, 'I ain't got no business around China's.' And Bud told him he was a fool to turn loose a woman like China; she just wanted to be played for a little bit, and that it was time he grew up.

He hadn't been able to grin and say 'Sho', Mister Bud' then, but just sat there stiff-faced, staring at the table—held by the queer mixed feeling.

And when Little Bob Colquitt had brought word the next day that Andersons at the mouth of the Ohoopee wanted big-river pilots to drift their logs on to Darien and Bud had said, lifting his chin and looking down his nose at Ratliff, 'This is a job for men and pilots'—his neck had swollen and he had choked and couldn't speak.

However, Bud took him along. Bud said those damned Ohoopeans not only couldn't pilot a raft down the Altamaha (being scared to death of it), but they couldn't make a tadpole that would drift decently. He said he reckoned he could use even a skirt-scared boy to do better rafting than the Ohoopeans. Ratliff remained swelled up, but he kept his mouth shut and hurried on with Bud and Josh to get the Ohoopee before the Andersons could re-raft their skiffs.

He might not be a pilot, Ratliff told himself, but he would God-damn well show Bud he was a man and a raftsman. He had never seen a tadpole raft so close at hand before, but he kept his mouth shut and watched Bud. Tadpole-rafting seemed simple enough under Bud's direction: three skiffs to each float, two bound abreast for the body and one on behind for the tail. Though, as Bud said, it wasn't the arrangement, it was the binding that made the difference. Ratliff knew it wasn't any big thing to show, but his work did stand out: he didn't have to ask even Bud any odds on pinning a raft.

They spent two days rafting the skiffs. It could have been done in one, except that more Andersons and more skiffs came in on the second morning. When they got them put together, there were three tadpoles. Bud was named to lead the way on the first one with Ratliff as his bowhand. Josh was to pilot the middle raft and Little Bob to take the cow's tail.

Bud had nodded his head approvingly over Ratliff's work more than once, but it didn't satisfy Ratliff. The thing that kept gnawing at the pit of his stomach as they bunched the skiffs was the hope that somehow he might be called to pilot—though he knew the notion didn't make sense. There were plenty of good pilots to take care of what rafts were there. And he didn't have it coming to him, anyhow.

Then before day on the morning they were to turn loose, another Anderson, Uncle Dick, and his boy and his nigger brought in three

144

more skiffs. Bud yanked Ratliff out of his quilts by the heel and saw the three of them shivering around the mended fire. 'Got another litter of Andersons and skiffs out theah,' Bud said, growling. 'Think you kin shape up their tadpole in time for it to turn loose with the rest of us?'

Bud probably just wanted more sleep and wasn't hankering to get out in the cold, but it woke Ratliff clean up, limber and hopping: Bud's turning the job over to him. 'You heeled a fellow who'll try,' Ratliff said.

Bud squinted at him. 'I'll name you pilot of the cow-tail if'n you kin git 'er ready.'

Ratliff grinned for the first time since they had been on the Ohoopee. He stepped into his shoes and shook his feet down in them. 'Where's yuh auger, Mister Bud?'

By sunup Bud was ready to untie and anxious to go. A freshet had been making up since they first got there, and the Altamaha had risen fast during the night: it was close to bank level. The crest would send the river into the swamps. But Ope Anderson (Ope was short for Oceola Powhatan) hadn't come with the rations. Bud said he could never be sure that Ope was a fool before, because he couldn't make out his blabbering words, but he knew that now. He had told Ope to bring rations into camp on the previous night, without fail.

Ratliff didn't stop to find out the trouble, but he was thankful for any delay. He was getting little help out of Uncle Dick Anderson's crew in rafting his tadpole. The crowd was scheduled to turn loose after breakfast. When meal-time came, Ratliff didn't stop to eat, but went on swinging his maul—trying to get his binders pinned down.

After the others had eaten, he saw Bud board the raft at the head of the line. Ratliff knew he would never make it with the rest: he hadn't even cut his oars yet. He sent the Anderson nigger down to Bud's raft to tell him that he couldn't get off with them, but he would follow within an hour. He knew he would not be able to make it that

145

soon, except through a plan he was figuring on. It would take more than an hour just to hew the oars for his tadpole; he couldn't possibly spare the time to hew them, he had decided, he was going to use his tapering-sapling type of oar—hell, he had already proved it on one trip and Bud wouldn't know til he'd proved it this time.

But the other rafts did not leave: Ope had not shown up. Bud reared. The big river would be in the swamps in another hour. He had the greenest bowhands in the crowd, now that Sutton was piloting. He didn't want to try to run off the crest with Cousin Willie and Cousin Walter (as the Andersons called them) at the oar. Bud got off his raft and walked up the bank to where Ratliff's tadpole was moored.

By this time Ratliff had already brought his sapling oars out of the woods and had their blades shaped up. Bud noticed them as quick as he came aboard and his face clouded.

'I 'uz just tryin' to make the start with the rest of the crowd,' Ratliff said, speaking first.

'You're just fixin' not to make it at all,' said Bud.

Ratliff grinned quickly, his neck beginning to redden. 'You know I tried one once after that time—' He stopped, as if he had bit his tongue, and his face got dull-looking.

'I got the responsibility for yo' pilotin' on this trip,' Bud resumed. 'Now go cut you a regular oar and take yo' time with it—you kin ketch us.'

Ratliff looked away down the river at the string of rafts. Make it or not, he had to wear his horse collar. He laid down the lazy-pin he was shuttling on and put up his knife. 'Sho',' he said.

When Bud got back to his raft, Ope still hadn't come. He waited awhile cursing and spewing, then a sharp wind rose and he said he wouldn't wait any longer. They had enough cooked victuals for dinner and the crowd was all going to camp together at night anyhow.

The Altamaha was plenty swift, driving past the mouth of the Ohoopee like a big greased moccasin passing a fishing worm. Still Bud wasn't prepared for the way Willie and Walter carried on. They were great big fellows, both as thick through the body as field pumpkins, and stout-looking. Walter came within a couple of inches of being as tall as Bud. And they were grown men, had drifted skiffs down the Ohoopee for years. But they had never been out on the Altamaha before. Bud could see their scare when the raft swung into it. Their eyes were like blue marbles, and they kept cutting them from side to side at the river. They were slow getting off together on the oar at Bud's call and they wouldn't clean their licks to the edge of the raft. They never knew when to stop pulling, either.

The Altamaha kept rising and, after a couple of hours' drift, a sudden, hard rain blew up. The raft was in crooked river, and Bud had too much on his hands to think of the fire until the rain had already beaten it out. This didn't disturb him so much till he found that there wasn't a match in the crowd: they had expected to get matches from Ope. After a while the rain stopped, but the wind got rougher, slithering up the river like a razor blade on a whipcracker. It slowed the raft, too, so that the crest of the freshet overtook them, and before dark the river was well out of its banks.

'Whut we goan do?' Willie asked. (He had left the oar and come midway the raft and stood, cupping his red ears with his hands.) 'This wind cuts yo' eyeballs out!'

'Do, hell!' Bud yelled above the roar. 'Keep a-goin'!'

But they didn't go far. Dark clapped down on them like a gallows cap as they got into the Narrows. Bud went forward with Willie and sent Walter to the stern. He had to feel his way along. They were a little above Mad Dog when he heard the swell of it. He knew where he was, though he hadn't quite figured it out: they were moving so fast in the reach that he hadn't calculated just how little current there'd be in the channel on the bend and how much in the swamps.

147

But he felt it dragging them toward the suck as soon as they got into the bight and they could have pulled out.

It wasn't his judgment of the river that got them into trouble, it was Willie. He went cow-wild at the roaring water he couldn't see. He pitched around, got on the wrong side of the handle and bucked at the oar. By the time Bud had knocked him down and taken over, they were already in the swamp and hung up.

They were there an hour before they first sighted the fire on Josh's raft. Bud had finished cussing Willie out and they had fumbled around in the dark with pike poles (they didn't have an axe: Walter had forgot to put it on) enough for Bud to see there wasn't a chance to get loose before day—if then. They were out of the worst wind, but sleet had come to take its place. Bud had figured that as full as the swamp was, it must be a mile to dry land.

He yelled to Josh. They were hung up in the suck, he said, and didn't have any fire. No use to try to help them get loose in the dark; drift on past and throw them a chunk of fire.

'Ood 'Awd, we 'ain't 'ome dwown 'ere!' Bud heard in response. It's Ope Anderson, Bud thought, with those damn store teeth he bought four sizes too big for him. He couldn't make out Ope's words, but he could tell by his tone of voice that he didn't want to come. He called again and didn't get any answer. He could see that the raft fire had got stationary and figured that they had tied up in the reach, about half a mile above him.

This is cow-freezing weather, he thought. Already he had no feeling in his legs below the knees and his nose and ears were numb. He couldn't see Willie and Walter, but he could hear them jumping up and down on the footwalk. One of them was making a noise like crying.

Bud kept calling Josh until he finally answered. He yelled that Mister Ope wouldn't let him drift past to throw Bud fire. Mister Ope was afraid that they couldn't stay out of the suck and would pile up with him in the swamp.

Bud bellowed out a stream of oaths. He got so mad he warmed up enough to make his ears and nose ache. But he didn't stay warm. The sleeting had stopped and still, hard cold had set in. It sank into his bones. He could hear ice cracking between the logs when he moved about. He thought: This thing's gettin' serious. The red spot of the raft fire above, as he stared at it, raised his dander again. He cupped his mouth and yelled: 'Say, Ope, you mush-mouthed, blabberin' bastard, if you don't let that nigger bring his raft by heah, I'm goin' to hold on through the night just to cut yo' guts out!' Bud decided Ope was gambling on his freezing to death, because this didn't budge the fire.

Then Willlie came running down the raft, falling and splashing ice and water as logs dipped with him. 'I kain't stand it, Bud!' he yelled. 'I'm freezin' to death! I kain't stand it!'

Walter wasn't yelling and he walked the boom log, but he came right behind him. Bud knew there ought to be a maul on the raft somewhere. Scratching around in the dark, he found two of the wooden sledges. He set the cousins to mauling on the butt of a big log. When they had warmed up enough to grip and swing their mauls, they hammered away, blindly, furiously. Willie was the first winded and Bud took over his mallet to warm himself. He was so stiff by this time he could scarcely grip the handle.

He didn't see the second raft fire until after it had come to a halt up above Josh's, but he yelled to send whoever it was on down to throw them a chunk of fire. Men on the rafts above shouted back and forth to each other. Bud could only make out that it was Colquitt's raft, that Ope's brother, Rob was on it, and the he wouldn't let Little Bob take the chance. He himself tried yelling to 'Sneaky,' as he called Colquitt, but the distance was too great.

'Looks like we goin' to have to keep maulin' the rest of the night,' he told Walter and Willie after his efforts had failed. 'Take it easy—just swing fast enough to keep limber. I wonder what in hell happened to Snake Sutton!' Gradually, Bud lapsed into silence. As their rotation at the mauls dragged on, there was no talk, except a soughing 'Heanh!' when one pushed his handle through the dark to another. The flat sound of their licks echoed through the swamp like the beat of a clock, counting the hours.

Bud was swinging numbly, sensitive only to the aching in his belly, when Walter grabbed him by the arm and told him that Willie was down. Willie lay on his back on the walkway, his legs already stiff. Bud stumbled over the updrawn knees in the dark. He pumped Willie's legs and arms, slapped his face and chest. Then he and Walter got on either side and jerked him up and down till he was limber. Bud forced a maul into his hands and helped him hold and swing it until he could grip the handle. Willie whimpered softly.

The slow, uncertain licks sounded like faltering gasps in Bud's ears, as he moved away along the boardwalk. His feet had no feeling, but they were like lead to lift. His knees and hip joints were sagging. It would be damned sweet to ease down on a log for a minute! He turned and stared through the darkness toward the raft fires. They seemed to blink. By God, were there three, or was he crazy!

The sight of the flickering yellow finger of the upper raft fire brought Ratliff a deep sense of relief. He had a profound distrust of drifting on such high water.

When the other rafts had floated out of the mouth of the Ohoopee that morning, he had yet to cut, hew, and mount his oars. By the time he had finished his feverish labor, the muddy swilling Altamaha had overspread its banks and only the bluff tops stood out. It was no longer drifting water: that was plain to anybody. From the bow of his raft, Ratliff had stared at it with hot, suffusing eyes. Goddamn Bud

150

and his hewn oars! Why had he listened to him? But there was a louder voice than Bud's, a bigger man, telling him then to hold on.

It was near dusk in the afternoon before the freshet had receded to bank level and Ratliff had untied his tadpole. Soon after midnight, he had run onto the crest of the freshet. He had not been able to see that the river was spread into the swamps, but he could feel the cross-currents. Only the knowledge that, until he found his companions tied up, the other rafts must be adrift on the same high water, and a hungering to catch up with Bud, to have a chance yet to show up before him in a better light—only these things had kept him feeling his way through the roaring, slippery dark.

A few moments after he had sighted the first fire, Ratliff saw a second below it. As he approached Colquitt's raft, he called to find out where Bud was tied up. Little Bob told him he thought Bud's raft was hung up in the swamp and that he had better tie to the first tree he could snub. Ratliff wondered if Bud could be in trouble: such a thing seemed incredible. He gave his river holler, then kept hallooing as he drifted on past the upper raft.

Finally he heard a distant voice. It was Bud's. 'Ope, you clabber-mouthed, rattle-jawed ape! Yo' Cousin Willie's done froze stiff!' The words were tiny, but clear. They came from the black wall of swamp ahead. Realization swept over Ratliff like fright: Bud's raft had no fire! Was hung up in the swamp! They had been there a long time—freezing!

He came abreast of the second raft fire, called shrilly, 'What's matter you sapsuckers ain't helpin' Bud out?'

'Don't go down theah! You'll tear up!' a voice said. Ope hollered, too, but he could not understand him.

Ratliff laughed, a laugh that began like the dubious, questioning hoot of an owl and rose to a harsh, high racket. 'Damn dog-asses!' he said. 'Hey, Bud!' he shouted. 'Tell me whur yuh air—I'm comin' on down!' Anger blazed in him. He leaned forward and glared into the open-mouthed, retreating face of his bowhand, a few inches away on the other side of the oar. 'Git to hell around on this side!' he said. He was suddenly warm all over, clear-headed. He felt a swelling in his chest that pulled the tendons of his heels.

Bud's voice came again hoarsely. 'Just chunk me a stick of fire! Dropdown on me antigoslin'—my stern's stickin' out in the bight a leetle.'

'Keep hollerin' so I kin tell whur yuh air!' Ratliff yelled. He told his bowhands to pull on toward the white side. He hurried back to the lean-to, snatched a pine bough from it, and used the straw to pick up a stick of fire. The raft was swinging into the bight: he could feel the current drag it toward the suck. He moved on to the stern with his fire. 'I'm goan make a stern slam!' he yelled to Bud.

The raft picked up speed. 'Go to the hill with 'er!' Ratliff called to his hands. It turned and drifted toward the swamp almost sideways. It bore down upon the uncertain shadow of Bud's tadpole. Ratliff could make out Bud's bunched hulk on the stern walk. He braced himself and raised the fire above his head. Bud's eyes were shining like a 'gaitor's. The raft sterns collided. Ratliff was jolted into the air, amid the muffled ring of bouncing timbers. The logs beneath Ratliff settled down, halted. With arms outspread, he regained his balance. Then he paused and carefully tossed the stick onto the walkway of Bud's raft.

CHAPTER

15

UNDER A FULL APRIL MOON, the crooked Ocmulgee flowed in soft light and shadow. On it (nearing the mouth and adjacent to a point called Okey Bluff) drifted a solitary raft, bright as a lye-bleached scrub-bench. Aboard the raft, Ratliff stood beside its lean-to, a jug on his shoulder, gazing across whited logs at Bud True. 'It all started 'ith a drink of liquor,' he said. His face was tilted toward the moon and there was a heavy-lidded, loose-lipped smile on it.

Bud leaned against the stern oar. The black shadow of his hat-brim covered his eyes and his cheeks below it looked flattened and glazed in the light. He did not respond.

Ratliff spoke again after a pause. ' 'Bout time you 'uz takin' one, ain't it, Bud?'

'Nope," said Bud. 'Naer you, either.'

Ratliff put his lips to the mouth of the jug and swallowed rapidly, then he pushed the cork into it and let it slide from his shoulder. 'Yep,' he said. 'Just time for me.' He walked back to the bow oar with elaborate care and took hold of the lazy-pin on his handle.

He had come away from his high moment at Mad Dog, his succor to Bud on the swamp-entangled raft a month before, convinced that it had been a reward for his trying wait at the mouth of the Ohoopee to let the freshet crest pass, for sticking to river law. Fast upon that chance to prove himself—the following day—had come other rewards. Bud had taken him into full partnership and had let it be known in the master way. At Wesley Horn, while they waited for the tide to turn, the crowd had held kangaroo court over Ope and Rob Anderson—it was put up like a big joke, but it aimed at more -- and Bud had named him the judge. At his say, Willie and Walter had given their uncles a frying that put everybody else in a good humor.

The intervening month had not lessened his interest in the fuller view of raftsmanship, or weakened his new conviction, but these had been gradually dimmed in his consciousness by the grace that had come upon him, by the flattery of Bud's favor and the laughter set off at Wesley Horn. Bud's imitation of Ope, when he opened his mouth to holler at the first lick and his teeth fell out, had kept Ratliff roaring over miles of echoing river. And the equality of terms on which he and Bud (he had become Bud's sole bowhand) had since been rafting had turned his self-reflection into a self-satisfaction.

He was not now conscious of any of this, of anything before his present spree, but a cumulative sense of that pleasure stayed with him.

There was a surge in his throat and he broke into song, without having known that he was about to sing, or what he was singing. His voice cut through the soft night: 'Run, Mister Bug, yo bee gum's gone . . .'

They were at the end of the reach. He depressed his oar handle, the blade came from the water, rumpling the soft surface sheen, dripping ephemeral pearls. He swung it beyond the edge of the raft and waited. Bud called out and he sank it again. The raft made a bend to the left, then a wide round in the opposite direction, before it came into river straight enough for Ratliff to halt the oar midway and again lean against the handle.

He pushed his hat to the back of his head. He pulled out his shirt-tail and wiped with it, then bellowed air over his dripping belly. 'It all started 'ith a drink of liquor,' he murmured, half-chanting. Immediately, he felt the presence of illuminated recollections, moving along beside him, in front, behind, like dew-glistened bird dogs in a sunrise. He smiled and his attention fastened on the image of Bud, skinning a liquor jug out of a croker-sack at the mouth of the lean-to, saying, 'The river's wrong: we got to git right!' They had both taken a stiff pull at the jug and that had started the thing off. Three days down, three days there, three days back to here, Ratliff counted. It was nine days ago that they had got into the raft race, and happenings had come hell-for-breakfast ever since.

He knew that drink had done started things; he had said so at the time—it had started the twenty-dollar bill in the store-bought pants, the game of skin they cleaned out the crowd with. He had set down his empty glass on the bar in the Timber Tavern. "Hubbie-de-buck!' he had said. 'Just a little twist 'twixt the fist and the wrist—I knew that drink done started things!'

Did he remember saying it at Hobson's Old River, or remember, remember saying it in the Tavern? Ratliff laughed. Makes no difference! He had laughed in the Tavern, he was still laughing: the humming had been in his chest then; it was still there—the humming that didn't make any sound, but made everybody happy, everything full of fun. He didn't aim ever to let it go! The smoky circle of Tavern faces formed before him now.

After me and Bud had done skinned by those sucks and cross-currents in the old river without a bobble, danged if we didn't hang on a sunken tree-top at Mosquito Bight, there in the open. With the quickening faces, there came to him the stout words and fine lift of his yarn. Bud had come forward to get him a piece of fire for his pipe. We didn't hang up, but that snag turned us hind-end foremost. The two niggers on the big company rafts passed us in the reach below, and the Grantham boys did, too, before we ever got righted.

The Grantham boys fell out at Jack's Suck in a fog, but it was two nights later and nearly morning before we came up with Zeke and Bear Ike. It was in the Narrows, above Mad Dog. One of these big mile-a-more sawn rafts had done hung up there and boomed the river. I saw her 'way off, danger fires on her, lookin' like Goliath's red-eyed 'gaitor. There was a mushy moon, hadn't gone down yet. I could just see the shadows of Zeke's and Bear Ike's rafts, tied up against the swamp—'sleep, I reckon, they were—figurin' we'd have to stop, too. But those rabbits didn't know the old gopher they were runnin' against.

The notion struck me pretty nigh as quick as I saw that sawn timber stretched across the river, and I don't know why, except our gum logs, floatin' so deep and slow, were on my mind. Bud caught it right off, wild as it was, just like he had read my thoughts. All I said was, 'Git the maul!' and we started movin' at a run: we tore down our oar benches and gathered up our stuff.

I'll be a big-mouthed bastard, boys, if that sinkin' gum didn't skin right under that lumber raft—sounded like tearin' a tarpaulin. Me and Bud jumped onto the sawn timber, ran across it and got back on our own logs. I had to swim after our oars, but the biggest trouble was in stoppin' our raft to put them back up again. Bud tried to lasso a stump, but it turned out to be a hog bear!

(Ratliff felt a scratching on his eardrums; the sleepy smile on his face straightened and he frowned. Without conscious reckoning of Bud's words, his hands swung the oar blade from the water, made a stroke to the right.)

We didn't lose a thing, except our plank walks. Bud saved his liquor jug: there was just a good slug apiece in it and we killed that.

When we saw old Rag Point ahead, there in that mornin' sun, we had our oars workin' ag'in and we knew we were way out in front—we were feelin' fine. Bud said he felt like leavin' his right arm on the bushes. We could have left our jug, if it had been a jug of liquor, instead of a liquor jug: we didn't want to insult old Rag Point. And them turpentine shirts of ours weren't much more'n kite-tails. So we just shucked off our breeches and pitched them onto the briars.

It was pretty lucky we didn't make Darien till close to midnight, being a shirt-tail. Ratliff tilted his head back and looked solemnly about him at his visionary audience. Then he grinned. He was still laughing, the humming was still in his chest.

There was a scraping sound beneath the raft and Bud called out; 'What's the matter up theah? Looks like I better take over the bow.'

Ratliff was busy with the oar, but after a moment he looked back over his shoulder, frowning. 'Yuh not wantin' both ends, air you?' He kept looking, but Bud did not reply. A smile overspread his face and he turned around.

But it was all hitched together, he told himself. It was all intended, it was all mixed into the first drink. You never knew why you told old Friedburg you wanted a pair of pants like those yellow corduroys he had on, but you knew it was right. The image of Friedburg, later, across the counter, his hands working up and down, came again before his eyes. 'No, no, no! Those fresh pants—just come—I went upstairs and got 'em—nobody had 'em on, not in my life!'

'Just wanted to be sho',' he had said, 'just wanted to be sho' it waun't yo' twenty-dollar bill I found in the watch-pocket.' He laughed. He could still hear old Friedburg having a spasm.

By then he and Bud were flush—riding a royal flush! You could have given the old man his twenty back and not noticed it, he told himself. But not that same yellow back, with the conjure-lode in it. He could feel the bill about his wrist now, the greasy, limp paper, as he flipped the cards from the deck—around the table. Slap, slap— dead on the turn! Slap—topped him! Slap—hubbie-de-buck, you always put down more than you pick up!

He and Bud had won all night, but that nigger game, that game of skin—cleaning up for breakfast—what an idea that had been! The crowd thought they had put old yellow-back out of the play and you wrapped him around your wrist and won right on: seven hundred dollars all told, when you and Bud got it out of all your pockets and counted it there on the bed. Bonanza! Bonanza !

'Aces backed and plenty of queens!' he murmured, as he turned and stepped back to the lean-to. He uncorked his jug and swung it up to his mouth. Bud eyed him silently. Back at his oar, he smiled at the pale softness of the swamp foliage, resting on the water like pink pin cushions. The pin cushions dissolved, became airy skirts, whirling lightly—arms, faces, bright hair above them. Then superimposed on the dancing skirts were figures in frilly drawers and chemises—then the lights of the room lowered, the grind of the music grew deeper—shadowy bare legs, bare bodies shuffled around in and out.

Ratliff grinned. What a frolic! The whoopingest, rooting-tootingest good-time ever in the Birdcage. It had been old Bud's idea, said he'd seen such a show in a Savannah house. And China had been stiff-necked till he passed that roll of twenties under her nose—'We'll buy yo' Goddamned place!' Ratliff chuckled as he swung his oar blade into the shadow of the right bank. I can see Roof Bostick's loping legs in those long drawers, runnin' down the hall after that Portuguese girl, now, he thought.

Suddenly the oar was jerked from his hands. He leaped forward and grabbed it. There was a smothered, slapping sound from the water and he teetered backward, holding to the handle. The blade had caught behind a root, had been broken off.

Bud was down on him like a snorting steer: 'Now we're in a hell of a fix! I figgered somethin' of the sort would happen. Yeah, you know what you 'bout—you 'bout drunk!' The words were harsh, the sound was hoarse in Ratliff's ears. It halted the humming in his chest, made his head jolt.

He quit listening. 'All we got to do is tie up and cut us another un,' he said, crouching on the right hip of the raft. He would jump ashore. They would be close enough for him to jump in a minute—in a minute. The raft passed the near point, drifted crookedly around the bend toward the opposite bank, kept drifting. Then he saw a shadow against the bluff below: it was a raft, tied up. He loped across the logs to the other hip, with the feeling that he was floating through air. 'Hi-hey, theah! Hi-hey! Give us a hand!' He waved his arms nonsensical-ly.' 'Give us two hands!'

Bud, behind him, holding the rope, called too. No one stirred on the raft. They came closer and Ratliff saw feet sticking out of the lean-to, shoes looking as big as fish baskets! He called again. Now they were alongside it. He jumped across the wavering stretch of wa-ter onto its boom log. He yelled, 'Throw me the rope, Budipus!' Grin-ning, rope in his hand, he ran along the log, past the middle binder, past the hips, across the bow, to the oar bench. He wrapped the hemp around the oar, two half-hitches. Then he was running again, jump-ing, floating back to their raft.

They moved on, the long line drew taut. On the raft behind them the oar handle flopped around, the bench squeaked loudly, the big sweep bucked up, like a supplicating devil horse, and splashed into the water. Ratliff stood watching. The oar was now trailing at the end of their rope. A tall man came out of the other lean-to. He stepped to the edge of the float and urinated. Then he turned back, kicked up the fire, and spread his hands over it. He had not seen them, he did not know what the squeaking was, that he had a rudderless raft. Rat-liff could hear Bud's hoarse, whispered cursing from the stern, but he was hauling in their shanghaied oar. Its blade glistened like the bare back of a woman! Ratliff laughed: the humming had set up in his chest again.

'How many mo' drinks you got in that demijohn?' Bud called from the stern.

Ratliff stood by the lean-to, slowly shaking the jug in his hands. He had drunk and corked it again. He looked up at the sound of Bud's voice, but he did not speak. They wouldn't make Cypress Sook's tree before afternoon—it was an hour yet till daybreak. Bud was right: he must lighten and lag behind on his swigs. He set the jug down carefully on a croker-sack in the lean-to. 'Hunh?' he grunted, straightening up. 'Oh, 'bout three-fo'. We'll be a long time gittin' to Sook's.'

'You damn right, we'll be a long time!' Bud called after him, as he moved back to the oar.

At breakfast-time Bud took an eye-opener with him. Afterward he found there were no more than two good drinks left. He held off then, held off till the feeling in him had died down to the faintness of a 'coon-hunter's coals. But he couldn't let it go out, not plumb out. After another drink, he tried to figure what reach he would take the next one on and he waited for it to show up, but the raft slowed down so: looked like Bud was holding her back. The sun was out, but somehow it put a gloomy light over everything and the woods looked sharp and dry. And the things that came into his head, he couldn't get at them right. The cracking of his oar blade kept sounding in his ears: it made him jump and have a sickening in his stomach.

Bud mouthed about his borrowing Noah Ammerdick's bow oar like he did—could see no joke in it. Noah was a regular raftsman and a first-rate fellow, Bud said. Ratliff hadn't known it was Ammerdick's raft, but Bud still called it a hell of a come-off.

Ratliff winced and shook his head: was he riding a raft, or a wagon bed on a pebbly road, behind trotting hard-tails! He went back to the lean-to and drained his jug.

The sun was straight up and down and the river was as hard and glittery as a knife blade when they came in sight of the Ohoopee Cut. Ratliff didn't make anything out of it, didn't look at it. He was seeing a tall-topped, funnel-butted cypress in the deep swamp shade: the hollow tree where Sook kept her moonshine.

'Looks like a drownin'! Bud called out.

Ratliff blinked his eyes. He saw rafts tied to the right bank in the distance ahead of them. Beyond the rafts, near the mouth of the cut, moved two boats. In one of them, men were feeling along the bottom with pike poles. In the other a man paddled slowly behind a bundle of fodder, watching it as it floated downstream.

Ratliff and Bud tied to the uppermost raft and got out on the bank. As they moved along the edge of the swamp tangle, Ratliff heard a distant voice, coming from a group of men who stood about the fire in a small clearing downriver. He heard clearly the words 'Little Bear' among uncertain sounds and addling echoes.

Bud spoke behind him. 'That's B'ar Ike's boy!'

As they reached the clearing, Ratliff found Bear Ike on the river bank talking to another negro, an overgrown calf of a boy. From the fire beyond them, the crowd looked taller than Bud, though with Bud close at hand, Ratliff could see he was scarcely as tall. He was black and gaunt and sinewy, like a burnt, weather-hardened pine. Bud had told Ratliff that Bear Ike got his nickname by killing a bear with his hands—he had wounded a hog bear and thought to finish him off without wasting another charge. The bear wasn't anywhere near as far gone as Ike figured and wrestled him, but Ike had choked him to death. Ike was a fine pilot: a little of a fool with brutes, but not with the river.

Ratliff gathered that the young negro had been a bowhand on Little Bear's raft: he saw, tied across the river below, a small mixed float, hind-end foremost.

'He hadn't bin sober since us sot out a week ago,' the boy was saying. He had thick, bluish lips and they trembled as he spoke. 'Had 'im a keg—said he stole it somewheres—he didn't say where. Us-ez raft had done hung up five time and de other boy wuz wid us—he run off.'

He sniffled and wiped his nose with the back of his hand. 'Li'l B'ar wuz staggerin' when 'e got on de raft dis mornin' and he took holt de stern oar and he never did move—just stood deah at de edge of de raft, proppin' hissself wid it. I yelled at 'im, but he wouldn't holp me none on the bend above hyur.' He turned and pointed across the river. 'When de raft come out'n de bight yonder, she wuz headed 'cross de river wid de current toward de point of dis hyur island and driftin' antigoslin'! I couldn't git 'er right by myself and it didn't do no good to yell at Li'l B'ar.'

Ratliff saw the boy's hand shake when he lowered it and a sickening quiver stirred in his own stomach.

'Fo' Gawd, Mist' Ike, I did my best not to head into de island,' the boy went on. 'I pull my heart up into my windpipe. And Li'l B'ar just stood deah a-lookin' at me, weavin' and a-holdin' to his lazy-pin. I thought sho' my end done hit, but it turnt, right at de swamp. I reckon it turnt out fo' I knowed—I waun't lookin', I wuz pullin'—kaze de fust thing come to me wuz de stern slammin'. I looked up just in time to see Li'l B'ar fall over de side of de raft.'

Ratliff was staring fixedly at the boy when Bear Ike interrupted. The sudden motion of Bear Ike's long chin and thin yellow lips was like a blow, a slap in the face, that broke the rigidness at Ratliff's neck, drew his eyes to the speaker.

'You ain't to blame. You did whut yuh could, son. Dat boy of mine had it comin' to 'im.' Bear Ike looked toward the river, his deep-set eyes staring at the boiling yellow water. 'He'd tore up rafts from Dublin to Darien—and run off and left 'em. He wuz mostly drunk, but when he waun't drunk he wuz just plain sorry—not fit'n for a rafthand, naer nuthin' else. He'd bin run off de river long time ago, 'cept on account o' me.'

Ratliff watched Bear Ike turn away, nod to them as he passed, walking toward the fire. But he did not nod in return: nodding might send him from the shaky limb he was trying to keep himself on—a

162

limb of assurance that his drinking had nothing in common with Little Bear's.

The group made room for Bear Ike. He stood with his back to the blaze, looking off into the swamp for a while; then he turned around. 'You men bin draggin' de river six-seven hours: you bin heah long enough—too long. De river's risin' purty fast and 'twon't be long befo' it be in de swamp. It's time for all of us to git away from heah.'

He was silent for a moment, then said: 'Gawd called dat boy to a halt. He'd done seen 'twaun't nuthin' in him wuth savin'. And if He'd aimed fur us to bury 'im, He'd done a-turnt 'im loose down on de bottom deah and let 'im come up.'

Worth saving! Ratliff winced. On the bottom! Bottom! He couldn't dodge the licks from his perch on the limb—he was falling—falling a long way. He saw again Poss's stiff, shriveled body as he had taken it from these same muddy waters—saw it bent double, the arms far outstretched, the knees drawn up and the legs poised in motion, in desperation trying to walk on footing that ever let him down, that wasn't there. And the look on the gray face: the eyes bulging and the mouth stretched in an open, urgent grin, stretched wide, as if by a violent desire that had finally lost its meaning. He felt his bones grow cold—the chill was familiar—it had haunted him for months after Poss's cramped legs had been straightened, his tense hands folded on his chest, and his body wrapped in blankets, in a box, in the ground.

Ratliff shivered and he stared hard at Bear Ike as he broke in. 'Look heah, you not goan leave that boy's body in the water?' The negro shifted the dark sockets of his eyes toward Ratliff. He went on. 'River bottom's no place to leave nobody—no human being!' He stopped and stared at the impassive faces about him.

Bear Ike's yellow strip of mouth was straight as he returned Ratliff's gaze. Finally he spoke. 'He ain't worth buryin'. River's as good as any other place fur his carcass!'

Ratliff lowered his head and watched fearfully, as Bear Ike turned away and walked along the bank toward his raft.

CHAPTER

16

TWO WEEKS LATER to the day, Ratliff and Bud were again at the
Birdcage. It was neither by chance nor persuasion that Ratliff was
there, sitting beside Bud on the overstuffed sofa—sitting a little stiffly, his hair wetted and combed, surveying the bizarre furnishings of
the room. He was there out of what he regarded as necessity.

It was his second visit to Darien since the afternoon on which he
reluctantly followed Bud and the other raftsmen away from the boiling, rising water at Ohoopee Cut, leaving beneath it the body of a
man, a negro, maybe, but a human being—at least, God had created
him human—leaving him there for the alligators and catfish.

On the first visit—two days after the drowning—he had not gone
to the bawdyhouse, or even to a saloon, and he had been able to eat
but little. He had had no stomach for such.

It had been a shocking realization to find that there was nothing a
man couldn't lose his right to, that however God created a man, he
could throw it away, make himself lower than a hog. And it had been
a grisly thing to know that liquor had done this to Little Bear. It had
been peculiarly shocking and grisly, because of the strange hold the
liquor he had drunk on their riotous spree had taken on *him*. It had

made a big fool of him. But his concern went beyond this: he hadn't had the sense, hadn't been able to quit drinking, like Bud, when they left Darien. Liquor had never got such a hold on him before!

He frowned now and glanced away from the lavender quilted chaise-lounge beneath a shaded floor lamp across the room. He had been scarcely conscious of them, yet his sense had registered their noxiousness. You felt more than a man, he told himself, more than human: that humming in your chest and walking on air, that grin on the face of creation. You were damned near crazy and didn't know it!

His gaze fastened on Bud, who was lighting his pipe, then moved on to the bay window at the end of the room, to the purple damask curtains, showing through the loose open-lace valances. Reflexively, his jaws tightened. He couldn't chance such a drunk overtaking him again. The pledge he had made himself—he had scarcely considered giving up drinking: that would have been dodging the issue—the oath he had taken was that he would never again let liquor get a hold on him. He had had guarded drinks already at Hammersmith's saloon tonight, but to prove himself it had been necessary for him to come back to the Birdcage—the scene of their craziest ruckus—the place where the humming had first set up in his chest. His eye lit upon the floor lamp again; he had the half-conscious impression of a monstrous toadstool. He drew in his lips tightly. That kind of lunaticking won't do!

A whisking of skirts from the carpeted stairway brought his hands from his pockets. China and the black-haired girl, Lou, were approaching the wide parlor doorway. His eyes fastened on the sorrel hair coiled low on China's rounded bare neck, and then narrowed.

The women paused in the doorway, China smiling. 'You hellraisers back heah again!'

He heard Bud's gusty laugh break out. He eased back in his seat. China seemed paler than the memory of her he had brought away from their spree—like the green on her satin wrapper.

166

'Back and rearin' to go: bring on yo' show,' Bud said.

Everybody laughed.

'Show me your bank roll,' China said. As she came across the room, her eyes settled on Ratliff's sobering face and her voice had changed when she spoke again. 'No: I was joking. I wouldn't let you all tear up my house like that again for the Bank of Darien!'

He moved farther away from Bud—though they were not close—to let China between them. He wondered at the change in her manner—wondered, with fleeting excitement, if the drunken ruckus had been too much for her, too. Then he thrust the thought from him.

Bud asked China if she had fixed the stairway banisters where Roof Bostick had butted them out, and Ratliff joined in the laughter. But, as Bud went on recalling Roof's pursuit of the Portuguese girl, he grew suspicious of the feelings that stirred in him and the grin on his face set woodenly.

Delia, the maid, brought drinks and he swallowed his slowly, listening to China add funny bits to Bud's tale. He could feel the warmth of the liquor in his stomach, its effervescence in his head. It's all right, he told himself, you've got yourself in hand. And when China had turned to him, drawing nearer, smiling with her wet, full lips, asking him why he had been so long in coming back to see her—he told himself that he had her in hand, too.

Then the black-headed girl climbed into Bud's lap and Ratliff stared and dropped his gaze. There was something about the way she had done it. He frowned and got up. China had done it like that—and he had caught her up in his arms and toted her up to her room—his feet on air, his head reeling, his chest singing!

As he moved toward the doorway now, China followed him. 'Looks like we're makin' a crowd heah: let's go up to my room.'

He encountered the maid with a trayful of drinks and turned back, still frowning. China had caught up two of them and held one toward him. He stared at her with a tightening face. It was not China

167

in a pale green wrapper, quiet and quizzical, that he saw, but her sweat-slick body writhing in a belly dance, her yellow eyes distended, burning—as the hot, forbidden urge had carried him away, lost him to everything else.

'What's the matter, Snake?' China was speaking to him. He blinked and shook his head. He looked down at the drink she had put in his hand. 'It's whiskey,' she said.

He turned the glass between his fingers. You didn't order another drink, he warned himself, through the haze enveloping him. Look out here, look out!

'It ain't what you think it is: it's whiskey.' China's full lips were pushing out, twisting indulgently.

He grinned back at her with glistening eyes and brought the drink to his mouth. He tilted his head and the liquor trickled into his throat. Suddenly sweat broke out on his face, he spluttered and dropped the glass. He had been losing his hold: the sense of dissolving control had closed his gullet, stiffened his fingers.

It was with a feeling of satisfaction that he thought of this evening at the Birdcage, a week later. He had kept his drinking in hand, even if he did drop the liquor glass, he told himself, as he lay on the boardwalk on his raft, where he and Bud had tied it at Old Soldier, awaiting an out-tide. The April sun was warm and the river breeze was pleasant and he felt lazy and at ease, lying on his belly, remembering how different he had found China from what he had expected, when they got up to her room. He looked out at the wide, tawny surface, rumpled with wind waves, and saw again China's downcast face—eyelashes shading her cheeks and her pointed chin lowered, softened—as she sat on the edge of the bed talking haltingly. She had never before let herself get drunk like on that crazy spree, she had told him, and she would never have done it with anybody except him.

'I don't like getting so drunk you don't know what you're doing,' she had said, tingeing a little at the neck and shaking her head.

The transparent image he saw above the rippling waves evoked again a measure of his momentary feeling of surprise, of wonder and warmth. Though when she had looked up, lifting only her eyes, looking calf-like, and had said: 'Nobody could have made me that drunk but you—don't you do it no more!' he had got a hold on himself again. He had taken her hand gently, then squeezed it and grinned. 'What about Henry?' he had said.

That look on her face had frozen stiff for a second, just a second, then her mouth crooked and she said, 'Henry who?'

He had to laugh. And he'd still felt like a purring cat, telling himself that he guessed Henry was practically nobody—nothing to him. But he had said, 'I won't be coming heah to git you drunk.' And turning her hand loose, had added, 'If I come at all.'

She was quick on the come-back and stout enough. 'You dog!' she had said, grinning. But she hadn't been able to hold his eye and he saw the pinched look that came around her nose and mouth. China wasn't stringing him!

Or was she? He turned over on his back and sat up, a familiar feeling, a suspicion of his heedlessness, stirring within him. He got out his tobacco and bit off a piece, narrowing his eyes, as he turned the chew over in his mouth. Look a-here, you didn't aim to take up with China again when you set out this time, he told himself. He spat to punctuate the sudden force of his realization.

As he gazed down the long reach, he was swept by misty misgivings. Bud, here—and liquor, he thought. And what about Captain Henry? What about—He blinked and did not finish the question. A cloud had passed from over the sun and suddenly the waves on the river were a million rippling suns, stretching off, off to a marsh of blue wild hyacinths. Staring, staring until he felt the sweet swelling in his chest pass softly into an ache, his inquiry no longer seemed important and he forgot what he had been going to ask.

169

In Darien, he found answers enough for his questions: they brought him no alarm. Bud's right, he told himself on the way to the Birdcage: there's nothing to it but a good time—just something to do while you're in this damned place. To a dead certainty he had a hold on his drinking now, and China, too. As a matter of fact, she was about the soberest woman he could find in Darien. And as for Henry, he, Ratliff, had not seen or heard of him since he came back to the river. Hell, China didn't give a damn for Henry! And he reckoned Henry had found that out and quit her long ago.

On the long reaches of the river he felt less sure and questions continued to niggle his mind. But in Darien—while April passed into May—he answered them confidently, if he happened to recall them; he saw China regularly, and they never got drunk. Indeed, they found better things to do—funny things that he had never thought to be doing with a woman out of a house.

On a mid-May afternoon the blonde, soap-shiny face of a new girl appeared at the Birdcage's front door to let him in and he was surprised that it was not the black maid's, Delia's, but he moved negligently into the hall, across the parlor and to the taproom, saying, 'Run tell China I'm heah.' He drew himself a beer at the bar and sat with his leg stretched out under a table, drinking it with a slow relish. He had finished the second and sat, his chair tilted back, drumming on the table when he looked up to see Delia halt suddenly in the doorway.

The yellowed whites of her eyes showed as she stared at him. 'How'd you git in heah?'

'One o' the gals let me in,' Ratliff said, smiling briefly. 'What in hell's keeping China so long?'

Delia's lips swelled out and her nose flattened. She continued to wall her eyes. (Ratliff thought she looked like a setting hen that had just been shoved off her nest.) She snorted. 'That's that new gul. She must-a bin brought up in the barn wid de mules!'

'What's wrong with her lettin' me in?' Ratliff got up and pushed his chair under the table. 'Where's Miss China?'

Delia shifted so that she blocked the doorway. 'What's wrong? What's wrong? Nobody 'ceptin' me and Miss China s'posed to let mens in this house.'

'Does she know I'm heah?' Ratliff asked, taking a step toward the door.

Delia glanced right and left hurriedly, gave a sniffling snort and got out her pocket handkerchief. 'That gul dooz something wrong ever'time she steps out'n her do'.'

'What's eatin' on yuh, Delia? China upstairs?' Ratliff moved toward the maid, shrugging, his hands in his trousers-pockets.

'Miss China ain't heah—she gone to Brumswick.'

'What the hell! That gal told me she was in her room.'

'That gul don't know nuthin'. You don't reckon Miss China goan tell that gul where she gwine? She don't talk her business to none of these guls.' Delia spread her arms to bar Ratliff's passage. 'You kain't go upstairs—you kain't go to her room!'

'Well, I want to change my clo'es, anyhow.'

'Nawsuh. You kain't go to a lady's room when she's not theah!'

'Say, Delia, what the hell's this all about? I know China's heah— who's up theah with her?'

Delia put a hand on either side of the door-frame. She swallowed. ''Tain't nobody wid 'er. She's got business to tend to.'

'Thought you said she waun't heah?'

'I ain't said she wuz. Today's her day to tend to business wid de man that owns de house.'

Ratliff paused. 'Who owns the house?'

Delia batted her eyes. 'Yeah, she got no time for mens: she got business to tend to.'

'Well, I want to put on some more clo'es.'

'Hold on! I'll go git 'em for yuh.'

Ratliff's hands came from his pockets abruptly, stopped still at his sides. 'Is Cap'n Henry up theah?'

''Twould be all right if he wuz: he's the landlord. You wait heah.'

Ratliff stared after her. There was a sinking in the pit of his stomach, followed by a rush of blood to his head. The Goddamned old goat! He felt a pulse in his neck and realized with surprise that he was angry. Damn it! You reckon Henry does own the house? he asked himself.

He remembered now a trip to Darien two weeks before when China had left word with Joe at the Timber Tavern that she had gone to Savannah, but would be back the next day. He had thought he saw Henry in town, too! Below the bluff. You ought to have guessed it then, he told himself. Well, what the hell! He put his hands back in his pockets. After all, he had the log branded before you came along. Don't string yourself; you knew, should have known that she was seeing him. But the pulse in his neck did not subside and he clamped his teeth together.

Delia reappeared and came toward him with her swelled lips spread in a wavering smile. 'Miss China say to please come back in the mornin'—'bout noon.'

Ratliff stared at her straight-faced. 'Where's my clo'es?' he said after awhile.

'I couldn't git—Lawd!' Delia broke into a laugh. 'I—I plumb furgit 'em.'—I 'uz so s'prized to find Miss China theah—that's why I furgit 'em.'

Ratliff turned away quickly and moved toward the front door. After he was outside and had fastened the picket gate behind him, his long face reluctantly spread in a smile. Hell's bells! Why get sore? he thought. Bud would say, 'For Christ's sake, rafthand, you've slept in the captain's bed for a month and a half now: you ought to be willing to let him have it one day!' He walked on, taking the sandy path toward Darien. But Ratliff found that Bud's view did not put his insides at rest. He couldn't make himself feel that the bed was Henry's. An obscure sense of befoulment clung to him.

Henry who? China's question and twisted smile flickered through his consciousness. His neck and ears were suddenly warm. Yeah, who, who! Her big gray owl, Henry, who made her nest. He lurched forward in a lengthened stride. No, she didn't want to get drunk—get drunk with you; she wanted to keep you quiet—scared Henry would find out about it!

But even as he jerked his feet through the sand in reckless heat, a sense of weakness insinuated itself into his anger. Hell, you knew he was still going to see her—had to be, he told himself finally. Why do you think the thing kept coming up to you, there on the river—away from Darien and that woman? He spat out the chew of tobacco taken at the gate, and twisted it into the ground with his heel. You knew you were sneaking around with the woman of a man who once kept your family out of the poorhouse. A long-forgotten, yet familiar feeling of shame stirred within him. Your friend, and you sneaking into the house he bought for her, the bed, when he wasn't there! His dereliction now seemed craven, crazy, strangely unlike himself. You let her *get a hold on you,* he thought, a cold compression in his chest, a stiffening in his neck. He had started on and he halted. The gaunt face of the negro, Bear Ike, at Ohoopee Cut, had formed before him, staring at him from black eye-sockets. He blinked and squinted his face. 'Yeah, like liquor!' he murmured hoarsely—'like river bottom.'

But the distance to town was considerable and he had time to wonder how this hold of China's had come about. As he turned into the path from Cathead Bluff, he relaxed his stride, remembering his first visit to the Birdcage, after his return to the river, after the long lapse. That time China had refused to see him, had sent down another girl. She hadn't shown any hankering for him then! And he left in anger and chagrin, aiming never to come back.

It had been liquor that brought him back the second time, and Bud—Bud's notion that they had to have some fitting way to spend their poker take. It had been liquor talking in him—and China? Her face, as she had sat stiffly in the chair across from him and Bud on the sofa in her back parlor, came back to him. She wouldn't hire out the house to them, although Bud had upped his offer to two hundred and twenty-five dollars. Then he, Ratliff, had leaned forward so she would have to look at him and had taken out that bill-roll big enough to choke a bull.

'We aim to do it, if we have to buy yo' damned house,' he had said.

China only glimpsed the roll. She had looked at him, had kept staring at him, getting stiff in her chair, like a chicken with the roup. But she had nodded her head.

'Knew you couldn't turn that down,' he had said.

Then later, when he and Bud got up to go, China had come to her feet slowly. She had looked him in the eye, not smiling. 'For one reason or another it looks like you don't aim to leave me alone,' she had said. She kept standing there by her chair, as they walked out of the room, but when he went through the door, she had called out, 'Snake!' And she had come to meet him as he turned back. Her face was dim in the shadow, but he could see that yellow light burning in her eyes. 'If you put your hands on any other girl heah tonight'—she took hold of his wrist—'I'll claw that damned wooden face of your'n!'

He smiled fitfully, then frowned. Still he couldn't say she had been laying out to get a hold on him, not before he came there. And the third time he had gone only to prove that he could hold his liquor and his head. It had come about strangely. It looked like neither one of them had intended it.

As he passed the first stores on Broad Street, he slowed his step. There was a remembered noise, an echo over his shoulder. He heard again the rasp of rubber-tired wheels on shell road—wheels of the buggy he and China had ridden around Brunswick in—over his

174

shoulder, as he looked at her sharp, white forehead under her bright hair, and the smile that played around, but never quite touched her mouth—recalled her words: 'I'd rather have a water bottle in bed with me than that store clerk—he couldn't even warm up my toes!'

The good, easy feeling of the ride came back to him. It seemed unconnected with any of his recent feelings about her, about himself, about Henry: it seemed immediate. His suit-buying in the store had bothered him and China had been so salty about the store people, had made it all look funny. He felt in his pockets for his tobacco plug.

He climbed the Tavern steps and inside encountered Bud, sitting at a table alone, smoking his pipe.

'Whut you doin' heah?' Bud uttered the words amid a burst of smoke.

Ratliff was fumbling in his hip-pocket, looking back at it. 'Oh, just foolin' 'round.'

'I thought you'd be a-layin' up with that red-head by this time.'

Ratliff's gaze wandered on to the doorway behind him. He remembered now what it was like: he had wondered every time the clear, fluttery sound was in his ear. He thought: It's like the whistle of the pewter bird on the old kettle at home: China's whispering. He felt the nearness of her shadowy cheek. She says things whispering that she'd never say out loud—lying there on the pillow. Suddenly, by the cheek on the pillow there was a florid, bulbous face! Ratliff glared at Bud. 'Red-head, hell! Let's git our stuff together and git goin'.'

CHAPTER

17

WHEN THEY WERE in the railroad carriage on the way home, Bud said he had just as lief get out of Darien with his money on him this time. 'Ibby's bin so mean and jawin' I couldn't come nigh 'er for more'n a month now,' he said, speaking of his wife. He gave Ratliff two twenty-dollar bills to keep for him. 'She'll git all I got and then won't be satisfied—it's bin a spell since she's found anythin' in my pockets worth the trouble of gittin' up for.'

Bud thought he'd stay home till the river started rising—if he could stand it that long—the water was too low for picking up timber. Ratliff aimed to stop by his place to get a boat, but he wouldn't tarry: that old house was too lonesome for the living—and he was fed up on houses and whores! If he couldn't float logs, he could fish. When they separated at Bell's Ferry, Bud had agreed to rejoin him at English Eddy on the Altamaha, after the river changed.

Ratliff did not find a log he could float, as he idled along the pockets, bights, and creek-mouths of the Oconee the following morning, his batteau loaded with rafting tools. But he had brought along gigs and poles, too, and the fish were biting. Logging did not seem urgent, and fishing was more to his liking in this May weather. And he was in no hurry to catch fish—a half-string made him a mess—for the sun was warm, the river breezes cooling, and the swamps were a show to see.

It was spring, just turning summer, and everything that could was blooming, looked like. The willow piles had turned from gold to green, May haws and crabapples were dusting the ground around them, like a miller's apron, and wide-open bay blossoms were shedding their matches. In the pockets and ponds, yellow and white and blue water lilies spotted the pads, and in the low swamp there were fields of flags. The redbirds and kingfishers kept a bright flicker moving up and down the river banks, and the white cranes and curlews in the sun were so bright it hurt your eyes to look at them. Ratliff thought he had never seen the sandbars higher, or whiter, and the muddy old Oconee had cleared to where you could see the bottom three feet under, and had turned a yellow-green. At sunset, on the reaches with the wind riffling it, it looked like muscadine wine.

He was glad the smell of Darien and the Birdcage was out of his nose; a whore was a whore, whatever she made out to be. As his first day on the river drifted into a second, the port town grew more remote in his consciousness until it seemed a half-remembered campfire yarn. His solitude and idleness and the spring weather took him back to those early days at Uncle Mundy's when he played alone in the swamp. He thought of the tall ash at Steamboat Bight that he used to climb up to look out of and see the top of creation, as he figured it then.

On his second afternoon, Ratliff found seven hewn logs in Moses Old River at Devil's Elbow. Somebody had moored them there, probably aiming to start a pick-up raft, he thought, but he looked them over closely and found no brand on them. Anyhow, they won't be wasted, he told himself, drifting them out into the main stream.

As the sun dropped down toward the swamp line, he lay on these logs, watching a water spider. His skiff was grounded on a sandbar in the Altamaha a few miles below the mouth of the Oconee. It was nearing supper-time, time to make camp, but his appetite had not prodded him. He circled the spider with a willow switch to prevent her escape and studied the tusti bowl on her back. 'Uncle Mundy said the Indians believed you brought the fire,' he murmured. 'And you still got it theah in yo' bowl.'

He recalled the first time Uncle Mundy had shown him the fire-coal on a spider's back. It had seemed wonderful and strange, but not past belief. Hell, I still say the Indians may have had it right, he thought, but he knew he could not wholly believe this—the thing sounded different now. It was the same spider, the same sand shallows, the same willow piles and swamps, with the deer and rabbits and moccasins running through them, but they didn't seem the same as in those days. That was before you knew so many people, he told himself. He raised up on his hands and looked across the water at the swamp. Shadows stood behind the solid barrels of the trees, purpled the distant turning of a moss-hung corridor. He remembered the little white deer, that fleeting form he had so often seen, or fancied he'd seen, at far turnings, in those days. He kept on staring. Those days are across the river! He got up hurriedly and went to the boat to get his fish and frying-pan.

With the night, spring musks grew heavy on the swamp air, and after the moon had risen, he stripped himself and put his clothes in the boat. He tied the batteau behind his log skiff and pushed off. Later the air cooled and he got into the warmer water, and swam until he was tired. For a while he floated on his back and looked up at the moon. It seemed to be drifting downstream, as he drifted. Uncle Mundy had said the moon was bad company to keep, but he felt no caution. A sweet musk was wafted into his nose and its warmth spread. A moment later he heard the mating call of a bull 'gaitor in the river below. It vibrated through him. He lowered his feet and turned over in the water. He filled his chest full and joined the 'gaitor's bellowing.

Later he thought he'd had a token. While he stood in the boat putting on his clothes, he was startled by a loud popping and he looked up to see, at the far end of the log skiff ahead of him, something as high as a man's head and spinning like a paddle wheel, but it wasn't a wheel. It blazed white in the moon light and seemed to be whirling toward him. He felt his throat close up and he dropped his shirt. But before it got halfway, it suddenly shot off the skiff into the river and the noise ceased. He saw that it was only a sturgeon, ballywhacking down the logs. He laughed and damned himself and the moon. Still he couldn't get rid of the notion that it might have been a token.

Next morning on Golden Grove Bar, as he looked at the wide sand plain before him, he saw the bright motion of a woman's dress in the distance and he started. Yet he moved toward it, as if it were beckoning to him, as if he had expected to find it there. At closer range he saw that it was a girl, wading in the shallow water, and there were two small boys with her. She was long-legged and slim as a willow switch. He came near and spoke. They were catching minnows. He stopped and stared at them.

The girl raised up and nodded her head, moving her lips without sound. Her eyes looked out from under a sharp-edged forehead fixedly. She bent down again and went on with the minnow-driving. The tow-headed boys behind her stood still in the water and returned Ratliff's stare. The smaller one had on only a shirt.

'Ketchin' many?' Ratliff said.

'A-few.' The girl was bent over with her hands in the water, trying to herd the school toward a submerged keg, and she did not pause.

'They don't like a keg,' he said. The girl gave no sign that she heard him, though he noticed a hard curve in her nostrils. He went on. 'I got a minnow net heah—just goin' to cut a switch for a hoop.' He took a small net out of his shirt-front.

She raised up, bringing the mouth of the keg from the water. Her eyes wavered on his face a moment, then fixed on the net. 'Reckon we kin make out 'thout it,' she said.

His gaze was on the pointed bulges in the front of her dress. One side of his mouth crooked in a smile. 'Want-a do it the hard way, hey?'

She saw his eyes lower to the length of her thighs between her tucked-up skirt and the river surface, and she moved out into deeper water.

'Look-out!' he said, 'you're a-wettin' the tail of yo' dress.'

Her mouth and nostrils tightened and she waded on, as if he had not spoken, but color came into her cheeks. The little shirt-tailed boy suddenly ran at Ratliff and kicked water on him. 'You ole Snake Sutton!' he said shrilly. 'G'on way!'

Ratliff laughed and raised his fish net, as if to catch him in it. The boy fled down the beach, his shirt-tail jerking up over his backside. The older boy burst into laughter and the girl joined in, sudden, flat sounds jolting from her throat.

Without further assent, Ratliff entered the minnow-catching. The girl now chased a flashing school of silversides toward his net, unmindful of her bare legs. When she caught him staring at them, he thought her eyes grew bluer, before she looked away. He pulled up the net and she went with him to the covered bucket on the sandbar and awkwardly picked the bright, tiny fish from the mesh, while he held it open. He looked at her nose and wondered if the nostrils were always hard. Her jaw was as smooth as a bay blossom. An odor came from her pale yellow hair that made him breathe deep.

The minnow bucket filled up, but the girl seemed in no haste to leave. She waded into the river with Ratliff, to see how far she could go. They went a long way out and she let him take her hand as they got into deep water. When finally it wet the bottom of her dress, she looked up at him and held on tightly. They laughed.

A treble cry came to them from the shore. 'What's the matter, Petey?' the girl called. Petey was afraid they would drown. They laughed again.

'I got to git back,' said the girl.

'Where yo' fo'ks fishin'?'

'In the bight below.'

'The boys kin tote the bait back.'

'I got a pole of my own set out.'

'The fish done got away by now.' Ratliff smiled.

She looked at him with her steadfast gaze a moment, then dropped her eyes.

Swarms of minnows had gathered about their legs in the water, and began nibbling at them. Ratliff grinned and drew her closer. 'Feel them sand roaches?'

She shook her legs and grinned back. 'Tickles!' she said.

He stared boldly into her face. 'Lucky little scrapers!' He felt the pressure of her fingers pulling away and shifted his gaze. He looked toward the sandbar and saw a flock of buzzards alighting far down the curve of the beach. 'Ole buzzard's gittin' ready to hold another funeral,' he said.

'I got to go now.' She started moving.

'Ever seen 'em hold a funeral?'

'A funeral? You mean after they done et up the corpse?' She paused and giggled, her curved nostrils puckering upward.

'Sho'. They line up and hold theah wings back and march up and down.'

She stopped giggling. 'Aw! I don't b'lieve it!'

'Come on. We kin git behind a ridge and watch 'em.'

'I got to go now.' She looked hurriedly toward the sand-bar where the boys stood and started moving.

He followed her. 'Come on back after while: them buzzards air a show to see.'

'We got enough bait to do us—I 'spect.'

'I'll be heah tendin' my lines till late.'

They had drawn near the boys and she did not reply. She picked up her sunbonnet and took the bait bucket from the larger boy's hand. The three of them set off.

'Leavin' yuh keg!' Ratliff called.

She looked back and nodded her head.

The afternoon was far spent when the girl came back. Ratliff made up his mind again to go in a minute and was at the lower end of the big sandbar where the willow grove approached the swamp. He was sitting in the shade of a tupelo, whittling a wooden shuttle for net-making, when he saw her. It was her bare feet, stopping in a quick halt, that he first saw. The flounce of her dress swelled out, then settled back. She was almost upon him.

''Bout thought you'd gone!' she said in a rush of words.

As he came to his feet, he saw that she had been running, that she was breathing hard and trying not to—that she was alone. And I'd about thought you weren't comin', he told himself, but he said, 'Bout had.'

Her flushed face grew redder. 'Thought you'd be t'other end of the sandbar—'s-a-long walk from up theah.' She said *walk* with emphasis.

'But I didn't give you plumb out,' he continued, moving nearer and smiling.

She looked around her hurriedly. 'I kain't stay long.' Her face was cooling, she smiled. Then her gaze lifted to his dark, staring eyes and the smile dried up. The skin over her cheekbones tightened and her pupils grew big. She could not look away.

She's willing, he thought, yet she's scared: she don't know how to begin! This astonished him. He realized suddenly that he was going to have to take the lead: he had never had to, before. He wanted to seize her arm, pull her to him, but the fright in her eyes, something, put a restraint upon his hands. His legs trembled.

The shrill burbling whistle of martins sounded close by and he looked off toward the river. A pepper cloud of the small birds was gliding over the air toward its surface. Suddenly they swerved, as one, and shot upward again. The whole flock looped in the air, keeping their formation. The swarm sped again over the soft, reflected blue and white and green, then it dipped and shattered the mirror.

He felt the tenseness leave his arms. 'Just like one bird!' he said.

'Yuh reckon how they do it?' Her voice was husky.

'Made that way—made to do it.' He looked at her, as she lowered her eyes.

Her glance fixed on his shirt. 'Law', look! A sun-darter!'

They were in the shade of trees, where the sun's rays shone through and were reflected by the shifting water. She pointed at the illusory spot of light fluttering over him and laughed.

The sunflake, her laughter, something, passed into the muscles of his arms. He grabbed her hand quickly, and whirled her around so that the light flitted across her face. He held her and kissed her cheek. Her voice rose to a squeal. He kissed her again and again, pretending to aim at the sun spot. She stuggled in his arms. 'Same as mistletoe!' he said, breathing heavily. Then he kissed her on the mouth and her struggling quieted. When he lifted his face, she tried to shove him away, she beat on his chest, her eyes straining from side to side. 'Lemme go! Lemme go! I just come to see the buzzards!' she cried.

He relaxed his hold. 'Sho! The buzzards. Sho'!'

As he released her, she jerked away and ran down the beach, her loose skirt whipping behind her. He stared: her running away revived the long-forgotten ache a distant fleeting thing used to leave. He smiled and set off after her, first at a walk, then sprinting. She ran swiftly, but he gained on her. When they reached the elbow of the long bar, he had almost overtaken her. Suddenly she dropped to the sand, and he had to jump to keep from falling over her. She leaped up and darted toward the river, wading out into the wine-colored water.

He did not follow her: he looked off at the horizon, where a blood-red sun drew an ocher haze around it. "Bout time for the buzzards—I'm goan git to my stand.' He moved up the slope toward the graying willow grove. A little way off, he suddenly stooped over and picked up a shell. He remained leaned down, examining it.

Her voice sounded close behind him. 'I bet I know what 'tis.' As she knelt down, he put his foot over the shell and she pretended indifference. Then he handed her the shell, looking off toward the skyline.

'The Injuns said the ole buzzard was the fust critter to come down to the world,' he said. 'The rest of them sent 'im to look for dry land.' He got up slowly, still looking away, as if he were unconscious of her gaze. 'Fust thing he found 'uz a sandbar—that's why he likes 'em so good.' He walked on toward the grove. She was moving at his side.

He had selected a bed of soft sand, shadowed by feathery willows and screened on three sides by white dunes. When they reached it, he entered the hollow and went across to the opposite slope, without noticing her. He lay face downward and looked out over the top of the ridge. In the distance, buzzards circled over the edge of the beach. He turned his head and saw her sitting beside him, stiffly upright. 'Git down!' he said. 'They kin see you.' She lowered her shoulders, then stretched out beside him, peering over the ridge. There was the quick, soft sound of her breathing, and he felt the warmth from her body. After a while he looked at her again. 'I kin smell yo' hair,' he said. (She turned toward him and her jaw loosened slowly until her lips had parted.) 'Smells like candy-root!'

She swallowed and laughed nervously. Her dress was pulled smooth across her breasts. Gazing into her eyes, he laid his hand over one of the rigid mounds. Something in her look, for a moment, made him wish that she were still running away down the beach. He felt her shiver, but she did not move away. A scorching urge took him and he lowered his glance. Then, forcing a smile, he pinched the breast. 'Green gourd, yuh got under theah!'

'Quit!' she said and grabbed his fingers, but she did not draw them away. Her mouth quivered. 'Green—' she said.

He leaned over her. 'I'm the one to ripen 'em!'

A flat, shrill voice came to them from far in the swamp at their backs. 'Madie! You Madie!'

The girl jerked to her knees, as if the sound had burnt her.

'Lemme go! Lemme go! That's ma!'

He held on. She beat at his shoulders, his face. 'Oh, my Gawd! Lemme go!' The distant call came again and she struggled on. 'I kain't let ma see me with you!'

'Why kain't?'

'She knows yuh a-sight—knows who you air—she says you a river rogue.'

He laughed and held her tighter. Then tears came into her eyes and she tried to bite him. His jaws clamped shut. 'You feel that-a-way, too? What's matter with a riverman?'

Her face was now red and broken with angry crying. 'Ma says you triflin', no good—she says, no good for nuthin', 'cept to git a gal in trouble!'

His face stretched in a taut grin and he spoke through his teeth, holding her out from him to look at her. "Hell, I might marry yuh! You kain't tell.'

'That'd be worser!' She broke his relaxing grip and jerked to her feet. 'Ma'd run me off—she and pa both!' The girl was walking down the slope across the hollow.

Ratliff did not move from the sand. He rested the back of his head on his hand. 'Sho'! You don't have to marry me.' He went on in an injured tone, 'You don't even have to tell me good-bye!'

She halted at the top of the opposite ridge and shook out her skirt. She looked back. Then suddenly, she ran down again and bent over him. The impact of her kiss almost shoved his head off his hand.

He did not try to detain her, but lay listlessly on his side. 'Think I'm gonna make my bed right heah tonight.' He paused and looked after her. 'The moon'll be full—it'll sho' be fun a-wadin' off the bar!'

She had gone back to the far slope. She turned. I kain't git out—I—'

'Oh, sho', sho'! They's plenty more bars twixt heah and Darien—and gals, too!'

'Go'n git yo' gals if that's way 'tis!' She kicked the sand at her feet.

'You ain't leavin' me no choice.'

She hesitated on top of the ridge. The shrill call of her mother came again, nearer by. The girl looked back hurriedly. ''Bout moon-rise—if'n I kin find a way to git out!' She slipped through the willows and was gone.

When Ratliff returned to his boat at the upper end of the sandbar, he found Bud True sitting on its prow, smoking his pipe. He was surprised that Bud had reached him so quickly. Bud said the sawmiller at English Eddy had told him where to look, and it wasn't so quick: the river had been rising since early morning.

Ratliff started to gather firewood to cook supper, but Bud stopped him. 'This ain't no place to lay up,' Bud said. 'We'd better drop on down to Jack's Suck.' Ratliff shook his head. They couldn't look for logs before morning; needed more water to float them, anyhow; and there wasn't a good camping place near the Suck. Bud said he didn't know what he was talking about and they argued. 'What you got hid out on this sandbar?' Bud said finally.

186

Ratliff was silent, then he borrowed Bud's smoking tobacco and smiled reluctantly. 'Got sump'n treed,' he said. 'Just leave me heah till midnight and I'll be ready to go to hell-and-out with yuh.'

Bud laughed and knocked out his pipe on the gunwale. 'Listen, if you and yo' gal lay out on this bar, yo' back'll be wet long 'fore midnight—and you not a-lyin' on it, neither. Theah's a freshet in the Oconee and the Ocmulgee, both. Boy, we got water and we got work to do—this no time for sandbar sparkin!'

Ratliff did not give up his intention to meet the girl at the willow grove even after they got under way with the log skiff. It would be but a two-mile paddle, now that the river was high enough to come through the Suck: he'd come back after supper.

Bud was in fine spirits to be on the river again with plenty of water. As they drifted on, he talked about what he called the liabilities and lack of accommodations of sandbar sparking.

'Why don't yuh git a woman for that ole house of yo'n?' he asked. ''Twouldn't be so lonesome then.'

'Git married?' Ratliff sensed that the sound of the word had been recently in his mouth, but differently. His eyebrows puckered. 'You a hell-of-a-feller to—thought you said a married man 'uz like a raft peddler in the Darien market: kain't go back and got no place ahead—got to take it. Waun't that it?'

Bud did not reply. After a moment he snorted and broke into song:

> *Come all ye Georgia ladies and listen to my noise;*
> *It'll never do to marry a sawmill boy.*
> *If you do, your portion it'll be:*
> *Corn bread and bacon in a dish you'll see,*
> *Corn bread and bacon in a dish you'll see.*

Below the Suck they passed a chain raft tied up. It was the raft they, along with its Coventry hands, had tried to get off the sand the week before. Now it floated above the bar, apparently deserted. Ratliff and Bud both stared at it in the gathering dusk.

'Reckon them niggers had to quit'er,' Bud said.

'Looks like this might be our stoppin-place.' Ratliff, standing at the stern of the skiff, lifted his pike pole and looked back over his shoulder. 'I don't see nobody 'round.'

'Nope. 'Twouldn't do, said Bud. 'I don't want-a take a chance on no lawsuit with no big company.' They had drifted on almost a mile when he spoke again. 'We'll just pole in heah and tie. I got a little treatmint I want-a give that raft, I think'll put it in shape for pickin' up more legal like.'

They left their skiff and paddled back to the chain raft. Ratliff secured it with a rope they had brought along with them, while Bud shifted the rope with which it had been tied from the bank to a cypress in the water. He moored it close to the tree and took deliberate care with the knot he tied in the rope.

'That's got 'er,' he said, from the bow of the boat, coming up off his knees. 'When the river rises three foot or more, she'll pull loose of 'er own accord—and come hell-bustin' around the bend, headed for the swamp!'

Ratliff nosed their batteau around the stern of the raft and loitered alongside, holding to it with his paddle. He gazed at the long float of pine logs. Must be ninety thousand feet in her, he thought. She'll bust up in the bight and strew timber for ten miles. He felt the push of blood under his skin—the freshet current dragging at his boat. What a day's work we got cut out! High water and floating logs! Then he looked away. He saw again a girl's flying legs, her loose skirt whipping behind her, on the bight strand of Golden Grove Bar. He shook his head slowly and pushed the boat off. He raised his voice as he paddled on:

Come all ye Georgia ladies and listen to my noise;
It'll never do to marry a river-runnin' boy.

CHAPTER

18

CHINA SWANN WAS COMPLACENT at first when Ratliff did not return to the Birdcage—complacent and even a little relieved. The month and a half of their revived intimacy had been a mixture of a drunk and a wake for her—reckless fun, somehow given an elevation of finality, a plaintive tone of remembrance. She thought she wouldn't mind clearing the giddiness out of her head. And even if old green-eye had got Ratliff, he'd show up again. It might make a man mean, but he didn't quit you.

She told herself this through the last of May and the first of June. The good sense of it was unquestionable. But her good sense became a diminishing consolation, as June wore on. The giddiness she'd got out of her head and was replaced by much less pleasant feelings. And before the end of the latter month she was disturbed by the suspicion that Snake Sutton didn't behave according to good-sense rules—and certainly the damned fool didn't *have* good sense! He had been coming to Darien regularly: three times during the four weeks, according to her check. She had had no word, seen no sign of him.

In late June he came again and she sent her negro boy, Eef, to tell him that she wanted to see him. He didn't reply and he didn't come.

On an afternoon in early July she stopped him as he and Bud True were coming up from the Boom. He kept looking over his shoulder at Bud—walking slowly on—as if he wanted to be going, too. She didn't talk around. 'You ain't gonna let a wheezy potbellied old man run you off, are yuh?' she asked him.

Ratliff wouldn't look at her. He was wooden-faced and cold. 'Cap'n Henry's a fine man: I got respect for him,' he said. 'The only thing I got ag'in 'im is his ruttin' around with you!'

She winced, but then she knew green-eye. What she didn't get was that Christian-hearted pose about Henry. 'What's the matter, Snake?' she asked, as quiet and frank as she could make it.

'You kain't –' he said, beginning to get hot, then he changed his voice. 'I just got respect for 'im.' He turned around and started walking.

She caught up with him and took hold of his arm. 'Let's get this straight, Snake: what's this talk about Seborn? He don't mean a damn thing to you! Or me, either, except he owns my house. You know I got to deal with him.'

'Deal with him!' he said, and laughed. Then he shook her hand loose. 'I don't pay a debt by foulin' a fellow's bed—even if he is fool enough to keep a woman like you in it!' He left, and that was all China was able to get out of him, except the look on his face: like there *was* something between him and Seborn and he didn't want to talk about it.

Her memory of that look remained vivid and disturbing. It shattered every assurance she had felt about his behavior. Any way she figured it now—whatever he might owe to Henry and whether he was only jealous, or not—it added up the same: she had to get rid of Seborn to get Snake back. And with the growing certainty of her belief grew her sense of denial, until it dwarfed the importance of her tie with Henry, the importance of her house itself. Getting rid of Seborn became, not a choice, but a necessity for her.

191

There remained one hitch, however, one big hitch: he still held title to her place. It was hers by right, she felt. He had been promising to deed it over to her for three years—God knows she'd paid for it! She may not have believed that he really intended to, but she had always felt sure that she would wangle him into it sometime. Suddenly that time had become immediate, the need urgent.

During July and August her conviction that she must rid herself of Henry developed into a course of action. On each visit he made to the Birdcage, she reminded him of his promise. She invented plausible advantages to her business that rested upon this transfer of title, she spoke of his reputation as a man of his word, over her foolish reliance on his promise, she browbeat and bullied him.

Henry never attempted to deny his promise, nor did he admit any weakening of his good intention, but his cunning at delay and the toughness he displayed under her coaxing astonished her. She saw that persuasion was not enough.

On a Sunday evening in late September, she sat at the tall secretary in her room thinking of what she had just done: Seborn had come to the house and she had refused to see him. She had sent Delia down with a prepared note, saying, not only that she wouldn't see him, but that he need not come back until he brought the deed. He had followed the maid back upstairs and had talked to her through the door. He couldn't get a deed drawn up, he had said, because it was Sunday and it wouldn't be legal. But she refused to unlock her door. He had hung around an hour, drinking in the taproom, and had finally gone away.

She shifted the inkstand on her desk. She felt taut and nervous. She was taking a strong hand with Seborn. He could blow up and take the place away from her. Have her run out of town! She did not think he would. Still, she was treating him pretty rough: they had always got on agreeably. She knew, had always known, that Seborn deliberately held on to the title to keep strings on her: just as a matter of practical sense—though this had never been intimated by either of them.

She opened a gray-backed ledger by the inkstand. Well, you brought his game out in the open, she told herself. He can call a bitch a bitch if he wants to, but he knows what that'll make him! He probably won't come back at all for a while, and he's sure to come drunk, when he comes—and no deed.

No deed: no China, by God!

She thumbed the ledger pages, not looking at them. You don't know how well this thing's going to work out, she told herself again. Getting rid of Seborn in too rough a way might only serve to set Snake more against you. She wondered if he really did have some sort of obligation to Seborn: when she had brought up Ratliff's name casually early in the summer, Henry had said he knew him only by sight. She was sure Seborn wasn't hiding anything. His open, wide-mouthed face passed through her mind and she half-smiled.

I'd almost rather buy the place, if I had the money, she thought. The pages of the ledger revealed only twelve hundred dollars to her credit in the bank. That wasn't half enough. Well, by God, you're not going to buy what's already yours by right! What you've paid plenty for, she told herself. She put away the ledger and locked the desk.

China guessed wrong on the hour of Henry's return. She was in the hallway on her way to her room that night, when the clinking of broken glass from the front door announced his arrival. He had broken out the doorlight with his pistol butt and let himself in. She reached the stairway landing in time to see him kick a chair across the reception room and into the parlor. Three girls and a customer had jumped up from their seats and stood in the parlor doorway staring.

His cap pushed back from his red, puffy face, Henry rocked on his feet drunkenly. In his right hand he waved a pistol. "Smy house, Goddamnit! And I'll tear 'er up if I want to!'

China felt her face flush. She had not looked for this. Seborn was making a fool, a drunken sight of himself before the customers and her girls. The shame she felt was in part for herself. My God, what will the girls think—say to each other about this! she thought, as she hurried down the steps. She took him by the arm. 'Having a good time, Sebe?' She smiled indulgently. 'Come on, let's put it to bed.' He shook his arm loose and looked down, as if to say something, but she spoke first. 'Come on up to my room, Sebe,' she said in an undertone.

'All right, then! That's better! More like it!' He twirled the pistol around his finger by the trigger guard, almost dropping it, then followed her up the stairs.

She got him into his big chair in her room and rang for Delia. Delia didn't need to be told: when she appeared, she bore a platter of cold meats and bread. She'd be back with hot coffee in a minute. Henry wagged his head about and tried to grab China around the knees: he didn't want to eat. But she was insistent and got food down him. She pulled up a chair by his side as he began his second cup of coffee, and sat down.

His broad, blunt face tightened. 'Thought I 'uz too thick to catch on, I reckon,' he said, squinting his eyes to better focus them on her.

She looked at him over her coffee-cup. 'Catch on to what, Seborn?'

'That you want to take on some pimp and 'ud like to git shed of me now.'

'Sober up, Sebe!' She set her cup on a table. 'You know damn well I got no pimp—that I've never had a pimp. That sort of chinch won't never be caught in my bed and you know it! If you were sober you wouldn't say that.'

He stared at her, his eyelids lifting unnaturally, then looked down at his cup of coffee. He fumbled with it, as if meditating her statement.

China went on. 'As a matter of fact'—she suddenly saw her opportunity and her voice gathered force—'as a matter of fact, the shoe's on your foot. I'm not sayin' you've got another woman—I'm not puttin' on, I'm talkin' to you straight—I'm not sayin' you got another woman, yet, but it's plain you're gettin' set to.'

Henry shifted the cup in its saucer, gazing at it, then an uncertain smile gathered slowly on his face. 'Might at that—may be!' he said.

'And take this house away from me and move her in!' she said, with quick vehemence. Henry looked startled, but before he could reply, she went on. 'I don't aim to let that happen—that's all, Seborn!'

'You're just talkin' to hear yourself talk!' he said huffily.

China's yellow eyes grew dark, and red spots came into her cheeks. 'You gave me this house three years ago—said you'd deed it over to me legal. I didn't press you about it, 'cause I thought we'd both live and enjoy it. Every year I've put back in it every cent I cleared: fixin' it up, buildin' new parts, gettin' new things—better beds, an icebox, that chair you're settin' in. I got twice as much in this house as you have—but you got the deed! It's mine in every way 'cept title, and heah you are tryin' to take it away from me to put some other woman in!' She stood up.

Steadier now, Henry came to his feet, too. He was shaking his head and his lips were pursed. 'No, China. By God, you know better than that! I'll take a paralyzed oath—'

'You took a paralyzed oath you were goin' to get me that deed!' her hand clutched the yoke of her purple wrapper.

'No, I didn't now! Not on an oath, not yet. But I'm goin' to have the deed fixed up—in the mornin'. I'm swearin' to it now—and I don't want to hear you say anything more about it.' His face straightened and he drew himself up. 'Nobody can accuse Seborn Henry of ever breakin' his oath—or promise, either, for that matter.' He reached out and took her hand. 'Even to a nigglin' woman.'

The buff skin beneath China's eyes hardened. He looked sober to her and serious to the point of swelling up. I guess he means it, she thought. Her arm relaxed. He'd never let himself be accused of breaking his oath (I can count on that), the big-headed bull-ox!

Henry drew her hand away from the wrapper. The yoke, where she had held it, opened, and he could see the moulding of her erect breasts. Her face was still sharp with emotion. He smiled. 'Smooth your hair down, red-head!'

'Nope! We can wait on the deed, Seborn!'

'But there ain't no way to git the deed tonight—wouldn't be legal. I'll go from heah as soon as I wake up in the mornin'—go right to Sid Ross's office.'

She gazed at him steadily. 'Can I go with you?'

He drew her toward him. 'Sure as shoutin'!'

Her body relaxed.

The next morning Delia despaired of getting China's petticoat to hang evenly. They were before the hearth in China's room and Delia knelt with pins in her mouth. China walked away toward her dressing-table, unconscious of Delia's outstretched arms. She picked up a brooch and juggled it in her hand. You should never have gone on with him, anyhow, she told herself. She looked at the clock on the mantel: it was now five minutes past ten. He's had time to get deeds drawn to half the houses in town!

A glimpse of Henry's slightly reddening face and his hand drumming on the back of a chair passed through her mind. 'I can do this a lot quicker without you,' was all that he had said. But she had known that he did not want to appear in the lawyer's office, in the courthouse with her. Henry was respectable, and she was, after all, a sporting woman. It wouldn't be liked in Darien; such a thing didn't go. When she agreed to remain at home, she had been thinking largely of herself: she didn't want to get respectable Darien down on her.

But you thought he was sober, she told herself. She had waited the first hour under that foolish assurance, impatient only with the clock. Then the hand had advanced, and it grew plain that her sobering him up was not working, that his oath was not holding—that she was being taken in. The damn soak is probably off drunk somewhere now! she thought. Her cheeks grew warm. She dropped the brooch, not remembering what she had wanted with it. The low-down hog! Don't even give a damn for his oath. She felt undone, undone by a low trick, and her anger rose. But you've always been able to hold him to his oath, before!

Delia had moved forward on her knees and caught hold of China's skirt again. 'Please'm, Miss China!' she said, through the pins.

China stood still. After a moment she said in an unnatural, quivering voice, 'It's a hell-of-a-thing to be disappointed in somebody you've had respect for, Delia.' Even if he is a man, she added to herself. Suddenly hot tears ran down her face. 'The Goddamned cheat!'

But when China appeared at the lawyer's office, her manner was deliberate and there was a bland smile on her face. Only the set and color of her eyes evidenced her grimness. As she entered, the lean, smooth-worn man at the roller-topped desk raised his spectacles and smiled. But his answer to her question jolted her. He hadn't seen Captain Henry: no, the captain hadn't been to the courthouse—he hadn't seen him all morning.

China turned away and walked across the room to a window. Seborn hadn't even come uptown. The lying, lowdown scum must have gone straight to his boat, she thought. Her chest swelled. She stared through the dusty window-panes toward the river with burning eyes.

When the lawyer spoke to her, she turned around hurriedly. She and Captain Henry had up a deal for the house she lived in, she said. She didn't know what had happened to him, but they wanted a deed drawn. She told the lawyer to fix up the paper and they would be in to sign it. Her deliberate manner had vanished when she strode toward the narrow stairway that led to the street.

On the sidewalk, as she turned hurriedly away from the staircase, she almost collided with a man, but she did not pause. 'Oh, h'llo!' he said, in astonishment. 'Law after you?'

As she swept on, her glimpse of him leaning against the wall, his cold heckling voice, registered on her brain. It was Snake Sutton. And his words came back: 'Cap'n Henry's a fine man.' She suddenly whirled around. Her face was stiff. 'All I got to tell you is, your fine man, Sebe Henry, is a lyin', crooked, overrated son-of-a-bitch!' The epithets came as separate explosions, but swiftly. She caught hold of her skirt that had spread out around her and paused. Her voice lowered. 'And when I'm through with him, he'll admit to it!' Her eyes hardened. 'And he won't show up 'round my place again!' Turning abruptly, she spoke over her shoulder as she moved away. 'Not that that means a damn thing to you!'

Ratliff stood, fumbling with a bill of measurement. His thoughts had been far away from China, when they bumped into each other, but now he felt a strange stimulation, as he watched her go along the riverfront street to its end and take the path toward her house. 'Jesus!' he said, aloud. Like a buzz-saw on the loose! I've never seen that bitch so mad before—except one time, he amended. He entered the buyer's office and stepped into line to get a bid on the raft he and Bud had brought, but his attention did not return to his earlier reflections. Like a shooting star, he told himself, remembering China's sudden appearance. It surprised him that such a likeness should have entered his head. He hadn't seen her at close range since that time she waylaid him, coming up from the Boom. Danged if her hair wasn't red this morning. He smiled. She's pretty hot for old man Henry to handle!

Later Ratliff saw her come out of the entrance to the lawyer's office again. She was still curt, forbidding. This time she turned, not in the direction of the Birdcage, but toward the freight wharf. She strode rapidly along the loose shell walk. That's where Henry's boat's tied up, Ratliff thought. He got into motion deliberately, but with lengthened stride, and followed her down the street. Something's bound to pop when she gets that sore!

As he reached the river depot, he saw China ahead of him, already crossing the gangplank to Henry's boat, the *Pollyann*. He halted behind a row of cotton bales that gave him cover and a clear view of the stern-wheeler. He saw that China, as she got into its deck, opened her pocketbook and took out a pearl-handed pistol. The door to the texas, a few yards away, shut with a slam, but she advanced on it without hesitation.

Ratliff moved closer. He was wondering with a sense of tension if he could get aboard the boat without getting into the mix-up, when he saw Henry and a negro hand come out of the forward cabins, moving aft. He decided to remain where he was. The negro looked back over his shoulder, but Henry moved quickly to a deck vent and pulled up the lid. He lowered himself into the Boat's hold. The darky replaced the covering, then hurried toward the engine room. Ratliff had watched the pantomime with a frown and tightening jaws. Suddenly he laughed. What kind of a son-of-a-bitch was it she called him?

When China found Henry in the boat's hold, squatting on a beam with his feet in watery mud, he got up quickly. He walked toward her, snarling, 'This damfoolery's gone too far—git out of heah!'

Then he saw her face in the half-light from the vent above. It was as smooth as a metal plate, the whites of her eyes were glazed, the pupils empty and black. She did not speak. The gun barrel glinted in his direction and he looked at it. He picked up his foot, but put it back down where he stood. 'You gone crazy?' he said, and his voice cracked on the inflection. 'Look-a-heah, this is highway robbery!'

'A hog-killin'!' she said, almost whispering.

'All right,' he said. 'You'll be—'

She interrupted him with a wave of the gun and he did not finish. He moved toward the vent and climbed out of the hold.

In the front cabin, China laid the deed that had been prepared by the lawyer on Henry's desk and he signed it, sitting down to steady his hand. As he stood up, he started to speak, but she silenced him. 'Sign the nigger's name for a witness and he can make his mark.' She said, nodding at the roustabout who had helped Henry hide and who now stood against the cabin wall. Then she folded the signed document with one hand and pushed it into the bosom of her dress. Henry watched her, his eyes fixed as if in irrevocable amazement. She turned quickly and went through the open cabin door onto the deck.

Ratliff had moved up to a pile of turpentine barrels at the wharf edge and had been able to see in through the cabin window. He could not hear their words, but as he had watched the signing of the paper, China's violent promise, 'when I'm through with him, he'll admit to it,' echoed in his ears and he smiled.

When China appeared on the deck again, Ratliff saw Henry stick his head out of the cabin door behind her. He stared after her until she reached the gangplank. 'You'll be damned sorry 'bout this before it's over!' he barked.

China looked back. 'No. I 'uz sorry beforehand,' she said, and started on.

'That deed ain't worth the paper it's written on!' he laughed extravagantly and slammed the door.

Ratliff saw a grim smile on China's face. She was almost across the gangplank. The sunlight struck her hair and it shone like burnished copper. Her final words, in front of the timber office, came back to him resonantly: 'Not that it means a damn thing to you!' He laughed and stepped out from behind the barrel. She looked up and saw him and he held out his hand to her. 'You called the turn, all right!' he said.

CHAPTER

19

BUD SNORTED. 'That woman's a hellcat! Better look out she don't use that pearl-handled popgun on you.' He spoke to Ratliff gruffly.

They were standing on the upper deck of a small river steamer headed up the Altamaha on the morning after Ratliff's unexpected reunion with China. He did not reply, but stared at Bud with dark, absent eyes, a still tension on his face. He turned away, frowning slightly, and moved to the deck rail.

'Hellcat,' he said tonelessly, scarcely knowing that he said it. He could not pause to consider it now: he was getting hold of something else, something bigger. China had given him something to think about. The feeling had struck him when he saw her coming back across the gangplank, that high, shining look on her face. And it had stirred in him deeper, lifted him more, as they were together through the evening. When, finally, standing by her mantelpiece just before they went to bed, she had said, 'I aimed to have my house, but mainly I wanted to prove to you what he was like and get rid of him, get rid of him for both of us'—when she said that, it had put the feeling in him good and solid.

Then lying awake in bed there—his eyes batting like bell clappers—the notion had come over him: China and Jake Pettigrew! He couldn't put it together then, he was too full of it. But the new light on China that had come to him had shown up Jake, too—they had something that put them apart from Bud and the ruck of folks he had been running with.

He turned around and looked at Bud uncertainly for a moment. Something, but nowhere near alike, he thought, moving slowly away toward the front of the deck.

The offhand, you're-just-like-the-rest voice in which the stranger called on him to step and get Bud's auger there at Jack's Suck, had got under his skin at the start, though now it was hard to see any good reason why. And there had been other things during the day, while they sweated over the Coventry chain raft, trying to get it off the sand—things like when the fellow sung out for him to grab a hold on the prize pole—pretty damned short, though of course he was straining at it himself.

All of that had been in his, Ratliff's craw, when he had taken occasion to happen to notice the lazy-pin on the stranger's bow oar and say, 'See you're usin' one of my lazy-pins.'

'Oh, you the one thought that up?' the man had said. 'It's a fine thing—sho' has saved us poor oar-pullin' devils' backs.'

Letting that strange, second-rate (he had thought then) raftsman know he was no scrub bowhand to be ordered around had done him a lot of good, and he had gone on to tell him all about how to go about it and didn't give a damn anyhow—glad to see everybody get the use of it.

The stranger had said that was a fine way to look at it—like he was impressed, but for manners' sake, too—then, hadn't talked any more, but had got busy cooking supper.

It hadn't been till after they had eaten, had turned loose and were adrift that night, that Bud named the stranger to him, snorting, 'Hell, don't you know Jake Pettigrew, the fellow who invented the sharp-shooter raft?'

It had come over him in a flash, in Bud's tone of voice: every-body—even the Coventry niggers they had been trying to help—knew the big inventor of the sharpshooter raft—everybody, but him. Pettigrew had known that and was just making small of him, letting him run on. He had felt his ears burn even there in the dark. He had put Pettigrew down as a damned smart-aleck, had been sore all the next day, till he ran into China.

It's a bigger sort of thing, he told himself, gripping the railing and gazing down at his hands. Like China: you'd never known her before—what she would put out to get the man she wants—had in her to put out!

He thought of the married woman with the gold rings in her ears who had come to his bunk at English Eddy. He had been worked up then, but now she seemed like a loose-sneaking bag. The flying legs and whipping skirt of the girl running away from him at Golden Grove Bar passed through his mind—it was always the way he remembered her. That had caught him up, but after all there was nothing to her, she was just a cottontail on the run.

It had come to him, when he saw the bigger thing working in China, that he hadn't been deep enough to figure Jake out, either. He leaned against the railing on his forearms and stared at the smooth yellow water slipping under the boat's square bow. Pettigrew's horse face, with its solemn yet easy-going look, formed before him again.

Jake's got more in his head than all the common ruck he runs across and he knows it, Ratliff told himself: that's what's in that look. He don't have to have anybody telling him what he's done and he don't have to tell anybody. That's it: he knows he's a man among men! It would have been so easy for him to let it out that he had invented the sharp-shooter just to see your eyes pop out, but he didn't give a damn about that or what you happened to think of him. He knew he had sense enough to lend you some and then out-smart you!

Bud, who had taken a seat on a deck bench and lighted his pipe, gazed at Ratliff's back and his big mustaches twitched. 'So you kain't make up yo' mind to admit it?'

'Hunh!' Ratliff twisted his head around suddenly and stared at Bud.

'That she's a hellcat.'

Ratliff grunted and looked away. China had said Henry called her that, too. Henry: mention of the man gave him the feeling of mist clearing up off the river—mist that had hung over him since he was a boy. Jesus, he had seen now that the fellow was nothing but a clumsy, stupid coward, who'd crook a woman! He turned back to Bud with the strange feeling that the face of things familiar to him was shrinking—like the lake behind Uncle Mundy's house that now seemed only a pond. And as he gazed at Bud, he saw too—in further revelation—that Bud's eyes were set far apart and had a simple look in them. 'Hellcat?' he said. 'That's what I want: I ain't no ordinary hound!' And he knew without thinking that his days under Bud were ended.

Nevertheless, the new partnership Ratliff formed seemed a little strange in the making, when—two months later—he hooked up with Sneaky Colquitt. It had grown out of a poker game in the Blue Goose Saloon at Darien. The crowd had got so hot in behind Sneaky that he couldn't use his tricks himself and he had dealt the cards to Ratliff. They had cleaned out the bunch. The idea of throwing the game to another man had never occurred to Ratliff before and he was impressed. Instead of dividing their winnings, Sneaky had proposed they pool them, buy stumpage and cut timber together.

On the following day, Ratliff lounged in a seat of the train to Lumber City and thought the thing over. He had heard of Sneaky's shrewdness for a long time, remembered his slick part in the joke they played on the Ohoopeans the winter previous, but he had never thought to team up with him. It seemed strange. He sat up, gazing at the plush back of the seat ahead. I reckon it would feel funny to be pardners with anybody, except Bud, he told himself. At first, it would. When the Ochwalkee timber operator had hired him as a pilot during the September freshet and he and Bud had separated, he had had no real notion of quitting him. And now it seemed a little sad.

You were lucky to learn the river under Bud. Nobody knows it better—nor the rafting game—but Bud's gittin' old and his tricks are tame. He couldn't appreciate Sneaky if he tried to, I reckon. Bud still holds it against Sneaky for not bringin' him the fire at Mad Dog, even though Sneaky wasn't on his own timber and couldn't swim to boot. Sneaky's deep and sharp as a prickly pear. Ratliff took a plug of tobacco out of his pocket and cut himself a chew. He felt sure of his estimate, though Bud's words, when Sneaky had proposed to Ratliff soon after their tadpole-drifting that they throw in together to cut timber, came oddly to mind. 'I wouldn't cut a watermelon with 'im,' Bud had said. And when Ratliff had wanted more of an answer, Bud added: 'He gits by all right, he aims to do that; but he ain't a fellow to get messed up with. Sneaky'll run under you.'

You swallowed it just like Bud put it out then, he told himself. It didn't come to you that Bud might mean he didn't want to be around a fellow who could outsmart him! Ratliff spat into the cuspidor at his foot. Run under you, he repeated to himself. He grinned. The notion seemed womanish. You ain't worryin' about Sneaky, or no other son-of-a-bitch runnin' under you. Sneaky's the slickest one you've ever seen and he may know more tricks, but he ain't too slick for you. That's what you are after: somebody smart enough to keep you lookin' out. He leaned his head against the back of the seat and dozed, wondering drowsily what Sneaky had in mind to do to the fellow up on the Ocmulgee whose stumpage they were going to buy.

Later he felt the presence of someone near him and roused himself. Sneaky—his lowered face, with its loose cheeks, looking like a cadaverous pocket gopher's—was standing by the arm of Ratliff's seat. 'You ain't seen my time-table book 'round heah, is you?' Sneaky asked. 'What's that on the flo'?' Ratliff reached down and retrieved a pamphlet, but it wasn't the missing time-table. 'I don't know what could a-happened'—Sneaky looked back down the aisle, then again at Ratliff. 'Well, gimme a chew and lemme go.'

Ratliff's left hand, by force of habit, started back to his hip, but halfway it halted. His eyes were on Sneaky's blousing shirt-front. Quickly he grabbed the flap where a button was unfastened. He reached inside, as Sneaky struggled, and brought out the tobacco plug. He cut off a piece and handed it back to Sneaky. 'Heah 'tiz,' he said.

'Tch-tch-tch! If I'd-a just knowed I had that 'backer,' said Sneaky, giving Ratliff a solemn, straight-faced wink, 'I needn't to bothered yuh.'

Ratliff grinned. 'It'll chew just as good,' he called out, as Sneaky moved back down the aisle. He felt pleased with himself. Still he'd heard about that one. Setting out, Sneaky always hooked something from his pardner—knife, liquor bottle, or something—then asked to borrow it. Ratliff had had the signal: he was looking out for the first move.

What Ratliff considered Sneaky's first move came four days later. They had bought stumpage in the Ocmulgee swamp near Jacksonville and had returned to Lumber City to get log-choppers, when Sneaky's hurry to get going suddenly petered out; he said he couldn't get the hands he wanted and left under the pretext of a visit to his kin. But Ratliff had had his eyes skinned: the newspaper piece on Green Bentley's death that interested Sneaky on their boat trip to Jacksonville, he had read, too, and he had heard the captain say that the old man left a fine swamp of cypress. He figured he could call Sneaky's hand on that one and he did.

When he entered the Bentley swamp with his short-handled axe on the morning after Sneaky had left, he saw that he had guessed right, that Sneaky was already in the swamp belting the cypress. He cruised around to the upper end of the tract and started belting trees himself and before long Sneaky came to him. As Sneaky stepped out from behind a tree in front of him, he said, 'Thought I'd yelp you up.' Sneaky gave his straight-faced wink, then grinned. They finished belting the best of the timber that day and made plans to cut it in February, come first high water.

As they rode back to Lumber City in the mule and buggy, Ratliff mused on Sneaky's words: 'Thought 'twaun't no use to bother you till after I got it belted: one axe makes less noise in the swamp than two.' Sho'! sho'! Sneaky, he said to himself now. He looked off at the pine trees circling past them along the sandy road. He cut his buggy whip through the air and its shrill whistle smote his ears. It was a good sound. He felt like that.

Ratliff was holding his own, but his admiration for Sneaky did not slacken. During the remainder of October and November they cut and drifted three pine rafts from the land of the man near Jacksonville with whom they had traded. They cut three, but Sneaky contrived to pay for only two, tricking the tenant farmer the landowner had looking out for him. Ratliff had to hand it to Sneaky for headwork. They began the second of their rafts one afternoon, quitting for the day with only the bow and boom logs laid. They left the swamp with the farmer, but that night they came back, finished the raft, and started another. Ratliff left with number two, while number three was just where number two had been when the farmer arrived in the morning. 'Who the hell does he think we are, a-puttin' a danged clodhopper down heah to watch!' Sneaky had said.

And Sneaky showed Ratliff some new sleights to doctoring logs. There was a swamp clay with which a doty log could be painted that, after a little burning, made the red-heart mighty hard to see, Ratliff learned. And one day in Darien, Sneaky showed him an exhibit of knots and plugs laid out on the mantel in the main office of the Coventry, Dale Lumber Company. Ratliff hadn't seen it before, he had never been behind the outer room railing.

'Their own inspector caught 'em in timber that had done got by the scalers at the Boom,' said Sneaky, picking up a large knot with a tag tied to it. 'Old man Dale calls it his "odd collection." Most of it's rough work, but it'll pay a feller to look 'em over and see why they didn't git by.'

They were in the courthouse at Mount Vernon—Sneaky said courthouses were good places to pick up things, for a fellow who knew how to use them—on the Monday after Christmas, when Sneaky saw the announcement of mortgages to be foreclosed that had John Y. Johnson's name on it. The court docket lay on a high counter in the clerk's office and Sneaky stared at it thoughtfully. Tch-tch-tch! Poor old John Y's going to loose that place of his'n this time,' he said. 'He's fooled around and let that mortgage git into the wrong hands.'

Ratliff, who had just come into the room and stood gazing about woodenly, turned toward Sneaky with kindling interest. He came close and looked over his shoulder. 'Who's sellin' him out?'

'He's got the finest swamp of floatin' timber on the Oconee River,' Sneaky went on, as if Ratliff had not spoken. 'Don't yuh know he'd like to git that stuff out'n theah 'fore old man McFerrin takes it over?' Ratliff squinted at him quizzically, but Sneaky had turned to re-examine the docket. 'Look-a-heah,' he said, 'court don't meet till last of February and then he's got another month 'fore a sale.' They sauntered out of the building in silence. On the doorsteps Sneaky spoke again. 'I know John Y—knowed 'im a long time—drifted timber fer 'im. He's a skittish sort of feller, but he aims to have what's his'n. I believe we could make a deal with 'im.'

They moved around the corner of the building and squatted against the wall in the sun.

'What sort of a deal?' Ratliff asked, following his question with a quick sidewise glance.

Sneaky took out his knife and picked up a splinter. 'To git out his timber fer 'im. Theah must be a million feet of the finest ash and poplar and gum and cypress you ever put yo' eyes on. Old man McFerrin'll be a-watchin' 'im so close now he kain't git in theah good his self—and he ain't much of a timber-runner, nohow.'

'You mean he kain't cut his timber, and the mortgage ain't foreclosed yit?'

'That's right: mortgage's on the timber, too.' Sneaky cut a long shaving from the splinter and waited until it had dropped to the ground. 'Of course we'd have to move mighty quiet ourselves with that old man on the lookout. He knows John Y ain't gonna let 'im have anything he kin holp, and he's a sharp old gobbler.'

Ratliff shifted his gaze from the splinter to Sneaky's face. 'Well, John Y's next to the swamp and the old man's across the river and fifteen mile away: how kin he watch 'im close enough to keep 'im out, aer keep 'im out nohow?'

'Injine 'im. Then soon as John Y cuts a log, old man Mac kin have 'im locked up.'

'What's to keep that old man from injinin' us—outside of ketchin' us?'

Sneaky smiled faintly. 'He'd have to go through John Y to git at us. 'Sides, he wouldn't know who we wuz to start with, nor where to look for us. We couldn't git nigh all of it, of course, but we could pick off some mighty fine sticks. It 'ud take three months of good weather to git it all—a-workin' open.'

Ratliff's lower lip slowly loosened, but he did not speak.

'They's ash in theah you kin git forty-foot lengths out'n. You know that timber: ain't it fine?' Sneaky's eyes glistened. 'I hate to think of messin' it up! Ought-a be some way we could git in theah long enough to do it right—' He broke off and started across the courtyard.

'And you think John Y 'ud agree to us a-doin' that?' Ratliff said, picking up a shaving.

Sneaky took out his tobacco plug and cut them each a chew. After he'd stowed his in his jaw and spit, he cocked an eye at Ratliff. 'John Y always calls me Bob.' He put the back of his hand up to his chin and wiggled two fingers to represent a goatee, and spoke in a gusty-artificial voice. 'Hah! Naw, naw—whut you talkin' about? I couldn't do a thing like that, Bob!'

He took his hand down and spoke naturally. 'Yeah, you right, I reckon, John Y. I 'uz just a-thinkin' about that old pappy of yo'n. All them years he turkey-hunted through that swamp, a-sayin', "No, I ain't a-gonna cut a stick of it—it'll always be heah for my boy, sump'n he kin fall back on in a time-a need!" I hate to think of that Tump Johnson swamp a-goin' to fatten old Ent McFerrin's pot gut.'

Sneaky resumed his artificial whiskers and voice. 'The God-damned son-of-a-bitch! You know he's already a-talkin' about injinin' me!'

Ratliff grinned and Sneaky kept up his dialogue, adroitly laying out his plan for cutting the timber on halves, persuading the imaginary John Y that the timber could be pirated without involving him, and giving him assurance of a fair accounting by allowing him to name the public inspector they should use at the Darien market. 'Well, now, Bobbie, how kin I-a keep you from goin' into that swamp? How kin I keep you from a-cuttin' that timber? Aer know anything about it a-tall, a-tall?' Sneaky concluded to represent John Y's capitulation.

Ratliff laughed, but his mirth dried up quickly and he gazed at the splinter Sneaky had resumed whittling. 'I know old man Ent,' he said slowly. 'Know 'im pretty well. I 'uz his second man in the warehouse for six months—cropped fer 'im before that.'

Sneaky's knife halted halfway through a shaving. He looked at Ratliff intently, his jaw slowly lowering. He began whittling again. 'Look-a-heah, what sort-a man I've tied up to!' he spoke as if to the splinter. 'He's got plenty of that gray stuff in his head—he don't talk

210

like no rafthand!' He smiled diffidently, then his manner became serious. 'You reckon he'd listen to a proposition from you?'

Ratliff batted his eyes. 'Sho', if he could see where he'd make a dime by it. You mean—'

'I mean he knows everythin' 'bout the situation we know—he's gonna be worryin' about John Y gittin' that timber out'n theah before he kin git his hands on it legal, just as much as John Y. Yessuh, by gum, danged if you ain't had an idea in that gober shell of yo'n!' He spat at a distant tuft of grass. 'A brand-new idea: the way to play this game is the two ends and the middle!'

They both stared silently at Sneaky's target. Ratliff wondered if he could handle Ent McFerrin. He had done a few tricks for him in the past, but that was chinquapin stuff. Old man Ent won't be nothing like so easy as Sneaky makes out John Y to be, he told himself. He stood up and yanked his hat down on his head. Great God! It'll be some shenanigans if we can pull it!

Early that afternoon he dropped by McFerrin's general store and found Ent on his high stool in the office. He did not mention the Johnson matter until he was getting to his feet to go. 'I see where you about to git into the timber business,' he said. 'John Y. Johnson's got the finest floatin' timber on the river.'

McFerrin was resting his lean body, that bulged like a squash below his vest, against the desk behind him. The eye-glasses on his clean-shaven face glintered as he shifted his head. He spoke in a soft, penetrating voice. 'I may have it on my hands. Johnson a friend of yours?'

'Know 'im to speak to. Never had any dealin's with 'im, Mister Mac, but I bin over that swamp.'

'Lies right down in the forks of the rivers, don't it?'

'Fronts on both of 'em. And it's never had an axe in it. Bet John Y'll hate to lose that timber,' Ratliff concluded, looking toward the fireplace across the room. He turned back to McFerrin and smiled. 'Wonder if he aims to?'

McFerrin's eyeglasses glittered. 'Don't guess Johnson would try anything like that,' he said in a toneless voice.

'It's t'other side the river and that's a long way from the sheriff's office in this county, anyhow you take it—must be fifteen mile, crow-flight—and two rivers to git out on—it 'ud be an easy proposition, sho'.' Ratliff took a forward step and spat into the fireplace.

'Not so easy with an injunction out against 'im.' McFerrin rested a hand on his smoothly parted hair.

'Sho', that might keep John Y out'n the swamp, but it wouldn't keep the timber in it.'

McFerrin leaned over and dropped a mouthful of ambeer into the cuspidor at his feet. He wiped his lips carefully with his hand and resumed his position against the desk without speaking.

Shifting his gaze, Ratliff moved toward the door. 'I sho' would like to cut that timber for yuh, but I reckon I won't git a chance—not and you a-waitin' to come by it legal.' He smiled at McFerrin slowly and left the office.

Ratliff knew the next move was old man Ent's. Inside, he stewed with impatience and doubt, but he loafed about Mount Vernon's streets like the town dog. On the third morning, as McFerrin passed him at the watering-trough, he nodded for Ratliff to follow. The old man was no less casual and quiet than before, but he was ready for business. From his high stool he forced Ratliff to do most of the talking, spoke with great circumspection, but they made a deal.

Neither questioned, when they came to discuss it, that Johnson would try to get out his timber. Ratliff was to bring McFerrin word as soon as Johnson made a move and McFerrin was to clamp an injunction on him. That would let John Y know to stay out of the swamp, that the law was watching him. They both agreed that this wouldn't prevent him from having somebody else steal the timber. But Ratliff could make terms with John Y's thief (to hold Ent off of him) and still keep John Y in the dark, especially since, having his own man in the swamp, he wouldn't want to be seen there himself.

Ratliff agreed to employ a negro log-chopper who McFerrin said was owing him, but who Ratliff knew would be Ent's spotter. McFerrin agreed to finance Ratliff for half above costs.

At the end, when Ent sat on, uncertain and trying to think of something more, Ratliff talked pretty stout. ''Twon't be no trouble to handle John Y's man: them timber rogues don't think nuthin' of a lawsuit, but they hate to sleep in jail.' (Squeaky had given him that one.) 'I'll gua'ntee to git our share, Mister Mac!' He pulled his hat on solidly and walked out of the store in a steady, heavy-footed stride. He kept his measured gait along the sidewalk past the store buildings, around the corner and down the public road till he came in sight of the river. Suddenly, he ran down a brushy slope, turned three cartwheels in the sandbed at the bottom, and moved off at a dogtrot.

CHAPTER

20

RATLIFF CALLED IT the old sow of all shenanigans, the old sow 'coon of 'em all. He would have liked to take full credit for the idea of playing both sides, but he knew that he had been only fumbling with it. Sneaky had seen it clean through. Sneaky was quick as a mink. And he had his wits about him at every jump. When John Y pushed one of his spotters on him, he took the nigger as if he was glad to get him and put him to chopping logs with a boy he could depend on to keep him out of the way. It was Sneaky's idea, too, that they operate together in the swamp, so that they would look like one crew, and that the logs be gathered in three or four places on the banks of both rivers to mix up the spotters. The nigger choppers were not told who they were cutting for: they were told not to know. Only the white loggers, who assembled the logs for rafting, were let in on the double-dealing. Ratliff was using Lum Dexter, under whom he had first learned logging in the Sumner swamp, and Sneaky brought his logger from over on the Ocmulgee.

During the first week of the new year trees fell in the Johnson swamp and were snaked to the river banks. Before the end of the second, Ratliff and Sneaky had each drifted an ash raft to Darien in the interest of his own partnership. It was like playing a game of fire-ball shinny with two balls, Ratliff thought, and he played it with zest.

Sneaky was feeling full of himself, too. Ratliff noticed a sort of glow—it wasn't as much as a flush—under his skin—as if he'd had a stout drink—every time they checked with each other in the swamp to see that things were moving right, though during the second week Ratliff began to see that Sneaky wasn't plumb satisfied to let things alone: he kept breaking off in his talk and looking away as if he'd forgotten to eat his breakfast and was trying to recollect what had slipped his mind.

As Sneaky made ready to leave with his second raft on Saturday, Ratliff learned what was gnawing on him. 'We ain't half workin' this game,' he said, putting on his leather jacket. 'It's you and Ent, and me and John Y, but we bin about to forget to deal ourselves a hand.'

Ratliff grinned. I might have known that Sneaky didn't aim to let it ride like it is, he thought. Giving me credit for the old-man-Ent angle, he feels like I'm ahead of him. He said: 'You ain't furgittin' nuthin', Sneaky—I see that. But how we goan work it?'

'I got a plan. I'll 'bout have it worked out by the time I git back,' Sneaky said, and boarded his raft.

Ratliff felt it would have to be a good one, as full as their hands were already. He'd figured this game had about as many angles as it could take, but old Sneaky was deep. He wondered how in hell Sneaky would work it. On his way back to the Oconee side of the swamp—Sneaky had turned loose from the Ocmulgee—he grinned at his own excitement and curiosity. They were damn sure goin' to break the record on roguing timber!

But a thing happened three days later that, having it on his mind when he heard Sneaky's plan, made him feel funny, made him turn against the idea altogether. He was taking down his second raft and was in the Beard's Bluff bend—one of the widest on the Altamaha—and out of the boat channel to boot, when the sidewheeler bore down on him. He saw her over his shoulder and yelled to his bow oarsman to pull like hell for the hill, though that one look told him it was useless: the boat was close and making ten or twelve miles an hour. Her bow drove right up to his stern before the pilot wheeled her and skinned past the raft, a sidewheel hammering on his boom log.

Steamboats had walked his float in the past, but never before had one followed his raft to the bank to get him. If his rifle hadn't been in the lean-to, he'd have taken a pot shot at the pilot. Glaring up at the pilothouse, he called the man inside everything he could lay his tongue to.

The fellow was looking ahead as if he didn't know the raft was on the river, but he glanced around once and Ratliff recognized him. It stopped Ratliff in the middle of a long-handled oath: the pilot was Seborn Henry. The last time Ratliff had seen him he was running the stern-wheeler *Pollyann,* but there could be no doubt.

The boat had knocked Ratliff's boom log loose completely, but he and the bowhand succeeded in drifting down onto the next point and tying up. While they were re-rafting the disordered side of his float, he puzzled about the thing. Suddenly he laughed. You reckon Henry's telling me to stay away from China Swann, he thought—like some yearlin' boy would? It's sure the only thing I can think of. And after China done run him off, too—the sorry old dogbottom, the yellowbelly! I reckon he thinks I got him run off. Hell, he got himself run off! He ought to have been run off: a fellow who would let a whore make a monkey out of him with a peashooter! He ought to have been run off long ago, if half of what China says was true.

He dropped his maul at the mouth of the lean-to and ordered his hand to loose the raft. China had told him that Henry had never even suspected about them; that Henry had stayed away from her house of his own accord since she treated him so rough, thinking to make her sorry. And Ratliff's name had not been connected with the story of the 'pearl-handled deed,' as the boys called it, that got around Darien. But Ratliff didn't give a damn about Henry's finding out that he was going with China. It just made Sneaky's proposition, coming right afterward, sound queer to him.

Sneaky had waited in Darien to talk to him about it: he met him at the Boom and they walked on up to the Timber Tavern together. Sneaky said that they themselves wouldn't be able to bring down the timber for this other pot they were going to play to: they'd have to find a nigger pilot they could count on. And they couldn't take a chance on his selling it at the Public Boom. They would have him drift it directly to the private boom of one of the companies and get them a front man in Darien to deal with the company.

They were sitting at a Tavern table and Ratliff was smiling, when Sneaky gave him the jolt. 'I got the very man for it,' he said—'Sebe Henry.'

Ratliff let his chair-legs drop to the floor, picked up the bottle between them and poured himself another drink before he spoke. 'Does Cap'n Henry know 'bout it?'

'Yeah,' said Sneaky. 'I didn't make him no proposition, but I felt him out.'

Ratliff stared at his glass. 'Well, he don't know I'm mixed up in it and he'll change his mind when he does—if'n he does,' he said. 'And I'm not a-wantin' him to hear it.'

Sneaky asked what he meant, but Ratliff didn't answer at once. He had a feeling against giving his reasons. He had never known about Sneaky's women—Sneaky let on like he didn't have any—and he didn't aim to tell Sneaky about any of his. Two times he had said something to Sneaky about going around to the Birdcage with him, and Sneaky had talked like he didn't go to houses, though Bud True had told him once that he had seen Sneaky there. A thing that China had said about Sneaky, when she found out they were running together, came back to him: 'He won't do, Snake.' Her back-biting had made him pretty sore then. He didn't take advice from any woman about his pardner—let alone China. And she couldn't lay her tongue to what she meant by it—just an idea she'd picked up from somebody like Bud. He still thought that: Sneaky's naming Henry did not change his view, but it gave him a funny feeling—made the whole thing look queer somehow. 'Me and Henry don't gee,' he said finally.

Then Sneaky asked him to put up a man. Ratliff didn't know anybody to suggest, but he had lost his tooth for the plug as well as the chew. 'Don't know as I favor the idea 'tall,' he told Sneaky. 'I'd ruther let 'er go till I kin sleep on it.'

The next week Sneaky brought it up again while they were in the swamp, but Ratliff's notion against it still dogged him and he put Sneaky off. After that Sneaky dropped it and he was relieved. As it was, they were running the timber down as fast as they could keep count, and making real money out of it.

On the second Friday in February, John Y visited the Ocmulgee side of the swamp, as Sneaky was getting ready to leave with a raft. He did not come all the way to the river, but stopped in the low swamp and sent on the negro he usually kept with him to tell Sneaky that he wanted to talk to him. It was the first time John Y had approached Sneaky at the scene of their logging. Sneaky told his bowhand to go ahead with the loading of the raft. He followed the negro back into the swamp and found John Y leaning against a big ash stump.

As they drew near, John Y stood up and started walking back and forth with his eyes on the ground. He was a big man and looked stiffback even when bent over. 'What's a-happenin' to my timber, Bob— what's a-happenin' to my timber? As he spoke, he looked up. His plump red face was still, but his eyes kept twinkling after they had fixed on Sneaky's face, as if he were embarrassed. The little goatee on his bottom lip, within and separate from the main growth of chin whiskers, twitched.

Sneaky had spit and glanced over his shoulder as John Y started speaking. Now he waited with a quizzical look on his face.

'Rance, heah'—John Y nodded toward the long, reddish-skinned negro who had moved a little away—'Rance has been cruisin' the swamp and tells me at least ten, maybe twelve rafts is bin cut out'n heah and you ain't turnt in but fo' so far—that's all the scaler at Darien know anythin' 'bout, too.'

Sneaky looked at the negro, who was resting the stock of a rifle on his foot. 'Ten or twelve!' he said, with an audible intake of breath. 'Yo' nigger don't know what he's—'

John Y cut him off. 'I ain't relyin' just on Rance. Looked it over some myself yestiddy and this mornin'.' He took a step forward, his eyes still fixed on Sneaky and twinkling faster. 'I ain't bin a-layin' around Mount Vernon as close as you think. I ddin't expect to git all yet cut, but my Gawda-mighty! I ain't a-gittin' my bait back.'

An embarassed smile touched Sneaky's face briefly. 'Tch-tch-tch! I don't know 'bout no ten, aer twelve, John Y—I got one big un—'

Suddenly John Y's eyes were still and staring: his left fist shot out and hit Sneaky in the mouth. Like clappers, Sneaky's arms flew out from his sides and he dropped to the ground. He lay on his back, his legs sprawled apart. John Y stood over him. 'Don't try to lie to me! I bin over this swamp. Speak up. By Gawd! Where's it gone?'

Sneaky's eyes were as wide as the eggshell rims of their sockets, and they looked black. He never took them off John Y's face. Slowly he put a hand to his mouth and touched the blood trickling over his lips. The loose folds of his left cheek began to twitch. A bluish palor spread over his face.

John Y stepped closer and raised a foot, as if he were going to stomp him. 'Gawddamnit, you better start talkin' fast!'

Sneaky hunched himself away rapidly on his elbows. 'It 'uz sump'n I couldn't holp, John Y! I din't have no part in it.' He sat up and pulled out a handkerchief. 'I 'uz threatened and I couldn't see whur talkin'—He got to his feet, holding the handkerchief to his mouth. 'Just gimme time.' His hand shook as he brought the cloth down. 'Ent McFerrin's got a man in heah—got a man in heah a-stealin' yo' timber. He told me if'n I cheeped to you about it they'd throw me in jail—and you, too.'

John Y's lip whiskers bobbled. 'Ent McFerrin! Ent McFerrin! W'y, that hawgish son-of-a-bitch!' He stared away into the swamp, his goatee suddenly still. 'McFerrin's done bin too graspin' this time,' he said. 'Too damn shifty, too smart, by damn!' He looked back at Sneaky. 'So it's Ent. Where's this fellow that's a-cuttin' for him? I'll just fix McFerrin. He's plain stealin', under the law.' Sneaky did not speak, and John Y raised his voice. 'I said, where is this fellow—what's his name?'

'You better take kyur, John Y—you done enjined, yuh know.' Sneaky put the handkerchief to his mouth again.

'Take kyur! I'll take kyur of all of you! You come along with me to find 'im right now. Who is he?'

Sneaky glanced at the negro, as he swung the rifle across his shoulder. 'Fellow's named Sutton. He's over on the Oconee side, about the rock pile, a-startin' a raft.' He looked quickly at John Y. 'It wouldn't do for me to go over theah—it wouldn't do for any of us to go—not now, John Y. He and his bowhand and his logger all got rifles—and they lookin' to have to use 'em. They're tough fellers, I tell you.' He picked his hat up from the ground and knocked off the leaves on his knee. 'I'll tell yuh when to git 'im: time to git 'im is when he comes out'n theah this afternoon—he'll be by himself then. He'll come right out to the Bell's Ferry road 'round sundown, aer a little befo'.'

'I don't aim to have no shootin'.' John Y looked at his negro, then back at Sneaky. 'Just aim to show him where he's in a bad hole if he don't fall in with me and holp.'

Sneaky's voice was extravagantly sympathetic. 'That's right, John Y. And he'll do it if you put it to 'im right. But it wouldn't do for me to be along—you know, you ain't supposed to know I'm in heah, you ain't supposed to know nuthin' 'bout me 'tall. It 'ud just git us both in trouble.'

'All right,' John Y said, and motioned with his head. 'Come on: you kin stay back in the swamp.'

But Sneaky did not move. 'My raft's all ready to turn loose and the bowhand's a-waitin' on me now.' He looked off toward the river. 'It may be the last un we kin git out if'n this business blows up—we better make sure of 'er.'

'You better stay with me till I git holt of this feller, I reckon.'

'You don't want that bowhand to know anything: he'll find out you're in heah, sure as hell, if we hang 'round. The further away that raft is when this thing busts, the better it'll be.' Sneaky crumpled his wool hat in a shaking hand. 'You kin come see me off—once I'm on the river, I'm gone for sho'. Kain't drift upstream, yuh know!'

John Y hesitated, then nodded to his negro. They followed Sneaky to the swamp edge. When Sneaky and his hand had untied the raft and poled it into the current, he stepped out on the bank and watched it drift around the bend.

An hour and a half later, Sneaky appeared at the rock pile on the Oconee where Ratliff was putting his raft together. Sneaky had tied up at the mouth of the Ocmulgee, a mile and a half below the point of his departure, and had walked up through the swamp. As he stepped out from behind a crabapple bush and sauntered toward the log-strewn river bank, Ratliff looked up.

He had one foot on top of a big ash log, which he had been examining, and his mouth loosened good-humoredly as Sneaky drew near. 'You just the bully I bin a-wantin' to see.' He lowered his eyes again to the log and remained silent for a moment, then went on. 'Gittin' back a day early from Darien and not bein' in no hurry to start

221

again, I walked out to Okey Bluff from Lumber City yestiddy, takin' my time.' (Sneaky's gaze was on the log. He looked away, glancing narrowly at Ratliff as he did so.) 'I got the notion, comin' on down the river bank to the forks, that y'all—you and yo' podner, John Y—didn't aim for me to get no breathin' spell in betwixt trips'—his gaze settled on Sneaky's face—'a-raftin' my own logs—' He halted, batting his eyes. 'Humph! Who busted you in the mouth?'

Sneaky's mouth was distorted with swelling and its expression seemed at odds with the rest of his face. He spoke brusquely. 'Go on! Go on!'

'Yeah, it looked to me like y'all were puttin' rafts together powerful fast. How often you a-turnin' out a raft, nohow?'

'Bout every other jug of liquor.' Sneaky's voice now matched Ratliff's in drawling good-humor. Two negroes with a crosscut saw approached the log that lay between them. He looked at the negroes. As they laid the saw on top of the log, he stopped them. 'Say, what y'all goan do heah? Hell, don't cut off that butt—theah's two hundred foot of lumber in it. That knothole kin be doctored.' He seemed to have forgotten Ratliff. Axe in hand, he went off into the swamp, found a limb, which he cut off and trimmed. He began driving his plug into the knothole. Then he glanced up at Ratliff. 'What 'uz that you 'uz sayin' about raftin' logs—'bout me and John Y, my podner, as you call 'im?'

Ratliff remained silent for a moment, watching Sneaky's log-plugging with a frown on his face, then he went on.

'Well I come on by the mouth of that big slough—you know that un that marks the upper line to John Y's land?'

Sneaky interrupted him, without looking up. 'Yeah. The line's this side of it.'

''Tis? Well, anyhow, the raft I'd figgered must be mine, the one I seen tied on the upper side the slough yestiddy, wuz gone this mornin'—no sign of it 'tall.'

Sneaky stopped his axe-tapping and looked at Ratliff steadily. 'What you tryin' to tell me? You ain't seen no raft up theah, sho' nuff?'

'I waun't drunk.'

'Wy, 'i God, that ain't hardly a mile above where I was a-raftin' and I never heard nobody up theah! 'Course I didn't start till yestiddy morning. Must be somebody cuttin' that Foust timber that jines John Y.'

'I didn't see no signs of loggin' as I come through the Foust swamp.' Ratliff studied Sneaky's swollen face.

'That's a cur'ous thing! Sho'!' Sneaky began tapping on the plug again. 'You didn't see no signs where they'd brought timber down the creek that makes into that slough? I reckon you couldn't hardly tell that, though.'

Ratliff turned away to the timber bunched on the bank. Hell, it must have been those Foust boys, after all, he thought. He motioned to his negroes and they put their hand sticks beneath a log and rolled it into the river. He went on with his rafting.

Later, standing on his boom out in the river, he looked up at the bank. Sneaky had finished plugging the log, but he still sat on it, gazing at the ground. When his eyes met Ratliff's, he reached in his hip-pocket and drew out his tobacco.

'Who was it spiled yuh looks?' Ratliff called.

'My podner, John Y.' Sneaky cut himself a chew. 'Who'd yuh s'pose!'

Ratliff grinned and went on moving logs into place with his pike pole. 'Git that new rope?' he asked after a while.

'Rope? Yeah, I got it.'

Ratliff continued to move logs for a time, then looked up again. 'Yuh bowhand come this mornin'?'

'Unh-hunh.' Sneaky spat between his feet. 'Yuh know I kain't figger out 'bout that raft.'

'Oh, I reckon must-a bin them Foust boys.'

After a time Sneaky responded, 'Must-a bin.' He got up and walked around the timber on the bank and turned as if to go into the swamp, but he came back and sat down again on the plugged log.

Ratliff looked up to find him staring at him. 'What in hell you hangin' 'round heah all mornin' for—ain't yo' raft ready to go?'

Sneaky jerked himself to his feet. 'I 'uz just axin' myself that same thing!' He moved off at a quick step. 'Got the body trouble, I reckon— this mornin'.' At the edge of the clearing he slowed down and looked back over his shoulder. 'Tch-tch-tch!' he said softly. He disappeared into the swamp.

Ratliff encountered John Y that afternoon, just at sundown on the public road, where it turned to go down the bluff to the ferry landing. He looked hurriedly about him and halted uncertainly.

John Y began speaking as he walked toward him, leaning a little on a walking-stick. He knew what Sutton had been doing, he said, knew all about it, from his deal with Ent McFerrin to the inspector they were using at the Boom.

In his first embarrassment, Ratliff had thought: the old man's bluffing! As John Y went on adding details, he asked himself: what the hell? And later: how in the name of God did he get all the insides? (The image of Sneaky's face flashed through his mind.) Couldn't have been his spotter, he thought. A deal with Ent? That don't make sense. (Sneaky had said John Y hit him—said it like a joke!)

'You and McFerrin kain't steal my timber right under my nose,' John Y was shouting, 'and git away with it, by God!'

You reckon Sneaky would turn up a raftsman, his pardner, to an outsider? Ratliff asked himself. You reckon he would? There seeped into him the distress of an old betrayal. The feeling was familiar: he did not yet recall its origin.

John Y paused, bending forward on his stick and thrusting his stiff beard close to Ratliff's face. 'Sutton, looks like you done let that sleight-a-handed son-of-a-bitch, McFerrin, trick you into trouble!'

Ratliff's thinking ceased. He met this inspection with a dull, droop-eyed look. 'Seems like you lookin' for trouble yourself.'

John Y's whiskers bobbled. He wanted no smart talk out of this damned young rogue!

'And you just a damn lie, if'n you call me—' Ratliff didn't get to finish it: he saw John Y's stick coming up and ducked. The cane glanced off his forearm and did not upset him. He lunged forward butting John Y in the stomach and sprawling him on his back.

He had heard a noise in the bushes across the road as he dived; now, as he regained his balance, he saw a tall negro advancing on him with a leveled rifle. 'Nigger, drop that!' he shouted, raising his hands. He began to back away along the road. The negro moved toward John Y, groaning on the ground. His gun barrel lowered. Ratliff jerked a pistol out of his shirt-front and held it on them. 'Don't try nuthin'!' he said, still backing away. He gained the shelter of a big cedar tree. From behind it, he watched the negro help John Y to his feet. 'You Goddamned, sorry, lyin' stealin' river scum!' John Y yelled, half-crying. 'You kain't git away with this! If'n I ever ketch you 'round my place ag'in—' He turned away with the negro holding to his arm.

Ratliff stared after them till they were around the bend of the road. He took a rag from his pocket and mopped his face. 'Jesus!' he said aloud, and turned back toward the ferry landing. An uncertain quivering stirred in the pit of his stomach. His legs began trembling and he halted, standing with them spread apart. He felt empty, hollowed out inside. So it was Sneaky! He stared at the ground. His throat swelled, clamped shut. A vertigo seemed to be sweeping him off his balance, stifling him. 'Coward! Son-of-a-bitch!' he cried out.

The unnatural sound of his voice startled him. He looked around at the gathering darkness, and hurried down the slope toward the ferry. But as he neared the landing, he halted again. No, by God, you're not clearin' out of here yet, he told himself. You're goin' to take that raft with you! He looked to his left at the swamp below the road. The trees and bushes seemed suddenly still, as still as a waiting bobcat. Already they were blurring into darkness. The silence drummed tightly in his ears. Trouble was crowding in around him.

He wondered what kind of deal Sneaky had made with John Y. John Y will figure you to try to make off with the raft, he told himself. He ain't got the stuff in him, but that nigger has: that nigger'll shoot if John Y tells him to. Still he can't see to shoot in the swamp—can't see till you get on the river.

He entered a path and moved swiftly through the woods. When he had reached the camp where his loggers and bowhand were cooking supper, he paused only to get his rifle and the corn meal they had on hand. He told the oarsman to follow him: he had no time for talk.

They moved single file through night-hidden trees to the banks of the Oconee. From the swamp edge, his raft looked like a long shadow. Beyond it, the vague river surface was touched with opalescent light. As the negro put their supplies aboard, Ratliff took off his wool hat and carefully pulled down the leather sweatband. He stood gazing at the spot where Sneaky had sat upon the big ash log. Sneaky didn't figure on John Y's knockin' hell out of him, he thought. Nor me a-catchin' on to that other raft. Ratliff put on his hat. And that son-of-a-bitch just kept sittin' there on that log! Sittin' there making up his mind! Ratliff picked up his rifle and stepped onto the float.

CHAPTER

21

RATLIFF STRODE along the boom log, reached down in the darkness and brought up a pike pole with the precision of an acrobat. He spoke quietly over his shoulder. 'Push from the hip!' He moved three steps farther along and thrust his pole into the water, striking at first try a sunken snag. As the pole bent under his weight, the raft was released and began to move away from the bank. He looked up quickly and stared back at the blackness of the swamp with his head cocked to listen. Then he moved on to the stern oar.

The raft was nosing out into the current, beyond the shadow of the trees, into a ghostly twilight. 'Three to the white!' he called to the bowhand in a low, carrying voice. His head was canted a little to one side, his face was still. He breathed shallowly as he pulled at the stern oar. The float moved slowly through the dusk. No sound broke the stillness as it angled across the river and into the shadow of the opposite swamp. When the raft straightened with the current, Ratliff brought his oar to a halt mid-stern. His breathing grew easy.

After they had rounded the bend to the right and were drifting down the reach, an early moon rose above the tree line ahead of them. He moved to the end of his footwalk and looked up at it, then lowered his face and studied the river. Its surface was a pewter pathway, between black borders.

His negro oarsman watched him from the bow. 'Sump'n up, Mist' Snake?'

'Stick to yuh oar, Dunk,' he said, turning back along the walk.

The negro remained facing him and his voice sharpened. 'You must be lookin' for trouble—no fire and all.'

'No talkin', neither!' Ratliff's voice gained resonance as he spoke. 'Not a-lookin' for trouble, but I aim to take kyur of what comes.' They were swinging around the long, shallow curve at the end of the reach when he added, as if to himself, 'not till I git shet of this raft.'

Ahead of them the river turned sharply to the right, then farther on the curved back in a spoon-handle bend. On their side the swamp receded at the bend and a sandbar extended out into the stream. The current swung to the far bank.

Ratliff moved to the outer edge of the raft and held his oar blade poised above the water. 'Hug that p'int!' he said slowly, in a low voice. The raft moved out of the swamp shadow into the moonlight. It gathered speed. For an instant he stared across the river at the nearing wall of blackness, then he thrust his oar deep and threw his weight behind it.

They came into the bend and the current carried them past the middle of the river. The Altamaha loomed in the distance below them, but neither Ratliff nor his bowhand looked up from his straining, swinging stride. They drifted nearer the opposite bank. Below, where a slough made into the river, it began to recede. Now Ratliff was running. He swung his free oar to the raft-edge. The swamp wall was no more than twenty yards away. He paused as he dipped the blade and wheeled about the end of the handle to shift his direction. A jet of flame stabbed the blackness before his eyes. A bullet clipped through the crown of his hat. Ringing detonation ripped open the river's quiet.

He sucked air in with a shrill gasp, shuddered, and for an instant held rigidly to the oar. Then he swayed toward the raft-edge and, by looking over his shoulder, loosed his hold. But before his body could drop, there was a second flash from the swamp. He spun around with a bullet in his shoulder and fell into the river on his face.

He dived deep, pulling with one arm. The water was cold and thick with mud. He kicked off his unlaced shoes and began swimming under the surface toward the bank whence the shots had come. He did not swim back upstream, but angled down with the current toward the mouth of the slough. His eyes shut, he kept pulling forward and down with his right arm, forward and down. His belly pumped for air like a bellows, but he pushed under the water until his hand touched mud. In spite of the jerking in his throat, he turned upon his back and rose gradually to the surface before he inhaled. He was a long time taking his first lungful. He did not stir until he had eased his breathing. Then he turned over and climbed to his feet.

He was in the mouth of the slough, within the darkness of the swamp. For a moment he stood in the shallow water and stared about him. The course of the stream was dimly outlined by darker banks and tree growth. Then he drew a long-barreled pistol from his trousers-pocket. He shook it and unbreeched it with his right hand. He blew on the cartridges in the chamber, then snapped it together and stuck it in his belt. He took hold of his left hand with his right and with effort slipped it into the other trousers-pocket.

Lifting his face toward the vague moss-tailed boughs above, he shook himself vehemently, then squatted in the water and climbed quickly up the mudbank on his knees. On top he stood a moment listening. There was the sound of a dead limb cracking in the swamp above. It was at a distance from the river. He turned and slid back down the bank into the water. He took the gun from his belt and waded again into the stream. Holding the weapon above his head, he treaded water until he crossed the slough to the other side.

When he had climbed the bank, he moved carefully into the swamp, feeling his way. He found a cypress stump and, turning to his right, walked swiftly along a pathway between the invisible trees. Soon he struck the slough again and moved more slowly, halting frequently to listen. He came to a footlog and got down on his knees. For a moment he stared along it toward the far side. Then he began putting his hand to the mud about the near end, touching it lightly with his palm. He found no returning footprints. His breath spent itself slowly through spread nostrils. Holding to a tree-root, he lowered himself down the bank to the water's edge. He stood up with his face suddenly twisted and a lip between his teeth and took the hand of his wounded arm from its pocket. Then he squatted in the blackness beneath the log and cocked his pistol.

High above the log, patches of sky were visible through the trees and a vague gray-blue light sifted down upon it. A shrill cry came from the distance to his left, but he did not turn his head. In a moment there followed the 'who-who-who-a-a' of an owl. There was a noise above the bank behind him and he gripped the pistol handle, but it receded and he relaxed his hold. He remained still a long time. Resting on his knee, the fingers of his useless hand began to jerk, but he did not look at them. Mucus began to dribble from his nose, but he did not sniffle, or blow it. His only movement was the steady shifting of his eyes.

There was a rustle of dry leaves and a faint footfall within the tall bank of blackness across the slough. He raised the gun from his knees. The bushes near the log moved. Then the whole swamp was still. Sweat broke out on his forehead and trickled down into his eyes. He blinked them without stirring.

Into the dim light above the slough moved the silhouette of a man, tapping the log with a rifle butt. He put out his other arm to balance himself. He began to move along the footwalk.

Ratliff came up noiselessly, deliberately. At the instant he was upright, his pistol flashed—twice, quickly.

The man on the log gasped with a harsh, catching suction of breath. He waved his arms as he fell backward. 'Ah-ah-ah!' he cried almost soundlessly. There was the splash of the rifle, then the man. The black surface of the slough slopped outward and closed over his body.

Ratliff faced the spot with his gun barrel raised. The man's chest broke through the rumpled water. A gagging, gurgling noise came from him. Ratliff leveled the pistol, but did not fire. The body went under again. He looked quickly around him, then back at the smoothing surface of the slough. He stood watching it. The body did not reappear. The water grew still.

CHAPTER

22

RATLIFF FELT swollen soreness and dull aching. He could not at first locate it: it seemed to be about his head, his left side, his shoulder. He opened his eyes and turned on his pillow: he was in bed and badly hurt. The dark carved wood of the bedstead top looked unfamiliar. Where in hell am I? he asked himself. The ceiling, the counterpane, the green-tiled hearth: he had never seen any of them before.

He had a sudden sense of falling, of remembered falling, and weakness from pain: his feet stumbling on the footwalk of his raft, as he held on to the oar; a pallid, dimlit stretch of river before his eyes, and the slate-gray swamp of Marrowbone Round. Yes, getting that damn raft to the Boom! Holding on to the oar against the pain: that had made up the whole trip. It seemed to have gone on and on, to have had no beginning.

Now he saw again the wavering mouth, the whites of the eyes of Dunk, his bowhand. God, what a face! Ratliff smiled feebly on his pillow. He had pulled Dunk out of the lean-to on the raft: Dunk, shaking all over, wet and wrapped up in a blanket. 'Gre't Gawd! is it you, Mist' Snake? Is it you, sho' 'nuff?' And he had told the nigger to get the hell up from there and help untangle the raft. It had been caught under the bow oar of another raft, right at the point where the rivers meet—in fact, a little on the Ocmulgee side—tangled up, by God, in Sneaky's raft!

Jesus Christ! How long were we coming down the river? he asked himself. The hurting in his shoulder had kept getting worse: sorer, then more throbbing, then hot, tearing pain—like a dog chewing at his back, a dog that was hung in a fence and gone crazy. And all he could do was to hold on to the oar—he had to hold on to that oar! There had been day, night, another day and night. It hadn't seemed that he was at the Boom when he got there: not his eyes looking at the hazy stretch of timber; not him turning loose the oar, throwing the rope and walking off the raft, telling the nigger to stay there with it and see the scaler in the morning.

He had almost fallen from the dyke, crossing to the bluff. Then he smothered sound of that doorbell—whirring, ringing; whirring, ringing—at the front door of the Birdcage. He must have gone out holding to that knob, ringing.

Ratliff raised his head from the pillow and looked around him again: it might be China's, but he had never seen it before. As he lay back, the dim, black, sluggish ripples on the slough rose before his mind. Yes, he remembered that slough and a gun in his hand—

At this moment the door across the room, beyond the foot of the bed, opened. China stood in the doorway with a napkin-covered tray in her hands. She smiled and came toward the bed. 'Perkin' up, hey?'

Ratliff saw that she kept smiling and had on a white apron and a gray plaid dress. She laid the tray on the bed-table and fixed his covers. 'How long I bin heah?' he asked.

She lifted a cup of beef tea toward his mouth. 'Since before day, yestiddy. You been plumb out most of the time, but the doctor thinks you doin' fine now—says you too mean and tough to die!'

Ratliff smiled feebly and drank. Then he stopped and lay back on the pillow. 'I feel kind of common: draggin' my bloody tracks into yo' place—but I 'uz so nigh out.'

She gazed at the cup in her hand. 'It makes me feel just the opposite. Don't let it worry you none.' She shook the cup. 'Heah, drink up!'

Ratliff finished the tea before he spoke again. 'Well, I won't forgit it: I aim to pay you good board.'

She turned quickly and put the cup on the tray with a clatter and left the room without speaking or looking at him.

He stared after her and at the door, when she had closed it. Now, what did I say? he thought. You didn't put it in the right way, I reckon. She's sort of a fool about her nursing. The warmth in his belly was pleasant. Guess you couldn't pay her for that, nohow, he thought drowsily. He closed his eyes.

It seemed that he was scarcely asleep when a jet of flame flashed before him—the flash from the swamp, from the gun he could not see. He wakened with fear gripping at his throat. A throbbing had set in at the base of his skull. He raised up on his elbow.

Hell, you knew it was Sneaky soon as the ball went through your hat, he told himself. Rising anger laid his feeling of fear. No son-of-a-bitch can turn me up! Can double-cross me, then waylay me and try to kill me! By God, I outfigured him and outdared him, too!

His anger was suddenly spent and he felt weak. He lay back on his pillow. But you didn't know it was going to be Sneaky, he told himself—didn't know till he shot at your head. It might just as well have been that nigger. You were lucky! Ratliff looked back over events leading up to the shooting: he felt as if a mist were rising about him, as if the grip of his senses were slipping. He hadn't been sure till the shot—the uncertainty did not begin with the shooting. Where did it begin? he asked himself. Christ! You didn't figure Sneaky to turn you up. That was the thing you didn't look for, but you'd never heard of its ever being done and it didn't make sense.

Anyhow, I figured him to know he had to get shed of me, to try to bushwhack me. I said I'd take care of what came and I took care of that yellow-bellied snitch! His chest tightened with a sense of returning strength.

Then the aching in Ratliff's shoulder sharpened and he felt tired. He stretched his legs and shifted to relax his muscles. The smell of China's hair came back to him. His thoughts began to blur and tangle. He slept again.

The next day, he awoke from his after-breakfast nap feeling clear-headed and stronger. In his sleep he had dreamed that Sneaky had made the mysterious raft he had seen in the Foust slough sink by urinating on it. Now he recalled the dream. That's sort of what he did to you, he told himself. You're lucky he didn't sink you! Yes, just plain damn lucky. You were sharp enough to stumble onto that raft, but you would never have figured Sneaky to spread out so big, to get so reckless that John Y would catch on to him. You took up with him thinking he was the smartest man on the river—and he was just a *fool to prove he was smart*—smarter than anybody else. Then he didn't have no guts. Hell, he didn't give a damn for anybody but Sneaky! He wasn't a raftsman, he was a polecat: there wasn't any way a fellow could run with him. By God, you had to kill him! Ratliff was surprised that such a concern should have come into his head.

He felt restless and uneasy. He sat up and shifted the bandage in which his shoulder was bound. Suddenly the image of China, walking out of the room after breakfast, saying over her shoulder, 'You talked silly as a preacher that first day'—the scene—came back to him. Her offhand words seemed ominous now. You ain't been yourself, he thought, and his face hardened. Putting your hide in a whore's hands! He threw the cover back from him and lowered his feet to the floor. When he stood up, he wobbled so that he had to catch hold of the bed. But he got down on his knees and made it to the chair where his trousers were hung and pulled them on. He was crawling about the floor in search of his shoes, when China opened the door.

'Snake, my God!' she said.

He looked up at her without moving, or speaking.

She held on to the knob to steady herself. A shiver ran down her spine as she stared at him. This wasn't the same Snake she had brought breakfast to. His eyes had the look of a strange cat's, like Smut's, after pa had run him off from the house and he went wild.

'What'dju do with my shoes?' Ratliff said.

'I'll get 'em for you, Snake.' She hurried toward him. 'The doctor'll gimme hell, Snake, 'bout your bein' out of the bed—please get back in bed!' She tried to help him to his feet, but he shook her off. Then he wabbled weakly as he stood up, and she supported him. 'Please—the doctor'll gimme hell!'

He permitted her to help him into bed, pull off his trousers and cover him up. 'I'm tired of this damn bed,' he said. But he knew that he was thankful to have it under him: his head was whirling and his middle was empty and watery.

He lay still after China went out of the room. The feel of her arms and the smell of her body had been pleasant, but it wasn't these that held him, staring at the ceiling. It was the scared look on her face when she had seen him on the floor. He had never before seen the breath so taken out of her. He felt relieved that she hadn't known what was going on in his head; he somehow felt like a fool, too.

Maybe you are trying to play this thing too smart, he told himself. You are lucky to be in this bed with a slug in your shoulder—maybe you better stay in it. That's what ailed Sneaky: too smart—for anything, or any rules. *Run under you!* He recollected Bud's phrase with a sense of discovery and a new respect for Bud. Yeah, you were so smart you had to let Sneaky run under you.

He raised up on an elbow. But Sneaky didn't get away with it: you stopped him! You played the fool, but you still knew your own bunch,

236

the thought, staring at the wall, suddenly feeling Bud's presence, as if he were in the room—the presence of many raftsmen. A warming emotion of kind and kinship spread through him. It seemed vast in extent, enveloping, yet contained in, coming out of his own body. You've been *made* to know them!

His head had become quiet and clear inside. He had the feeling of looking out from a tree-top. Sneaky made out to be a raftsman and got by: sooner or later he was bound to get some of us in trouble, he thought. The river is better off to be shed of him. If it hadn't been you, it would have been some other fool—who might have got killed! He sank back on his pillow, feeling that his having killed Sneaky was not accident, nor lucky, not his own calculation. He saw himself, as he had squatted beneath the log over the slough, waiting to get Sneaky, saw himself as if he had been another man. He had not felt lucky, or confident: he hadn't felt anything—he had just known, within that burning pressure inside him, that he was going to get Sneaky. It was put upon you, he told himself.

Three days later, China sat with him at a table in the taproom, talking. He had put on his clothes and come downstairs for the first time that day. It was in the afternoon and China felt lively. She had an impulse to ask Snake questions. It was none of her business who shot him, or why, she knew, but she couldn't quite leave it alone. 'Any chance the bee you say stung you in the shoulder to come lookin' you up?' She glanced at him sidewise.

Ratliff grew still, then he smiled briefly. 'No bee don't sting me but once. If'n he don't' git me that time—' He stopped and looked at her. 'You a-wantin' me to shove off?'

Her face straightened quickly. 'No, no Snake! Hell, you know better'n that! I can count on you not to git me in trouble, if I can count on anything. I 'uz just uneasy—' Delia stood in the doorway beckoning to her and she got up. 'Be right back,' she said.

He watched the door swing to behind her. Count on me! he thought. The question of China's safety had not occurred to him before. A sense of guilt pervaded him. Well, there wasn't any danger, he told himself. And she sure don't want you to go. Suddenly his head tilted. Wasn't she a little too anxious about it? 'I can count on you,' he repeated China's phrase to himself. Just the way a woman would figure to throw you off. He gazed out of the window.

When China had followed Delia into the hallway, the maid told her that Captain Henry was in the reception room. He was sober and he wanted to see her. China's face hardened at the mention of Henry's name. He had not visited the Birdcage since she had forced him to deed it over to her, six months before. But when she approached him, walking back and forth near the doorway with his cap on, she smiled.

'What brought you back?'

Henry looked at her solemnly and took off his headgear. 'I come to bring you some bad news, China. I hate to have to tell you, but Little Bob's dead—bin killed. Somebody shot him.'

China's smile vanished and she came to a stop. 'My God!' she said.

'I thought I ought to tell you. Some niggers fishin' found his body up in the Oconee swamp this morning. In a slough, I hear. Two bullet holes in him.'

China's face was pale and the paint on it made red patches over her cheekbones. 'I might-a known—' She broke off and looked away.

Henry went on. 'I reckon they're goin' to take him back over on the Ocmulgee where he was stayin'—unless you want his body brought heah—'

She had turned and walked toward the parlor with her gaze on the floor as she spoke. Now she raised her head and interrupted him. 'Here?'

'I thought maybe you'd want to do something,' he said.

She glanced at him keenly, her face stiffening. 'How'd you come to find it out so quick?'

His mouth opened and he blinked. 'Me?' I got it up at English Eddy. I just got in off the river—heard it from some rafthands.'

She moved toward him. 'You thought I'd want to do something?' She fixed him with her yellow eyes. "I already got the man who killed him in heah to nurse!' She paused. 'You kin take care of Bob.'

Henry stared at her and his florid face grew yellow.

I thought this had a smell to it, China told herself. (She had seen Seborn and Bob together on the street, twice since Christmas.) She spoke, her eyes darkening. 'You put Bob up to bushwhackin' Snake Sutton and got 'im killed. Don't come to me with it—you bury 'im!'

'You taken leave of your senses? You must be crazy!' The color came back into Henry's face with a rush.

'Don't yell! You want Snake to hear you? She looked over her shoulder toward the taproom. A hard smile broke the lines of her face. 'Come to think about it, I might just tell 'im you hired Little Bob to do the job that was too big for 'im. Tell 'im now.' She moved toward the door at the back of the room.

'Wait a minute! Theah's bin trouble enough—' Henry got into quick motion with a long stride. He grabbed her arm. 'I didn't have a damned thing to do with this and I don't want you gettin' me mixed up in it!'

China shook off his hand and spoke vehemently. ' You don't think I believe that!' She stopped short, and after a moment turned to him. 'All right. But I can't stand the sight of you. If you want me to keep my mouth shut, git out of my house—git out and stay out!'

When she had closed the door behind Henry and returned to the back hallway, she met Ratliff coming out of the taproom.

'What's bin keepin' you so long?' He paused and gazed at her face. It was stiff and pale.

She came close to him and slipped her fingers into his shirt-front. 'Le's go sit down.' She pressed him gently backward without looking at him. They moved through the doorway into the taproom.

'What's up, China? What's a-matter?' he said as they got into their seats.

'I just heard Bob Colquitt's been killed.'

Ratliff had hold of the table, adjusting his chair. His hand gripped the table-edge and he halted. He looked up at her slowly. 'Killed?'

'Body found up theah where y'all cuttin' timber.' She kept her gaze on the table-top.

'Yeah.' His lower lip loosened and his head tilted. 'Well—what's that to you?'

'Not much. Just he was my brother—half-brother.'

Ratliff batted his eyes. He felt his neck swelling. "Jesus, China! Godamighty! I didn't know—' He got up awkwardly from his chair, and stood staring at her. She can't prove anything, he thought, but she knows! China's hostility and condemnation would be a hard thing to bear. He must get away. He turned, as if to leave.

'Don't go, Snake!' she said, rising. 'He waun't no part a brother to me—not since we 'uz little. The only times he got kin to me was when he needed money—he'd slip 'round heah and dig me for what he could.' Ratliff's gaze was questioning, lowering. She met it and stood still, looking up at him. 'I don't know what happened, Snake.' The pupils of her eyes grew big. 'I don't need to know. All I know is *I'm on your side.*'

Ratliff was silent. He saw that she meant it: she was on his side—against her brother, against everybody! He had never looked to see a woman there, he hadn't believed a woman could be counted on—till now. He swallowed and put his hand on her shoulder. His neck grew red, then his face. 'All right, China,' he said. 'if you feel that way!' He turned hurriedly and left the room.

CHAPTER

23

'DIDN'T LOOK TO SEE YOU back here!' the inspector said in a soft drawl, as he sauntered onto Ratliff's raft at the Public Boom in Darien. The crown of his felt hat reached scarcely as high as the mouth of the negro turner behind him. He fixed Ratliff with sharp black eyes, then put his dip rod into the living water at the top end of a cypress log, without awaiting a response.

Ratliff's face still appeared lank and bleached out from his wound of a month past and its confinement. There were new lines about his mouth and it seemed wider and less withheld. His eyes—an effortless steadiness in their intent look—remained on the man's face for an instant, then he glanced over his shoulder at his negro oarsman near the middle of the raft. 'Give the turner a hand, Dunk!' he said.

The inspector measured several sticks before he spoke again. He did not look up, but glanced at Ratliff out of the corner of his eye. 'I hear somebody killed your pardner, Sneaky Colquitt—up on the Oconee.'

Ratliff was standing three logs away, watching the rapidly moving dip rod, and his gaze did not waver. After a moment he turned his head and skeeted a stream of tobacco juice into the water. ' 'At's what I hear.'

The inspector began setting down figures in the notebook in his hand. 'Who do they say killed him?'

When he lifted his face, Ratliff met his eyes casually. 'I hear they say I killed him.'

Their gaze was joined for an instant, then the face of the inspector crinkled up. He took the dip rod from under his arm and turned to the log. After a while, he spoke again in a warmer tone. 'It ain't none of my business, Snake, and I hadn't thought to make it mine, but I'll tell you the sheriff's got a warrant out for you.'

'Warrant?'

'Under that new ordinance the town put through in January, making it a misdemeanor to plug a log. Dawson and Clare's man caught one in that ash raft you left with your nigger for me to inspect last month.'

Ratliff's face remained impassive but his voice was scoffing. 'You mean that kinky-headed feller? That son-of-a-bitch claim he found a plug?'

'Oh, they found one all right: it come back on me to the tune of ten dollars—you know I wouldn't have paid it if they hadn't! Think they mean to make an example out of you—if they catch yuh. Doubt if you can sell this raft, either—not in your own name. The law closes the market to you.'

Ratliff stared at the brown corrugated back of his raft and at the muddy gray water beyond. He felt incredulous. Embarrassment grew in him. He had not known about the new law, but that was not the point. Never before had a plugged log of his been caught, not merely by the public inspectors, but never even on second inspection by the company men.

The scaler finished his inspection and held out the bill of measurement. Ratliff took it without looking at him and turned away, but he glanced over his shoulder. 'Sorry that last un came back on yuh.' He grinned and his still sallow neck reddened. 'Sump'n funny 'bout it!' he said, moving off, his face hardened.

When he had come out of the fifth timber-buyer who declined to bid on his raft, he stood a moment in the shade of the covered sidewalk and looked off at the sun-glazed sand in the street. The smile on his face—it had grown more set and dry with each rebuff—broke up. His swelling neck muscles corded, constricting his throat. He turned back and gazed at the glass-fronted office door. Suddenly his mouth twisted and he spat. Tobacco juice splattered on the glass. Damn crooks are all one crowd! he said to himself. Think they can run creation! Think they are God Almighty!

He moved on to the offices of Dawson and Clare, Ltd., whose private inspector had found the plugged log in his raft. Inside, he handed his bill of measurement across a high counter, the outer edge of which had been deeply notched by whittling. A lean, grizzled man took the bill. As he glanced over it, the tiny folds of skin under his eyes gathered like a closing fan. He went back into an inner office and returned with a tagged wooden plug. 'We have a little memento of your last raft you might be interested to look at,' he said, with a taciturn smile.

Ratliff looked sharply about the office, then at the man, taking the plug from his outstretched hand. His eyes settled finally on the irregular-shaped piece of wood. I figured it would be this one, he thought. He stared at it and a chill ran down his back. It was as if Sneaky had reached out of his grave and grabbed hold of him.

'Look familiar to you?' the man broke in.

Ratliff cleared his throat. 'It ain't my work.' He paused as if he might say more, but he did not.

'Found in your raft.'

A vague smile touched Ratliff's face. 'That's right, too,' he said softly. After a while he laid the plug on the counter. 'I see what's wrong with it.' He looked up. 'Well, you goan bid on my raft?'

The grizzled man met his gaze without response, then picked up the plug. 'What do you think is wrong with it?'

Ratliff's lip loosened. 'That clerk you sent out to fotch the sheriff ought to be about gittin' ole Shade out of his rockin'-chair b'now.' He reached over on the counter and picked up the bill of measurement. 'Gimme my bill!' At the doorway he grinned. 'He'll have on his shoes in a minute and be a-comin' down heah!'

When Ratliff told China of the warrant for his arrest, she grew silent. They were sitting in her room, drinking beer. She drained her mug and set it down before she spoke. 'That big deputy, Lemons, come heah regular: he's Lou's man—has been for two years.' She put her handkerchief to her lips and wiped them absently. 'He's done some things for me. I believe he can git it fixed for us—so as you can git out with just a fine, anyhow.'

Ratliff set down his beer with a clomp. 'Pay those bastards a fine? To hell with that!'

China winced. 'They run this place, Snake!'

Putting his elbows on the table, he looked off at the wall reflectively. 'They think they're might slick at ketchin' plugs—that kinky-headed smart-aleck who makes 'em pop out, hitting the log with his hammer, I can beat that trick, I reckon. Ain't nobody ever had to try much before. They didn't ketch me on my own pluggin', nohow.' He faced China. 'They kain't! When they do, I'll take my medicine.'

She stopped him as he got up to leave the room. 'Looks like you done made up your mind, Snake. I'm with yuh, any which-a-way.'

He looked at her fixedly, then smiled. 'I'll leave my bill of measurement with you to give to Bud, or either to Ike Pippin. Tell whichever one comes heah first to sell my raft and I'll see 'im.' He moved toward the door. 'I've got to git out'n heah, and I gotta do around 'fore I go.'

Another month had passed and April-blooming bushes were in full color when Ratliff tied up at Hall's Landing in the Altamaha, just below the forks of the rivers. He found Bud True in the swamp near the landing. He wanted Bud to sell another cypress raft for him: a raft pinned and plugged so tight it would take dynamite to blow her apart, he said.

There were two men with Bud at a log pile, and one of them—the one with patches on the seat of his breeches—showed Ratliff a sweet-gum timber he had wanted his companions to try to plug. 'Looks like they all gittin' feather-legged since the companies put in that law,' he said, rubbing his gums with a stick toothbrush. 'I wanted a man that don't scare to look at it.'

Ratliff's face remained impassive, but he ran a switch into the hole. 'She kin be plugged, if she's plugged right,' he said.

Bud got up off the log he was sitting on and stretched. 'I ain't got no plugs in Darien showcases, naer no nigger deputy out lookin' for me—and I don't aim to!'

Ratliff's face stiffened as he came to his feet, but finally he smiled. 'You better come look over this raft you 'greed to sell for me, then—she's full of plugs.'

Bud and the two men followed him to the raft and went over it from end to end closely. All they were able to point out were two heartshakes that had not been doctored.

Ratliff grunted when they gave up. 'There's nine plugged tops, one butt, three plugged knotholes, and two splinter draws fixed up,' he told them. Then he brought out a canvas bag from the lean-to. 'This my groover,' he said, holding up a long-handled tool. 'A plug ought to be bigger at the bottom, just like a pin. But to put 'er in theah so she'll stay you ought to groove the hole inside.'

When he had finished showing his tools, he turned to Bud. "Course I"ll be theah to take the blame if anythin' goes wrong, but you don't have to tetch 'er if'n you don't want to.'

Bud snorted and sent up a cloud of smoke from his short-stemmed pipe. 'They ain't a plug in that raft that I couldn't git it by Saint Peter,' he said.

Ratliff grinned. After his face had straightened, he kept on looking at Bud. He spoke gently. 'The plug they caught, Bud, wuz a little piece of property Sneaky left to me—the day he died.'

'Gawdamighty—' Bud said, his face slackening. He stared at Ratliff thoughtfully.

Bud had a right to know and it came natural to tell him, but Ratliff kept a tight mouth two days later, when the detected plug was thrown up to him again. He had tied at the mouth of Phinholloway Creek, loafing along so that Bud's raft could catch up with his. Son Jacobs and some men he didn't know were rafting cypress there and he offered to plug the wind-shake in a top. Son kept quiet, but a tallow-faced stranger bugged out his eyes at him and said, 'I'm afeared of yore doctorin'—I'd ruther take a little less than to git a warrant along with it.'

Squatting beside the log, Ratliff looked into the fellow's pop eyes. He could have said: Not my doctorin'; the plug that fixed me was Sneaky Colquitt's—he could have said he had never had one of his plugs caught. These things were in his mind to say, but he didn't. He felt a smile coming, felt it down in his gullet. 'Sho'.' He stood up. 'If you're a-feared.' As he walked back to his raft, his smiling put him in mind of Jake Pettigrew: he knew deeper now how Jake looked at things.

Ratliff sold his raft through Bud without trouble, and the doctored logs, it appeared, were not detected until they had lost their identity and were sawn at the mills. By early May, he had sold—through Ike Pippin—a second, even more heavily doctored. And he had been able to move quietly in and out of Darien without being arrested. Still he felt low in his mind, dissatisfied. This sort of slipping by was not enough, it didn't get him anywhere. He wanted to stick in the craw of the companies, he wanted somehow to make them think they had stirred up a hornets' nest. Moreover, the new law and the warrant out against him seemed to be making ninnies out of most of the raftsmen and had almost put a stop to log-doctoring.

During May he tried to quiet some of the buck ague over the law and to bring more barrels to bear against the companies in his own behalf. He talked to raftsmen on the train going back upriver and he stopped by a half-dozen timber camps in the Oconee country. In the railroad carriages the timbermen listened respectfully, but shook their heads at his claim that the law was a bluff. In the camps they laconically declined his offer to doctor their logs. And he knew that out of his sight they laughed. Once he overheard a pilot drawl, 'Better not let Grenade heah him braggin' like that!' (Grenade was Darien's negro police officer and always a subject for jest among raftsmen.) After that he quit talking: it was going to take more.

Early in June, Ratliff brought a raft to Darien with Ike Pippin as his front man. He did not quit it on the outskirts of the town, as he had on previous occasions, but piloted it to the Boom and remained aboard while it was being inspected. The traffic was lively that morning and the scalers and rivermen were moving about the long train of logs above his raft.

Their inspector had just handed Pippin the bill of measurement, when Ratliff noticed men on the timber above looking at a big-shouldered negro approaching along the Boom. Ratliff recognized Grenade readily, but he was incredulous when the snuff-colored deputy sheriff halted beside his raft.

Grenade was coatless and wore his official shield pinned on his galluses. A pistol barrel stuck through the bottom of the holster he wore on a sagging cartridge belt. His long face was immobile, his straight mouth broke open. 'Mister Sutton!' He crossed his arms on his chest. 'Uh—High Sheriff McDooly sont me down heah.'

Sitting on the middle binder, Ratliff stared at him. Whatever he had expected, he hadn't looked for this. He wondered if some raftsmen had staged it, but he couldn't believe that Grenade would lend himself to such a fool trick. Grenade was quiet and respectful to whites and minded his own business, policing Darien's large black population.

The negro lowered his big hands uncertainly to his sides. 'The sheriff told me to read a warrant to you and tell you to come up theah.' He reached toward his hip-pocket. 'I got it right heah in –'

Ratliff cut him off. 'Not so fast! Do you mean Shade McDooly sent you down heah after me?'

Grenade brought his hand down. 'Now, don't git het up, Mist' Snake. It ain't me comin' after you: it's this badge heah whut's come, it's the law.'

Ratliff glanced at the men drawing near the edge of the raft above. He spat. ''Tis?' His voice grew soft. 'Yuh reckon your totin' the law might not git you hurt, if'n I happened to put a bullet hole through it?'

Grenade's wide mouth stiffened. 'I got to take a chance on that.' Ratliff was coming to his feet, gazing toward the lean-to. 'Now you better leave yo' rifle–' Grenade began, but he broke off suddenly, staring at the pistol in Ratliff's belt.

'And you better keep them black hams hangin' natural by yo' side!' Ratliff said, putting his hands on his hips. There was a pause and he spoke with a restrained gentleness when he resumed. 'I've always liked colored people—I'm known to like 'em. Two of 'em took me in and brought me up. I thought as much of 'em as anybody in this world. Up and down this river most of my best friends have bin black.' His voice was suddenly harsh. 'But they ain't a nigger alive kin arrest me—and you know that, Goddamnit! Grenade, what the hell you mean comin' down heah with that warrant?'

The negro shifted his feet uneasily, but folded his arms again and stood where he was. 'Mist Snake, it waun't my choosin'—I had to—I got to!'

'Why didn't Shade come?'

'Mist Snake, he don't hardly ever go to 'rest nobody—he's the high sheriff.'

'Where's that damn big Lemons?'

'He's in Tatnall County.'

'Well, that cock-eyed un?'

'He say he had *indiegestion.*'

Ratliff snorted and there was a guffaw from the adjoining raft. He resumed. 'So they picked you for the goat?'

'Sheriff told me I had to come—he told me I had to bring you back, too.'

'He didn't say nuthin' 'bout me a-bringin' you back, did 'e? And a-throwin' yo' black carcass down in front of the jailhouse?' The negro was silent. Ratliff spat between the logs and went on. 'Listen, Grenade, them fellows framed you. You don't think them other two deputies like you, do yuh? You gittin' all the nigger fees, which is most of the fees in this county. Yessuh, they aimed to get shet of you right heah—and you fell fur it! You the one ought-a had that *indiegestion!*'

The negro wet his lips and glanced at his feet. 'I kain't say 'bout that—but the sheriff told me not to come back 'thout yuh.'

Ratliff caught his gaze as he raised his eyes, and held it. 'Look heah, Grenade, you bin totin' that big artillery on yo' hip and draggin' drunk niggers to jail so long you done got a leetle off balance. Look at it a minute. What you thinkin' 'bout a-tryin' to come down heah and arrest a white man? I ain't never felt nuthin' but kindness for you, but—'

'Gawd knows it waun't my notation to come down heah, Mist' Snake.' The negro lowered his head again. 'I don't want to 'rest no white man—and most 'specially you.'

'Well, you go tell Shade McDooly—'

'But, Mist' Snake, you goan git me fired—you goan git me fired sho', if'n you don't come along.'

Ratliff laughed and the crowd laughed with him.

Grenade's face remained sober. 'The sheriff done swo' to it!'

Ratliff glanced up at the sun overhead. He spat out into the water between his raft and the Boom. His lip loosened. 'Well, Grenade, I meant it when I said I had kindness fur you—I ain't none of that nigger-baitin' white cattle like you work fur. And just to prove to yuh friend, I'll help yuh out—Dadburnit, I'll go along with you!' He moved to the lean-to and picked up his jacket, amid a sound of shifting feet and murmuring from the next raft. At the edge of the Boom he halted. 'They's just one thing, now: I want you to take me to the sheriff himself—the high sheriff.'

As Ratliff had guessed, when they reached the jail the sheriff was at dinner, in his home in the front part of the building. He and Grenade walked around to the front door. The trusty who opened it to their summons attempted to close it behind him, but Ratliff put his foot in the way. He entered the hallway quickly, following the trusty. Glancing through the doorway to his right and another adjacent, he saw the dinner table and the sheriff's broad body at he far end of it.

He spun the trusty around between him and Grenade, ran quickly down the carpeted hall, and opened the dining-room door. His eye fell on the sheriff's gun belt on the table beyond the dishes of food. He swung the door behind him, leaping for the gun. He yanked it out of the holster and leveled it at the sheriff's widening eyes. 'You Goddamned, pussley-gutted son-of-a-bitch!'—As he spoke he seized a baked sweet potato from the table—'What you mean sendin' this nigger down to arrest me?' he mashed the potato in his hand and

250

slapped it into the sheriff's face. He moved on, running out by the upper way, as Grenade opened the door through which he had entered. He dashed across the hallway and slammed the front door behind him, brandishing the sheriff's gun in his hand.

Fifty rafthands had watched Ratliff cut the fool and carry it off with the nigger policeman. A greater number had been on the streets when he came out of the jailhouse, parading Shade McDooly's, the high sheriff's, artillery. It was the beatin'est thing, the daresomest damn piece of impudence that ever came off the river, most of them agreed. Ratliff was not present, but they drank more-power-to-him at every bar in Darien that night.

And the story spread quickly, the story with the potato-smearing, and other details that grew with the telling. It circulated up the Oconee, the Ocmulgee, the Ohoopee, wherever timber was cut and drifted. For the regular raftsmen the job had been done to a turn, and even stiff-faced farmers, who only brought down rafts after laying-by time and before Christmas, got a laugh out of it.

Ratliff himself felt well satisfied, as he paused briefly at China's before taking to the swamp. It had been a natural, rolled out for him. He couldn't have thought up such a top-notch shenanigan if he had been given the whole halter. China had heard about it before he got to the Birdcage and was lively and full of questions and wisecracks. She kept him going every minute he was there, showing no symptom of the bilious foreboding inside her.

During the weeks following, everywhere he went, Ratliff found himself known to timbermen and looked up to by most. He had figured he'd hit a lick to help himself, but he was surprised at the to-do over him. Ratfthands, loggers, and choppers alike limbered up when he came around. Some raftsman dubbed him Sheriff Snake and the name spread.

When summer low water stopped his picking up timber on the river, he turned to log-doctoring. He would have liked to spend a while with China, but anything more than a passing-through was impractical for him in Darien now—the damn company law had ruined the place! Still he found to his pleasure, as he swapped tobacco with timbermen, that its spell had been broken. Raftsmen and loggers had begun throwing it into their jokes along with the fat sheriff who hid behind a nigger.

He drifted about logging works both in the Oconee swamp and pine highlands, with his log-doctoring kit on his back. And, timbercuttting in anticipation of the September freshets being general, he in time moved into the Ocmulgee country, also. He had no trouble now in getting timbermen to let him doctor their defective logs. His contempt for the new law had infected them, and moreover, it had got around that he had been caught on a plug he didn't make, and that he had ignored to tell about it. Usually he got a fee for his work, but he made no secret of his methods. He told them his way of plugging a knothole to make it hold against an inspector's hammer, how to paint and burn red-heart not to show, how to take advantage (instead of losing by it) of a windshake to swell the size of the top end of a log.

When Ratliff set out he had no idea of going over to the Ocmulgee, he hadn't even thought of covering all of the Oconee country. He had time on his hands and he calculated to use it to cut a bigger chip for himself in his quarrel with the companies, and to pick up a living. But as he went along he found that even strangers he called on were clever to him, he got to like meeting new folks, and he got to feeling close to them, somehow. The thing that soaked in on him, though, was the fact that practically every timberman he met had some grudge against the companies, too.

And now that he had set his mind on it, he began to learn things about the Darien market that he'd never picked up before, or had paid no attention to. At Hard Bargain he learned from a spectacles-wearing fellow that the Darien people didn't elect their mayor and council, but the companies, working through some of the grand jury, named them, so that the public scalers got their jobs at the hands of the companies. An old man named Ashley on Fodderstack Island could remember when the rules of measurement on timber were a lot fairer to the raftsmen. He said the companies put a bill through the state legislature, changing them. Of course everybody who had ever been to Darien knew about the rules. As Candy Cox put it, "They all say, "Take off for the company"; naer one says, "Put on for the raftsman." ' The thing the old-heads said most was, 'The damn companies know they got you when they get you there, because you can't take your raft back home.'

Occasionally he ran into a fool who said he didn't believe in log-doctoring, who wanted to take the Darien companies' dose like they gave it. There weren't many, and he even got to arguing the point with them. A fellow like that, at Mosquito Bight, argued that the timber ought to measure up to the rules, that it all came out right in the price: the seller had a chance to get the best price, because the companies all bid against each other. But Ratliff told him that they just made it look so, that he knew from his own experience they were all together.

As Ratliff thought about it, swapping talk from place to place, he wondered how he could have ever had the notion that selling timber in Darien was a horse trade. He came to see it plain. As he told the Mosquito Bight fellow: 'It ain't even a gamble. The damn companies stack the cards and cut 'em, both. They keep the deal all the time, and if you put into theah place you've got to play theah game. The only card you ever could slip in was log-doctorin', and it waun't much, but now they're tryin' to put yuh on the chain gang for that.'

Even before Ratliff quit the Oconee country, he had almost lost sight of his own quarrel with the companies, listening to other people's, and arguing with fools. He came to see that it was all one scrap and every timberman had a share in it. And a curious feeling about it grew in him: it was as if—he found near the end of the summer—he had a responsibility for the whole thing: as if it were intended for him to see that every timberman doctored his defective logs and to see that they got by.

From the middle of September on, the rivers were full of rafts and Darien Creek choked up with them. Ratliff knew that most of them from the Ocmulgee and Oconee had doctored logs in them and a good part of the doctoring was his. He called his plug 'Sutton salutes'.

Early in October he and Ike Pippin came into Darien with a pick-up. He spent a night with China and had a drink at every bar in town, keeping a couple of jumps ahead of the sheriff's men—half the rafthands there were looking out for him. He heard that McDooly had another warrant for him. Joe at the Tavern said it was for assault with a sweet potato.

During November, on a trip back, in the aisle of the railroad carriage, he ran into old Marmaduke Pitt, the Dawson and Clare man who had shown him the caught plug. Pitt asked him, 'What you doin' now, since the sheriff stopped you from bringin' timber to Darien?' And Ratliff answered, 'Bringin' timber to Darien.' Old Pitt's smile was a tight one. Then Ratliff said, 'How's the run of yo' logs now that you've stopped me from pluggin'?' And old Pitt snorted and walked on. Ratliff enjoyed that snort all the way home.

When he came to Darien on Christmas Eve—he picked that time, for even the law lets up on Christmas—he got off the raft below Reap Hook Bend and walked in, going straight to China's. There wasn't much business at the Birdcage, but he lay low to keep any of the customers from seeing him.

China said he sheriff's men had been nosing around her place a lot of late. And even the sheriff had sent for her to tell her she had better tip him off the next time Sutton put in there. Ratliff urged her to string McDooly along: all he wanted was shirt-tail distance to get away from that crowd. China didn't laugh and seemed pretty jumpy about it all. But they spent the night and Christmas Day quietly.

Late the next night, after they had been in bed a long time (Ratliff would have been asleep, except that China kept picking at him about his upriver women—just pilfering questions), Delia came running up the hall and hammered on the door. The sheriff was on the front porch with a posse, she said.

Ratliff and China both jumped out of bed like burnt cats. But when China lit the lamp, her hand was steady. Ratliff already had on his pants and shirt by that time and he told her to dress. They could now hear the big-footed deputies blundering around downstairs. China didn't answer him, but stood in the middle of the room in her nightgown, looking around.

Then she moved swiftly, shutting Ratliff's satchel and handing it to him. She spoke. 'Go out that window. Climb from the side porch roof to the kitchen—from the back porch you kin jump to the garden.' She paused to blow out the light, while Ratliff raised the shade and sash. Some of the sheriff's men were thudding up the stairs.

At the approaching sound, Ratliff halted before the window, irresolute, his eyes shining like a cat's. 'Hell, China, the bastards might handle you—'

'It's a straight shot from theah to Cathead Creek,' she went on. She hurried to him, her gown billowing in the breeze. 'Goddamnit, git goin', Snake!' She hooked one arm around his neck and kissed him quickly on the temple. The boards squeaked under the carpet in the hallway and somebody tried to open the door. She pushed his receding shoulders through the window and dropped the sash.

Heavy knocking filled the room as she moved across it, rapidly unplaiting her hair. She relit the lamp and poured her basin full of water at the washstand, easing the pitcher to the floor, amid the sound of foggy shouting. The shouting came again. 'Come out of there, Sutton, or I'll kick the door down!'

China's voice rose in tremulous soprano. 'Oh, you can't come in! What do you want?' She snatched her nightgown over her head and stood naked in the chill air.

'The hell we kain't come in! Sutton, you under arrest—don't try to git out-a-window, either: we got the place surrounded!'

China put a piece of lightwood on the embers in the fireplace. She ran back to the washstand as someone began kicking the door. 'Don't! I tell you!' Her voice rose to a scream. 'You kain't come in! Theah's nobody heah!'

The thumb latch gave way and the door burst open. Two pistol barrels punctured the lighted gap. Behind them stood the fat sheriff and his deputy, Lemons.

China cringed, her bright hair falling loose about her hips. She held a dripping washrag before her and shrieked.

The men blinked and their eyes widened. They seemed unable to move.

'Shut that door!' China yelled. She scurried behind it and began swinging it to. 'I never heard of such a thing! And you call yourself a sheriff!'

The men were abashed and backed away. 'Miss China, I told 'im—' Lemons began.

'You told 'im! You told 'im! You the one kicked my door in! And you call that law enforcement! I kain't even bathe in my own house— after all, I am a woman, ain't I?'

The sheriff cut in. 'How'd we know you were takin' a bath?'—it's a strange time to be bathin', anyhow. We want Sutton.'

She pushed the door almost shut, saying, 'Wait a minute and lemme put on some clothes! You can wait a minute!' Deliberately, she picked up her chemise from the back of the chair. She kept talking.

Through the lighted crack, the men intently watched her disappearing and reappearing figure.

256

CHAPTER

24

RATLIFF LEARNED BEFORE he returned to Darien after his Chrismas-night flight that the sheriff had arrested China for harboring him, though she was later released for lack of evidence. He had seen it coming, still it was a mean, underhanded lick that hurt sharp. But that was only the beginning. During February McDooly raided the Birdcage twice, while customers were there. He wanted to let China know that when he told her to help him trap Sutton, he meant business. The cases cost China more than two hundred dollars.

Ratliff grew yellow with his pent-up bile. Finally he called for counsel, sent word to Bud True, Ike Pippin, and Roof Bostick to meet him in Darien. Early in March they gathered secretly at China's, though none of them had an answer to take the glumness from his face. It looked tough, Bud admitted, as they sat drumming knuckles on the dining-room table, looked like McDooly had the pincers on Ratliff.

But when the men had lapsed into silence, China spoke out defiantly. 'Say, you limbernecks, I just got warmed up! If I couldn't think faster than Shade McDooly, I couldn't stay in business. I'm movin' the Birdcage to Brunswick—and everything I can take with it. We'd like to have you fellows' business!'

They stared at her. Then her idea dawned on them and they grinned, laughed out. Ratliff began talking fast, his eyes on China's face. They would tell the river crowd that the sheriff had run China out of town, stir them up, and get them to quit trading in Darien. The biggest part of them went to Brunswick to catch the train, anyhow.

He could not remain for their campaign, but he spent the afternoon before he left making plans and thinking up arguments. They must seek out the Birdcage's customers in particular, but should buttonhole every rafthand who would listen. Tell them that Darien doesn't give a damn about the timber-runner, doesn't want his business, and that the companies are at the bottom of it.

Upriver, Ratliff went back to his log-doctoring, making timber works all the way from the Ohoopee to the Ocmulgee. He kept his talk to timbering. But when someone who knew him well enough said, 'I hear the sheriff run your woman out of Darien,' he replied, 'The companies made him do it: they don't like the brand of pluggin' we're puttin' out.'

During the second week following the Darien meeting, he learned through Bud that China had opened up in a big two-storied house on the outskirts of Brunswick and was doing good business. He learned, too, that Jack Jolley and four other raftsmen who had girls at the Birdcage had joined in the canvass, that they had spent the better part of a week in Darien and had talked to more than three hundred men.

Ratliff found fruits of their efforts as he moved about. In every camp he visited, regulars assured him they wouldn't so much as buy a drink in Darien now, and even some of the contract men and farmers (some of whom had never been in a bawdyhouse) agreed on the principle of the thing. The way timbermen were taking up his fight made Ratliff feel powerfully good. He grew sanguine over putting the

258

pressure to Darien. When he visited China's during the first week in April, he learned that more than a hundred had brought their timber checks with them aboard the *Hessie* and had come to Brunswick to frolic and buy their goods. He got a little drunk over it. He felt like a bull 'gaitor smelling spring musk, he said. He had friends from the Mouth to Macon and he was a pardner to every one of them: the raftsmen were jimming together now.

Then the Glynn County sheriff closed China's place up, told her she couldn't run in the county. Ratliff heard the news at English Eddy and took a boat to Brunswick. China said she believed the other madams had had it done and tried to be cheerful about it. She told Ratliff to keep the boys steamed up over the Darien boycott while she found some way to get next to the sheriff.

But Ratliff knew that the long arm of the companies was behind it, that there was nothing either one of them could do. To hell with the boycott: China was out of business! She couldn't get a toe-hold in Brunswick and, so long as she was his woman, she could not operate in Darien. Even if Ratliff didn't go about her place, McDooly would hound her as long as the timber-plugging charge stood against Ratliff—and now he had heard the grand jury had returned a true bill in the case.

He brooded over China's situation after he had gone back to the Oconee country. He had become a tar baby for her. And the fact that she hadn't turned on him, was standing by him, only made him feel lower in his mind. On his first visit to Brunswick in May, he found China's steam pretty slack. She no longer tried to contend she had a chance to do business there. She claimed to be hopeful of some change in Darien, but she was down. Ratliff had planned to slip into the timber town for a look-around on his way home, and he told her he might just better give himself up. He wasn't more than half-serious, but this roused the fight in her and she wouldn't let him leave till she had his promise not to.

Word of his arrival in Darien spread quickly and a dozen raftsmen scattered themselves about to form a lookout for him. He still put up a front there. He carried a jug of liquor with him and handed out drinks to the boys in the Tavern, saying that he even brought his liquor when he came to Darien now. Everybody laughed, including Joe behind the bar. Ratliff grinned and asked him when he was going to have to close the place.

It was just then that Marmaduke Pitt's handyman came in and called Ratliff to one side. Pitt wanted Ratliff to come to his office, he said. Ratliff only snorted, but the man said it was business. Ratliff told him to tell Pitt to come to the Tavern if he wanted to see him, and come by himself. The man left, but after a while he came back, bringing word that Pitt would see Ratliff aboard the Macon train, if he was going home that night.

Pitt was on the train when Ratliff got aboard and they found seats at one end of the carriage, remote from the handful of passengers. They sat facing each other. Pitt's lean face wrinkled in a smile. Its warmth seemed unnatural to Ratliff.

'Sutton, I've had my eye on you for some time,' the older man said. 'You're no run-of-the-mill rafthand. I've been in the game thirty years and I know a timberman when I see one.'

Ratliff spat in the cuspidor between his feet and tightened his jaws. Since he had got the message, he had been trying hard to figure out what Pit could want with him. This don't make sense, he told himself now. What in hell's the man after?

Pitt went on. 'I think you've got the makings of a real timberman and I want to offer you a chance—an opportunity.' He touched Ratliff's knee with a long finger that shifted with the motion of the train.

Ratliff drew back, glancing at the empty seat across the aisle. Jesus Christ! The old devil can't be offerin' me a job, he thought. His ears began to buzz.

'Now, I know you've been something of a hell-raiser around Darien,' Pitt went on. 'Some people look on you as a sort of outlaw. Your trouble is, you just haven't got the right slant on things yet: that often happens with a young man full of piss and vinegar. I can put you on the right track to make something out of your energy and ability.' He paused and looked at Ratliff, as if for a nod of assent.

Ratliff's immobile face tilted backward.

'Dawson and Clare can use another inspector.' Pitt resumed. 'It's a good job: we'll pay you well and give you a contract.'

Ratliff was suddenly on his feet, coughing. 'Just a minute!' His tobacco cud dropped out of his mouth. 'Need a drink-a-water,' he said, moving out into the aisle. He felt a sweetish swelling in his chest. Confusion jerked at him. China, saying, 'It would mean the gang, Snake!' her mouth twitching, kept coming before him. He lurched past plush seat-backs. As he filled the tin cup at the cooler, he asked himself: Hell, how can you inspect timber from the chain gang? But he knew that Pitt was preparing to withdraw the case against him— have things straightened out between him and the other sheriff—he'd have to—and that would fix things for China!

Ratliff took his seat again deliberately, leaned back and looked at Pitt from under lowered lashes. 'To put it plain: you want me to pick out them plugs I bin learnin' these rafthands to put in theah logs?'

Imperceptibly, Pitt's face unwrinkled. His smile became taciturn, habitual. 'We'd expect you to work for the company, naturally.'

Ratliff felt his mouth tightening. He licked his lips and gripped the arm of his seat. 'I don't quite git yuh, Mr. Pitt. It sounds like a fine job, but you know I couldn't work fifteen minutes in Darien before the sheriff 'ud have me.'

'The point now is your attitude toward the job: if you go to work for us, there won't be any trouble with the sheriff.'

Ratliff felt short of breath and his teeth clamped harder. He looked away at the empty seat again, then he suddenly leaned forward. 'I got to know: will the company git shet of the case altogether?'

'As soon as you go to work—or sign the contract to assure us you really want the job.'

Ratliff's lip hung loose, but the muscles at the back of his jaws were working. He felt as if he were on a swift current, drifting toward a shoals. Goddamn fellow tryin' to buy you off—git shet of you, he told himself. Git shet of you! He spoke. 'I don't need no contract.'

Pitt's eyes wrinkled up. 'The company wants to show its good faith. We'll give you a two-year proposition: a hundred and twenty-five a month the first year and, if you make good, we'll raise you to a hundred and fifty the next.'

Ratliff's jaw muscles kept working. 'I couldn't go to work right off,' he said, and swallowed. The carriage creaked. Down the aisle, the baggage racks swayed. He felt himself bobbling on the drift.

'Any reasonable time,' Pittt assented.

China would be tickled to death over my workin' in Darien, Ratliff thought. Shut up: are you plumb crazy! His face looked as dull as an imbecile's, but a tic had set up in his neck. He continued silent.

Pitt spoke again. 'Well, what do you say?'

'I'm yuh man, I reckon.' The words bolted from Ratliff's mouth. He laughed. It was like the rattle of paper.

'I thought you'd see it,' Pitt said. His smile was warm now.

Ratliff looked at him without loosening his grip on the seat-handle. Hell, the dogasses would have done the same, he kept telling himself. You don't owe 'em a damn thing!

He spoke hurriedly. 'They's one thing stands in the way, though.' Pitt had been about to speak, and he paused questioningly. 'I got stumpage on a poplar raft bought—got a lease—paid a feller a hundred and fifty dollars cash fur it—he needed the money—it ain't got but 'bout two months to run.'

Pitt smiled. 'We'll buy your raft and meet the best bid you can get.'

Ratliff took his hand from the seat-handle and rubbed his chin. He spoke more slowly. 'Not and that true bill ag'in me, you won't.

'Well, you'll be ready to go to work when you get there with the raft, anyhow—won't you?'

'Sho', sho'.' Ratliff exhaled a measured breath. 'I reckon so.'

The door he was facing popped open, letting in a trainman and a roar of noise. The man swung rapidly along the aisle. Each time he paused at a seat, he cried out in a strange, barking way. Ratliff stared up at him. What in hell! What in hell's he trying to say. Oh, Jesup! We just coming to Jesup?

Ratliff got off the train at Lumber City, in darkness. He had felt as if he was waking from a drunk when the trainman shook his shoulder in the carriage, and unpleasant recollections somersaulted through his mind while he descended the steps with his croker-sack of tools. As he limbered up for the long walk home, his head cleared. Near the wooden bridge, a gray gap above the shadowy creek on the town's outskirts, his thoughts returned to the poplar raft. His mind grabbed at the memory, leaving behind the nauseous sound of Pitt's droning voice and embarrassingly stout words of his own. He wondered why he had talked so hard about a raft: he hadn't put out a hundred and fifty dollars, he didn't even have a lease, though he had about traded to cut some gum and poplar in the swamp above home. But he had known then, without figuring how or why, that he was grabbling for a loophole, not to cut himself clean off. Yes, he had known.

The hammering of his heels on the bridge sounded reassuring to him now. I tied a boulden knot for you, he told himself: sure as shootin'. You can take him that raft—he'll have to kill that case against you before you tie it to his boom. Don't sign nuthin' till that's done. Then you can say to hell with the job. He felt his back stiffen. Yes, sir, that knot'll hold and pull out, too. An owl screamed in the bay to his right and he mocked the bird.

Then China's twitching mouth rose before him in the dark and his plan tumbled about his ears. Who the hell you think you were dealin' for, anyhow? he asked himself. Killin' that case ain't goin' to help China. Old Pitt'll be sore as hell when he finds you tricked him. They won't let up on China: they don't have to have a warrant to hound her! Ratliff's face was suddenly hot, and sweat did not cool it. His brain fogged.

But as he moved along, the circling mist in his head kept bulging with Bud True's big shoulders. He stared at the dim gray road and dug his feet into its loose, sliding surface. Beyond the road, beyond the rim of his vision, were vague gray forms, watching raftsmen—he did not look at them, but he knew they were there, knew their faces. He climbed the hill, descended it and went on, pulling through the sand with quick, heavy steps: the gray forms clung to the rim of his consciousness.

Finally he came to a footlog, where the road crossed a branch. He set his croker-sack down and pulled off his hat. I knew you never aimed to take that job, he told himself, his forehead cooling suddenly, pleasantly. Hell, huntin' plugs for a Goddamned company—your own plugs! He snorted. 'Ain't no bitchin' woman in the world kin make me do that!' he said aloud, and slung the sack to his shoulder. And a whore at that! A whore! A whore! he kept repeating to himself as he went on.

Once he eased his load to the ground, staring at the dim form of the bushes by the road, then slung it back to the same shoulder and walked hurriedly on. As the bridge at Tillman's Mill Creek rattled under his feet, he broke into song.

> Come all you Georgia ladies and listen to my noise;
> It'll never do to marry a river-running boy. . .

His voice brought distant, broken echoes as it rose through the stillness.

. . . And the name for to give it is doughboy dough!

Approaching dawn sifted the gray above the black swamp line of the Oconee. Ratliff had been walking a long time and was nearing Bell's Ferry. He jerked up his head suddenly and halted in the road. He was looking toward the horizon and he squinted his eyes harshly. You're a damn liar, and you know it, he told himself. He let his sack slide to the ground. The hell you didn't aim to take the job! Pitt had you runnin'—whinin'—hung up with a slut—you snivelin' Sneaky Colquitt.

His eyes burned as he stared, and tears ran down his cheeks when he blinked them. Pitt can't get away with it! He cleared his throat harshly and spat out cotton. 'I'll fix 'im if Gawd lets me live!' he said, aloud. He rasped his throat and spat again. I'll show the son-of-a-bitch how a rattle-snake comes back! He swung up his tools and walked on toward the ferry, hawking shrilly as he went.

CHAPTER

25

WHEN RATLIFF GOT HOME he cooked and ate breakfast. Then, without sleeping, he set out for Doss Kelso's to close his timber trade. He walked at a hard stride, his head tilted and his eyes hidden in their lashes. From Kelso's he went on to Longpond to round up log-choppers for the following Monday: he might not know his mind by then, what shape his comeback against Pitt would take, but choppers had to be seen ahead of time, and besides he had to keep walking.

The next day he walked the Kelso swamp. His excuse had been to cruise the timber and pick out the sticks he wanted. But he had to walk. There was plenty of room in the swamp: it ought to come to him best amongst the trees he aimed to cut. Likely it was something that had never happened before, but Ratliff never doubted that it would come.

He cruised the swamp from one end to the other, stopping often to stare up and down the length of a gum or poplar. Then he began over again. At times he walked slowly with his eyes on the ground, his rifle across his back and his hands hanging limply over its ends. Then he strode in haste, breaking his way through underbrush and wading through sloughs. Once he cut down a great black gum, chopping furiously until the trunk began to crack. When it had fallen, he walked about it, sat and studied the grain of the wood and the bark. ''Tain't no log-doctorin'll do,' he muttered as he left it.

Later he took off his boots and climbed a tall straight poplar, climbed it to the top, and sat a long time gazing out over the swamp. He fired his rifle through a hornets' nest once, and stood staring at the circling hornets until one popped him on the neck.

On the second afternoon, he shot a big moccasin, took out his knife and ripped him open. He watched the exposed heart beat until it ran down. At dark he clomped up the high steps across the puncheon floor on his log house and threw himself on the bed to mutter and chew his tongue in fitful sleep.

But on the third morning, he was again in the Kelso swamp, walking. Near noon he halted and, pushing his hat back on is head, gazed at the trunk of a poplar. Its gray shaft reared upward, round, smooth, impervious. Like a million more. Suddenly and without aiming, he threw the axe he held in his hand. Its blunt edge struck the tree and glanced off, carrying a large fragment of bark with it.

He blinked at the naked spot on the trunk and walked toward it hurriedly. He stood staring at it. His legs began to tremble. His breath came harshly. He no longer saw the white spot, the tree. For a time his gaze remained fixed, then the smile of a sleeper spread over his face. 'Gawdamighty!' he said in a hushed voice.

He gripped an arm about the gray trunk and clung to it. He looked up, he leaned backward and gave a prolonged river yell.

The next morning Ratliff put the choppers and a team in the woods and got the bowhand, Dunk, and his huge deaf-mute brother to help him. Beside a narrow pocket slough he halted and looked at his negro helpers from a stiff, still face. 'I kain't use no questions, Dunk: just do what I tell you,' he said.

The three of them set to work throwing up a mud dam across the slough to cut off a sixty-foot segment at the end. They fixed a makeshift wooden floodgate in the dam. Then Ratliff had the negroes haul a dozen loads of stones from an old hog-killing grounds near the swamp hill. He had marked the trees for his choppers to cut and he ordered his logger to haul them to the slough. Ratliff built three big fires beside the log trough he had cut off and heated the stones. Then he raked them into the trough, until the water was scalding hot.

The logger had already dropped a dozen of the long poplar pieces—ranging from forty to fifty feet—on the bank of the slough by the time Ratliff got ready. He studied his log before he called to the hands. He moved with intent deliberateness as he and the negroes rolled it into the trough and turned it in the scalding water. Then he ran it quickly through the floodgate into the main body of the slough. Boring an auger into the butt end of the log, he fixed a stout hand-hold and put Dunk on it.

As Dunk turned the log slowly, he tapped it with his hand stick. He hugged it in his arms and gave the bark short, careful jerks. Suddenly the whole husk was sliding. He held to the top edge, while Dunk pulled on his hand-hold at the other end, walking backward. The naked log drew out of the long cylinder of bark, leaving it whole.

The negroes and the logger on the bank all stood for a while, staring silently at the bright timber and its gray sheath in the water. Ratliff squatted down and looked through the cylinder. His face sharpened. Putting his mouth close to the end, he shouted, 'Goddamn!' The curt sound echoed flatly through the hollow bark.

With the aid of his logger, he snaked the bare timber out of the water and sawed it into three lengths to secure a thirty-foot middle section. The two short ends he rolled back into the slough. Then he and Dunk worked the ends again into the bark cylinder, fastening a pole between them, where there had been solid wood before. Ratliff spun his reassembled log over in the water. He pressed down on its hollow middle with his hands and the gray bark sank evenly beneath the yellow surface. A grim smile flickered across his face. He looked up at Dunk. 'You kain't tell what's in a aigg by its shell,' he said.

He and his crew spent nine days removing mid–sections from the poplars he had cut for the raft. The hollow-bark logs were drifted to the mouth of the slough and rafted along with the extracted pieces and twenty sticks of peeled gum. He had bought, he had cut and hauled sixty-seven sticks of timber; and now he had a hundred and seven to take to market.

When Ratliff reached Darien, the grim fevered look his face had worn for more than two weeks had been replaced by his usual loose-lipped tranquillity. He tied up at the Public Boom and had his raft scaled; then he visited a lawyer's office—China had once suggested this to him—and employed counsel in the log-plugging case. After he had made a round of the other buyers to get bids on his timber, he went to the offices of Dawson and Clare to look for Pitt.

Ratliff had waited an hour when the agent came in from the company sawmill, hurriedly. Seeing him, Pitt smiled and asked if he were ready to go to work.

'Just about,' Ratliff said, and handed him the bill of measurement.

'Wish you'd brought it on to our boom. We're needing poplar logs right now,' Pitt said, looking at the bill.

'You wouldn't break the law would yuh, Mr. Pitt?' Ratliff grinned slowly.

The agent did not appear to him, but put the bill under his arm, saying, 'All right, I told you we'd meet the top bid: let's get it down to our boom.'

Ratliff did not move. 'What about the law?'

Pitt looked at him sharply. (Ratliff's face was sober and questioning.) 'You ready to go to work now?' he said.

'As ready as I kin git till y'all take the sheriff off'n me.'

Pitt's mouth twitched. He drew out his watch and sprung it open. 'Guess the ordinary's still over there,' he said. He wrote a note, telling

269

Ratliff to give it to the company lawyer and go with him to the court-house. Ratliff slipped the note into his shirt-front.

When he and his counsel and the company lawyer came out of the ordinary's court two hours later, the log-plugging case had been legally quashed and he was again on civil terms with the sheriff. He went back to the offices of Dawson and Clare. Pitt met him at the outer counter. 'Get on down to the Boom and take your raft to the mill,' said Pitt. 'They're waiting on it.'

'Sho thing,' Ratliff said, wheeling back toward the door. But as he pushed it open, he paused. He turned hesitantly. 'Say, Mr. Pitt, my niggerhands—some choppers who come along on the trip—bin down theah waitin' on theah money since early this mornin'—they ain't had a cent since they started cuttin'.' He grinned wryly. 'I kain't go back down theah 'thout sump'n to hand 'em.'

'What'll it take?' Pitt asked, drawing out his bill fold.

Ratliff glanced sharply at the pocketbook as Pitt opened it. 'It'll take fifty-one dollars and thirty-nine cents—got it figured up.'

Pitt sighed and turned toward the inner office. 'All right,' he said. 'Come on in here.' He took the bill for the raft from a hook on a high desk. 'We might as well settle for the whole thing—comes to four hundred and fourteen dollars—let's see. . .' He set figures down on the bill. 'Less fifty-one, thirty-nine in cash—'

Standing by the desk, Ratliff fired intent eyes on Pitt's face without varying the smile on his own. 'If we goan have a settlemint—I reckon I ain't yelped loud enough. I'm ragged broke. I want to buy me some right sort of clothes to go to work inspectin' for Dawson and Clare, L-T-D.' (He pronounced the letters separately.)

Pitt frowned and looked up at him. 'All right,' he said, turning away from the desk and going toward a large safe. 'Make out your receipt in full.'

Ratliff ran into Bud True at the Boom, as he prepared to drift his timber to the Dawson and Clare mill. Bud came onto the raft, followed by Roof Bostick, Jack Jolley, and five other raftsmen.

'Snake, theah's some cur'ous talk goin' 'round,' Bud said, taking his pipe from his mouth and looking at it. 'We all hearin' it. It's talk a feller in yo'r place kain't let stand—yuh ought to stop it: it's got some fellers wonderin'.'

'Yeah?' Ratliff faced him with an unruffled smile.

'It's 'bout you and a inspectin' job at Dawson and Clare's.'

'Yuh ain't meanin' to say I'd pull plugs for a company?' Ratliff's face was unchanged, but as he gazed on at Bud his neck began to redden.

Bud put his pipe in his mouth and looked at him. 'I ain't meanin' a damn thing: I'm askin' you.'

Ratliff's eyes shifted to the other men. 'Just had my case killed in court, and I'm a-sellin' Dawson and Clare a leetle raft of poplar—takin' it to the mill now.' He paused and his gaze met Bud's. Behind his smile, his jaw muscles hardened. His voice was slower, softer, when he continued. 'Come on down: you'll git my answer when they derrick them logs out'n the water.'

That afternoon, as the *Hessie* plowed along her blue, circuitous course and a widening green gulf of marsh grass leveled Darien Bluff behind her, she bore on her deck a loud and stinking crowd of rafthands. Their hickory shirts were open at the neck and they sweated freely from river-caked bodies, long unwashed. Added to the smell of this, there was a soured-liquor odor. Most of them wore black wool hats, still more carried dark-barreled rifles. They jostled about and their mouths broke open in raucous shouts, or widened in rough laughter.

As that little steamer approached Buttermilk Sound, a lank, stoop-shouldered fellow, whose hatbrim shoveled upward, shifted his way to the lower deck rail. He brought his rifle to his shoulder and aimed at a buoy, a hundred yards to the right of the boat. The gun barrel spat orange in the slant sunlight and the red-bellied buoy bobbed under the water. 'Got 'er!' yelled several voices. The man shouted above them. 'Theah goes another poplar log!'

A roaring guffaw went up from the raftsmen. Their bronzed and reddened cheekbones bumped out and their eyes glinted.

Near the middle of the deck, Bud True's bewhiskered head reared above the mass. His short-stemmed pipe sent up whorling smoke. At his elbow, Ratliff sat on a capstan, smiling tranquilly.

The boat drew near a dyked point. Two buoys appeared along the channel, close at hand. Men crowded for the deck rail and a dozen rifle barrels were raised. The buoys sank in a splattering of lead and water. There followed another roar of shouting and laughter.

'That 'uz the axeman cuttin' into the raft!' said the stoop-shouldered fellow when the shouting had subsided. A fat man leaning against the rail pushed his hat to the back of his head and faced the crowd. 'That nigger wouldn't believe it even when he seen them logs 'uz hollow bark!' A voice cut him off: 'Hell, he waun't no different from me!' The fat man went on. 'They looked like shingle-backs when—' He paused and looked up.

A bright-skinned negro, dressed in a mate's white cap and coat, was standing at the rail of the upper deck with his hand raised. The crowd quieted and he spoke. 'The captain says this shooting must stop, or we'll turn around.' His accent was English. 'This is a public conveyance—'

A shot interrupted his words. It came from the prow of the boat and the men twisted their heads to see who had fired.

The mate waved his arm and shouted over his shoulder in a shrill voice. 'Turn her around! We'll take 'er back to port!' Then he looked again at the crowd. From all parts of the deck, gun barrels were leaning toward him, gun butts drawing up against hard faces.

The fat man barked, 'Keep 'er headed for Brunswick, you yellow bastard!'

The mate's hands had jerked up into the air. He was backing away.

'Kill the Gawddamn faughiner!' a tall negro raftsman yelled.

The mate wheeled and ran through an open door.

'Looked like old Duke Pitt!' said the shovel-hatted man. There was laughter and the gun barrels came down.

A moment later the captain appeared on the lower deck. He was a short, keen-eyed man with a salt-and-pepper mustache. The crowd of raftsmen parted as he advanced at a stiff-backed stride. He halted in front of Bud True. 'I'm goin' to have the law on you rowdies,' he snapped. 'Who was it drew his gun on my mate?'

Bud glanced down at him, then deliberately raised a foot, knocked out his pipe and put it in his pocket. Suddenly his hand shot out and he seized the captain by the collar. He lifted him from the deck like a child, and squatting, stared him in the face. 'Look heah, sailor, us river rats headin' for a leetle celebration in Brunswick, and we don't aim to do it in Darien—thass all!'

The choking captain plumped to the deck, going down on his back. He put his hands to his throat. Then he got up hurriedly and walked back into the cabin between the loudly howling raftsmen.

When the noise had subsided, the shovel-hatted man moved toward the capstan where Ratliff sat. 'Hey, Snake, you ought to get Bud to try that out on McDooly.'

Ratliff grinned. 'Theah ain't nuthin' 'twixt me and the sheriff now—not even a baked tater.'

The crowd laughed and quieted to hear the man again. 'The hell they ain't—if'n they ain't they will be soon as old Pitt kin swear out another warrant!'

'Nope, I 'uz a-lookin' ahead on this un.' Ratliff spat in the clear space between him and his questioner deliberately. 'They got to make 'em some more law 'fore they kin hook me on them poplar logs.'

There was a throaty hum among the raftsmen. 'Gre't Gawd!' the shovel-hatted man yelled, leaping into the air. He clapped Ratliff on the back. 'Pitt put out you 'uz goin' to pull our plugs and you pulled his leg!' Everywhere men began laughing and slapping each other.

Smiling, Ratliff got up off the capstan. He felt clean and hard and free. Yes, I reckon old Pitt won't try any more of his tricks with me, he thought. An inspecting job! He turned and looked off at the horizon behind the boat. His smile slackened. The sky glowed softly above the tree-line, far across the sound and the marsh, where Darien lay. He fancied he could make out a speck of bough above the rest: the top of the live-oak in China's yard. He had picked it out many a time coming down the river, he thought, with a tightening in his throat.

CHAPTER

26

ECHOES OF THE TIMBER market collapse did not prepare Ratliff
for what he found when he reached Darien in May of 1893. While the
two rafts he and his hands had brought down were being measured,
he noticed with surprise that the Boom, although cluttered with timber, appeared deserted. There were few timber-runners, and there
was neither the usual stir of scalers with their dip rods nor the swing
of company crews moving the purchased stuff onto private landings.
But he had come first to look the thing over, he told himself, and to
market his own timber.

When he climbed the bluff from the rice-field dyke, he found
Broad Street littered with tight clumps of raftsmen. They were not
only on the sidewalks, but in the sandy road. 'Panic' and 'Cutthroat'
he heard above the noise of their talk. The buzz of crowds came from
the swinging saloon doors. Men, bent a little forward, were pulling
through the sand to and from the buyers' offices. He watched a
bushy-whiskered fellow step down to the sidewalk from Stuyvesant-
George Company's doorway. His eyes had a fixed stare and his brin-
dled brush suddenly gaped open. 'Plain robbery!' he barked with a
metallic muzzle ring. Ratliff had known that the word he got was of

no ordinary market grousing, but this thing had the look of a lynching!

He edged into a group at the first street corner, feeling as if he had gulped down a slug of raw liquor. A square-shouldered fellow in the corner was saying, 'Pitt claims it's the money market—I claim these damn thieves tryin' to take our timber 'way from us!'

'Yeah—know they got us heah and we kain't drift our logs back home!' said a voice in the crowd.

'Old man George goes on 'bout the free-silver boys.' The lank, stubbly face speaking, Ratliff recognized, was that of Jerry Ballantine.

'What's up Jerry?' he asked, pulling him away from the clump.

Ballantine blinked at him vaguely. 'Damn companies cut timber prices ag'in today—claim bottom done dropped out of the lumber market—panic on.'

Ratliff released Ballantine's arm slowly and grinned. 'Looks like I picked out a po' time to drift my spring's cuttin' in heah!'

Ballantine's eyes focused on him hungrily. 'I got eighty thousand foot of hewn pine at the Boom—wisht I knowed what to do 'bout it.'

The eyes, their appeal, at once excited and restrained Ratliff. The look was familiar and stirred a feeling of kinship and obligation deep within him. He shifted his gaze and his face grew suddenly still.

Ballantine put a hand on his shoulder. 'What you aim to do, Snake?'

'What's this animule they keep jawin' about 'round heah—pank? pankt?' Ratliff grinned. 'I got to git a good look at that feller first.' He started off. 'I don't never shoot till I see 'is eyes.'

He had subsided in a truce with the companies after his big comeback at Duke Pitt of the spring previous. He had landed his lick to his full satisfaction and his interest had lapsed. During the ensuing summer weeks he thought about the long quarrel and what it had meant to him—mulled it over, as he loafed along in the swamp shade near home, fishing. In a way he had left China in the lurch, he decided: but to hell with that! He was a raftsman, not just a river-jack drifting logs to Darien to get to a woman. It hadn't come easy, his raftsmanship, but he had had it knocked into his fool head and he didn't aim to forget it for a woman, or anybody else. His crazy big-headedness hadn't caused him to drown poor Poss and his fool smartness, to have to kill Colquitt, without leaving him some notion of what it means to be a raftsman. And he thought soberly, over his cork and line, of the sore temptation Pitt had put him to.

With the return of drifting water, Bostick and Wall and Pippin and other of his running-mates had begun stopping by Dead River to see him and to renew the hour of triumph over the companies that they had shared with him. The passing log traffic also brought raftsmen he knew only by sight and some he had not seen before, men who found need of fresh water from his cypress spring and time from the swollen Oconee's seaward urge to swap talk and tobacco at his tall front steps—men from as far upriver as Dublin, and some of them with graying heads and wrinkled faces in sharp contrast to his smooth forehead and stubbly blond beard. Talk ranged from fish bait to fall prices, but it rarely failed to touch upon his long quarrel with the companies and his master stroke.

Ratliff came to see that it was for more than himself that he had fought the Darien buyers—that he had spit out Pitt's sugar-coated bait—that he had publicly twisted Pitt's tail. River-jacks had seen how to be stouter raftsmen for these things. He had the feeling before, but now he was convinced that it had been put upon him to do them. God and the river had marked him, his rafting, for more than himself.

Of this new sense of responsibility, he had conceived no peculiar purpose, or enterprise, when it came to him in the early fall. He had resumed timber-running, after he found that the market (excepting Dawson and Clare) was not closed to him, and he had taken up again with China. Months before the Birdcage had reopened without official interference and there no longer seemed any reason to stay away. But the feeling had remained always close to his consciousness, coloring thought and act and carrying a vague expectation for the future.

When Dunk had brought him word, second-hand, in the Dawson swamp that the buyers, all in cahoots, were dropping prices hell-for-breakfast, he had wondered what it meant, if it were true and meant anything. He had decided to take his timber—already cut—on to Darien to see for himself. The disturbing quiet and confusion he had met with at the Boom and on the Bluff—the look in Ballantine's eyes—now convinced him that it was for more than himself and his logs that he had come.

He made a round of the buyers with his bills of measurement. It became plain enough that the bottom had dropped out of the market: the best bid he received on his timber was scarcely half the price he had got for the raft he brought down in February. As well as he could gather it, the buyers claimed the lumber market had gone to pieces on account of the railroads and Wall Street—that silver money had scared the goldbugs, or something of the sort, and there was this thing they called a *panic* on. They all talked the same way and made out they didn't give a damn whether they bought his timber or not. He wondered just how solid their indifference was, but, when he had quit the last office, he was no nearer an answer to Ballantine's question.

At the Tavern, where he stopped for a drink, most of the men seemed to be storing their rafts and waiting for a better price: they couldn't afford to take what was offered, they said. But they were uncertain. When they asked him what he aimed to do, he saw in their faces the same sort of look Ballantine had worn. It deepened his deliberate quiet. 'I ain't talkin' yet,' he said. When they had turned away, they did not move on. They hung around, as if they thought he was withholding inside information. Your dodging only makes them worse, he told himself. He quit the Tavern for the Birdcage.

He found China in low spirits and fractious. Raftsmen were too worried and hard up to come to her house and there were few sailors in town: business was dead. She sipped at her beer, as if it were medicine, while they sat talking in the taproom.

'The freshet comes and the timber comes,' China intoned querulously. 'And the freshet won't take it back.' She looked at Ratliff. 'Hell, you suckers will get what the companies want to give you. And when it's all over they'll make a killing. I've heard they always do.' Her lips pushed out, twitching uncertainly. 'If you as smart as you make out, looks like you'd quit the river and git in the money-makin' end of this game. The smart men I see work in Darien.'

Ratliff frowned, but after a moment his face smoothed out. 'Last time I locked horns with a Darien smart-aleck, I didn't come off so bad.' He downed his beer and stood up. What the hell! China wasn't any help when it came to making up his mind.

He went by the store of a squat German Jew named Marcus, from whom he bought his hardware. Marcus was powerfully sharp about business and he could talk straight when he wanted to. Marcus told him it was no company trick, it was a panic—a thing that scared money everywhere and made it hard to get hold of. And there was no telling how long it would last. Marcus had seen it happen before. Later he cornered Tavern Joe on the street. Joe said about the same thing: it was a sure-enough panic.

Ratliff had the answer: the thing to do was plain, but he deliberated. His answer must serve the crowd and the butt-heads weren't ready yet.

He went back to the Tavern, where raftsmen were still loudly talking. His face wore a complacent smile. He moved among them quietly and said nothing. When the question was asked him, he grinned and said quickly, 'Got to git a good look at this heah panter, first,' as if to divert the questioner from some secret intention. He visited other saloons to be questioned and to answer his confident 'Kain't say yit.' There were more than a hundred raftsmen in Darien and he managed to excite and leave suspended the curiosity of most of them before he went to bed. But the crowd wasn't ready for the answer yet.

During the next morning Pippin, Jolley, Bostick, and Boze Wall looked him up. He told them to stick around and they attached themselves to him in a conspicuous satellite group, moved with him to the Boom, about the streets, into saloons and eating-places. They kept idling questioners at a distance and took over the role of spokesmen. 'He ain't sayin' yit,' they answered each in a confidential tone. Ratliff maintained a self-assured but watchful silence, as the coming and going of raftsmen about him grew.

He sold his raft late that afternoon, taking twenty-five cents 'on the average' less than he had first been offered. From the buyer's office, he hurried through falling rain to the crowded Tavern. His henchmen trailed him and silently lined up beside him at the bar. When he had downed his drink, he turned to Pippin and the men in the saloon got quiet.

'Well, Ike'—his voice penetrated the swish of the downpour—'I bought stumpage on one raft and by workin' hard—and kyurful—I got heah with two.' His mouth loosened as he paused, and there was a chuckle from the crowd behind him. 'Sold 'em both fur just about what my labor and the stumpage fur one cost me—and a half-fare ticket back home. But I could have done worse, heap worse: I could have hung around heah and let storage eat up my timber and got nuthin'—kaze this heah panter's done *took up* at the Darien market!'

He turned toward the listening men behind him, as if he were just discovering their interest. He looked them over. 'I don't know what *you* bullies aim to do, but Snake ain't rustlin' no timber fur a joy-ride down the river.' He moved toward the door. 'Boys, I'm goin' fishin' till the panter leaves.'

By word that got to Longpond later in the week, Ratliff learned that most of the raftsmen had followed his lead in selling out and quitting Darien. Indeed, so many of them had sold that on Tuesday the market went off another quarter 'on the average.' 'Sho made sheep out'n them river goats,' he said with a grin, feeling a trifle low-down to have done it to his own crowd. 'But sell was the only thing.' And he felt, too, a tenderness for them, new and strange, and a surge of warmth at his success.

By the middle of June the Oconee and the Ocmulgee were too low for drifting logs and low water lasted till late July. Very little timber went to market and prices improved. Ratliff grew suspicious: the market seemed to be behaving as it always did on low water, panic or no panic.

Then came news of freshets up both rivers and the market jumped a dollar a thousand. Before the end of the first week in August, the Boom was hemmed with rafts and the price had dropped two dollars and a half. Ratliff's suspicion was confirmed: this panic wasn't all stranger, by God, it was part home-grown: the companies were helping it along, and the raftsmen—suckers for their bait—were doing their damnedest to help along the companies! His admonition to go fishing till the panic was over didn't carry very far. The damn fools! Hell, the thing hadn't got into their potato patches, their cornfields, their hogpens. They could keep away from the panic and starve her out.

With fresh zeal, Ratliff set out for timber works over the Oconee country. The place to stop the timberman was in the woods: the time, before he got to market. During August he spread his argument un-flaggingly. The men he talked to readily accepted his theory that cut-ting off the supply of timber long enough would break the panic on the Darien market. Many of them agreed that they could make out to eat at home, without selling their timber, and some even promised to hold their logs in the woods till the panic was over. But more often he heard, 'I'd stay away if the other fellow would,' and, 'It won't help for me to hold mine and the other fellow a-takin' his.'

Then early in September there was a big rise in the Oconee and rafts went drifting past his place like homing geese. It was clear he couldn't head off the timber in the woods. He hired out as a pilot and went to Darien.

The Boom—when he reached it—looked like a great furrowed field afloat: logs everywhere—gray-back, brown-back, and white, hewn flat. The sight of it raised his dander. He tied next to old Deacon from Lapsley's Landing, who had sworn to 'move naer stick' out of his woods for the 'duration.' Ratliff said nothing, but the old man volunteered, looking out at the river, 'She was just such fine driftin' water— and I thought maybe the market mought-a picked up a leettle.'

On Broad Street the raftsmen stood about talking, as they had when he last saw them in May. Now they were not so hot under the collar and were saggier at the knees. On the sidewalk in front of a buyer's office he passed a rib-like man with a lost look on his hound's face, muttering, 'Forty thousand foot of timber and they want-a gimme ten dollars more'n I got in it!' Before Stuyvesant-George's place lank men stood, tapping bills of measurement against their fingers and staring off into space.

He entered the Blue Goose, trailed by a dozen raftsmen. The saloon was filled with a noisy clump of men. He approached the group. Recognizing him, a squat frog-faced man took off his hat and waved it over his head. 'Heah's the bully knows how to handle the companies!' he called out. 'Let's sell 'em some mo' hollow logs, Snake!'

Close-packed, the men shifted their bodies and faces to locate Ratliff. He pushed his way to the inner ring. 'This ain't no time for tricks,' he said. His big lap was straight and stiff. He looked around the circle. Several of them had quit Darien with him last May for the duration of the panic, he said, and as many more he had seen in the woods and had tried to persuade them not to bring their timber here.

It looked like he hadn't done much good. But he was trying again. He had come to Darien just for that purpose: he wanted every raftsman there to agree to get out and stay out. And, instead of running timber, to spend his time getting his neighbors to agree to stay away. 'Don't stand 'round heah bellyachin' and damnin' the other fellow—go git 'im to join in,' he concluded.

There was a pause and the men in the circle shifted their eyes, looked vaguely away. A man behind him muttered, 'Them jiners won't pay my taxes!' Old man Deacon, who had followed Ratliff up from the Boom, shrilled, 'Sutton, you don't seem to 'low for the contrary people on the river 'tall!' And a man across the ring asked, 'What about the contract men and some of these damn farmers?'

'Git next to 'em: they're in the same boat,' Ratliff retorted.

The squat man interrupted: 'And these damn 'Hoopeans! You kain't tell them fools nuthin'!'

A crook-backed man turned his buffalo's hump toward Ratliff and moved away. 'Hell, I thought you wuz goan tell us how to git a purchase ag'in them thievin' companies!' Ratliff kept talking, but the group gradually disintegrated.

He doggedly visited other saloons, talked to raftsmen on the streets in twos and threes, cornered them singly. They could follow his argument of cutting off the timber supply to better the market, but when he spoke of a joint movement of raftsmen up and down the rivers, they shook their heads; it wasn't reasonable.

By the third day he had dried up in disgust. And that night he had a row with China. It began in the afternoon, while she was fixing her hair. His complaining gave her the opening.

'You just findin' out you kain't tell a rafthand nuthin'?' she said, taking hairpins out of her mouth and laying them on her bureau. 'They're born suckers and don't want-a be told!'

The sweet odor from her body was suddenly oppressive to him. 'Shut up!' he snarled, and he stalked out of the room.

But later, after they were in bed and he was ready to go to sleep, she wanted to talk. 'Snake,' she began in a small, uncertain voice, 'I didn't mean to make you mad this afternoon. I'm a friend to these rafthands—they good fellows'—she slipped a hand under his pillow—'but I kain't shut my eyes to the fact they're blunt—they kain't take it all in.'

Ratliff mumbled and shifted his head.

'You kain't believe it 'cause you ain't the same gauge as them—you expect 'em to see all you see.' She paused, but he made no response. 'Snake? Why don't you come to Darien? They's an openin' heah for the right sort of an eatin'-house'—she raised up on an elbow and stared at him through the dark. 'The Darien men run this show: you kain't git ahead bein' a sucker for 'em!'

He slung his hand out violently and hit her in the mouth. . .

When he left Darien the next morning, he told himself that he was through with the damn place. And China, too—for a month of Sundays. Back at home he set to work gathering the corn that he and Dunk's oldest boy had made in the swamp field, and his sugar cane for grinding. He kept hard at it and his hands were quick to pull the ears and cut the stalks, but he couldn't make his mind stay with them. The freshet comes and the logs come! China's saying kept running through his head. It had always been that way. How the hell could he change it! How the hell?

By October, the timber traffic was light again and he heard the market had improved a little. But that, he knew, was just the let-up before the downpour. He got to thinking about it while he was skimming his juice at Doss Kelso's cane mill, where he made his syrup. The gully-washer is just making up, he told himself. Farmers are not getting anything for their cotton this fall and every damn one of them in reach of a river will take a raft to Darien for his Christmas. By the middle of November the rivers will be full of them.

He let his syrup scorch, troubling about it. A slough of farmers always brought timber to Darien just before Christmas. Hell, the companies will knock the bottom out of the market this time, he thought. And they'll get enough logs to let us regular timbermen starve till spring! The prospect harassed him. And a sense of failure gnawed at him, too: he hadn't handled those fellows right; talked his head off like they did. Still he told himself that he was through with the Darien market. Hell, raftsmen were lone prowlers—scattered over six or seven hundred miles of river. They couldn't get together on anything—never had—and it looked like it wasn't intended.

But the specter of the timber deluge pursued him: his eyes grew feverish and his hands as restless as caged cats.

He was splitting rails to mend the swamp-field fence—he had run that low on tasks—the old saw that China liked to mouth had been dogging him and he was singsonging its final words, *the freshet won't take 'em back*—when the notion ran through his head. It seemed foolish at the time and he went on swinging his axe. But late the next afternoon, as he was about to finish his mending, the thing came back to him at a different slant. It suddenly began to make sense, to add up into a plan. Hell, rafthands had to be slicked into helping themselves! He quit the unfinished fence and walked toward the house, still staring at the ground. When Dunk's boy, who had cooked supper, called him, he wouldn't come to the table, but kept sitting on the tall front steps in the dark, chewing his tobacco. Late that night, he sent the boy by Dunk's place to tell him to get his hat and come on, and on below Longpond to tell Bud True to meet him in Darien.

Ratliff got to Darien on the first day of November with a short pick-up raft. Space alongside the Boom was pretty well taken up and he tied at the lower end. Raftsmen were straggling glumly along the walkway and eight or nine came down to his float.

A bent, brushy-whiskered fellow got aboard. 'Thought you waun't goan sell no mo' timber heah on the panic?' he said, raising his voice.

Ratliff watched the inspector dip his rod at the top of a log, then looked up. 'Will if I kin git my price.'

For an instant the old man and the others standing behind him on the walkway gazed at Ratliff in astonishment, then their mouths loosened briefly, in an effort at smiling. Their faces grew glum again. The old man looked away. 'You better be easy satisfied.'

'Won't take less than seven dollars a thousand.'

The old man jerked his head toward Ratliff. 'You'll take a damn slight less, if you sell.'

'May not sell.'

The old man's jaw worked at his tobacco irritably, then he spat. 'Storage is high and the river won't tote 'er back for ye.'

Ratliff raised his eyes to the men. Their mouths sagged and their cheekbones stood out. They stared at the moving dip rod, as if held by its familiar, inevitable certainty. 'It don't pay to be too sure about nuthin', Milt,' he said, with a steady smile. 'Stick around.'

When he climbed the bluff, he found the usual litter of timbermen on the dusty riverfront street, but now their roar of talk had dwindled to a drone. And they were not standing spread-legged out in the driveway: they squatted and leaned against buildings, or got up to walk aimlessly along the sidewalks and squat again. They still wore their ragged, mud-caked river clothes; some were barefoot. They put him in mind of a rusty, helpless herd of 'gaitors trying to keep wet in a drying mudhole. As he drew near, he saw gaunt faces and wandering eyes that settled nowhere.

He strode past them, as if intent on his destination. Some of the men recognized him, called out, got to their feet.

Luke Haynes grabbed him by the arm. 'What's yuh hurry, Snake? Le's heah yo' notion about this thing.'

'Didn't come to talk about it,' Ratliff said, and was moving again.

A tallow-faced man blocked his way to say he couldn't clear enough on his raft to fill his meal barrel, and he didn't have a dusting. Ratliff looked at him impassively. 'Talkin' kain't fill it,' he said. He cut off a group who halted him at the corner without hearing them out. 'You kain't talk trouble away.'

The crowd stared after him, as he strode on toward the Market Street timber offices.

When he had got bids on his raft, he set out to look for Bud True. In the Tavern he encountered a straggling group. They sat talking, or tapping their bills of measurement on the table-tops. Several of them called out to him. Had he sold his timber? He did not reply, but looked searchingly about the room. He moved rapidly toward Jake Pettigrew, standing near the fireplace. 'Ain't sellin',' he said over his shoulder finally.

There was an abrupt quiet, then equally abrupt laughter. It had a flat, harsh sound. 'Goan let storage eat it up,' someone called to him.

He and Pettigrew were walking toward the doorway. 'Ain't goan store it neither,' he said, as they went out.

Ratliff had counted on Bud's help, but he had not thought of Pettigrew until he saw him in the saloon. He was in luck if he could get the help of the sober-minded inventor of the sharpshooter raft. They walked deep into the alley and squatted against the side of the Tavern.

Raftsmen who came out of the saloon to find where they were going, looking down the alley, saw that Ratliff's face was creased sharply, that his hands moved quickly, drawing on the ground with a stick—that Pettigrew remained silent for a time after Ratliff had ceased talking, that finally he nodded his long head and shook Ratliff's hand. But neither had anything to tell the questioning group when he came away.

That evening Bud stayed a long time in Ratliff's room at Hammersmith's boarding-house and issued from it shaking his head dubiously. But he played up to his part, when the men downstairs in the saloon drew around him. What the hell was Sutton up to? He moved

287

off, as if he had important duties to perform. 'Stick around and see,' he said.

With the darkness raftsmen stuffed their soiled and worn bills of measurement into their pockets and moved into the saloons and eating-places to speculate about it. A blurting Ohoopean, in the Blue Goose, said Sutton was up to some damn foolishness. But a half-dozen growls called him down. It was no time for foolishness and Snake Sutton knew it. Most of them guessed that Snake was rigging a trick to beat the market. Roof Bostick said it might be a way to short the companies on measurement, though that couldn't help much: the price was so damn low—and logs kept coming, piling up at the damn Boom to stay—to stay till storage ate them up or a fellow finally took what the companies pleased to give him.

When Ratliff appeared on the street late the next morning, Bostick and Boze Wall asked him point-blank what his business was. He looked at them with a sober face. 'I'll tell you when the time comes,' he said, 'if you're theah.'

A few minutes later he came out of the hardware store, followed by his bowhand, Dunk, bearing two cases of Winchester cartridges. On the sidewalk, raftsmen squinted their faces and loitered along behind him. He entered the Blue Goose and came out with a jug of liquor in each hand. Then he and Dunk went into a grocery store. They finally emerged from it, with bulging croker-sacks on their backs, and headed for the Boom. Squint-faced men blocked their way. A tall fellow, his head canted and his mouth half-open, blinked at them. 'Sho' nuff now, Snake. Tell us whur yuh goin'?'

Ratliff stared off at the river. 'Takes more than tellin'—aer takin' for granted.' He nodded toward the Boom. 'Come on and see.'

He and Dunk crossed the rice-field dyke as the tide began coming in. An irregular line of raftsmen stretched out behind them.

A thin man, leading the silent, heavy-footed column along the walkway of the Boom, twisted his head toward Ratliff's small raft and blinked his eyes. As he halted beside the bow, his glance moved hurriedly over its familiar form: sapling oars, elm binders, pine-bough lean-to: his mouth sagged a little. The faces of other men drawing up behind him, turning, made the same hurried survey, showed the same disappointment. But they remained sober and there was no word spoken, as the walk filled and the column spread over onto the timber above.

Ratliff moved toward the bow of the raft with a pike pole in his hands and the semicircle of eyes fastened upon him. His own gaze was lowered beneath pale, weighted lids. He halted at the hip and turned toward the men. His head tilted slowly backward. There was a smile on his face, though taut lines crow's-footed the corners of his mouth and the skin was tight across his cheekbones. He lifted his eyes. Their clear green was gone: they were dark and shining. The men across the intervening logs sought his glance, but they could not look into the big pupils, they could not catch the gaze. It seemed far away, fixed on the distance above their heads. There was no recognition. Tension grew upon the faces of the men.

Then a cloud covered the sun and its shadow lay a gray pallor over Ratliff and his watchers. The raftsmen's bodies shifted and they lowered their eyes. Ratlif dropped the end of his pole quickly and set it against the Boom, beside that of his bowhand. Sweat popped out on his face. He glanced up at the sky, then gazed down the river. He took a quick breath and swallowed. 'Heave!' he said, and he and the negro began pushing the bow slowly away from the bank.

As it moved outward, the men along the edge of the Boom spat and stared at it. The spitting came quick and often. A fellow with plaited pigtails kept twisting the end of one around his finger. A sallow man with a gaping mouth picked his nose. At the front of the bulge of men on the adjacent raft, a wild-haired fellow slapped his knee with a limp wool hat. Ratliff began walking along the raft-edge, leaning on his pole. He seemed not to be breathing. The triangle of water between the raft and the Boom was slowly widening like a bright, unfolding fan. A man standing near its vertex with a set smile on his face gradually drew in his chin and bore backward, as he stared at it. The fellow with the hat belched and the semicircle of faces twisted briefly.

From the rear of the walkway came the sound of scuffling feet and the front row wavered outward. 'What the hell's he doin'?' called a scuffler. The crowd gave a heavy, short laugh, that left no smiles. Current caught the bow of the raft and it moved more rapidly out into the river. 'Headed for the Atlantic Ocean, looks like,' the man with the pigtails said. 'No, 'tain't—tide ain't right,' said the thin man frowning.

The river now had hold of the front end and for a moment poised the float at a right angle with the Boom. Then, under a sudden burst of sunlight, the raft began to pull away from the cluster of men. Foreheads twisted above the staring eyes. There was a sound of heavy breathing. The man with the hat began hiccoughing. The sallow man's eyes protruded. 'Whur you goin', Snake?' he cried. Ratliff dropped his pole and looked toward the crowd. His face shone like cobalt in the sun. From the seaward distance, a breeze stippled the gray surface of the river, zigzagging toward the raft. It rumpled his hair and he smiled. The float was moving with the tide. He turned and ran toward the bow oar. His movements had become quick and easy.

As the raft rounded the train of timber alongside the Boom and straightened out on the river, there was a giant shout. 'Boys, she's goin' upstream!' It came from Bud True, whose head reared above the crowd. The faces in the semicircle winced, broke open, spread falteringly in grins. 'I'll be Goddamned!' said the thin man. The hiccougher stuttered, 'Jeez-hus!' Shoulders and feet shifted and hoarse laughter rose.

'He kain't be headed for home,' said the man with pigtails.

'He'shovin' off, ain't he?' Bud retorted. 'And he's takin' his timber back with 'im!'

The nods from the crowd came unsurely.

'Come on, Bud: what's the ole rattlesnake up to?' said the man.

Jake Pettigrew raised his voice. 'There's a way to find out, you know!'

The crowd loosened stiffly and began to move along the Boom. Now Ratliff had taken the stern and Dunk was at the bow oar. Almost imperceptibly, but steadily, the raft was moving up Darien Creek, past the train of logs along the bank. Men who had been at the rear of the crowd ran out onto the timber and yelled at Ratliff.

He stopped pulling and faced the shouters. 'Them that air game to try a new way to beat the companies, come on! I kain't use nuthin' but game 'gaitors!' He turned back and put his shoulder to the oar.

On the timber, along the Boom, on top of the rice-field dyke men stood and stared as the raft rounded the bend, and passed the mouth of Cathead Creek, headed up the river.

CHAPTER

27

RATLIFF REACHED CLAYHOLE Creek, twenty miles above Darien, before day the next morning. The drifting had taken two tides. He and Dunk secured their raft at the creek mouth and climbed the slope of the low bluff above it, bearing their tools and supplies. They made camp on top of this sandy, sparsely grown river bank, building brush lean-tos and a high-blazing fire. It kept them busy while they waited.

The next incoming tide brought five more rafts and eleven men, including Bud True and Jake Pettigrew. Ratliff opened one of his whiskey jugs to help while away the time, but he watched close to keep the drinking light. He did not drink himself, feeling no taste for liquor. The men were restive and heckled him with questions, the strain of waiting brought him fatigue, almost *uncertainty*, but he held on to his assured good-humor and his secret. Those he could, he enlisted in fixing up a large campground.

The day stretched out and the tempers and patience of the men shortened. The afternoon tide added rafts, stragglingly. When it had spent itself at sundown, there were thirty-six men on the bluff and fourteen rafts tied below. Ratliff had hoped for more, but he realized he could not delay longer: there could be no more before midnight and all who had come were game and, for the most part, seeing men.

As a yolk-like sun floated down against the tree-line, he stood up from where he had been squatting before the fire and walked over to the edge of the bluff. 'Take yo'selves a dram to open up yo' heads and come on over.' He looked back at the men around the fire getting to their feet, and the stragglers coming up from the lean-tos and the woods. Now that the waiting was over, the raftsmen took their time. They sauntered up from the liquor jug (those who drank) in twos and threes. As they gathered within the sandy clearing, he walked back and forth, his eyes dark and fixed on the distance, where the smooth yellow river crooked out of sight.

When he turned to confront them, they stood a little away in an irregular semicircle. Their faces wore a taciturn, an habitual immobility, the eyes were observant, and each head was shifted a little to present a close ear. They remained standing.

He glanced back at the river and swallowed. 'One reason I—I wanted to get you all off up heah,' he said, putting his hands in his pockets, 'was so you could listen—n-n-not be deefened by Darien jabber'—he stammered at starting, then bolted his words. ' 'Specially by a lot of contract guineas and clodhoppers!' He shifted his weight and looked at the ground. 'I—I—I'll be quick as I kin.' He pulled his hands from his pockets and looked up, stretching his mouth in a stiff, hurried smile. 'I don't want to put no tax on Roof Bostick's kidneys.'

The faces before him did not loosen, kept on looking at him. The thin man who had led the raftsmen onto the Boom to watch Ratliff's departure from Darien lifted his sharp nose. But there was a slackening of posture among the men, and three or four slowly lowered themselves into a squatting position.

Suddenly Ratliff's shoulders straightened, his hands quit moving and clenched at his thighs. 'I wanted to tell you to see that everything you've heard and takened to be a fact has to be that way.' The twitch-

293

ing in his lower lip ceased. 'A notion can grow up and look as solid as a light'ood stump and be doty in the middle. But the main thing is, that I wanted to get hold of them who were game to try a thing that had never been tried before—kaze that's the kind of business I got cooked up for us.' The words now came even, urgent, rapidly—took off, like a covey of quail. 'If a rock-balanced grist of corn makes too big a load for yo' ole mule to git to mill with, you kin cuss and talk about it the rest of yo' life, but you got to get over the notion of rock-balancin' a grist of corn to lighten the load so the jarhead kin tote it.'

Several of the men shifted their feet. Roof Bostick and the wild-haired man of the nervous hiccoughs nodded their heads.

'All y'all who've took time to think' Ratliff went on without pausing, 'know you ain't seen no bad timber market yet to what lies ahead. The time the companies has bin layin' for is purty nigh heah: the killin' they bin holdin' out for: the Christmas-time timber that ever' damn-fool farmer on the river—and regulars, too—always brings to market. And it's goin' to be worse this year.

'There's bin a lot of talkin' 'bout the panic and the market and what ought to be done—a hell of a lot. And I've done my share, though I had more'n talk in mind. I've argued with you up and down the river—in the woods—in Darien—and got nowhere. The loophole has always bin "the other feller"—always the other feller. Well, I got that loophole chinked now—I got the answer—I got a plan to take care of the other feller. I didn't bring you off skylarkin' to show you how far you could drift yo' rafts up the river: I got a proposition, I got a way to make raftsmen jim together.'

He halted and gazed around the semicircle rapidly. 'They's thirty-six of us and fourteen rafts: that's plenty.' He wheeled about, looking out across the river. 'She ain't more'n a hundred and fifty paces wide here and well banked. Three-four rafts tied together will boom 'er.' He faced the men. 'And that's what I aim for us to do: boom 'er, and not let another raft git by to Darien!'

They blinked and stared at him. Wind rustled the dry oak leaves, a tiny sand whorl came over the brow of the bluff and collapsed. The three men who had been squatting came slowly to their feet. The wild-haired man dropped his pipe in taking it from his mouth. Bud True looked off at the river with an uneasy, querulous face.

Ratliff was now standing with his legs spread apart, leaning a little forward and balancing on the balls of his feet, as if the earth beneath him were in smooth motion. His voice sharpened. 'We want to put a bunch up at Swan's Lake and along, where most of 'em will be stoppin' to wait on the tide, or, in case the tide's right, to hail 'em down—tell them they kain't git by—get them to jine in with us.'

Dog moons gleamed in his eyes as he gazed slowly around the circle. The faces before him squinted. Three men whose jaws had dropped slowly tightened them. The flesh on Luke Haynes's cheekbones was gathering in hard knots. The thin man knocked out his pipe.

'Some of the boys'll be hot when we stop 'em.' Ratliff clipped out the words strongly. 'But they'll be in twos and threes—never more than six or eight—and we can handle 'em—we can take 'em in the lodge. Soon as word gits back up river that we mean business—that they sho' nuff kain't git by—they'll quit comin'.'

The men dropped their heads. Their bearded faces had become swollen, their eyelids heavy. They looked like a herd of goats under attack. Bud True stared off at the river.

'But, Snake, what about the companies?' Roof Bostick's voice came with a whispering sound. 'It's the companies we're foughtin' with, hain't it?' He subsided in an embarrassed, mirthless grin.

Ratliff tried to catch his eye, but he dropped his gaze to the ground. Only Jake Pettigrew's face remained calm and open. Ratliff pressed forward, his forearms tense before him. His voice rose. 'Boys, if we kin hold up this Christmas flood—block this river for sixty days—the damn companies'll be beggin' for timber! The Darien mar-

295

ket'll have to open up—the combine'll be busted—they'll be cuttin' each other's throats to git timber!'

A brushy-whiskered old man, whose jaw had been working rapidly at his tobacco, looked away and spit. 'I'm afeared I don't follow ye, Sutton!'

Ratliff jerked his head toward him. 'Kain't yuh see, Milt? Kai'nt yuh see—it would be simple to boom the river heah at the bluff. Once we cut off the timber supply, the companies'll cave in!'

The thin man put his pipe in his pocket. 'You lack a hell-of-a-lot showin' me how to cut it off!'

Ratliff's eyes looked black. He turned and took a step nearer the declivity. 'It's sound—it's simple. Tie above the bluff—he pointed across at the smooth, vine-laced swamp—'and slam a bow right into them bushes—I can cite you the root to tie to—'

'Hell, Snake!' A lean man raised his hardened face. 'You'd bring ever'body down on us—includin' the Gover'mint!'

'Yeah, the Gover'mint would danamite us, aer the damn steamboats!' said Jerry Ballantine.

'I'd figgered on the Gover'mint,' Ratliff went on quickly, looking back over his shoulder. 'We kin fix a shiftin' boom: it would work like this: when a boat come along, drop out a middle raft to let 'er by, then drop another un down in 'er place, soon as the boat got through. Then we—'

'Gover'mint, hell!' Haynes said, looking off beyond the edge of the bluff. 'What about the river? The ole Altamaha wouldn't stand for being yoked up no sitch a damn way for two months.'

Ratliff had not closed his mouth from speaking, his cheeks glowed, creased sharply. 'We don't aim to dam the river, Luke—just a floatin' barrier; you kin hold one together on a fresh—I've seen it done. And I know t'other swamp—there ain't no slough or water road they could use to git 'round us—case they did come a big rise—'

296

Haynes had dropped his tobacco cud into his hand while Ratliff was still speaking. 'Great Gawd, so this is what you brought us heah for!' he said, and threw the chew away. He turned his back and started walking down the slope toward the creek.

'Kain't help it if yo' head's too thick, Luke!' Ratliff barked. He stared at the downcast faces of the men. 'Look at me, boys!' His mouth was flared out, his lower lip moist and moving. 'I ain't never give yuh no bad steer! This's the only thing that'll stop the timber—crack the market. Timber-runnin' game's changed—old ways won't do!' He searched out True's face. 'Bud here kin tell you, I got this thing figgered out—from gall to gizzard!'

Bud looked away and was silent.

'Jesus Christ, I thought you were goan have a plan to bust up the companies, aer at least trick 'em!' Bostick said. 'Not git into a fight with raftsmen!' He turned away without looking at Ratliff and followed Haynes.

The men in the circle stared at Ratliff now. Their necks were stiff, their faces hard.

'Hell, we couldn't tell them fellers they kain't take theah rafts to Darien,' said a glass-eyed fat man, tightening his belt. 'That don't make sense!'

'My pappy's aimin' to bring a big cypress raft down about the last of the month—I kin see myself standin' theah telling him he kain't git by!' said Boze Wall. He tried to laugh that rose shrilly and broke. 'He'd scorch my tail with a Winchester!'

'Christ, I thought you had a trick that 'ud work!' said Jack Jolley.

Ratliff's cheeks grew splotchy and twisted. His mouth clamped shut. He still leaned forward on his toes, his eyes on the grim, retreating faces, but he did not speak.

Men edged away in twos and threes, turned their backs. They walked off into the gathering dusk, went down the path to their rafts. The old man with the brushy beard stepped forward and paused. 'Ye

297

mought-a argued me into firin' Darien, or bushwhackin' some of them company men'—he turned aside—'but nuthin' so onsensible as you talkin' 'bout!'

Ratliff looked away without speaking. Gray, feathery ashes covered the coals of the campfire and darkness moved up the slopes of the bluff. He turned toward the river. Night was changing the far swamp into a black wall, rising from the water's edge. The squeak of oars and the foggy call of voices rose to him. He peered through the dusk at the river's slate-colored surface. 'The blind, butt-headed bastards!' he said finally.

'Tain't their heads,' a voice murmured.

Ratliff glanced behind him to find Jake Pettigrew standing near, but the dazed wooden look on his face did not change. From a farther distance Bud True moved toward him. 'Why, boy, you bin on the river as long as you have—'

'It goes for you, too!' Ratliff blurted. 'Both of you'!' He turned his back on them and stood staring at the river.

Late the next afternoon, he returned to Darien and sold his raft. When he had paid Dunk his wages for the trip—they were standing at the mouth of an alley on Broad Street—he shoved a string-tied bundle toward him. 'You kin have 'em, Dunk,' he said. 'I won't need 'em any more.' In it were a broadaxe and a club axe, an auger and a maul. He faced about and headed for the Birdcage.

PART THREE

Robbie

CHAPTER

28

ON THE AFTERNOON OF Gallatin Jackson's funeral, Ratliff put on his Sunday suit and closed the tavern. 'Gat Jackson's about the only man in this 'gaitor hole I'd close up for,' he had announced in the bar earlier. To a dead certainty, his fourteen months in Darien hadn't made him think *more* of anybody in the place! He had known Gat Jackson since his first timber-running days: Gat had been the squarest of the public scalers, to his mind—squarest with the raftsman.

But he was not meditating on Jackson's virtues now, as he buttoned the coat of his iron-hard gray suit against the January wind and quickened his pace along the path that led from his side door. He had felt strangely excited when the notion first jumped him that morning in the kitchen. Again the same feeling ran in his blood, as the question returned to him: Why not get Jackson's place? He had never set public timber-scaling down as a thing he wouldn't do: he had never thought of it before with respect to himself.

At the first measured stroke of the church bell, he had unconsciously quickened his step. Now, as the bell tolled again, leaving a lingering vibration on the wind, it seemed to repeat his question more insistently. Public scalers had always been sort of halfway men to him—polecats more or less. They were beholden to the buyers, but some of them didn't sleep in the same bed with them.

Why did the notion stir him so? You are hungry to get your feet back on a stick of timber, I reckon, he told himself. God, you ought to have had enough of that! But scaling logs would be different: no wind and weather, lonesome river, hard work for short pay. Public scalers made money, a hell of a lot—some of them. A lot more than running a tavern turned out! His had little more than broken even: six hundred dollars for the whole year, and half of that was China's.

Well, hell, you had to learn how! he told himself. Bill Hammersmith's got big rich at it. A stride farther on, he added: But he don't aim to let you! He was suddenly conscious of a metamorphosis in the personality of Hammersmith. An upriver man himself, Hammersmith had been the loud-cursing, river-rough friend of all raftsmen. Ratliff had often obtained his food and lodging on credit, had borrowed money from him to get home on after an unlucky game of cards. It had really been the example of 'Big Bill' that drew him into the tavern business. But since becoming a fellow tradesman, Ratliff had met his closed fist, not open hand. The other tavern-keepers had joined in, but Hammersmith, the biggest, had taken the lead: had kept Ratliff from getting any suitable location for his establishment, made him have to pay cash for his stock of liquor, started a local complaint—he believed—over the noisiness of his place.

Funny how different Bill looks to me now from what he used to, Ratliff thought, turning his head and skeeting a stream of ambeer beyond the edge of the shell sidewalk. And tavern-running, too!

He raised his eyes. The site of the funeral was in view—the clapboards of a church gleamed white between the gray trunks and moss-hung boughs of the live-oaks. There were lines of carriages and buggies under the edge of the trees on either side of the street; beneath the tall spire where the bell tolled, people were entering the doorway. Ratliff unconsciously bent his head to avoid a moss-tail, without taking his eyes off of them. He had never been to a funeral in Darien, nor any other churchy gathering. This was a different–looking crowd from what he was used to seeing. The women held themselves so high and the men all had on derbies. He straightened the broad-brimmed black wool on his own head and stepped up.

Near the doorway he found an empty pew. The church was already half full. He recognized a polished, tufted dome down front: old man George of Stuyvesant-George. The bushy-haired man beside him must be one of those foreign-country fellows—consuls. Hell of a lot of women in the house, Ratliff thought, glancing about, unable to find a single one who looked familiar. His gaze fixed on three young ladies, sitting still and erect, across the church from him. Beneath perched-on hats, their soft white faces seemed shadowed in respectful reverie. Their profiles were not similar, but somehow they looked enough alike to be triplets. Ratliff had seen Darien's big rich driving by in carriages, but not these hand-raised house cats.

The whole town's turning out for old Gat, he thought. He drew his hat nearer him on the bench, as a frock-coated fat man pushed in between the pews and sat down at the other end. Hell, Gat Jackson was well-to-do! He had been making five or six thousand a year for twenty-odd years, I reckon. Nothing wrong with that: not in Darien. It's like China says: the only Mister in Darien is Mr. Dollar Bill. *You* could make that much on the Boom! Maybe more. There's damn few running the river who don't know you—rafthands stick to an upriver man—and you—it ought to be a killing. Ratliff batted his eyes, then his gaze drifted off to a sealskin cape, a wine-colored velvet collar, a gold-headed cane that leaned against the arm of a pew.

After a moment he frowned. Hell, there's nothing really wrong with being a public scaler! He doesn't *have* to be a son-of-a-bitch.

The deep, vibrating tones of an organ spread through the church—the people around him were getting to their feet. Ratliff stood up and listened to the intonations of the preacher, as slow-

303

footed men bore the black coffin down the aisle. In his seat again, he gazed at the surpliced choir behind the pulpit. Their faces were lifted, their voices rose above the low moaning of the organ. It was a sad, floating-away sound.

As the singing continued, his mind drifted from the scene. He saw again—as if it had been yesterday—the semicircle of raftsmen before him on the Altamaha bluff at Clayhole Creek—the shaggy-eyed, taciturn, questioning faces; felt the hard, jerky force in his chest surge up through his throat—take off in a whirr of words: his plan handed down from Up Yonder. Yes, he was sure then that the Old Marster had put it on him to lead the raftsmen out of bondage.

The singing ceased, the organ died away. He lowered his gaze and settled down into this straight-backed pew, the fine-clothed, rustly crowd about him. From the pulpit, the preacher spoke in sententious tones. Ratliff wondered if he had taken the paper money out of his cash drawer: he couldn't recall hiding it under the loose floor-board. Then he remembered that it was in his pocket.

Somehow, rafthands had come to look different to him during the past year, he reflected irrelevantly—different across the counter from him. The image of Josiah Well's loose-legged, crumpled form lying on his tavern floor rose in his mind. He had flattened Josiah out for getting smart-aleck over a plate of eggs. Then the whole Wells tribe took it up, not to fight, the scum, but to mouth around with decent raftsmen and try to stop them from trading with him. He had finally had to back water—to do some explaining out amongst them—or shut up shop! And he had been coming up short every month as it was.

Ratliff frowned down at his hat. Still, it's not so much the raftsmen as it is the job: you weren't cut out to be a grub-toter, nor a drink-pourer. By God, you're a timberman!

Fleetingly, the circle of men on the bluff reappeared to him. Their faces had lowered, their heads were threatening him—like fighting goats! His big lip loosened, twitched. You took off, but those butt-

304

heads wouldn't follow, he said to himself. You knew you had been appointed, but the Old Marster had forgotten to say anything about it to those bullies. His face spread in a smile. He glanced quickly about him, then went on with his thoughts. I reckon that song's done sung! And somebody's goin' to scale their timber—one way or another. You could give the rafthand all he's got comin' to him—take care of those slick enough to deserve it. Hell, a public scaler is a timberman—he don't have to have fleas on him! The measured step of the pallbearers sounded in the aisle. He looked up. Behind the coffin the corps of timber inspectors walked in a body. That was the bunch he wanted to talk to.

It was the first of the following week before he finally ran up on John Holden on Broad Street. He had chosen Holden as the scaler he liked best, next to Gat Jackson. It had been Holden who had measured that first raft of mixed logs he and Poss brought to Darien—'way back, when he was a boy—Holden who gave them the five dollars to get home on. The old man stood at the corner, rubbing his flaring nose, as Ratliff approached, speaking.

'Who's out for Gat Jackson's place?'

'Why, I don't know'—Holden wiped his now white mustache as he drew down his hand—'I guess that boy who's been night watchman at the Boom will apply. Who've you heard?'

'Nobody.' Ratliff leaned against the brick wall of the building beside them. 'Except I bin studyin' 'bout it.' He paused. 'I might be willin' to take it myself—if it ain't too much trouble to get.'

The frog-throats beneath Holden's eyes pulsed as he blinked at the faintly smiling, serious face in front of him. 'It isn't got,' he said finally.

'Oh, I know: the council picks the man,' Ratliff returned in haste to clear his meaning, yet even as he spoke he felt a strangeness in Holden's reply—he had expected a different response to his announcement. 'But they don't know a timberman from a log-turner! Who tells 'em who to pick?'

Holden straightened up. The stiff-fronted shirt and standing collar he wore—he had finished his day's work and had re-dressed—increased his rigidity. 'It is to be supposed that only timbermen will apply. The council is concerned with the character of the man it selects for such a public trust: his probity and citizenship.'

Ratliff opened his eyes in astonishment. Was the old man freezing up on him? 'I thought you scalers had a say in it,' he said.

'That would be improper, Sutton—highly improper!' Holden turned away.

As he moved off, Ratliff stared at his stiffened back. Jesus, he said to himself, I wonder what's eatin' on the old water turkey! Swiftly, his mind reviewed the recent past: Holden had never been in his tavern, but he had hardly expected that in its out-of-the-way place. What could he have taken exception to? It didn't make sense: he had seen the old man only a half-dozen times since he came to Darien and he had always been friendly till now. Ratliff stood away from the wall, slowly rubbing his jaw. It used to be 'Snake' when he was scaling my timber, he thought. Probity, probity: what the hell is probity?

During the succeeding week he broached his interest in the vacant position to three other inspectors and to Inspector General Spalding, without enlisting any support, or even gaining a clear idea of where they stood. All of them could not be holding an unknown grudge against him, yet they were strangely cold and close-mouthed. He could not get over his surprise at their complete disregard of fitting experience for the job. He, Ratliff, knew more about timber and timber-runners than any man in Darien, yet every single one of them ignored this fact. It grew to be annoying.

Finally he concluded that it was the case of the tavern-keepers again, and a little worse. The damn dogs figure you might take a little business away from them if you ever got on that Public Boom, I reck-

306

on—and I reckon you would, he told himself, as he leaned against the doorjamb of his tavern, watching Eddie, the barkeep and general handyman, polish glasses, and waiting for the morning's first customer.

For a time he felt inclined to ease his effort for the job: he had counted mainly on the scalers for help—and it looked like they weren't after a timberman, anyhow. To hell with these people, he thought: they don't know a timberman from a log-turner. And he sensed about him a curious, town-mannered, web-covered hostility that he did not define, but that kept him uncomfortable.

Still he did not give up his quest. He had really known that he would not—if Darien didn't know a timberman when she saw one it was up to him to learn her. He decided to lay his problem before Marcus. China couldn't, or wouldn't, help him. She wanted him to stay with the tavern, not quit just as he was getting a start, she said. The Jewish storekeeper had no connection with the timber business, Ratliff knew, but Marcus kept himself informed about everything.

That night, perched on a high stool in his hardware store, Marcus regarded Ratliff with heavy-lidded impassivity and heard him out before speaking. He seemed in no eagerness to commit himself, even when Ratliff had ended and sat looking up at him. He scratched his gray head.

It was his guess that the timber merchants had the biggest say in who was to be picked, certainly in who was not to be taken—though the inspectors' objection would be heard, too. He was afraid Ratliff had handicaps he had not considered. They would unquestionably favor a Darienite, and Ratliff, in their eyes, was hardly a Darienite. That was not the worst of it: among the buyers, Ratliff must recollect, he would be remembered, not so much for his knowledge of timber as for the fact that he had—here Marcus paused and chose his word—'skinned' them on the logs they bought.

Sure, Ratliff expected them to remember it, but he failed to get Marcus's slant. He had counted on that to help him, he said: an assurance that he wouldn't get skinned by the timber-runners: it would be to his own interest not to.

Marcus doubted that the buyers would take that view—and he was even more dubious about Ratliff's open relationship with China, but he only shook his head and said, 'Maybe so.'

Ratliff found that he had no friends among the scalers who would pull for him; he had never been friendly enough with any of the buyers to expect it and he didn't even know the names of the councilmen.

Marcus scratched his head at length. Ratliff couldn't use what he didn't have, he said finally, he had best work with what he had. The negro policeman, Grenade, was a friend of his. Talk to Grenade. He had been in town and county politics a long time and knew a lot. McIntosh County's big negro population had no vote; still, it had political influence. A newcomer could not be choosy about his help.

Ratliff looked down his immobile face at Marcus, but finally he smiled. 'Sho',' he said. 'Grenade's a good nigger and I have favored him more'n once. I could take help from him.'

During the past fall, Ratliff had opened a bar and lodging-room for negro rafthands in the upper story of the old residence housing the tavern. Grenade had paid it occasional visits and usually Ratliff had provided him with a drink on the house. But the snuff-colored deputy sheriff shook his head when Ratliff asked if he could offer a suggestion, or give him a hand. That was too big a turn for Grenade to tote.

'Christ! I wish I knew more about the set-up here,' Ratliff said, squinting tensely at the barroom door as the two of them walked toward it. 'There's obliged to be some way to get next to this job.'

Outside, Grenade started for the steps but turned back. There was one colored fellow in the town who might be able to help Ratliff: the Reverend Jonas Caldwell—he was really the leader of the colored people in McIntosh County and drew some water with city and county officials. Grenade would talk to him.

The Reverend Caldwell was slow to take interest in Ratliff's case, according to Grenade, but finally he sent word that he could get something done, if Ratliff were prepared to stand the expense—it would cost him five hundred dollars.

Ratliff looked sharply at Grenade's somber, brown face, when he received this message in the tavern bar near closing time—then broke into a laugh. But Grenade assured him that Caldwell could do something, if he said he would, and would, if he took the money. Ratliff said, 'Jesus, I wouldn't be after the job if I had five hundred bucks!' But he did not dismiss the offer. Upon reflection it sounded sensible that a Darien councilman would be out to make what money he could out of the job, and especially with an outsider like himself. Still he didn't have five hundred dollars in the world. He had only a little over two hundred of the three hundred he cleared for the year—and passing it up through black hands would be a dark and doubtful route. He returned Grenade with a counter-proposal and at the end of a week's dickering he had agreed to raise two hundred dollars. On a mid-February night Grenade took him out to the preacher's house in the negro colony, to do business.

Ratliff still doubted that the negro could be trusted with so much money, or had the connections he claimed (though he was intrigued by the notion of a councilman's having a negro preacher as a front-man for his slick business). He was not altogether at ease as he followed his escort through the darkness toward Darien's outer rim. He believed Grenade was straight: he had known a number of straight negroes on the river, and a straighter man never lived than Uncle Mundy, white or black—but a town nigger and a preacher!

In the dingy-walled room the Reverend Caldwell referred to as his 'parsorium', Ratliff found himself confronted by a great square chunk of a negro, rising from an armchair behind a roller-top desk. His color was lighter than Grenade's and he had loose, rounded jowls. He wore a black coat, a wing collar, and brass spectacles. He sat down and began talking.

'I have become recognizant through Brother Grenade, heah, of your truly faithful and laudashous friendship for our race,' he began.

Ratliff did not like the preacher's oozy bass voice and wordiness, but he continued to listen quietly, while Caldwell explained that it would be necessary for him to hold several shoutings with refreshments to get his people united in support of Ratliff, that he would have to organize a committee to accompany him when he visited his friends of the city council, that he could not undertake the project without money in hand.

'That's all mighty fine, Caldwell,' Ratliff said. His lip loosened, but his voice carried an edge. "However, I want to see the man who can deliver the goods. I aim to see that my money gits to him and that it gits me the job!'

The negro's short, thick neck bulged over his collar and he snatched off his spectacles. 'Don't you come heah and insult me!' he blurted. 'It looks like you got funny ideas 'bout this thing.'

Ratliff's face became expressionless. This damn town preacher was biggity, as well as proper-talking! He had let himself in for something by fooling around with these burr-heads. And the nigger's hands would be as oozy as his voice. He came slowly to his feet. But this is the only thing you've found that looks like a toehold, he told himself. And, hell, you're in Darien now—not on the river! His head tilted backward and he grinned. 'All right, preacher,' he said. 'Just furgit it.' He took two one-hundred-dollar bills from his pocketbook and held them up. 'Le's let the money do the talkin'.'

When he quit the Reverend Caldwell's parsorium, he had left one of the bills and a torn half of the other with the preacher. He would deliver the final half when his name had been presented to and acted upon by the council.

That body met on the first Tuesday evening in March and Ratliff watched its proceedings—secretly since the applicants were not expected to attend—from the courtroom gallery reserved for colored people. Screened by a black delegation, he sat in the seat behind that of the Reverend Caldwell. He felt well pleased with himself. The scalers, from whom he had a right to look for help—according to river ways—had refused to lift a finger, and were probably privately against him. But he had run around them. He had got next to the council without their aid, knowledge, or consent. He now had Caldwell's assurance that the skinny bubble-eyed councilman, sitting in front of the mayor's rostrum on the far left, would put him over. This was a new and none-too-choosy game for him, but he figured he had played it pretty well. His face was still and his loosened lips gave it an almost tranquil look.

The applications for inspectorship were considered. The skinny councilman rose and Ratliff leaned forward to look at him. He spoke in a thin, almost toneless voice—about a white man's country—the white man's responsibility for the colored man. This seemed pretty far afield, but Ratliff decided to give him time to head off in the right direction. He sat back in his seat.

Darien had always tried to live up to this responsibility, the councilman went on—had considered the welfare of its black population, even naming a colored police officer to enforce the law understandingly. And Darien's law-abiding colored citizens had appreciated it, were still appreciative. But there had been one long-standing oversight that had been brought to his attention lately. Although almost half of the raftsmen bringing timber to Darien markert were black and although there were eleven men elected to inspect their timber, there had never been a single man selected with a view to looking out for the colored man, to paying attention to him. For many reasons, the raftsman whose skin was black and whose mouth was closed where he came into conflict with a white man should have somebody specially commissioned to look out for him at the Public Boom.

The colored leaders of Darien and the rank and file had found a man of their choice, the councilman was happy to say, a man eminently fitted for the place. Ratliff leaned forward again and craned around Caldwell's back as the speaker enumerated his qualifications: 'a reputable citizen of our little city. . . a well-to-do business man. . .whose knowledge of timber and familiarity with the timber-runner, especially the colored man, is second to none. . .'

The fellow was dressing him up pretty fancy, but, by God, that last was right, Ratliff thought.

When the speaker sat down, an erect, gray-haired man across the chamber got to his feet, after a moment's conference with a neighbor. Ratliff's spokesman, whispering with the two members who had gathered at his desk, stared at him glassily. The gray-haired man was asking the clerk to repeat the applicant's name. 'I don't know him,' he said in a quick, firm voice, 'but the proposal advanced for his support is most extraordinary.' Ratliff frowned. He wondered which side this fellow was on. Then: 'Since when has the yaller nigger borne anything for the black rafthand, except an open razor?' The old jack-in-the-pulpit was right, but—Ratliff stopped thinking to listen. 'Who is this R. P. Sutton, and what is his color, may I ask?'

There was a hush, then the sound of chuckling spread over the chamber. Ratliff's face hardened and he lowered his eyes.

'I think I am prepared to answer your question.' The voice was suave and precise. Ratliff noticed that members were straightening up and smiling and that his man's face had gone into a dour squint. He craned his neck to look down at the speaker. He had smooth black hair, parted in the middle, and stood with his finger of one hand slipped into the pocket of his buttoned coat.

'I don't have the ambiguous privilege of an acquaintance with the man,' he said, 'but I have taken the trouble to investigate him, and I want to say that in the light of my findings, his application for the position of public inspector strikes me as even more fantastic than the argument of our curiously quixotic fellow councilman.' (The lines between Ratliff's eyebrows tightened, then he looked from the speaker to the smirking faces about the room.) 'I confess I cannot appreciate Councilman Jaeger's viewpoint, but I wonder if he knows, and if you, Major Macgregor, and the other councilmen here, know that R. P. Sutton, in the timber trade, goes by the fitting sobriquet of "Snake"—and that he is the same Snake Sutton who was indicted some years ago by a McIntosh County Grand Jury for doctoring his logs?'

Some of the negroes in the delegation shifted in their seats to look back at him, and below, upward flicking chins showed thin smiles, but Ratliff's face had become expressionless and he kept his eyes on the black hair parted in the middle.

'The question has been raised as to his color,' said the man. 'I have seen him and I will hazard the opinion that his face would be white, if given ablutions and a shave, but of course, I can't speak with authority on that point.'

Kaleidoscopic images of lifting eyebrows, twisting lips, shrugging shoulders below him, and broad, curious black faces at his elbow caught in the corners of Ratliff's eyes, but he did not shift their blazing gaze.

The council had never taken official cognizance of them, said the speaker, going on, but there had at times been rumors of the presence of 'women of questionable character' in the city for the 'entertainment of our commercial guests.' Possibly some of the members had even heard of one by the name of Swann, called China. He had been reliably informed that this individual was the *fille de joie* of this applicant for high public office. He must perforce be even blunter with his fellow councilmen: *fille de joie* was scarcely the word—kept woman. And that was wide of the mark still. It appeared that the woman was doing the keeping!

The color drained from Ratliff's face and his breathing came heavily.

As the man sat down, Jaeger rose haltingly to his feet. The gray-haired Macgregor was before him. 'Gentlemen, I am shocked! This whole thing is preposterous! I suppose a man so abandoned as this applicant has been described to be could have no sense of decency, but I am amazed that he has found a sponsor in this body.' He fixed Jaeger with his gaze for a moment, then turned and glanced up at he negroes in the gallery. 'I am confident that the colored citizens of Darien have been deceived in the character of the man who has been foisted upon them, for their support.' His eyes fastened on Caldwell. 'I say, I am confident they would not knowingly support a criminal, an ex-outlaw and a fugitive from justice, a whoremonger and a procurer!'

Ratliff was on his feet. His eyes were black, his face like hammered lead. He stepped quickly into the aisle and started toward the gallery railing, but Caldwell's great back blocked his way. The negro preacher had stood up and was speaking: 'Your honors, we have been foisted on—we—'

Ratliff stopped and stared. Then his eyes shifted to the black, ogling faces of the delegation. He wheeled about and left the gallery.

CHAPTER

29

RATLIFF MET CHINA on the landing of the softly lighted stairway, after an hour's heel-pounding had finally brought him to the Birdcage. When she saw his still, grayish face, caught the copper glint in the depths of his black eyes, a sweat of fright swept over her and she jerked to a halt. 'What is it, Snake?'

She had grasped his hand and, as he passed on by, she followed him back up the stairs to her room. She closed the door behind her and looked up at him.

'Let's get out of this Goddamned hole!'

She winced and stood away from the door.

'This sweet-smelling chinch-bed is no place for me, naer you, neither!' He drove the words at her with harsh, even emphasis.

'What happened, Snake?'

Echoes of a mincing, mocking voice pursued him. The hot eyes, looking through slits in his face, grew momentarily abstract. He'd got enough of the sleek-headed councilman's double-talk to know he'd been called a pimp and his blood questioned. The old man, too. 'We bin sleepin' with skunks,' he said. 'Got to burn our clo'es.'

'What skunks?' She saw his sweat-wet shirt, felt the heat from his body.

Images of the smirking, half-hidden faces in the pit, the staring loafers in the courthouse corridor, flickered before him. It had been this crowd—he had seen three constables and the two men opposing him for the inspectorship in it—that prevented his waiting for his defamers. But he had felt unequal to the crowd in more than a physical sense. They knew what the councilman's double-talk meant!—knew the big, mystifying words that so maddened him. 'I've been a fool one time,' he said, 'but I don't aim to keep on bein' one –aer let you!'

'How a fool?' She searched his hard-packed face.

He had felt baffled by the enmity of the men in the council chamber—as he strode along under the live-oaks in the darkness—the crowd outside the door. It had seemed both mysterious and corrupt. Finally he had settled upon the course that took him to the Birdcage. He clenched his hands at his sides. 'I can tell a rotten egg when it hits me, all right!' By God, China, le's sell out and clear out? Dead River, the swamp patch, is a damn sight better than this place—it stinks!'

'What the hell's it all about?'

'Look. We're gittin' married and headin' for the old place—marryin' you won't hinder me none up on the Oconee!'

China's eyebrows gathered. 'For Christ's sake! What ails you, Snake?' She put out a hand, but hesitated before his rigid body. He glittered like a knife blade driven into the floor. There was something fine and dangerous about his look. But this talk wouldn't do. 'Tell me what happened!'

He went on, as if she had not spoken. 'I want you made my woman by law, anyhow—my younguns to know their pappy and mammy, and be proud to know 'em!'

China looked beyond him at the dark wardrobe against the wall. When he had first quit the river, when they had begun laying their plans to open the tavern, and lawyer was drawing up the partnership papers, Ratliff had offered to make it a 'full partnership' with a marriage license. China remembered the moment: in this room, standing almost where they were now. It had made her swell up and want to cry. But there had followed a chill of dim consciousness that such a bond would turn over everything she had to him—though she had not admitted to herself the cause of her restraint even then, and now she did not remember it. She had declined, because marriage with her would handicap Snake in Darien. She was right, then, but now? Wasn't what he said about the backwoods true? Was it? She lifted an unsteady hand to her hair. 'This is all fine, but how in—Snake, break down just long enough to tell me what happened to you.'

He squinted, as if in pain, and lowered his gaze. The thought of reporting the insults renewed his humiliation—the more, because he was so unsure about them. 'No dandified tumblebug's goin' to make his ball—blackguard me and you both—not and get away with it!' he said.

The buff-colored skin beneath her eyes hardened. 'Oh, they pulled me into it, too—hey? The councilmen? What'd they call yuh—a whoremaster? Maybe a pimp?'

He blinked.

'It would be like some of those stiff-necked, pious-puking hypocrites!' She paused for an instant, then accepted his silence as affirmation. 'I didn't want you to try out for that job, you know. I didn't tell you but I knew we weren't ready for it. I'm still named around heah as your woman—and, after all, I am a whore'—her gaze lowered—'At least, they call me that.'

He rocked on his feet. It hurt him to hear China admit to the name, but she could not very well help herself as long as she stayed in business. That was why he had come. After all, she was open to things the councilmen called her—in Darien. He broke his stance and took her by the shoulder. 'You won't be when I marry you—you won't be when we git to Dead River—there won't be anybody callin' you that on the Oconee, not where we can heah it. They won't make no point of it, nohow.'

But China avoided his gaze. Her vision of Dead River, the backwoods, was not his: she saw the broken, wild-rattled shanty on Buzzard's Ridge and her poor addled mother whimpering and rocking before a cold fireplace. Her voice was muted when she spoke. 'I kain't see it in the cards, Snake. God knows, I ain't in love with Darien and my business here—and I'd be ready to follow you to hell and back, but just now you mentioned children. That's another thing!' Her mouth grew hard. 'I didn't choose to be a sportin' woman, but I'm one: and I don't aim —whatever I do—to put my brand on any child of mine. Dead River wouldn't be half far enough.'

His hand dropped away. He felt weak in his vitals, as if she had cut him a lick in the small of the back. Goddamn! Was China lining up with his enemies—their enemies? He stared at her. 'I just mentioned young'uns in a general way,' he said. 'I ain't studyin' 'bout a family now. I ain't quittin' Darien to raise a family.'

She blinked and caught her breath. 'It's them councilmen—that's it! I should have guessed what was on your mind before this.' She drew closer, shaking her head. 'Look heah, Snake, you can't do that! On the river you can settle with a fellow who's been blackguardin' you and get away with it. But not in Darien. These fellows won't fight you, and if you kill one of 'em, you'll swing for it—sure as hell. You may be smart, but you can't get away with killin' a Darien councilman.'

'I ain't sayin' what I aim to do.'

'But I know.' She grasped his coat-front with both hands. 'For God's sake, Snake, listen to me. They are tryin' to make a sucker out of you—they want you to start some rough stuff'—her words came fast and at another time they might have sounded wild to her, but now: she had to talk Ratliff out of this madness—'so they can put you on the chain gang, or break your neck. Look heah, that ain't the way to settle with them. You want to pay 'em off in their own kind: somethin' they can understand, sweat and groan and puke about.'

'I can make 'em understand, I reckon.'

'But not in the way you're settin' out, Snake. You've got to beat 'em at their own game to make 'em swallow their words—to make 'em afraid of you and respect you. Money is the only thing that makes a man talk, or hold his tongue, in this town.' Panting, and relaxing her hold, she felt near enough to the truth. She went on: 'Those bastards don't even see they were low-ratin' you: you are just a penniless nobody to them. If you had been Mr. Ten Thousand Dollars, instead of Pocket Change, why you'd have met with bowing and scraping. You wouldn't have known yourself, the way they'd have spread it on.'

Ratliff had avoided China's gaze. Now he broke away. Her refusal to leave with him had shaken him deeply; not that he couldn't again live alone on Dead River, carry out his plans by himself, but he had grown used to thinking of China as a partner, as a part of himself. And to have her back down and want to stay on here in the face of being called a whore and his being called a pimp! He walked slowly toward the fireplace. To take it like she did knocked the props out from under him. But there was more that he could not well define: her saying she couldn't go far enough away to have children, somehow—well, it seemed to be admitting to a whole lot. He lowered himself into a chair and stared at the gray-feathered embers. How can you make these Darien rats scared to call her name, or yours—if she won't join in—back you up? he asked himself.

'Look at it right, Snake.' China pulled up a rocker beside him. 'You're tryin' to take the easy way out, to crawfish. You knew Darien was a son-of-a-bitch when you come here, but you aimed to make her your son-of-a-bitch. You swore to quittin' the river for good—to quit sweatin', stealin', freezin', fightin' over logs to make Darienites rich—raftsmen were born suckers, and you quit 'em to work your way into the big money, take your share from the smart men.' She gave him a sidewise glance. 'You knew, or ought-a known that you were startin' out from scratch, too.'

He did not look up, and she went on. 'The rules are different here, so are the things that count. You were the best shot and axeman on the river, but that ain't worth a dime here. You were the slickest of the timber-runners, but you can't slide on that in Darien. You settled your differences with a maul or a gun on the river, but that don't go a peg in Darien—won't get you anywhere, except the jailhouse. You've got to put those councilmen's names down in your books and bide your time till you are ready to pay 'em off—and first, you've got to catch on to their tricks, not get caught, not be a sucker for 'em.'

He reached for the poker and stirred among the embers on the hearth. Had it been the tricks that got him: that had made the job and the town all at once seem rotten at the core and covered over with highfalutin ways and words that he could not understand and did not want to be around? He had caught on when that peewillie called him a pimp! But he had been unsure, for a moment afterward had questioned himself. Could he learn such tricks? Did he want to?

She got up and leaned against the mantelpiece, facing him, 'Jesus, I had been waitin' for you to come by to spill some good news.' He raised the end of the poker, but stared on at the embers. 'Big news—if you're not runnin' away, skippin' out on me—if you still want to lick Darien with her own fancy coachwhip?'

He eyed her briefly, then returned his gaze to the fireplace. Could China be right? By God, he couldn't think of a better way to stop a dog's slobbering mouth than by putting a gunhole through it—and putting the fear of God in all dogs. Still, she was right about his not knowing what goes here, what he could get away with. Was he a first-timer, refusing to treat Rag Point? Had he tried to plunge too fast? Would he be flushing the covey again to quit Darien? The thing he hadn't figured on was having to leave without China—was he ready for that? He felt strangely mixed up over her. He pushed slowly back into his chair. 'Spill it,' he said.

'I got an option on the brick warehouse on the Bluff, there at Broad and North Way—can get a ten-year lease! We can make the biggest, best-payin' tavern in Darien out of it.'

He picked up the poker again, rolled it between his hands. 'I ain't cut out to be no tavern-keeper,' he said.

'You ain't had no chance to know, over there where you've been.' She put her foot down on the poker-end to enforce his attention. 'Besides, you wouldn't have to do the running of it for long. We could put in a gamblin'-hall. Make big money right from the start. After you've piled up the spondoolix, you can do what you damn well please in Darien. It's the chance we've been after for fourteen months—the thing every tavern-keeper in town has been tryin' to keep us from gettin'.'

'Sho'. That's a fine spot,' he said tepidly.

'Like as not Bill Hammersmith had found out we've got this option—like as not he paid that councilman to try to make you mad enough to lose your head and do somethin' to get run out of town about.'

'They didn't know I was hearin' 'em.'

'That don't make no difference.'

Ratliff stood up. 'No, I reckon not—not in getting' people down on you.'

'You buried Diggs McMillan's bad names for four years—when you were a boy—waitin' for the right chance, didn't you?' She slipped her hand into his coat-pocket and drew him toward her. 'All I want you to do is wait till you're sure you've got the right chance, Snake.'

'And the right tricks.' He looked away. 'To pit myself against a polecat.'

CHAPTER

30

EARLY IN JUNE, Ratliff sat in the small bedroom-office of his new Altamaha Tavern, eating a midnight snack. His ears were attuned to the noises drifting in through the open door from the gambling-hall, in which his cubicle cut off a corner. But this listening was subconscious. Stretched out in his chair, he gazed up at the ceiling and gave himself over to chewing on a ham sandwich.

Less attentively, he ruminated, he savored another satisfaction. The Broad-Street warehouse had been remodeled for his enterprise, and that day—completing the first full month's operation—he had found his take to be almost as great as his earnings for the whole of the previous year. His fresh comfort flowed into the gap left by a feeling about himself now absent, filled some of the emptiness, and he sensed his peculiarity without reflecting upon it. Temporarily, he had accepted Darien on her own terms and he had been forced to temporize with her estimate of him. But the climb upward had started: he was making headway.

He washed the last of the sandwich down with a draught of beer and stepped to the doorway. At the other end of the hall, under a shaded swinging lamp, a group of raftsmen and sailors clung to a dice table. The dealer's slender rake flicked across the green-baize top. To the right of the dicing group, a half-dozen rough-shirted men bent over a poker table, and at another, almost opposite his office, a ring of brushy heads were following the swift hands of the blackjack dealer.

Ratliff's gaze came to a halt, remained fixed. On the far side of the table a straw hat and slender face shone whitely among the black wools and whiskers. The man's shapely nose and chin flicked upward. The lingering taste of Ratliff's sandwich went bitter in his mouth. For an instant he had thought it was Anthony George, the younger member who had maligned him at the council meeting. He felt a touch of nausea.

But it was not George—this fellow was a blond. He had seen him before somewhere, too: the sharply cut nose, the look of amiable assurance about the mouth. His eyebrows puckered. Son of old man Dale of Dale and Coventry. The squirt had been pointed out to him the week before. Ratliff's frown deepened, and after a moment he sauntered over to the card game.

On the table before Dale, before the high-buttoned front of his gray coat, were stacked four chips: one blue, three red. Ratliff glanced at his dealer. He ought never to let that doorkeeper deal! He stepped around Dale's side and bent a smiling face toward him. 'Like to see yuh just a minute, podner, if you don't mind.'

At the doorway of the small office, Dale looked up, puzzled.

Ratliff's green eyes were like glass. "How much down are yuh?'

'Down? Why, I don't know—some twenty-four or five dollars. What is it?'

'And two-and-a-half makes twenty-seven fifty.' Ratliff counted the money off on his roller-top desk. 'No hard feelin's stranger. I know you didn't know, but this is a raftman's hangout.' He stuck the bills toward Dale.

Dale's arms stiffened at his sides and his face paled, then reddened dully. He took a step toward Ratliff. 'What are you trying to insinuate?'

Ratliff blinked, remained with the bills held out in his hand. Christ! The fool! He was trying to give him his money back—so he wouldn't go running to the law. 'Not a thing, podner. Just, you don't know the rules these river-runners play by—and I didn't want your gittin' in the wrong place to cost you nuthin'.'

'I'm prepared to withstand my losses!'

There was a pause in which the men remained facing each other: the one rigid, the other with his hand extended. Then Ratliff put the money in his pocket and drew out his chewing tobacco. He offered it to Dale, who shook his head. 'I didn't aim to git your dander up,' he said.

As Dale watched Ratliff put a chew in his mouth, his stance limbered and he grinned. 'I'm free, white, twenty-one, and then some—if you play any card games here that I don't know—or rules, either—I want to learn them. Even if it costs me a few quid.' He turned toward the door.

Ratliff stood gazing at his back irresolutely, then followed him to the card table. He sat down and assumed the dealership. He said, the lamplight giving his tilted face an inanimate glaze: 'Mr. Dale, heah, ain't never played skin. I'll run a hand.'

When Ratliff locked up the hall for the night at two o'clock, Dale accompanied him to the bar. He tarried for a nightcap. 'I remember you,' he said, following Ratliff's movements on the other side of the counter. 'Someone pointed you out to me when I was here three years ago. You are Snake Sutton.'

'Yeah.' Ratliff was pouring his own drink and did not look up.

'I thought I knew your face when we were in your office. I had always wanted to meet you, because of that fast one you pulled on Marmaduke Pitt: the hollow logs.' He grinned and downed his drink.

324

Ratliff was yawning, but he kept wary eyes on his customer. The fellow couldn't get sore: he had won twenty dollars—Ratliff had seen to that. And he would see to it that his thick-headed doorkeeper did not let him in again.

But Geoffrey Dale had every intention on going back, as he drove toward his home in the Ridge, Darien's fashionable suburb. He had found no other diversion half so interesting, since his return two weeks before. That was the drawback to Darien: dull, straight-laced, provincial.

The only son of Edward Dale, senior partner of Darien's largest timber firm, Geoffrey had spent little time in the scene and source of his family livelihood since he was fourteen: he had been sent to Harrow and then to Oxford, in paternal tradition. Though thirty years in America and married to an American, a Darienite wife, the elder Dale still considered himself an Englishman. Whatever else this education may have done for Geoffrey, it had sharpened his critical judgments of Darien and its mode of life. After a five-month flier at settling down in his father's business three years before, he had changed his aim to law and his residence to Yale University, whence he had recently returned to enter Dale and Coventry again.

Tonight, he reflected, he had had the stodgiest, most parlor-bound of evenings—until eleven o'clock! This riverman's tavern was as tough a spot as anything he had found during this stay on the Continent—with less pretension. And the raftsmen were colorful rowdies.

Sutton's still face flickered before him: almost tranquil, he thought, yet there was an underlying watchfulness about it. He slackened the horse's reins and the sound of the buggy wheels on the shell road softened. This Snake Sutton seemed to be as much of a person as he had ever fancied him to be. Funny about your flaring up, he told himself. You didn't grasp his meaning at all.

They were exclusive, these river-runners: didn't want to admit gentry into their sanctum. Or was it that? There was nothing of the

English lower order about them, to be sure—except, maybe, exclusiveness. No, they were really barbarians—red-beards from up the river—had their own slant on things, own customs. He had caught an inkling of this during his first stretch in the office—even as a boy, he had been attracted to them.

Shocking how little the people in Darien knew about them: to Darienites they were merely sheep in the corral to be sheared—though they had more of a goatish look and odor! Geoffrey slumped in his seat and put his feet on the dashboard. He had always wanted to get to know the raftsmen. Yes, you'll visit this Sutton again, he told himself.

In his room, Ratliff stood before the window staring out into the darkness and enjoying the warmth of the liquor he had drunk with Dale. As proper-talking as that bastard George, he said to himself. But George's name brought him no active sense of depression now. The day after that night, after the March meeting, he had learned that the council did not name anybody to the inspectorship, that a spokesman for the scalers proposed to cut off the job, reduce the number—nothing had been done. Ratliff had scarcely listened when he heard it, but somehow it had come to make a difference.

A sudden smile twitched at his lips and he rubbed his face with his hand. Christ! He hadn't any idea of being friends with this peewillie: he just wanted to see to it that Dale didn't make trouble for him. But there was something about the name: it talked timber, timber strength! Ratliff found himself remembering that the inspectorship had never been filled—remembering, with a feeling of excitement, suspense. Yes, Goddamn you! you still want the job, he told himself, turning toward his wooden cot.

Three days later, Geoffrey sought Ratliff out in his barroom, under the excuse of asking for assistance. His father had recently discharged the firm's private inspector, for getting drunk—or rather, for not getting sober, he said. A man out of the office had been inspecting logs for them, but he was worse sober than the other fellow drunk. Did Sutton happen to know of a good man for the job? Geoffrey was seated at a table with the julep he had bought and Ratliff stood leaning on the back of a chair.

The chair creaked. 'A plug-puller!' he said, and looked away. 'You want me to pick you up a plug-puller?'

Geoffrey clasped his hands together above his glass. 'Why not?' His eyes brightened and his jaw lowered so that his under lip curved and his upper lip protruded, his cheeks sloping inward. It was an habitual expression of amusement. 'I consider your opinion expert.'

Ratliff grunted and looked down at him without smiling. 'These heah plug-pullers are always gettin' fried for boozin'—I don't keep up with who's workin' and who ain't.'

Geoffrey sobered. 'We'd appreciate it if you'd keep an eye out for us.' Then he changed the subject, recalling the tale he had heard of Sutton's visit upon old Sheriff McDooly—memorable for its dramatic brevity. He implied his admiration and asked questions.

Ratliff followed Geoffrey's English way of speaking none too readily. He watched him closely and made taciturn replies. Fool way to talk, he thought, but I'd better try to get it. And he eyed Geoffrey's dress and gestures as carefully. China had called him one of Darien's glass-covered gods.

When he had gone, Ratliff sat down at the table and called for a straight whiskey. He repeated Dale's words: *keep an eye out for us.* They had never quite left the back side of his head, all the time the talk went on. It seemed strange, funny! Of all jobs, too! But there's something to this fellow's asking you that, he told himself, tapping an outstretched foot against the table leg. It's plain that he likes you. And you ain't takin' up time with this high-class Darien crook for nuthin'. You were thinkin' just now about studyin' his ways—but workin' fur him? A company plug-puller! He came out of his chair quickly and slammed it back under the table.

Later he told himself that he had a good business and didn't want to get into the timber game and that Dale wouldn't give him the job, anyhow. But he did not get rid of the suggestion with this dismissal. Dale visited his bar again later in the week and asked if he had spotted a man for the place.

Ratliff felt a strange tension in his arms, as he wiped on at the bar before he spoke. 'Nope,' he said. 'Not yet.'

Dale set his glass down. 'I was in hopes—I'd relied on you finding us the right man!'

Ratliff moved a little way down the bar, reaching for a yellow splattering of liquor. Hell the fool does want you to take the job, he told himself. And, does he expect me to give up a business, making me three times as much? Christ, you wouldn't have to do that! He straightened up to shake out his rag and his gaze fastened on Dale's. But it was not the questioning eyes across the counter that kept him staring vacantly. It was a vision of red-carpeted steps: the plug-puller's place, entrance within the timber crowd's stockage, old man Dale's backing—to the public inspectorship. That doorway stood open and luminous. 'I reckon I might take a—' The rag slipped out of his hand: his voice had sounded unnatural. He bent down to retrieve the cloth. Like Sneaky Colquitt's! Fool notion! Yet, he felt inhibited. He began mopping again. 'I might take another look around,' he said.

Dale had seen that for a moment Ratliff thought of proposing himself. He was surprised. He lifted his glass to drink. But not too much surprised: Sutton's behavior had been premonitory—this fellow loved the smell of logs—it was in his blood! Dale knew that. Would his father permit him to hire the notorious Snake? He finished his drink and turned away. 'We won't do anything until I hear from you.'

Later, driving home, he meditated on his casual enterprise. The job would place this Sutton where he could really have a look at him.

A more picturesque specimen of the Altamaha raftsmen could not be found: this fellow was a local Robin Hood—a Rob Roy, anyway.

At sight of the wrought-iron gate and the shell driveway, curving off through the grounds of the Dale home, he frowned. His father might prove difficult.

The younger Dale found justification for his suspicion when he set upon the elder after supper in the comfort of his library armchair. Edward Dale brandished his luxuriant side-whiskers—still wavy and yellow, despite his fifty-odd years. 'Oh, I say, son, the fellow is an outlaw—or was.'

Geoffrey sat on an ottoman, cupping a knee in his hands. 'Sutton only got caught at what he had been doing and believing in all his life—and what most other raftsmen still do: plugging logs. And he didn't want to go to jail for it. Besides, it was all settled out of court long ago.' He smiled ironically. 'Can't say but that I admire him for what he did to Pitt—you, father, have never approved of Pitt's practices.'

The elder Dale brushed a hand over his nose and forehead—as shapely, though bolder than his son's. He wondered if Geoffrey's leaving law school without finishing was the wise thing: the boy had education enough, was capable, but he must settle down. Geoffrey was urging his father to see the matter from Sutton's point of view.

'But this man,' the father interrupted—'your Uncle Don told me, after the council meeting where he had the brass to offer for a public inspectorship—this rowdy lives openly with a prostitute!'

Geoffrey was sure that the reports had been exaggerated.

The elder Dale's whiskers settled upon his chest and he toyed with the book he held closed on his finger.

Other men had been known to visit these women.

His father frowned and spoke resolutely: such a thing could not be winked at in Darien.

329

But prostitutes were taken as casually as bread by raftsmen—Geoffrey's eyes were glistening—Sutton had probably never heard of Darien's queasy disapproval. Give the fellow a chance!

His father opened his book without replying. Geoffrey released his knee and stood up. Not bad for the first sitting, he thought; better suspend.

Ratliff did not confront the decision he had deferred at the moment of his conversation with Geoffrey until he had locked up the tavern for the night and had gone to his room upstairs. He placed a chair by the window and lit a cigar—a taste he had developed with tavern-keeping. He had never been one to go against his raising, his nature—but what was nature and what was fool notion? He looked out of the window at a wet moon and let the aromatic smoke drain from his mouth. Let's look at this thing from where you are sitting: in Darien, he told himself. What's wrong with this plug-pulling job?

He felt his throat contract and he swallowed and spat out of the window. A wraith of his bitter rage against Pitt in the darkness that morning as he neared Bell's Ferry came back to him. He turned the cigar in his mouth. You were spitting cotton that day, he thought. But it wasn't so much the job as it was Pitt and what he was trying to do to you.

The gray rim of raftsmen's shoulders sprang up in his mind—the ghost that had dogged him earlier on the long walk from Lumber City—and he remembered the feel of the loose, sliding sand beneath his feet.

Ain't you got a blind hangover from when you were pluggin' their logs fur a livin'? he asked himself. A hell of a lot of sand has whistled under your feet, and theirs too, since then. Those log-jumpers wouldn't hold it against you—the thick-headed bastards would feel lucky that it was you takin' the last crack at their timber, instead of some other bully. And Bud? It seemed a long time since he had seen Bud. He bit on the cigar and wrinkled his nose. Christ, old Bigun would laugh—at you, maybe, but it wouldn't make him a damn bit of difference. It's just a lot of prejudice in you—it never was the job—nobody's tryin' to buy you off now.

He made a throaty sound up through his clamped jaws. Nobody's tried anything yet! Asked you nuthin'. And you moonin' around like a pregnant girl!

He took off his shoes and moved up to the edge of his bed. What he needed was sleep, not another job—he was making plenty of money with the tavern.

On the following day, as he reviewed his thoughts, he decided that it was not the particular job that was important: in Darien a man needed to know his mind, to be set to act quick when a chance turned up. You ain't runnin' with a ruck of rafthands now, he told himself; you are out to lick Darien, and she's deep and crooked as a snake.

But the occasion for the ready action, or any other kind, did not present itself. Ratliff remained near his bar throughout the afternoons and kept a watchful eye upon the door to his gaming-room in the evenings. Geoffrey Dale did not appear.

On Sunday Ratliff felt his head uncommonly level and his feet solid under him. He had wasted enough good time piddling around with Big I: he had decided to look Dale up and ask for the job.

When Geoffrey came out onto the porch of the frame building that housed Dale and Coventry, on the following afternoon, he paused near the steps and asked Ratliff to ride with him to their mill at Old Darien.

Ratliff remained seated on the rococo banisters. If it were bad news, he didn't want to ride two miles for it. ''Twon't take that,' he said, looking steadily at Geoffrey. 'The only plug-puller I can recommend to you is me. You may think I'm a fool, but I want the job.'

Geoffrey closed the watch in his hand carefully and slipped it into his waistcoat. 'Not at all,' he said. 'And I think the firm would be fortunate to get you. I hope you don't mind if I say that I suspected what was at work in your system, that you wanted to get back into the timber business.' He smiled, lifting his face and moving toward Ratliff. 'And I have talked to father and he agrees. Now do you mind finishing this while we ride along?'

As the buggy passed the outermost negro shanty, Geoffrey slackened the reins over the horse's back. 'Father raised only one question,' he began in a casual voice, yet measuring his words. He paused, then went on. 'It is of a personal nature: would you mind discussing it with me?'

Ratliff's eyes had been on the passing scene. He fixed them on the horse's rump. 'Shoot,' he said.

'I like the raftsman's manner of doing things, myself: downright even if a bit reckless.' Geoffrey jerked the reins. 'How does the song go?—

> *Rope around my shoulder, auger in my hand,*
> *And little brown jug from Darian.*

Ratliff smiled 'Bear down more on the *arm.*'

'Yes, indeed. In just a moment.' Geoffrey's jaw lowered. 'After running logs for hundreds of miles on high water, in all kinds of weather, with nothing for company except other raftsmen and alligators, at port he feels a need for women. And one could not expect him to be choosy about them. Darien holds that to be all right, so long as he is a raftsman, but once he becomes a resident! Well, really, the town's extraordinarily provincial in its manners and morals.'

The little lines that had been about Ratliff's mouth and eyes had drained away, leaving a blank smoothness. He started to reach for his chewing tobacco, but withdrew his hand.

'The point is that the report has come to father—and he is as straitlaced as the rest'—Geoffrey smiled deprecatingly—'that you have been seen about in public places with China Swann—the Birdcage madam.'

Ratliff stiffened. 'That's right: I have,' he said.

Geoffrey looked at the horse and slapped the reins together. 'It's stupid business, but these fool people here. . .I hope you know it's not my idea, Snake, but father told me to tell you that if you take the job, he will expect you to see that no more such reports get about.

Ratliff had pulled out his tobacco. Now he cut himself a chew, staring off at a pine thicket, as the red in his neck deepened. Deliberately, he shut his jackknife and returned it to his trouser-pocket. He turned the chew over in his mouth and spat. 'Sho,' he said.

CHAPTER

31

RATLIFF'S FIRST NOTION WAS to master Geoffrey's words and way of talking. The need seemed imperative. Darien would accept no outsider as a public inspector. He had to learn to pass for a Darienite—and one of the top timber crowd, to boot. As Dale and Coventry's plug-puller, he counted himself still a long way from the inspectorship pew—and the necessity of spending every odd hour in his tavern doubled his difficulty—but he was in the right church.

Geoffrey was hard to follow, not only for the way he said them, but for the words he used. Ratliff found it easier to reproduce the sounds than to get the meaning. But before the summer was gone, he could talk like him, and know what he was saying.

He had to change his idea about using this knack, however. On his first trial in the office, he told the bookkeeper, dropping his duplicate over the railing, 'Oh, I say, Dickens, here is the inspection inventory.' (Full of *d's*, shoved together and clipped off.)

Dicken's face came up—like a white-blazed mule's—and broke open in a laugh. But Ratliff recovered in time to laugh, too, when Dickens, added, 'By Joe, you're a good mimic!' He saw then that he had to put his own mark on it.

Geoffrey made out that he didn't think much of his education, but Ratliff could see through that dodge. All of the top layer had a lot of education. He pretended that he was not too serious, but he made him a trade: log learning for book. Geoffrey dropped his jaw; still he took him up on it. He was pitiful about logs, didn't even know that all floating timber except ash had a heavy side!

Despite Ratliff's misgivings about an uppercrust crook, he found that Geoffrey kept his bargain. During the last week in August he even helped Ratliff put in a double-entry system of books for the tavern—though Dickens did most of the work.

But Ratliff would never have thought of fooling with the McIntosh Light Dragoons—not if Geoffrey hadn't urged it on him. It all started with Ratliff's throwing an axe, while they were riding out some land lines near English Eddy. It was a good throw from horseback — about fifty feet — stuck in the blaze; but he thought nothing of it, not even when Geoffrey asked him if he was much of a horseman. More of a mule man, Ratliff had said.

It wasn't till after they got back to Darien that Geoffrey mentioned joining up. He was trying to organize a saber team, he said. Ratliff couldn't see what sporting a feathered hat and loping a horse around the town could have to do with his case. 'I ain't got time for that sort of flap-a-doodle,' he said.

They were leaning across the counter in the outer office. Geoffrey jerked up his head. 'Where're you going?'

Ratliff grinned. "Tain't no tellin',' he said.

But that night he looked up in a dictionary the word Geoffrey had used, the word *prestige*, and he changed his mind.

After the first Wednesday night meeting he attended, he figured he had been a glutton for punishment. He should have felt which way the wind was blowing when Geoffrey quizzed him about this application blank, about his middle name: Perrineau. But his father and Uncle Mundy had always been proud of Perrineaus, and Geoffrey didn't try to get into the other side of the family. Still, he should have known that any bunch of Darienites who wanted to look up his family would be uncommonly sneery.

They didn't do anything a stranger could take exception to. They were the politest crowd you could imagine. It was what they didn't say and do. He would have backed out that night if Geoffrey hadn't been trying so hard to make everybody act clever with him. And he had about made up his mind that this military lodge would help in getting to be like a Darienite.

He found his welcome in the drill hall no warmer on the following Sunday afternoon. They all seemed to have sudden blindness when he came around, except for his own squad leader and Geoffrey, and he overheard one tadpole call him 'that ruffian,' but he set his lip and kept his nose in the regulations book.

Later, when he was bringing in his saddle after drill, someone stood in the doorway to a small room off the hall, bellowing, 'Who left his saddle soap out?'

He saw that it was the fat sergeant who looked after things. 'I did,' he said.

The fellow bugged out his eyes. 'Hell, recruit! Don't you know this stuff costs money?'

Ratliff let his saddle slide from his shoulder and his face grew still. 'I'll pay for it, podner,' he said.

'Don't podner me!' The fellow's neck swelled. 'I'm Sergeant Catignani!' His glance shifted to include the other saddle-bearing troopers, halting behind Ratliff. 'And if I thought you'd take it to that pothouse of yours and use it, I'd let you, by God!'

Ratliff's fist caught Cartignani on the jaw, just as the cheeks were spreading in a smile. He dropped to the floor.

Ratliff whirled to back up against the wall, but no one offered to come upon him. The group parted and he strode from the building in silence.

When he told China about it that night, she laughed, laughed immoderately. He had slipped up the back stairway—his practice now—and they were eating a cold snack in her room. He thought her voice sounded shrill. The thing hadn't seemed funny to him. But, as her beer glass shook in her hand, the infection touched his insides and he chuckled.

'What business you got with that circus outfit, anyhow, Snake?' she said, her yellow eyes sharpening through her smile.

He did seem pretty silly to himself now, but he swallowed his beer without replying.

The conversation shifted to the tavern—as it seemed increasingly to do of late, the less often China saw Snake. She sat dabbing her face with her handkerchief against the perspiration of her laughter and the warmth of the evening. She had known that he must see her more covertly, more infrequently, as he made his way in Darien—had known it when she gave him the start, she told herself, but it had made a difference. As he left, she could not resist saying, 'Looks like you have to get your feelings hurt by your new pals, before you can find time to come around to see me now.'

He loosed his embrace, held her away from him and stared at her. Then he grinned broadly. As he walked home he thought: China's gettin' green-eye! And he felt flattered. But somehow it no longer seemed to be a matter of first importance.

Geofffrey sought out Ratliff at the firm's log boom on Monday afternoon. He had left the armory before the altercation of the previous day, but had learned of it in full account from members of the troop. As he knew, most of the dragoons privately disliked, were contemptuous of, Catignani—a retired Regular Army cavalryman, who served the troop as paid instructor and custodian. He was thought vulgar, a bootlicker, and a bully.

Ratliff laid his branding hammer on a timber pile and turned a somber face toward his companion.

Geoffrey grinned. 'Stout punch you pack in that right of yours.'

Ratliff only grunted.

'Stout enough to break the ice between you and the troop.'

Ratliff eyed him impassively, while he disclosed that most of the troopers were privately pleased that Ratliff had brought down Catignani, even at the cost of discipline. Then he explained the theory and meaning of military discipline, tactfully mentioned that he, as lieutenant, had been designated to apply it to Ratliff, in a face-saving fashion—and that, of course, Ratliff's was the first face he was interested in saving.

Ratliff grinned, grinned reluctantly. He had to admit this Darien podner of his was a clever fellow.

'We'll get this saber team whipped into shape yet—enter the state meet next year!' Geoffrey concluded, turning away.

Ratiff put his hammer under his arm and fell in behind him. Hell, don't forget it's because he wants to use you, he warned himself.

But Ratliff didn't think he was apt to forget that and it was a good enough trade for him. He went into cavalry training with an abandon that startled other members of the troop. By dawn each morning— before he began his long work day—he was at the barn, saddling his horse, riding out onto the track, while it was still in semi-darkness. And when it was scarcely light enough to see the leather heads— according to Catignani, who soon became an admirer—he was swinging his saber at the three-inch pine pegs beneath them—and hitting them most of the time. Before Christmas he had made the team.

However, Ratliff relaxed none of his attention to the safer bet: he might learn passwords through the troop, but he had to convince old man Dale that he was a topnotch timberman to get his backing. During the the winter the opportunity came oftenest in serving Geoffrey as woodsman and adviser in dealings with the contract men —a thing that usually took him away from his own work. He was proud of the chance, if he just had more time, he reflected—time: all that hamstrung him was the scarcity of hours in a day—it had become a Devil's Elbow every step of the pull to make them go around.

In February he was given an assistant at the Boom. The following month Geoffrey asked him to accompany him to the Oconee country, to Mount Vernon, for the trial of a damage suit against several contract men. Despite the use of a local lawyer, Ratliff would be valuable in picking the jury. It was a fine chance for him to impress the head of his firm. Still, he thought of it fretfully as he and Geoffrey rode northward on the train.

Raftsmen he used to run with had come to him several times since he started pulling plugs for Dale and Coventry, wanting him to let their doctored logs by. Someone of the scalers had agreed to ease up if he would, they said. Twice he had tried it, and the second time he got a kickback from the sawmill. He had to be agreeable with the boys who came to his tavern, and he did agree, but he hadn't let any more of their sorry stuff pass. They had about quit asking these *favors* of him now, and he was relieved. He didn't have time to worry with them, he had to keep his mind on his business.

And now the damn contract men are popping up, he told himself, biting an end of his cigar. They would, he knew, expect him to trigger with the case to help them. Well, by God you never did take any *contract men* to raise and you needn't to start this late, he thought. It's Snake Sutton you're out for!

There was one thing to look forward to, anyhow: he would get to see Bud True. For two months now, according to word that came to the tavern, poor old Bud had been abed with his legs and back broken from a tree fall. He had wanted to head upriver was soon as he heard it, but the news was two weeks old when it came and he just couldn't turn loose, break away. It hardly seemed possible for Bud to be laid out, the bull-ox! He viewed the prospective visit with mingled feelings.

At Mount Vernon, Ratliff did not stint his effort in behalf of the firm, and he eventually had the satisfaction of hearing the jury report damages for them; but it was a dubious advantage. In a quaint manifestation of justice to all, they jury also returned damages for the defendants, who had filed a flimsy counterclaim.

Ratliff was glad to get out of the Oconee country: he had found the sight of Bud, splinted and flat on his back, hard to bear, and the timber-runners of the opposing side had been pretty mouthy about him. Hell, Darien was a bad enough dose to take without swallowing the spew of a lot of contract guineas.

On May Day, Ratliff found the Darien dose bitterer than at any time since he had renewed his resolve to attain the inspectorship. This potion was administered at a festival given by the ladies of Saint Andrew's Church on the lawn of the Dale home. Until that time, he had not been bothered with the womenfolk of the top layer, but Geoffrey insisted that he come: it was imperative that the dragoons attend, especially the saber team, now in high favor. Two weeks before, it had licked the Brunswick Horse Guards, and only the day previous, had tied the second team of the celebrated Liberty Independents. The swordsmen were to stage a tilt to climax the program—winner selecting the May queen.

Ratliff was a little awed by the picnic's color and trimming, the silken pavilion and beribboned pole—he had never seen anything like it. Still, he felt that the dragoons made a pretty good showing when they rode in their blue uniforms and orange-plumed helmets past the animate beds of pink and lavender and white dresses—and he felt like one of them then. But when the parade was over and the troop dismounted, most of the men disappeared into the feminine groups.

He didn't mind staying with the horses, with Catignani, didn't mind that none of his fellow troopers made him acquainted with the girls. But the way these finicky women eyed him! It was the old hens who did most of it. They glanced over their fans, or their shoulders, when they thought he wasn't looking. It was plain that he wore a smallpox sign.

It gave him the itch, though he could have stood that. The trouble came afterward, long afterward. The team had ridden for points—Geoffrey was an easy winner and he had tied for second place—and the queen had been crowned. He was getting ready to mount his nag and ease out when Geoffrey ran up to him, holding this girl by the hand.

Somehow, Geoffrey disappeared and he found himself at the punchbowl with her, among a lot of other people. Geoffrey had said that she was his Cousin Robbie. She seemed nothing special for looks, sort of sallow-faced and too long of nose. But she was mannerly. At least she tried to be.

'I don't believe I saw you at the ball?' she said, as the conversation lagged.

Ratliff said, 'The ball?' and rubbed his jaw.

'The troop ball—' she began, then caught herself: 'But there are so many balls!' She looked down at her cup quickly and asked for more punch.

It was Ratliff's first news of the troop ball and he knew that she must know that now. He was glad to go for punch.

Then he started back from the refreshment booth and saw that another man had taken her arm, that her face was withdrawn when she said, 'Sorry: father's come for me.'

Ratliff halted with a cup in each hand: the hauteur of the gray head was familiar, the man beside her was Major Macgregor—of the council meeting—who had called him a procurer (he knew what that meant now) and a whoremonger.

He broke down and told China about it on the following night, while the bilious fever of his hate still burned in him. He had named Macgregor second man on his list –to be settled with some day.

This moment of confidence with her brought him scant relief. Something had happened to China. It seemed that he couldn't talk to her anymore—except on business. She had laughed and shown no concern, had broken off to tell him that Seborn Henry was back in town, had spoken of him as her man Sebe, trying to be funny and only making it sound common.

Later, mulling over the incident in his bed, he suddenly realized that after all China was a whore. The thought brought him upright: he had never quite admitted that before, not to mean it. And no longer such a fresh one, either.

But he did not brood over his changing relationship with China: he hadn't the time to settle his mind about her now. He had to get going, get something definite started about the public scalership job. He wondered if he could afford to let Geoffrey know what he was after. He had been with Dale and Coventry for a year, practically, and he hadn't made a direct move. And he was sick as hell of diddling with swords and blockheads!

On the following day, however, he found a new significance in his swordmanship, a new importance.

'You have become a public issue,' Geoffrey said, his jaw dropping. They were seated in the barroom of the tavern after work. 'The hens of Darien have their feathers spread—trying to hide their chicks from the Snake!' He laughed.

Ratliff looked at his whiskey glass with an impassive face, then tossed off his drink. The motherly alarm had developed at the festival, as the knights tilted for the May queen, according to Geoffrey. The mammas were suddenly aghast when Ratliff, fourth man of five, had tied the high score. They had held their collective breath until Geoffrey won. Geoffrey was being franker with him than he had ever been before. What was his own move—what would all this mean for him?

'For a moment your poor Quixote was changed into Galahad—for the matrons!' Geoffrey laughed again. 'Heavens, Snake, just a lot of silly old women. Don't be so owlish with me!'

There was an odd, a fitful change in the pupils of Ratliff's eyes: he had been touched by a fleeting impulse to confide in Geoffrey. Now his mouth twisted, loosened. 'They don't need to kick up such a dust,' he said. 'I ain't a chicken snake.'

He sat on after Geoffrey had gone, sat rapping his fingers on the crown of his new straw hat. Damn their daughters: he was out for bigger game. But a public issue—he had had a taste of that once! Could he hold on against the women—his job—remain in the troop? By God, the troop! He put on his hat and got up. His saber had suddenly become more than caparison, than a plaything: it was a real weapon—the best he could now lay his hand to.

Formerly he had ridden in the early morning; now he took off, as well, the late afternoon hours that he had devoted to his tavern. He thrust, cut, rode each lengthening summer day into darkness. He bought himself an expensive cavalry horse from Liberty County— taking Geoffrey with him on the preliminary inspection trip to pass on the animal's performance. Geoffrey found his action admirably smooth. He agreed with Geoffrey's view: the mount was vital to swordsmanship in a tournament. A man should have his horse so well trained to the course that he could virtually forget him.

Ratliff knew now that he was sure of his saber, as sure as he had ever been of rifle or axe. He must attain exact form, the fine points. His saber arm must become infallible, he told himself—he liked the new word.

He rode down the sandy Darien course one August afternoon, whirling a bright blade through the graying twilight. The first leather head went spinning from its post. He thrust the ring hanging below the cross-arm and tossed it into the air. Without pausing, in a continuous, even motion, his arm, his body swayed to the left of his

343

mount, came back—sending another head spinning. That's it—by God, that's it! he told himself, as he and the horse sped on, in the same rhythmic swing to sever other heads.

Timing was the secret: to form, to infallibility. He had scarcely been able to see the rings, the pegs beneath the heads. It was like a dance, never changing, never pausing. There was time enough—no sense in finishing under ten seconds—that left a second's grace.

Before the first cold snap of autumn, Ratliff had become regularly the high scorer in team practice. In early March of the following year, his swordmanship created public excitement. The *Darien Gazette* published a story about it.

The Dragoons had met the Liberty Independents in an informal contest on the local course, and while the home team had lost, the margin was very narrow indeed: five and a half points. The Dragoons' fine showing had been largely due, said the *Gazette,* to the amazing performance of Sergeant Sutton. Out of a possible score of sixty points (for the individual) he had amassed fifty-eight and a half in his three runs: four and a half points more than any other swordsman on the field.

Ratliff took Darien's demonstration impassively. It was satisfying to see that he had reckoned true: in making himself indispensable to the team, in confining himself to troop sport and giving the mothers and their daughters a wide berth. But his clatter buttered no bread for him. He bowed in his turn before the bandstand on the evening of the spring ball, then he moved along the flag-draped walls of the armory toward the door, without a second glance at the smooth arms and sweeping skirts of the feminine dancers. The thing on his mind, the question, was again one of timing.

Outside he collided with Spalding, the timber inspector-general and former commander of the troop, resplendent in the dress uniform of a militia major. 'Surely you're not leaving the ball,' Spalding said, in a warm, blurry voice.

Ratliff smiled briefly and started to move on. 'Don't dance,' he said, not altogether accurately.

'But you are the principal honoree.' Spalding glanced through the doorway at the ebb and flow of bright figures. 'And it's quite a show. Doesn't any of it interest you?'

Ratliff's gaze followed his questioner's and for an instant fastened on the undulant shimmer of a white dress. Then his eyes flickered and he spoke. 'There's just one thing that interests me, Major.' He looked Spalding in the face. 'A public timber-inspector's job.'

Ratliff had not awaited an answer from the astonished Spalding, but he felt the following week that he had not spoken too soon, for the focus of attention already had shifted. To the future: the troop was absorbed in an ambition to win the state tournament—only two months away—and the town reflected it. He was confirmed in his judgment before the week was out.

Spalding stopped him on the street and said, without preface: 'I have spoken to the mayor about you and he seems interested. But just now the whole town's attention is on the state tourney. Your performance was remarkable, but unfortunately, at an informal tilt. You will have to repeat it in Atlanta if it is to count for victory, Mr. Sutton. Wouldn't it be a fine feather in little Darien's cap if we could win that championship?'

Ratliff felt a little amazed at how simple his struggle for the inspectorship appeared to be turning out. It suddenly seemed a little silly, too, but he knew he could repeat his performance in Atlanta, or anywhere else. And he proceeded to prove this for himself and the team, by making, or bettering his high score (depending somewhat on the judge) six times in succession during the following week.

Then came the uncomfortable realization that what the troop and Darien wanted was the championship, not his score—even at sixty points. And this called for five swordsmen. He joined Geoffrey and Major Spalding—who had once headed the team—at coaching, and joined them in their headaches. The team was good, but was it good enough? Every man spun his heads and thrust his rings, but what about their style? Denton was wont to drag his saber over his shoulder from right cut, and Bostick to slight the outward thrust in making his carte and tierce points.

It took timing, Ratliff told them—the dance swing—and he explained and demonstrated, but this was not enough. He dreamed a wild notion, made them try it—had them go over the course blindfolded, swinging their sabers—to forget their mounts, the object in view—to fix upon the feel, the rate of progression—hours daily.

When the days for practice were spent and they were finally in Atlanta, awaiting the critical afternoon, the actual test of swordsmanship, there remained still one hazard, one weakness in the team's arms: Wilkens, a good blade and a high scorer in practice, suffered nerves in a tournament—was liable to go to pieces. Ratliff and Geoffrey lost sleep over this peril: Spalding could only suggest prayer. But as they were driving to the fairgrounds in their hired surrey near noon, Ratliff recalled an old huntsman's practice, at beef shoots, and he bought Wilkens a vial of laudanum.

News of the triumph of the McIntosh Light Dragoons had long preceded them, both by the telephone and the telegraph, when the *Hessie* docked at Darien Bluff with the saber team aboard. The swordsmen were not unprepared for welcome. Still, when Ratliff saw the web of blue and yellow bunting on Broad Street, the size and turbulence of the crowd gathered at the wharf, heard the measured pounding of the troop's field piece, found the mayor and the council in frock-coats advancing to greet him and his comrades, to lead them to a beribboned carriage drawn by four white horses—he wondered, wondered if he were the same renegade rafthand they had booted out of their chamber two years before.

346

But only for an instant: he brought his hand to his helmet in salute with other members of the team, and bowed from the hips to the ladies, while he drew a handkerchief from his cuff to hide his grin.

CHAPTER

32

BUD TRUE THUMPED across the barroom floor on crutches. His right leg was shriveled and crooked and the toe dangled uselessly against the staff. His broad back, as it swung between the arm rests, appeared stiffly bent and ridges of the brace beneath his shirt were discernible. His face wore a frown, though it lacked its old fierceness, and his cheeks had a puffy, dingy pallor about them. Climbing the back stairway in measured bumps, he muttered to himself. What the hell was keeping Snake?

Bud had been the official host of the tavern for three months. To comply with the law prohibiting public inspectors any outside business, Ratliff had legally transferred his share in the place to Bud. Actually the trade between them provided Bud a small interest in the profits for the five hundred dollars (left from the sale of his farm after he had paid off his debts) which he had deposited as down-payment in the supposed sale. And in addition, he received a salary of seventy-five dollars a month and living quarters for himself and Ibby, in the rear of the building.

But this arrangement was not the cause of Bud's mutterings. It suited him well enough, since he could no longer run timber or farm.

His dissatisfaction was with Ratliff. Snake had let Darien get a hold on him in a way Bud would never have suspected possible. Timber-scaling was an ornery enough job in itself, but for Snake to suck around with such doughfaces as young Dale and join the Goddamned church—get so stiff-collared he couldn't come into his own barroom! He even talked like that bunch now! Bud had figured out the flea in Ratliff's breeches, all right, but his conclusion did little to ease his mind.

He clumped across the upstairs hallway and entered the small office adjoining the gaming-room. He came to a sudden halt and shifted on his crutches to catch his balance. Ratliff was seated in the swivel chair at the roller-top desk, his mouth limbering in a smile.

'You gittin' worse'n one of these damn screegy boards—aer whatever you call 'em,' said Bud, turning toward a chair.

For a time they discussed tavern business, then Ratliff leaned back in his seat and stretched his arms above his head.

Bud eyed the straw sailor Ratliff held in his hand. 'You'll find a drink the drawer theah—if you can still take it barfoot.'

'No thanks.' Ratliff rose.

'Well, hand it to me—I ain't too high-toned fur it.' Bud looked up from his seat. 'And I reckon Ibby won't pray over me fur smellin' like I usually do.'

Ratliff put on his hat. Bud hadn't been cold sober since he took over the tavern. He wondered how much longer Bud would be able to carry his liquor and attend to business. He frowned. 'It wouldn't hurt you to miss one a little oftener.'

'The gals I run with don't care.' But shifted his crutches in his lap and reached over and pulled open the drawer. 'And I don't fiddle with them as does. Oh, I've seen smart bucks befoh go down to the altar to git 'em some calico—least they thought they 'uz smart, and mighty shifty.'

Ratliff watched him silently, as he pulled out the bottle and uncorked it. Bud was bringing business to the place, all right, he thought, if he didn't drink up all the profits—or give them away.

The open bottle halted before Bud's mouth. 'Ever' one of 'em I can recollect got hooked afore it was over. Church is just naturally a woman's element—and preachers are in cahoots with 'em—marry you quicker'n you can bat your eyes.'

Ratliff's lips loosened, then suddenly set. 'All the more reason why I should keep a clear head.'

Bud took down the bottle. 'Oh, so you think your head's clear! Well, ever'thing you've done around heah for the last month aer more shows it ain't, includin', right now, turnin' down a good drink of liquor.' He gazed at Ratliff and his shaggy brows gathered fiercely. 'God Almighty, Snake, you're the last rambler alive I'd-a thought would let his tally-whacker take him inside a Darien church.'

When Ratliff had quit the tavern, he headed toward his boardinghouse, walking slowly through afternoon sunlight that slanted under the widespread boughs of the live-oaks to brighten their dark trunks. It looked like Bud's troubles had upset his seriousness, Ratliff reflected. He hardly seemed a grown man any more and his manner was so rough Ratliff found it hard to tell him anything. He had a specific reason for not taking a drink that afternoon—even with Bud: after supper he was to attend a Sunday-School departmental meeting, where he would see Robbie Macgregor. At Robbie's instance he had taken the pledge.

He glanced down at the shell pathway, wiping perspiration from his neck, as Bud's phrase came back to him—*inside a Darien church!* Yes, he had to admit his getting into a church was surprising— damned amazing, when he stopped to think. But the explanation was simple: it was all a part of getting inside of Darien. Still, he might not have mixed up in such ticklish business if it hadn't been for Robbie.

350

He saw again her astonished eyes, politely restrained and serious, but rounded and dark under the moon—when he told her that he had never belonged to a church. They were riding alone in his buggy to a Sunday-School watermelon-cutting, and that in itself was surprising. When the stevedore's daughter he had been put with flounced off with another man, not deigning to go with him, Robbie had pretended there was some mix-up and that *she* was really his partner—just to save his feelings. Of course she had counted on their sharing the buggy with Geoffrey, but Geoffrey had picked up another girl and had ridden with her.

He could see that Robbie was a little uneasy to be alone with him—and that, he supposed, had started her interest in his religious life. Her face had softened with sympathy when he told her that he was an orphan, brought up by family negroes. Nobody had ever invited him to join a church.

'You don't just join,' she said. 'It's a serious step.'

He squinted off at the sunset. More serious than you had figured on when you set out, he told himself. The pulpit-mannered preacher had given him a slough of Bible passages to read and a book of church rules. And later, had knelt with him: 'O God, this young man . . . so deeply under conviction—give him the will to open his heart— bring him peace and understanding.'

He supposed the preacher prayed to the same God that he knew— had known—but it was a complicated, high-sounding rigmarole: this Darien brand of religion. And it seemed lunatic, if you took it for what it said—which, of course, Darien people didn't do. *Love your enemies, bless them that curse you, do good to them that hate you,* Ratliff quoted to himself. He grimaced and shook his head. All right, I guess—for the other fellow. Puts him right to get his clabber face smashed! But the pompous old codger wasn't so dumb: he had finally got down to brass tacks—began nosing into Ratliff's past history—his

351

running a gambling-hall and barroom. He had taken cold feet and started to back down.

Then Robbie had stopped him one Sunday morning as he was leaving church, and told him that the preacher had talked to her and that she hoped he, Ratliff, would take the step. That had put a different light on things and he had joined.

He had known that Robbie liked him ever since the moonlight ride: the change that came into her eyes when he started talking to her. Damn fine eyes, too! he thought: window-panes—but I doubt if she has any feelings she needs to hide. Nope, they all seem as—as modest and smooth as the breeze from a silk fan. I reckon she thinks she believes that Sunday-School stuff—and that it's your soul she's worked up over.

Christ! A sense of spiritual jeopardy swept over him and he pulled out a tin of tobacco and bit off a chew with a yank. What are you fiddlin' with this fool Darien girl for? Share your bed with a cuckoo-clock bird? And Macgregor's daughter, to boot? You'd be scared to go to sleep!

Don't worry, old Macgregor ain't goin' to let her marry you, anyhow. When he pulls the halter, she'll follow him right back into the house—forget all about your immortal soul! Suddenly his chest pounded and the blood ran hot in his veins. He spat out his tobacco violently and pushed open the gate in front of a large white-columned dwelling now silvered by the twilight—his boarding house, Darien's most select.

That evening when the meeting was over, he moved to the church door to intercept Robbie. Something was up. Among the white-frilled, fidgety row of young ladies at the front, her profile had remained fixed on the spot by the chancel rail where the participants in the program stood; she had not glanced in his direction. And her face had seemed grave; the tawny skin somehow darkened.

Obstructing her passage, he bowed formally at the doorway and smilingly hoped she was well.

Robbie had the prettiness of an Arab mare, the ease. She paused with a gentle backward swaying and tucked her Bible under her arm. Her eyes darkened and a sad smile touched her face. 'Hello,' she said, and moved away.

He followed her outside. 'What's wrong, Robbie?'

She halted in the half-light of the entrance. 'If *you* don't know, I suppose there's nothing wrong.' She started walking. 'I was just sorry to hear that you fell by the wayside.'

He grasped her arm. 'Wait a minute. Fell where?'

'You were seen coming out of the Altamaha Tavern this afternoon with the smell of drink on you.' She spoke over her shoulder, twisting her head a little.

For a fraction of a second he hesitated; then he turned her around and looked steadily into her face, ignoring a couple who brushed by them. 'That's not so.'

'Why, Ratliff! Oh, it doesn't matter—but Geoffrey saw you—passed you on the sidewalk.'

'Geoffrey? That's right, he did. But I was not coming out of the tavern and I did not have liquor on my breath.' So that dog was talebearing, he thought.

Her gaze wavered sensitively, but she continued to stare up at him, her lips parting, as he went on. 'I—I—this sort of knocks the props out from under me.' He winced and looked away. 'Coming from Geoffrey—I don't understand it . . .' He turned back, his face beginning to flush. 'You—er—Geoffrey's not in love with you?'

'Oh, of course not'—she swallowed, smiling—'he's like a brother—has been teasing me, saying your change of heart—but this afternoon he seemed in earnest.'

'Let's go find him! Right now!'

353

'No, Ratliff. It isn't necessary. Geoffrey may have been joking—but at any rate, I know now that he was wrong.' She touched his sleeve. 'Oh, I'm so terribly sorry! I've been so terribly unfair!' She whirled and ran down the steps and across the walk to a waiting surrey.

He stood for a time looking after her, not moving. 'It isn't necessary—' he murmured and, absently reaching over, he rubbed his ribs under his left arm. Suddenly, his face twisted and he turned away. The damn little fool!

The thought of Geoffrey's tattling disturbed Ratliff. It returned to him while he lay abed in his room, trying to read. He hadn't expected complicity of Geoffrey, but this was more than his laughter of the past. Geoffrey had been amused when he had joined the church: Ratliff had expected that. Geoffrey called himself a skeptic, didn't believe in churches and seemed pretty vague about God. And he had agreed with him at one time about the churches and had put up no argument against his views on God—it didn't seem unguarded to do so then.

Memory of the liquor-splattered bar and the empty glasses, and Bud and Roof Bostick and Geoffrey leaning against it on a Sunday late in May, came back to him. The week after Bud had taken over. Bud was pretty drunk that afternoon, and had been spinning the yarn about Hannah's ghost. And when he laughed with Geoffrey at Bud's claims for the haunted island, Bud swelled up and told about Ratliff's vision of the steamboat, just before he had wrecked his raft and drowned Poss. He hadn't thought of it in years, didn't know his mind about it, but he didn't appreciate Bud's telling it there, or Geoffrey's smiling.

Later, Geoffrey had put his philosophy theories to it: said that the vision was only in Ratliff's head—because he secretly feared some catastrophe. Geoffrey had done a lot of deep reading on the subject of the mind, and Ratliff was prepared to accept this explanation.

Then the story of his vision had turned up again three weeks ago, in an odd fashion. Geoffrey had told Robbie about it and she brought it up one evening after Vespers. Ratliff hadn't been surprised that she took it as he had taken it, when it happened to him as a boy—she was simple about her religion—but she said it was a manifestation of his innate piety (even as a heathen!). It recommended him to her.

Though the outcome had been curious. She had jumped him about his drinking with Bostick and Bud and even Geoffrey, and had asked him to take the pledge. He had been pleased at the chance to promise, not thinking about the pledge at all, but what her asking him amounted to.

Jesus, she's too easy to flimflam! he thought, closing his book and looking off across the room. She wants to believe in you. Suddenly his chest tightened under a sweetish pressure and he frowned. He opened the book and began repeating its words to himself.

On the following Wednesday night, Robbie was forbidden to see Ratliff again. He had driven her home from prayer meeting and, when she turned away from the door, she found her father standing in the middle of the hall, in his smoking jacket.

At first the usually firm voice almost stammered. His precaution was made necessary by the unprecedented presumption of the man, Macgregor said. A solitary light, burning in the crystal chandelier above him, gave his face a frigid pallor. He did not wish to impugn her intentions, nor her discretion, under anything like normal circumstances. 'I know this Sutton has been permitted to join our church, and I do not here judge his motives, but the man has led a life so depraved that you, in your innocence, cannot conceive of it.' He spoke of brutalized appetites. She must certainly know that he was not a gentleman.

The length of Robbie's nose was marked when she lifted her face to Macgregor's. 'Your concern is—is premature, father.' Robbie was surprised at the coldness of her voice, at the resentment she felt within her. Mr. Sutton had never asked to call on her—tonight he had merely driven her and another girl home after the services. She, for one, believed in his sincerity in joining the church. There were changes in his manner of life to show this. He had always been most gentlemanly around her. How could her father judge, when he did not know him?

Major Macgregor shook his head slightly, in impatience. His information was reliable enough—the man's behavior was a matter of public knowledge—and of public condemnation—even though he was tolerated for his attainments by some of the less responsible. Her susceptible Cousin Geoffrey had now come to see him in a new light. He paused imperiously: he must insist that she discontinue any association with this Sutton.

Robbie's face turned a sallow white and she moved her lips twice before she spoke. 'I'll always respect your wishes about whom I receive in this house, father. But I think I know my own Christian duty.'

Ratliff guessed, readily, that Major Macgregor had pulled the halter on Robbie, and his haughty gray head haunted Ratliff's sleep. But during the month that followed, he grew annoyed with himself and finally with Robbie. He saw her as usual at Sunday School, at church, at prayer service, but he could never effect a meeting, and she never managed more than a how-do-you-do.

Then he lay in wait for her at the Dragoon's Hallowe'en Ball—it was one of the few that she attended—and asked her for a dance. But she had not been taken by surprise. Too readily, she produced her program to show that it was entirely filled out. He turned quickly, without a word, and walked away.

Still he did not quit the dance and later was grateful for the hunch that held him on. She came to him near intermission time, as he stood alone by a shock of cornstalks, drinking punch. 'I've decided that I should tell you, Ratliff, that father has forbidden me to see you,' she said. Her face was almost grim and her voice shook a little.

The admission warmed his blood like drink, but he only bowed stiffly.

356

She went on to say, finding it hard to stop, that her father had been misled, that he was wrong in his judgment of Ratliff.

When she had ended he smiled slowly. 'You mean de white fo'ks' heaven ain't meant for me—' She dropped her head and color flared in her cheeks. He went on. 'What's that Bible verse—"Bless them that curse you"? Hadn't figured on havin' to start with one of my fellow church members—and a deacon, too!'

'Don't be cruel,' she said, finally looking up.

He kept smiling. 'Cruel?' he said, and his lips trembled.

That had dissolved her father's injunction for Robbie. She met Ratliff secretly at intermission, among the palmetto palms back of the armory and later, after evening church services, whenever the opportunity offered.

On the second occasion that he drove her home at night and she asked him to put her out at the corner, Ratliff felt the beat of blood in his temples, found it hard to bring his hands to rein in the horse—so hotly he ached to ride up the driveway, to let her into the house, to flaunt her before the high-headed son-of-a-bitch who called himself her father. He began to allude to him humorously as the Deacon, and Robbie accepted the term with little protest.

On the last Wednesday in November, when they had halted the buggy at the corner and sat a little while beneath a slack moon before parting, Ratliff kissed Robbie. He had led up to it with a speech earlier in the ride—a speech he had prepared beforehand, but he had got it off all right, he felt.

They had been talking of the nosiness of a Mrs. Dawson, who had hidden at the corner of the church to see them get into the buggy together, of an anonymous warning Robbie had got the morning before. 'I guess they are right, Robbie,' he had said, his arm on the back of her seat, loosely encircling her shoulders, and she had turned to him questioningly.

He would confess that he had been villain enough to cherish her company, sinful enough to think her beautiful. Here she moved away from his arm, but he had gone on, smiling, yet more than half-serious. He had even been blackguard enough to respect her piety, depraved enough to reverence her purity.

'No—you mustn't say that!' she broke in.

'I'm afraid I've committed the unforgivable sin, too'—he had taken her hand and was suddenly fervent—'I've fallen in love with you!'

She permitted, received the kiss, but he was not prepared for what followed: when he had released her, had lifted his head, she slid silently from the buggy and fled down the sidewalk.

Ratliff had sat watching her, as she ran, unable to move, and, after she vanished, he had fumbled with the reins for a time. But he told himself later that she'd get over it—she was young, young for her years—and only twenty-two.

He was conscious of his own pulse that night, but strong nerves restrained it and his thoughts were not absorbed in sentiment. What would an elopement mean for his position, his future in Darien? He sat long with the question. He was not blind to all its hazards, but a wife from a first family could not be a liability for him in Darien— even in the face of her father's bitter opposition—hell, he had that already! His blood moved with a slow, tingling thrust, as he rested on his haunches against a wall of his room, his hat still on his head, thinking of Macgregor's humiliation.

The old glass goat would never consent to a marriage, anyhow. That would be his argument with Robbie: it was unanswerable. But he must have more, must dress it up with the Sunday-School palaver. 'Pride goeth before a fall'—God, the man was proud enough—could she be made to see it in that light?

But on Sunday morning, Robbie did not appear for services, either Sunday School or church, and again in the evening she was not there. More than hunger for his vengeance crept into Ratliff's pulse.

Likely, a headache prevented her coming, he told himself; but it was a poor time for dawdling. On Monday he smuggled a note to her at home, through a son of the negro gardener, but he got no answer. He tried again as futilely on Thursday, and on Wednesday evening, he found with alarm her absence at prayer meeting.

Robbie met Ratliff, at her own suggestion, in the sacristy of the church, during services the following Sunday. And she seemed to him unchanged—she looked astonishingly calm, even tranquil. She frowned when he locked the door against surprise, but her hand trembled less than his when he took it. They stood where he had turned back from the key and he looked off through a small high window. His proposal for elopement suddenly became a difficult thing to say.

Then, he found that she was speaking—it seemed almost her Sunday-School voice, though lower pitched. She had thought and thought about them. It seemed terrible to her. So many things cut across them—so many obligations and duties and affections—but she knew, now, that the feeling she bore for him could not be wrong. She looked at him and her face flushed, but she met his gaze. 'It seems stronger and surer than anything else,' she said.

Ratliff winced and dropped her hand. He felt a tremor through his vitals and a weakness behind his knees. This was more than he had looked for. He strode the length of the small bare room. Hell, she couldn't mean it—couldn't know what she was talking about—a strip of a girl! Darien girl! The pulse in his body seemed like the slow surge of a river freshet. He swallowed twice as he walked back to her. He held to a fragment of what he intended to say. 'There's nothing for us, Robbie, but to run away—run away and get married. The -- your father—you know—'

'Run away?' Her eyes widened. 'Run away!' Her mouth opened again, but sagged weakly, whispering. 'Why, father would never forgive—we haven't asked him—'

Ratliff turned back and began walking. His feet made a loud sound on the uncarpeted floor. He did not look at her.

When she finally moved to halt his step, her cheeks held a greenish pallor and her lips were gray. 'We'll go—if there's no other way—'

As he brought his gaze to her face, he gulped air. He caught his balance and stood, spread-legged, staring at her . . . 'No,' he said, after a time. 'No. No, by God!' He shut his eyes and his body grew rigid. A thin, impalpable chill, a fire moved in his veins: it had been years since he had had the feeling, but it was unmistakable.

'Oh, Ratliff! Not the Lord's name!'

He blinked. 'Yes,' he said. 'In the Lord's name, by God!' He grasped her arm with his half-raised hand. 'And we'll ask your father!'

CHAPTER

33

RATLIFF FOLLOWED ROBBIE through the cabin door of the *Hessie* and they walked forward along the deck. It was New Year's Day. The mid-afternoon sun felt warm, despite a light breeze and the bracing air. They moved at a loitering step and Robbie was smiling.

'You and Bud must have been terrors,' she said.

The captain had been telling of the time that True picked him up by the collar and raftsmen took over the *Hessie*. Ratliff hadn't been too comfortable at Robbie's hearing it, but he laughed with them. 'Old Bud!' he now murmured absently and turned toward the rail.

The boat was moving along the narrow cut from Buttermilk Sound into the Altamaha River. He twisted his head about, to take in the whole range of sea and marsh that lay before them. Blue veins of bright water crooked and curved through the great gulf of yellow-brown grass. Clumps of live-oaks smudged the level distance with green. A sunny calm lay over all. He breathed deeply and his gaze fastened on the forward horizon, where lay Darien Bluff.

They were nearing the end of their wedding excursion—a journey that had taken them from Brunswick to Savannah, then by coastwise steamer around the Florida peninsula to New Orleans and back again. They had been married in Brunswick, without the consent of Robbie's father—or mother, either, but she had been there and it was not quite an elopement. Ratliff had suggested the plan, but Robbie had, with little persuasion agreed—it had seemed the only practical thing. She had led her mother to Brunswick on the pretense of shopping, while he made his bid for Macgregor's consent to his suit In case he saw no hope of getting it, he was to come on to Darien for an immediate wedding, and this he had done.

Her gaze had followed his off toward the skyline, but she turned back. She touched his forearm with gloved fingers. 'I'm glad I didn't know you all then: you'd have frightened me to death!'

He laughed a short laugh without lowering his eyes. Then he looked to find her staring after the foamy wake of the boat. Her profile was piquant against the sky. Her skin seemed to glow in the wind. His gaze took in the slim figure in gray squirrel pelisse and wine-red skirt. How could he ever have thought her plain that first day at the picnic! But it was more than these: it was the way she looked into the distance. So frail! he thought. And he marveled at the strength of will she had shown at the moment of final decision, on the hotel porch, before her mother's handkerchief-hidden eyes. But he had known the answer in the sacristy of the church—had known the joining was immutable—against the world—the way from there had been destined.

Destined where? She was suddenly looking at him, smiling, as if she had asked him the question. He shrugged. 'Bud's still a timber-runner—still guzzles everything in sight,' he said quickly.

Her gaze wavered and went away. 'Bud ought to give it up—that tavern,' she said.

They were coming into Darien Creek. The boat made a slow turn, and he watched the prow sweep toward the marsh grass for the far bank. 'Bud couldn't make a living where he was.' They would do well to talk of something else, he thought. But not of the future, not of *where*. It would be old man Macgregor's inning now, perhaps. Rob-

362

bie had said that her mother would bring him around, but Ratliff knew that nothing so easy made sense—not hard sense. Robbie knew less about her father's capacity for hating than he did. He had seen, finally, Macgregor's arrogance reduced, seen his baffled rage. What did he feel now for the old glass-eyed 'gaitor? Somehow, with the turn of things, his triumph had been tasteless, swallowed up.

The wharf came into view in the distance—a small, harsh yellow building, picketed by still, gaunt piling. The shadows under the eaves were like masked eyes. She spoke behind him. 'But that tavern is bad for all the raftsmen who come there, as well as Bud.'

He pulled her arm through his and moved slowly along the rail. "Now, Robbie, you got your hands full with me: you can't scrape the mud and sin off the whole tribe of raftsmen.' Yes, Macgregor might line up all of the buyers against him, certainly the Dales—probably had. He could see three men and a woman in a white skirt and blue cape, standing at the wharf-edge. Who were they? Why were they there? Dead certain, not for welcome!

He felt Robbie's forearm stiffen. She looked up at him and broke their silence. 'And think of his poor wife! I'm going to find out about her.'

He laughed, and turning quickly, swung her with him. They moved back up the deck.

On the ride to his boarding-house, Ratliff saw Spalding at a distance, saw him turn away. He may not feel too kindly toward you, he told himself—taking two weeks' leave without applying first. But he must have got your letter. And the rule has never been rigid. You couldn't afford to show your hand then, whether he likes it or not. He watched Robbie lean over and speak gently to the negro hack-driver. There had been no one at the wharf they knew, except the agent, who passed them hurriedly, waving a handful of bills. But they had written no one the hour of their coming.

363

In the boarding-house hallway, Mrs. Runceforte met them, her eyes bright and her smile bracing the sags in her cheeks. 'Ah, the honeymooners! Yes, I got your letter, Mr. Sutton.' But Ratliff noticed a stiffness in her neck, and he saw that Robbie caught it, too. 'A *temporary* bridal suite,' she said, with the same smile: she would talk to him later about his plans.

Ratliff opened their bags in the stiff-curtained, unfamiliar bedroom and departed. He must see Spalding and make ready for the morrow. Robbie had said she would hang up a few things and call her mother.

The timber inspector-general was seated in the drugstore when Ratliff found him, and did not rise at his approach.

'I was a little slow getting in my application for leave,' Ratliff said, grinning and sitting down. (The man had offered him no congratulations and still did not smile.) 'I hope—'

'I might as well tell you at once, Sutton, this is a serious affair,' Spalding interrupted, his blurry voice creaking. 'Three firms have filed charges against you: Stuyvesant-George, Dawson and Clare, and Atkins.'

Ratliff's mouth tightened. So the fight's on, he thought. Macgregor lost no time! The Dales must have stayed out to make it look straight. But he said nothing.

'They are asking for your dismissal.'

Ratliff's head jerked backward slightly. 'But you got my letter, Major?'

'I can't discuss the case with you, man. I'm—it's a serious business!'

Ratliff's face smoothed out, became expressionless. 'I see,' he said, and rose.

'You'd better get you a good lawyer,' Spalding called after him.

As he walked down the street, he felt his muscles tauten. You are not going to get soft-bellied, honeymooning in the place, he thought.

Spalding was probably right about the lawyer, but whom should he get, whom could he trust, how far did this thing go? Looks like they aim to throw you out, Darien wife and all, he told himself. Could there be any way to settle it, patch it up, so that Robbie wouldn't hear about it? Hell, no! You are already under suspicion. But I can break it to her easy—make light of it tonight, he thought.

When he opened the door to their bedroom, he paused for an instant on the threshold, then stepped inside and closed it behind him gently. Robbie lay face downward on the bed. She looked small in the middle of the broad counterpane—a child asleep. Beyond her, a suitcase lay open, still unpacked.

'Is it you?' she said, before he could move. She reared up on her hands and slid to her feet.

'I'm sorry I waked you!'

'You didn't,' she said, and turned quickly toward the washstand.

Even in the dim light he could see that she had been crying. Cold touched his spine like a knife blade. He stood still in the middle of the room.

She spoke with her back to him—bending over the basin. 'Father's had a stroke, Ratliff. He's very low.' Her voice broke off and she reached out blindly for a towel.

He stepped to her, stumbling, handing her the towel, feeling as if his own fist had been rammed down his throat. He touched her, felt her rigid shuddering, but she stood away. 'I'll drive you home,' he said, 'Now. To your mother.'

She moved back to the bed and sank down on its edge, sitting a moment before she spoke. 'Aunt Mag answered the telephone—mother is not well, either.' She lowered her head. 'Mother could not speak to me—father has—has forbidden it.'

'Good God!' he said, and gripped the knobby frame of the bedstead. He stood staring at her dumbly until she got to her feet. His lips twitched, parted twice before he spoke. 'I—I didn't look for this, Robbie—I couldn't have! Before God, Robbie, I couldn't have—' He concluded in a desperate whisper, 'I did what I thought was right—'

She took hold of his arm quickly, gripping it hard. "No, no you're not to blame!' She steadied herself. 'It's so strange—I can't understand—but I cannot believe we are in the wrong.'

Ratliff was amazed at the pain Robbie brought him. It was as if the hide he had toughened against Darien, against twenty-nine years of untoward existence, had been ripped from his back—though he was too full of the experience to define it. Her quiet, pallid face never left off hurting him. And everything touched the wound. First, there was Mrs. Runceforte, who hardly waited for them to unpack before she 'reminded' him that she did not board married couples—though he knew she had—and expected them soon to find another place.

Then Robbie received a note—she didn't tell him, he found it— from the Sunday-School superintendent, sympathizing over her father's illness and saying that another teacher had been selected to fill her place. None of her friends had come near them, and her solitary riding for exercise was to the Ridge to meet Geoffrey's younger sister for smuggled news of her father and mother. When they went out on the street together, they passed a paling fence of backs and turned heads.

And he knew again his friendlessness: most of the members of the troop were polite to him, but few indicated their sympathy. The breach with Geoffrey was complete. Even Bud seemed cut off by his silent disapproval of Robbie and the mess Ratliff had gotten himself into. He spent his time at work on his case before the council, though there was little he could do except worry. His lawyer insisted that if he wrote Spalding the letter and Spalding got it, they would not fire him. But Ratliff felt little assurance the Spalding would admit the receipt of the letter, against the pressure from the buyers, and he had never been able to determine certainly that Spalding had got it. Suspicions about his lawyer dogged him, too.

But the trial finally ended in anticlimax. Near the last of January, he received a heavily marked, twice-forwarded envelope. It contained the reply Spalding had written to him in New Orleans, criticizing his carelessness, but agreeing to request an extension of leave. Robbie took it as Fate's favor, an answer to prayer—her face brightened with thankfulness. The sight of her was a cheering thing for Ratliff, though the council's action, adding thirty days to the term of his suspension, brought him more bitterness than relief.

He was now convinced of a necessity that had been growing plainer to him for months. Long before his marriage, he had come to see that a public inspectorship was only a way station in Darien. The job was under the thumb of the timber merchants and got one the raftsmen's kicks, to boot. At first he had listened to Bud's foolishness and had taken care of a few that they used to run with; then a raft of Roof Bostick's had cost him ninety dollars on reinspection. That and his popularity with the rivermen had brought the buyers down on him like a bee swarm—all they wanted was an excuse to penalize him.

Since his suspension the other scalers—that green-eyed gang— were putting out poison with the raftsmen: if he ever scaled logs again, they said, the buyers would be so prejudiced against him he would have to lean over backward, couldn't even give them what was coming to them.

He hadn't stayed in Darien to take buyers' back-door handouts, always—always, his hat in his hand. Already he'd felt the cramp to put his battered sky piece back on his head. But the new compulsion dwarfed his earlier feeling. Now Robbie's head was bare to the buyers! They could shut their doors in her face, even their hangers-on could insult her, so long as he was their hireling. Only at their level could he command respect. These thoughts trailed him, bayed loud at his heels, as he helped her—she had finally been glad to get away from Mrs. Runceforte's insinuating questions—buy for and furnish the house they had rented.

But the total of cash he could scrape together—his savings and his hidden interest in the tavern—would scarcely make fifteen thousand dollars. He must have twice that sum to set himself up, not to mention the need of credit. He sought out August Schardt, head of the only firm that took no actual part in the action against him, but he got cold comfort from the old German. He tried to interest his Jewish friend, Marcus, in a partnership, but Marcus preferred to keep his money in something he knew more about. Finally, he tried a horse trade with a rapacious Atkins, whose business was as small and shaky as his reputation.

This was over Robbie's objection. He wouldn't have told her—he knew her Sunday-School notions and felt uneasy enough about his share in her religion, as it was—but they were together so much now and he sensed the pain that lay always behind her hearty smile. (Even though Macgregor was out of bed, she was still barred from the house, could only communicate with her mother through little Aurelia Dale.) He had to say anything he could to brighten the look of the future.

He knew Atkins was a hard bargainer. He first offered his capital and his services for a fourth interest, then a fifth and finally a sixth, without salary. Atkins still mulled over it, but early in June he sent for him and made him a counter-proposal.

Contract business was overshadowing the open market: Dale and Coventry must be getting half of their timber supply by this method, undoubtedly had thousands upon thousands of acres under lease. Atkins hadn't the capital to tie up in such extensive leases. He didn't mind furnishing timber-runners, furnishing them everything except timber. And there were still shifty fellows on the river who didn't ask anybody to get their stumpage for them. Sutton should know, Sutton should know, too, just where all of the Dale and Coventry's fine, unguarded leaseholds lay. Now, if he could head up a first-rate, inde-

368

pendent contract business for Atkins that didn't involve leaseholds—a silent partnership in the firm might be arranged.

Ratliff gazed on at the mud-gray, terrapin eyes before him for a moment after the man had ended. Then he lowered his own, slowly, casually. Sure he could still steal timber, get it stolen, but this would be a juggler's act, and a lot of tricky balls to handle! The wisp of Robbie's hair, the cheek it had fanned, that morning at the breakfast table floated through his mind. She had told him she was pregnant. Hell, it's a toehold, he thought, and, by God, you need one more than ever now! You don't expect Atkins to hand you anything—except a slick trick, if he can. And he can't! But this inner voice somehow sounded shrill. . . . He raised his eyes. 'Well, it took you a month to think it up. Guess I'd better not be too quick.' He drew his hands jerkily from his pockets. 'I'll let you know.'

Two weeks of pondering did not bring him to a decision, and then, he felt it had been taken out of his hands. He learned of Major Macgregor's second apoplectic stroke at the Boom, and when he got home he found Robbie in bed and a doctor at her side. He could hardly bring himself to look at her. Her face was grayish-white, had grown suddenly gaunt. She stared up at the ceiling. Her gaze was the only sign of life about her, and that a shadow. She did not move, or speak to him. But there was nothing for them to say: he could not have uttered a word.

The doctor told him that she had lost her baby; he had guessed that already. As he walked over to the window, the gooseflesh on his neck and head was as hard as hoar frost. He stood staring out at the gray-trimmed oaks—hearing far within his ears a shrill catch of breath, like a boy's, in another room—it kept catching, but the cry never came.

Without his knowing when or how, there formed in the shade of the trees before him the cold, grim face of Macgregor: chin still high above his pillow. He shook his head and the image flickered out, but he had seen it, seen it plain: a smile. He stared on, bemused, respect-ful.

Then, blood glutted his veins. It ebbed away under an acid chill and he shook from head to foot. The shaking brought him calm, a new assurance: he knew now the Atkins deal was off his course, that Robbie would not die.

She didn't. Ratliff found her stronger than she looked. Before the end of the month she was out of bed and seemed almost herself again. He forbore now his scheming, left ways and means to Other Hands. Robbie's need was immediate. The money he had saved for his timber business, he would use in building a house. The land was Robbie's, six acres on a salt creek near the Ridge; she had it of her grandmother.

At least this would take them out of Darien: beyond the averted faces, the whispers—the whispers they saw and felt, that somehow always got to their ears: 'It's that Sutton' . . . 'Who would ever have thought *Robbie Macgregor*' . . . 'White trash and a blackguard' . . . 'They'll kill her father yet.' Remote from the church bell, too, the pon-tifical face of the preacher, saying—on their first time at services after Robbie got out of bed: 'A godly, devoted member. . .again at the point of death. . .remember him in your prayers'—and stares; cold, vicious, indecent stares!

On the woody six acres they were away from all this—the two of them, with only the Irish and negro workmen. And each day brought its small enterprise, diverting problem. Robbie seemed caught up in it and he half-forgot the lag, the waiting for an upward turn. She vi-sited the place when he could not be there, brought Laura Gracey—the one friend left her, that she permitted herself—and even her queer Aunt Eugenia, who lived on a near-by plantation and who had taken their part. During July and August the house rose tall and gray, in its shingle covering, above its dormer windows, to the ridge of its steep gables.

If only her father would get well! (He was reported stronger, sitting up.) It was a strange prayer for him, Ratliff knew—for him, who had never asked aught of an enemy. But he would have nursed the old man himself, if it would have helped. Robbie was gaining health, would gain health, if only her father would get well. September was upon them and she must get away from this humid heat, this hellish coast and its people! She still weighed less than a hundred pounds, the pallor still clung to her cheeks, but there was no getting her to leave with her father ill—and the malady that drained his strength drained hers.

Macgregor did not get well, however. On the tenth of the month he had another stroke. And this was too much: Robbie's nerves broke halter. She went home, despite her Aunt Mag's warning not to come. It was only her father's fiendish sister who didn't want her. He would see her, had to see her! He didn't. And failing once, she went again, supported by her Aunt Eugenia. She got into the room this time, stayed there, but it was of no use: the light never glimmered again in the grim old face.

Robbie couldn't cry, couldn't cry even after she got away from the bedside and her Aunt Mag, even when she met Ratliff in the hallway of their home. It was a hard thing to see, her dead face and eyes, hard—but the feeling was still with him then—it did not shake his faith. He could even tell her then –though it throttled his voice once or twice—tell her, as she clung to his shoulder, that it had not been given them to lay the course, that God's love was like iron.

But after the funeral, after he had seen her off on the train with her aunt from Charleston, her mother's sister, for the trip to the mountains—seen her off, still white-faced and staring—Ratliff wondered.

They had gone unwelcome to the funeral and, unwelcome, they had sat with other members of the family, sat among the gray, embittered faces, surrounded by the harsh, condemning eyes. And now he

371

was by himself with the whispers—the deed was finally done, they said, and they looked at his hands. . . By himself, in the rainless, endless September heat. Even Bud had deserted him: wanted to quit the tavern, borrow money to buy back his farm. Once, he had wished to replace Bud, but now the thought of his going left him chilled, wondering, staring, as Robbie had stared.

The sun hung above Darien like a stovelid. High water held, logs came, and he stayed wearily at work during the day, trying to regain some of his trade. . . . The nights settled down on him like a motionless swamp slough, alone in his unfinished house, on his unfinished course alone. Was he alone, indeed? Deserted? Where would it end? He had foregone, on faith, his one chance to break the companies' bondage—he had bowed his head to the torture that Macgregor's desperate revenge had brought them. What could he tell Robbie, offer her, when she came back? . . . If she came back! Had this thing broken her faith in them? In him? What did her staring eyes see?

Ratliff stood on his porch and looked off at the moonlit marsh, heard its dry rustle, saw its limitless grass fade into the night. He shut his eyes. His body grew slowly rigid, swayed. He felt a smothering closeness on him, an iron frame—tasted iron in his mouth. 'Oh, Poss!' he cried aloud. 'Uncle Mund—' His swelling throat choked back the word.

CHAPTER

34

ON SATURDAY NIGHT, on the night of October 2, when the wind began to blow out of the northeast, Ratliff slept wearily, heavily in his bed. And in the morning, when the cook summoned him to breakfast, he was still not fully conscious of the storm, so long had his sleep, his drugged senses, been enveloped in the roar. But at the table, swallowing a forkful of fried egg, he paused and lifted his head. No small shakes of a blow, he thought, feeling a tremor through the house. After a moment he pushed back his chair, got his hat and jacket from the back hall tree, and moved through the kitchen toward the door. "Left my log book at the Boom,' he called to the negro man, standing over a waffle iron at the stove.

Outside, the sky was a muddy gray. The wind smote his face and made his eyes smart. He hurriedly saddled his horse under the creaking strain of the barn, thinking, this is enough to damage timber. Lone leaves shot through the air like quail. The saplings along the lane shuddered, hard bent before the wind. When he turned his mare into the shell road to Darien, its force caught them from behind, carried him against the animal's neck and sent her down the way at a hard trot to keep her feet.

The boughs of the great live-oaks churned angrily, their moss tails flung out like whips. In the wind, in the roar about him, was a deep, giant drum-roll from the marsh, from the sea. 'Nor'easter,' he said aloud, as if to think clearer. 'Hell, this is some storm!'

There were repeated jagged flashes of lightning as the horse galloped on, and Ratliff was suddenly swept by rain, rain that drove through his breeches-legs, down the collar of his leather jacket, hid the way under hurrying gray waves. At the bend of the road, he felt his mare's body twist beneath him as she was carried skittering obliquely across the pavement. 'The Devil!' he said. 'Your log book's not worth it.'

His voice sounded as if he were at the bottom of a well. He strained at the reins, brought the horse down to a walk that resisted the wind at each step. Turn back, you fool! he told himself. . . .But he did not. He felt his blood rise warm against the chill of the rain. There was a kindling stimulation from his wet cheeks, from his nostrils, his throat, the clutch of the formless, importunate gale.

Then he heard a faint cracking above him—almost soundless in the uproar—and the wind's veering thrust sent his horse sideways again. A bough brushed his shoulder and he saw, carried past him through the rain, the big limb of a tree. It struck the ground and bounced along in the blast. 'Close!' he said, expelling his breath hollowly. The danger touched him like an electric current, cleaned his nerves and his brain of lingering poison, dullness.

He narrowed his eyes. What in God's name's the matter with you? Go back! But he did not check the mare. An obscure curiosity, an inarticulate need, an unreasoning hunger stirred in him. He felt it in his belly, his loins, his arms. Go back to what? he asked himself.

At a point where the road ran close to the creek, where the woods gaped, the marsh came into view and he twisted against the wind to look at it. The rain had let up and what he saw almost carried him from his shifting seat: not a mud-bound creek, not a strip of water

374

bordering a great plain of grass, but a wide, gray, foaming gulf—water as far as his eye could carry in one glimpse. He doubted his senses, tried to look again, but he could not. 'God,' he said, 'God, what a sea!'

The wind forced the mare into a run, her head lowered, her hind quarters moving obliquely with her body. The great trees above, about him raged, lashed out with their limbs. A bough raked his head as he ducked. Horse and rider were carried off the road, against a vine thicket—the mare stumbling, struggling to keep her feet. He climbed down her trembling side, led her back to the pavement, went ahead on foot, his eyes black, his face sharp, his body braced back against the blast—but running, running soundlessly in the uproar.

Suddenly, as he reached the outskirts of Darien, the wind lulled with a vast, expiring sound, as if the engine of the universe were stopping. He felt his weight on his feet, the reins in his hand. But only for an instant: the hurricane veered to the east, struck him with a concussion that sent him into the air, floating, whirling—at the heart of a rising, rending howl—the roof of a house sailing before his eyes.

When, finally, he landed, halted his driven body, caught in and held to a palmetto thicket, his face and hands were bleeding and he found that his horse was gone, gone completely. But he did not think of the horse, or himself. He did not think: his mouth broke open and he bellowed. The grip, the pressure, the infinite force enveloping him, the frenzy that filled space with driven boughs, uprooted trees, riven fences, roofs, the deafening din of voices, blurred, broken, swallowed up in the outraged howl, the shriek of the storm, the gargantuan riot, all charged him with a wild tenacity to hold on to, to be a part of it.

On his belly, clawing at the palmetto roots, he inched his way into the wind, gained the shelter of a ditch by the road. 'God!' he shouted. 'Great and Almighty God!' The sound that passed his ears was small and fragmentary. He moved down the ditch into the town. Beyond a cross-street, beyond a cloud, a blast of sand, he saw the riven stump of a dwelling. God, indeed! Was He out to destroy Darien? He raised his head to the blast and laughed, laughed a thin, rattling sound.

With outspread arms clutching the ground, his tight-shut eyes and mouth pressed against it, he pulled himself across the sand-blast to the shelter of a tree-trunk. He made it to a picket fence. Then, holding to it, crawling beside it, he pushed his way into the wind. After an hour's hard driving, he came to the lower edge of the Bluff. He held to the trunk of a shuddering giant oak and stood up. For a moment he waited, then he looked around the tree.

A great gray gap, in violent motion, met his gaze. He ducked his head and wiped his eyes on a sleeve. Below him, the masts of schooners jumped, darted, swerved like raked straws—their hulls rose high, disappeared beneath monstrous walls of water—water that roared, smashing, foaming over the wharves, over the roofs of the depots.

He looked to his right, upriver, toward the bend, toward the Boom. There was no bend, no Boom, no river—no dyke, no rice field! Over the space of the field, against the Bluff, a boiling brew of logs still swung, shifted, beat the bank. He saw a great pine rear endwise, shoot into the air, fall, spinning, bouncing on the churning timber, driven by the blast.

'Gone! Scattered,' he said, 'from here to Jesup'—not hearing his voice, not knowing that he said it.

His gaze moved on to the storm-rifled buildings on the Bluff, the naked streets. Brick and mortar still stood: his tavern was there, though the sign was gone. Over bending tree-tops, in the distance, he saw a church steeple crumple, slide off in the blast. These things came in through his eyes. He wiped the water from his wind-bitten face. 'There won't be a wharf left, or a boat, or a boom,' said his tiny voice.

'The town may go!' He lingered, turning farther, but there was only the grove at his back.

Finally he faced the gap, looked into the distance. There was no marsh, there were no islands—only a tumultuous, tilting waste of white-tipped water—terrific currents, ripping landward. Out of the infinite gray sky, sweeping in from the gray horizon, mountains of sea rocked and rolled toward the Bluff. His mouth opened. His face twisted in hard furrows. He gazed on, his black, staring eyes crossed with a soft gleam.

Then suddenly, as if the lightning flash had touched him, he loosed the tree and staggered backward. 'Och!' he said. 'Logs! . . . Pick-ups!' he shouted. He got down on his hand and knees. 'The Old Marster ain't furgot!' He laughed at the ground beneath him. Ain't furgot you!' He began to crawl. Business on hand—plans—me and old Bud! He was crawling through the gale, across the Bluff, toward the tavern.

CHAPTER

35

DARIEN WAS SLOW to disentangle its wreckage after the hurricane. Men were shaken. In the town two churches and three houses had been demolished, a score had been unroofed, and an unreckoned number of negro shanties. Catastrophe had struck the islands. By Tuesday the reported number of drowned had reached half a hundred. And the rice plantations lay in ruins: dykes, houses, stock, fields gone. The tugboat men were hard hit, too. Their vessels had been capsized, broken, driven far into the marsh. One of them, the *Unique,* came to rest in a back yard on the Ridge.

But the timber merchants had suffered the greatest damage. There had been more than forty million feet of logs at the Public Boom and at their private booms, wharves, and mills when the gale struck. Scarcely a trace of it was left when the wind stopped blowing, and booms, wharves, and mills were wrecked.

Like most other able-bodied males, the men of the timber houses had turned their first efforts to the rescue of lives and the relief of human distress. And on Wednesday morning, when Ratliff returned to the place, he found them at their first tentative efforts of salvage. The thought of the desolation of the islanders disturbed him: he should have been there, though his absence had not been noted. It had been the timber on his mind, the timber—and it must be the timber only. He moved about the uptown streets and stores, his hands in his breeches-pockets, his head stilled to hear and overhear. He had his calculated plan, but he came alert for any advantage the situation might offer.

At midday, when he descended the steps of the Schardt and Schiewitz offices on Market Street, however, it was to resume his original intention of dealing with the terrapin-eyed Atkins. Schardt had sent for him, wanted his help: men were at a premium and most of the scalers were helping, for there would be no market at Darien for days to come. The old German had been the only timberman who had not joined in the suit against him, the winter before.

He spat beyond the sidewalk. You are playing these cards like they fell, he told himself, recollecting Schardt's mention of 'friendliness' without emotion. Not for Schardt: he was a damned buyer, too! The half-smiling embarrassment, vanishing into gravity, that he had seen on Edward Dale's face at the steps of his office earlier in the day flickered past his consciousness. Staring at Ratliff absently, he had spoken to him. Then, recollecting who Ratliff was, he had said: 'Ah, sir, this is no time, no time—catastrophe has struck us.' Dale and Coventry, the biggest, had been the hardest hit: eighteen million feet of timber carried away. The old man would have offered you a job if you'd hinted for it, he thought. But he did not sneer: he had no time for sneering. The only feeling he knew now was the vibration deep within him, in his chest—like organ music—comprehending him, dedicating him to his task, supporting the weight of his responsibility. It left no room for whims.

When Ratliff reached Atkin's small sawmill on Cathead Creek, he found him overseeing three negroes at work on the stump of a wharf. The white men walked away and leaned against the side of the roofless boiler shed and Atkins launched into the story of his misfortunes.

Ratliff heard him out, then stood away from the wall. 'I'll recapture that timber fur you—ever' stick of the three million feet you say you lost.'

Atkins batted his drooping eyelids. 'That's big talk! What do you want?'

'That can wait till the job's done.' Ratliff's mouth stretched, its corners turning up briefly.

'The Sam Hill, man! You don't know what you're talkin' about.' Atkins suddenly pushed himself away from the wall on an elbow. 'You can't get help—you can't get niggers for love nor money—can't find 'em.'

'Leave that to me. You just furnish the liquor and grub and wages.'

'Hell, Duke Pitt and the Dale and Coventry crowd's already got most of 'em, I hear—givin' 'em three dollars a day.'

'You goin' to have to pay for your niggers.'

'I'm willin' to pay that—maybe more, if we could just get a good crew together—get my timber out of the marsh.' Atkins wiped sweat from his lean face with his shirt sleeve. 'My God, if I could just get half of it back—it'll be hell to pick out your own logs.'

Ratliff grasped Atkins's forearm and looked at him levelly. His eyes were dark and held a copper glint. He spoke in an even, steady voice, but swiftly. It was foolish to think of picking out your own timber. Already the others were talking about an exchange to straighten up the brands later. The squabble was going to get bad after a while. Atkins was a little fellow and had better pick up his chips fast and get out of the way. The thing to do was to throw several crews to work up and down the river, pick up the easiest logs to get, without even looking for the brands. Ratliff had hired a naphtha launch in Brunswick. He could have fifty niggers ready by morning—get more later.

Atkins was silent for a time, running his hand through his thin gray hair. 'I reckon you want a partnership,' he said, 'and I guess I could use that fifteen thousand of yours before this is over.'

Ratliff thrust his hands into his pockets and turned away. 'It ain't unlikely. But we got to get goin'.'

Walking toward Darien, he thought: That's that—hell, Atkins is all right—if you've ever got him by the scruff! It was not Atkins he had turned down back in June: it was his proposition. With this job he would be footloose on the river and nobody to get in his way: it was cut to fit and he had cut it.

That night at the tavern, in the room behind the bar for negroes, he dealt with the colored policeman, Grenade. Grenade shook his head several times and rubbed a palm over his face. Hands who weren't burying their dead or rebuilding their houses were already employed by other buyers. It was dangerous business: sneaking company labor at a time like this.

'I never call on a friend except when I need him,' Ratliff said, looking at Grenade impassively. 'Thirty men will mean a hundred dollars for you—but they've got to stick.'

The next morning at sunrise, twenty-six of Grenade's contracted thirty appeared at a battered fish house below Darien Bluff and there joined twenty others that Ratliff had himself obtained. The air was crisp and a light breeze stirred with the turning tide. The negroes crowded the dock, grunted and grinned idly among themselves until he divided them up into crews and loaded them into his long, flat-bottomed naphtha launch and three rowboats.

The boat train moved up a now puny Darien Creek, bordered by banks of storm-swept and littered marsh grass. At the mouth of Rifle Cut, Ratliff dispatched one of the boats to pick up a derelict batteau, but he did not halt until they had reached the point at which the creek made out from Butler's River, a larger branch of the marsh-diffused, tidal Atlamaha.

He crawled upon the cabin roof of his launch. In the slanting sunlight the swollen carcass of a cow whitened the mudbank. He surveyed the scene. The dying grass lay twisted and flattened on the marsh. On the island to his left the broken limbs of a wind-rifled hammock were like bare bones. In the distance beyond it he saw the smashed gable-end of an overturned house. Ahead lay the black hull of a tugboat, its keel making a bright scar.

He twisted his head about and caught his breath. For miles in every direction, the marsh was splintered with logs, like a spring's scattering of magnolia matches under a blossomed tree. Here, there, yonder logs were clumped together, in fragments, in sections of rafts, but everywhere they littered the land and water. His chest quivered as he expelled the air, and he turned quickly and, with trembling hands, crawled back onto the deck.

'Mike, you drop off here!' He spoke harshly. 'Lay your boom on the white side, just above the creek mouth yonder. Put one man to a skiff—pole 'em down on the tide, then turn 'em up Cathead Creek and tie against the bluff.'

He threw a coil of rope into the boat where a gray-headed black stood listening, and his voice modulated as he went on. 'Remember these are all free logs, our logs as soon as we dog 'em. You are taking orders from me—nobody else. I'll be back after a little.'

The train moved on, leaving one boat behind. Beyond Reaphook Bend timbers lay thick upon the mudbanks. He detached another crew and a third at the high plunder of Cooper's Bar. Along his course he had found other blacks at work and here and there a white boss, directing them, but except for a nod or a raised hand, there was no communication. Every man and group seemed singularly intent upon the logs.

Above the bar he entered the Altamaha proper, moved out of the marsh land into the shadows of gray, cavernous swamps. There had appeared along the way the white bellies of dead fish, but, at the lower end of Piney Island, he passed the swollen carcasses of two alligators—killed by the hurricane. And on the jagged limb of a gaunt dead pine he saw the body of a gull impaled. Over the marshes the breeze had been tinctured with the smell of death. But now the sun was high and warm, and the swamp-walled, wood-strewn river reeked of fetid fish and flesh. They were stinking spoils! At the head of the long reach called Old Soldier, he set out his last crew and turned back.

He counted his naphtha boat a find. He had seen no other on the river. The thing would make ten miles an hour downstream. He could get about in a hurry, fast enough to keep his niggers humping, his logs moving—and white men from interfering.

Duke Pitt, in a boat pushed swiftly by six oarsmen, passed him at Piney Island. The lean, squinted face glanced his way, but did not appear to see him, absorbed in pointing out timber in the mouth of a slough. It was the same hungry look he had seen on all of their faces. The dogs will be growling soon, baring their teeth, but I aim to get my share of the bones, he thought.

Two of his hands were waiting for him at Cooper's Bar. They said a white boss and his crew had taken a float of ten logs away from them—that the man said the timber bore his company brand, then went on down the river with the skiff. 'Hellfire, that's no cause to quit!' Ratliff put them back to work. He told his engineer to hurry up the launch. He found the fellow below Reaphook Bend and recognized him—a Stuyvesant-George foreman—but did not speak. The engine ceased and his boat approached the negroes who were fastening the skiff into an unfinished raft.

'What you goin' to do with my logs, boys?' he called.

One of the negroes lowered his pike pole and looked over at his lank foreman, sitting in the stern of the batteau. The white man held his gaze to the logs. 'Keep movin', theah!' he said gruffly to the blacks.

The launch was now alongside the batteau. Ratliff stepped into it and reached the man in a single stride. He struck him in the face and sent him backward into the river, then got back into his boat. The negroes had quit work and stood looking at him. 'Jughead,' he said, addressing one of them, 'take that float on down to Atkins's mill. Tell the white boss I sent you, and to give you a drink of liquor.'

'Yessuh, Cap'n Sutton.' The negro began poling the skiff away from the raft.

'You can stay down there and work, if you want to,' Ratliff called after him.

'Yessuh,' the voice came back.

When the day had ended, when the logs gathered had been drifted and tied at Cathead Bluff, Ratliff went home to make a fresh start. He took a drink and bathed and ate supper. Then he re-dressed in the clothes he had taken off and saddled his wife's mare. He rode off into the night, northward. He followed roads and trails skirting the river swamp for nearly three hours, then turned into the jungle.

It was past eleven o'clock when he reached Swan Lake. The going had been rough, and he had dismounted in the low swamp and approached the reflected glow of the fire on foot. In the night, the thick-laced foliage, the wild, encompassing tropic growth above the camp, had the look of a cave. He saw a giant, jolting shadow lose its shape in the stalactiform. His blood quickened and his eyes smarted. He whistled. The three men around the blaze got up. Bud, propped on crutches, lifted his head. Ratliff stepped out into the light and they gathered about him.

'So Bud found you, Roof,' he said, taking the lank, loose-jointed Bostick by the arm. He turned to the others. 'How did your first day go?'

They nodded their heads. Bud spoke. 'We got three rafts tied out theah.' He looked off at the dark void beyond the fire, beyond the mud-cracked slope.

384

Ratliff followed his glance, peering into the shadowy gray mist that veiled the lake. He could see no shape. In the distance, beyond the reach of the trees, limpid stars were suspended in the black depths. 'Just three?' he said, turning back.

'Two more on the way—out-tide caught Dunk and Ike, I reckon.'

Ratliff shifted his head to locate a fire glow through the trees farther along the lake. 'Your hands camping over there?'

Bud nodded.

'Did you all run into any ganders?' Ratliff asked, looking at the fire-gleam in Bose Wall's glass-like eyes.

Wall smiled. 'Just logs—and ever' man tryin' to git around as many of 'em as he could 'fore somebody else.'

'Good,' Ratliff said. 'We can work in the open for a day or two yet. By the time we have to get under cover, I can spot you the skiffs and rafts to pick up. We'll have an incoming tide at night for ten days more to drift up here on.'

'We 'uz a-thinkin' about a drink,' Bud said, lifting his bushy eyebrows, and Ratliff nodded. The men were relaxed, but still excited, alert to the darkness. He paced back and forth before the fire, talking as Bud rummaged in a wooden box. The Darien crowd wouldn't get up this far and raftsmen would halt at the mouth of the lake. If a stray hunter or fisherman showed up, Bud should say that the rafts here belonged to timber-runners who were waiting for the Darien squabble to clear up and the market to reopen. Bud handed a jug to Ratliff and he drank.

He passed it on to Son Jacobs, who held it before him for a moment, batting yellow, light-glazed eyelids. 'When we set up our company in Darien,' he said, 'I aim to have me a demijohn like this 'un, a-settin' on my desk.'

The men about the fire grinned and looked at Ratliff. When he had sought them out on his trip to the Oconee, he had offered money for hands and supplies, his direction and protection for their craft and labor. He had proposed that they pool their booty, make it capital for a lumber company of their own, to best dispose of it. The need to gain their interest quickly, to hold them together and ensure their responsibility, had been imperative. Besides, he could not have afforded the outlay of a cash inducement. His mouth loosened and he spat into the blaze. 'It's early for countin' chickens,' he said.

Bostick, having taken his turn, smacked his lips and set the jug down. 'I like to a-got me a crow,' he said, 'the mornin' after the storm—soon after I clumb out'n that hollow cypress I spent the night in.'

The men smiled.

He wiped his bearded muzzle on the back of his hand. 'I 'uz pretty nigh the mouth of Little Buzzard in a dugout, when I looked up and seen the leaves a-shakin' in an overhangin' oak. That same ole bigun you shot the bar' out'n, Bud—and I thought I'd found another. I could glimpse a black head amongst the leaves.

'But just as I raised my gun, a voice sung out: "Gret Gawd, white man!" Damn if it waun't an ole nigger woman—blowed up theah by the hurry-cane!'

Ratliff watched the bearded jaws loosen, draw back in laughter, and finally he remembered to grin himself. The liquor went around again and came to him. He demurred, then drank, saying, 'Guess I'll need it before I get back to Darien.'

'Not tonight!' said Bud, sobering.

Ratliff handed back the jug. 'Another job, come sunup.' He turned away from the fire and moved toward his tethered horse.

The logs came to Atkin's mill—they came bearing his brand, other brands, no brands but they came. By Monday, Ratliff had added thirty more hands to his force upon the river. On the following day, he detailed a crew to go to work at one o'clock in the morning, to drift on the early tide.

Old man George had protested Ratliff's treatment of his foreman. And he and others complained to Ratliff's ignoring brands and drawing away their labor. Atkins cautioned him: he only snorted.

Manners among the timber merchants shortened quickly. They ceased to look for or talk about brands—at least on the timber each himself gathered. The wage for hands went up to five dollars a day, with free food and whiskey: all the buyers paid it —to anybody's negroes he could hire. The day after Ratliff started night-drifting, all field forces had such crews.

During the first few days (through Sunday) his log pirates had come boldly out upon the river in the daylight—there were many strange raftsmen, negroes, meddlers—few knew each other, the way was multifarious and wide, there was no order. Ratliff and his rogues made the most of it, for he knew it could not last.

But even as forces were becoming identified, scuffling broke out among the foremen, contention developed among the employers. Ratliff had foreseen it, helped it along: it fitted his ends. On his first evening's foray, he met his pirate crew at Piney Island, brought them to Cooper's Bar, Butler's River, set them upon the skiffs and rafts that Dale and Coventry's men had left for early morning drifting. The timber that was to have gone downriver on an outgoing tide went upriver on an incoming—more than three hundred logs.

Contention gave birth to suspicion. Edward Dale suspected Atkins, but he also suspected every merchant in the field. On the following night, the rogues made Stuyvesant-George their victim. On the following day, this merchant's suspicion fastened on Dale and Coventry. But while they whispered and considered, Ratliff made a third haul on the succeeding night at the booms of Dawson and Clare. Then the timbermen put all-night guards with their timber. This called for different tactics. He used he wily Bostick for his decoy. Roof, pretending to be fire-hunting deer, stopped by Schardt's boom at Rifle Cut, talked the guard into drinking with him, took him off on the hunt. But the enticement had taken more than two hours, and Ratliff's crews were unable to make Swan Lake—had to hide the rafts in sloughs and creek mouths until another tide. He cursed. Roof liked liquor-lapping too damned well!

The work of his right hand, the log-salvaging for Atkins, Ratliff had carried on with hard-faced relentlessness, from the hours of morning darkness to their evening return. Before the second week's end, he had put nearly two million feet of timber to Cathead Bluff. It was time to slow his output, or he would deliver himself of a legitimate excuse for being on the river before the logs were gone. It was time, he decided, that the work of his right hand should supply the want of his left.

Fewer logs went to the mill. They had suffered the suspicions of the others, now they were suffering their thefts, he told Atkins. And the Swan Lake hideaway continued to get timber.

But the strain of his task, the weight of his contingencies told on Ratliff. He seldom got more than three or four hours' sleep out of twenty-four. He had too many irons to watch. Atkins, the other forces in the field, his own rogues, had to be watched—it was a juggler's act and some balls were always in the air. And he feared that Robbie might come home to complicate it more, though he had written her to remain in Charleston with her aunt until the salvaging was over. He must have time to secure his gains, to realize his plans, to have something to offer her. His face grew gaunt: the lines became furrows between hard nostrils and hard mouth, his eyes were hollow in their sockets.

And the loot in Swan Lake harried his mind incessantly: the log store grew too slow, yet the growing made it harder to conceal. The buyers might find it, discover their brands on the logs; other thieves might come and steal; even his own rogues might make away with it. He could not have slept if he tried. His work schedule shifted with the tides, but during the course of each night, at some hour between sunset and dawn, he got to the lake to see his timber, to count the rafts and chafe at their small number, to reassure himself it was not less.

Atkins's complaints at the decline in output grew louder. When Ratliff had worn out the story of theft, he made bad logging his excuse: the logs grew daily more remote, more difficult to get. Two weeks, even with an increased force, had added scarcely a million feet. As the month ended, Atkins announced that he would quit. He had, he said, recovered about as much timber as he had lost: the three-million-foot figure was high. The recapture of logs was now not worth the cost.

Ratliff's hollow weary eyes, as he stared at Atkins there beside his desk in his office that Saturday afternoon, took on a mad glare. 'You're a Goddamned ninny!' he shouted, but he turned away, got himself in hand. He saw that the job was over: had to be. He left Darien for Swan Lake and remained there two days with his pirate crew. He tried picking up logs in the surrounding swamp at night, but the white men wanted to drink and trifle and the negroes were too slow, too clumsy in the darkness to warrant the wages he was paying. He tried one night foray on the company booms, but his negro, Dunk, got shot in the arm and barely escaped capture: they got no logs.

The white men had grown restive and wanted to go home, back to the Oconee. Home! With logs still loose on the river and their lake not half full! He railed at them, barking across the fire after they had returned to camp. Denied permission to go home, they wanted to celebrate, pitch a drunk. Fine *partners* they would make! He thought, listening to their mouthing, but he did not say it: he had not used the term since early days. He said they talked like shirt-tail boys. Roof said, hell! they had enough: four million feet or more; it would bring forty thousand dollars on the market. 'On the market!' Ratliff almost shouted, though he managed an indulgent smirk. 'It's a hell of a long way from the market, boys, and I guess you all would go off and leave it here!'

389

But that night he slept, till late morning, and when he arose, his head had cleared, he had recovered his grip. The negro hands he sent back upriver in the naphtha launch, under the wounded Dunk's care. Then he walked around the lake and again surveyed the great floating timber prairie. He felt renewed. Not all he had hoped for, but Roof's guess was scant. He got up on a cypress stump and gazed out over the even, furrowed acres of logs. There was capital enough for his timber house, enough to free him from the buyers, enough to offer Robbie! An ease came upon him, a release. He had taken all the scramble for logs would bear: he had not fumbled his high favor or failed his task.

CHAPTER

36

'WE'VE GOT A BEAR by the tail,' Ratliff had told his raftsmen *partners*, held unwillingly at camp to guard the timber. If the logs had been hard to put in the lake, he said, they were going to be even harder to keep there and harder still to get out. He and Bud had left. Ratliff knew he had not over-estimated the difficulty, and now in Darien he moved warily: his face wooden, except for the passion-distended pupils of his eyes.

He visited Atkins's office on Monday to discuss the partnership. The old man seemed cold. Ratliff feigned indifference, mentioning that he had had another offer—from a man in Ludowici with a huge tract of timber, and money to boot. But this had held a double purpose: he was not eager: he did not like the anxiety he saw in Atkins's face.

On the following day—but one day later—Dale and Coventry brought suit against Atkins in federal court at Savannah. When Ratliff heard the news, his pulse jumped and he felt thankful for his caution. It wasn't time to think of turning loose the bear's tail yet.

The next day, Dawson and Clare followed the Dale and Coventry lead into the law court—though the buyers were still stripping the marsh for logs—and Atkins filed countersuits against both of them. Ratliff's pulse beat hard again and his mind raced feverishly with questions, but in the end he grinned, grinned slowly, guardedly. It was incredible, incredibly quick, but a way was opening.

He went quietly into action: at the Bank of Darien he borrowed five thousand dollars on his home. From his old friend, Marcus, he got the promise of a loan of fifteen thousand on the tavern. By hook or by crook, he'd raise his own cash, cut and sell his own timber. Alone, combat the entangled timber lords.

Then on Saturday (it was the first week of November) the other two firms joined in the lawsuit: they had fallen far short of recovering their lost timber, the issue of brands was raised, there were claims and counterclaims. The litigation became general. Ratliff laughed grimly: this was beyond his hope, his calculation. It was more than his contriving, more than luck: circumstances were conspiring in the birth of his timber house. He did not pause—he could not—but he felt humbly thankful, and in the back of his mind there flickered a vision of Robbie's excited face.

While the dust and din of the dog fight were high, he must move quickly, boldly. He made a trip to Ludowici, where he rented two portable sawmills—hiring their operators and hands, whom he knew and could depend on—to move at once to Swan Lake. Through Marcus he leased a wharf and boom site on Mayhall Creek from an agent for Dawson and Clare, who held the property, but were now too embroiled, too buried in their troubles to suspect the move.

Circumstance favored him again with his would-be partners at the lake—though not altogether unexpectedly. He had continued to hold them there since his departure: the timber could not be left unguarded—or unexplained—for an instant. And when he visited them early in the new week, they pleaded that they must go home, wanted money. He was looking for money, too, he said, staring at them with his gun-hole eyes, now always black. It would take money to handle the timber, big money, and many months of waiting, a year—damned risky business at that!

They settled for three hundred dollars apiece, wages, and a vague promise that there might be more. Hell, three hundred was enough, enough for a full-length drunk even for Roof! And that was what they would put it to, whatever the sum, Ratliff told Bud in Darien, later. Bud's laugh was short. But he himself had not been sober enough since his return for Ratliff to use him, had been too drunk, almost, to sign the papers transferring Ratliff's share of the tavern back—now legal, since he had some time before resigned his inspectorship. Bud failed to realize that he, Ratliff, had put out, had chanced his hard money for those overgrown boys—and the money was not his, either: he had had to borrow it from China, against his share in the tavern's earnings.

China, too, had been moved by circumstance into the destiny of his enterprise, to yield a favor. The twelve hundred had been but an opener. Marcus had agreed to the big loan for three months only—it was more than he could handily afford, he had said. Ratliff had assured him freely of a first mortgage on the tavern. And Ratliff faced China confidently in the little back parlor of the Birdcage, where he had not been in many a day. 'I'm going to ask a lot this time,' he said, unsmiling, gazing steadily at her. She seemed almost a stranger then, for a moment, wearing a green, leg-o'-mutton-sleeved coat suit, sitting stiff in her chair, looking hard of mouth.

But he had got what he asked, before it was over. Although, he later reflected, the talk had taken a damned touchy turn. In telling of his chance, the big chance he had been looking for ever since he first hit Darien, he had said, 'I'm on the way to making her my son-of-a-bitch,' harking back to a thing China had said four years before when he was about to quit the place. Their eyes met and China's twinkled, showing their yellow gleam. And he had gone on about her words then, saying they had kept him in Darien, kept him after the damned place—'Kept you from bitin' off a couple of councilmen's thumbs, anyhow,' she had said, and they laughed.

Then he had told her about his destined timber house and what he wanted of her, but he saw she wasn't listening, that her eyes were on the floor, her face working, growing soft and finally hard. And he stopped and she came out of it slowly, saying that he was going on to the top of the heap, that she had known he would, and mentioning his marriage to a 'high-class woman.' And she had looked suddenly into his eyes and said, 'I'm glad, Snake.' She just hoped, she said in another voice, that 'she,' meaning Robbie, was half as glad.

It had given him a funny feeling, and he had wondered for a moment if Robbie *would* be glad, and it seemed suddenly that she was staying away a long time and writing seldom. But, God, he had urged her to stay and was not yet ready for her return! He went on and made the deal with China, promising her a written contract on stock in his company—when it should be incorporated—for her quitclaim deed.

It had been pretty touchy, Ratliff repeated to himself on the third Monday of his return to Darien, as he locked the deed, which had been recorded, and the contract, which had not—at his insistence—in the tavern safe. Touchy, but now he had the money, and he put on his hat and left for Swan Lake.

When he came back from the lake near the end of the week, leaving behind a steady whine of saws, he knew his shadow-boxing was at an end, that he must finally meet the buyers' fists. He could no longer escape their notice, skirt about under the dust of their fight. He had to sell his lumber, invade the market—their market.

It had had his watchful attention since the day he first began to plan his own house. He knew little lumber had been shipped since the storm: that little could be shipped with every log in Darien tied up by the court (though there was talk of its being bonded out), that three barques had been lying idle off Doboy for more than a week. He knew, too, that representatives of big foreign lumber dealers had come to town—Highsmith and Steele of Liverpool, Schulz and Hanby of Hamburg—that they had come to press Darien firms to fulfill their contracts; that the ships would soon be, if they were not already, costing the foreigners demurrage; that the Hamburg man had been there more than a week. He had seen the paunchy German visit Stuyvesant-George's offices twice during the morning before he left for his mills. And on each coming-away, the fellow's jowls had hung limper and his head heavier.

It was with the German that he decided to try his first thrust at the market, to strike to penetrate the tight-held trust of the timber ring, when on his return he saw the barques still in port, still empty. Herr Kraus, the agent, was in his room at Mrs. Runceforte's boarding-house and greeted him politely, spoke in careful English.

Ratliff told him that he had formed his own timber house. The doors had opened that morning. It was not so big as some, but it was free of court entanglement, unburdened by the cost of the storm, ready and able to deliver lumber immediately at a reasonable price.

The German got up gravely to congratulate him, but Ratliff dismissed the courtesy with brief grace, smiling only with his mouth, continuing his gaze steadily at his man. 'I see your ship is still idle here. I understand you can't get the lumber you contracted for by your firm?'

Herr Kraus shook his head and smiled painfully. 'Hurricane! The hurricane is all I can hear.'

Ratliff nodded slightly, sat still. 'How far behind are Stuyvesant-George on their contract?'

The sandy lashes concealing Kraus's small eyes blinked dubiously, then he looked up. 'I tell you, the lumber should be in Hamburg six weeks ago and I don't know anything still, but *act of God*—they claim an act of God.'

'If it's timber, not talk, your firm wants'—Ratliff spoke levelly—'I can have the stuff here to load that barque Monday—put it to the stevedores as fast as the niggers can throw it in the hull, have the boat ready to clear by the end of next week. I'll post a bond at the bank—forfeit two shillings the *load* for every day beyond that date the boat is held.' The tilt of his long head seemed to give continuing force to his words, after he had ceased and remained looking at the man.

'But, Mister Sutton, Stuyvesant-George have the contract!'

'I'm not selling promises, nor excuses—nor manners. Just timber.'

Kraus blinked and shook his head. 'Yes, I know, but we have done business with Stuyvesant-George a long time, we will do business with them again—before, they always fill their contracts—*und* a contract is a contract.'

'A *broken* contract ain't!' Glints came from Ratliff's big-pupiled eyes.

Kraus turned his head tentatively, his gaze still held in Ratliff's. 'But *act of God?*' he said, finally blinking and looking away.

'The federal court's got the timber tied up, not God.'

'Yes, yes, the court—I have talked to our vice consul here about that—he thought so, too, and I've been trying to tell them so, but—'

'Two hundred and fifty thousand feet of shipping timber—that's four hundred and eleven *loads*—aboard your ship, headed for Hamburg before sunset Saturday week.'

Kraus's sandy lashes lifted. 'Saturday week,' he said, and stared at Ratliff silently. '*Mein Gott!* we want timber—that's why I'm here—and they have cabled me authority to act to get it. . . . But you Darien merchants'—he threw up his hands—'all together—all have raised your prices!'

Ratliff's eyes seemed to widen, then to narrow, and he was still for a moment, but when he spoke it was with the same even insistence. 'I'm selling timber: I'm not with anybody on anything—no storm

396

troubles, no court troubles, no red tape. . . .What are Stuyvesant-George's contract prices?'

Kraus blinked, hesitated, but he did not look away. 'Two pounds, three the load for hewn shipping timber; three shillings more for sawn; six pounds, nine and the standard for deals—it was so.'

'And they want more? They are holding out to bounce your crowd for more—calling it an act of God!' Ratliff laid his hand on Kraus's knee.

Kraus cleared his throat. 'It begins to look so—'

'How much more?'

'Seven shillings the load, fifteen the standard.'

Ratliff gripped the knee, his head suddenly weighted backward. After a moment, he went on, but his monotone had become drawling, gentle. He'd beat the *original* price by six shillings the load—a pound, seventeen for hewn shipping timber, three shillings more for sawn, six pounds flat for deals—yellow-heart pine—in the barque by Saturday week—no red tape—no excuses.

That had cinched the sale. Ratliff had seen it in Kraus's bright blue eyes, before he blinked, exclaimed 'Six shillings!'—stood up, saying warmly, 'Mister Sutton, you may have talked us into trouble, but you have sold your timber.' And Ratliff bore away the contract, his admittance to the market, his pass within the timber stockade, in the breast-pocket of his coat, stiff against his chest.

He bore, too, a sense of shock at learning that the buyers were trying to kick their prices up almost three dollars the thousand—on old contracts, as well as new. Jesus, the storm must have cost them! Or were they malingering? He wondered. But this was only a fragment of the puzzle, the picture that came together when Bud True, in the office, made his report.

Bud's mustaches spread in a fierce grin, and he turned to the big-bellied bookkeeper at the high counter that bisected the outer room. 'Tell 'im what we bought, Pruitt.' Then he went on, not waiting. 'Nine rafts—ever'thin' that's bin theah this week, exceptin' three—at six dollars and down—it's rape!'

Ratliff opened his mouth, then shut it and frowned. He put his hand on his desk to steady himself and echoed Bud's word, 'Everything?'

'Hell, Darien's big dogs've got the log colic—the runners can't hardly give 'em stuff!'

Ratliff stood there, not moving, his hand steadying him, while his eyes slowly widened, burned. He turned away, as if Bud's face dazzled him, fumbling against the counter, moving uncertainly toward the doorway of his office. What? Was it possible? Hell, no!

He swung the door after him, not shutting it, and let himself into his chair with weakened knees. The September market had run high—they buyers had bought heavily, very heavily. Then the storm! He leaned on his desk and stared at a calendar above it, into the simpering face of a Floradora girl that he did not see. The storm had swept forty million feet of timber into the marsh. Then recovery had come dear—and loss piled on that—Stuyvesant-George had got back only little over half, he'd heard. (The bits of the puzzle were slipping into place, as if drawn by a magnet.) He had heard—and hadn't credited it till now—that the cost had been eighty per cent on their investment. All told, that tied up three-quarters of a million dollars and put it into court. They are tryin' to welsh on contracts, they are passin' up dirt-cheap timber . . .

'Great God!' he said aloud and solemnly. 'They can't! Their credit's gone—they're strapped!' His neck swelled. He gripped the arms of his swivel chair and swung toward the window. His face shone, as if in the glow of a fire. If I can just hop fast enough, spread myself thin enough! He came to his feet and staggered for a moment drunkenly. I'll run this Goddamned roost! His hammer head set on his shoulders, making a single powerful line with his jaw.

CHAPTER

37

WHEN RATLIFF WAS finally aboard the train for Charleston on his way to fetch Robbie home, he realized suddenly that it had been three months since he had seen her. He sat upright in his seat, winced and shook his head. Three months, lacking two days, since the September afternoon that he had put her and her Aunt Miriam Simonton into one of these carriages. He had known the time was long and daily growing longer—but three months! The dull sense of misgiving that had shadowed him for weeks, that had hung on at the back of his mind, that he had had no time to stop and consider, was suddenly sharp upon him, jerking at his pulses, whirling questions at him.

When he had got into another seat at Ludowici, feeling one train nearer his destination, he consoled himself with the thought that he had not *let* her come home, he had withheld her, he had written her that he was coming to Charleston—written twice. The first time, he remembered, was just before he went to the Savannah bank to get a line of credit, two —my God! had it been three weeks ago?

As he paced the lobby of the Savannah station, waiting for his final train, he told himself that he had been a fool, a blind idiot to keep on putting off the trip. But, God knows, he had wanted to come, to see her, to claim her. He had never gone to sleep at night—not in a bed—without the hurt of loneliness. The pain was at him now—pain and doubt.

But finally within the carriage that would bear him into Charleston, he felt reassured. At last, at last he had a place, a situation, a Darien to bring her back to. Already the contemptuous timber ring, the arrogant, were beginning to suspect that something was happening to them, had taken their logs out of hock. Though that would do them little good. It came too late, for he had broken their grip on the market, broken it to pieces. When he got his new line of credit with the Charleston house worked out, he would be set to buy every damned log that came to Darien for Christmas.

Yes, it did seem strange for a man married less than a year to allow his wife to go away on a trip and stay three months—but they had been no more married-couple-of-a-year, it had been no mere trip. Robbie had known that he knew she needed time, though they had never mentioned it in their letters, had known, too, that she must wait until he could make Darien endurable for her. He had scarcely more than hinted at what he'd done, made ready. And she had said little about her coming back, but she had been curious about what he was doing.

He arrived in Charleston early next morning. His inquiry of the white-capped negress in the deep vestibule of the tall brick house on Rutledge Avenue was only to reassure himself of the place. When her guttural sounds through the closing door were clear to him, he reopened it and followed her down the hall. He turned from its shadows into a brightly lighted breakfast room, close behind her.

There was a flutter of the folds and flowing sleeves of wrappers. He paused on the threshold, glancing quickly, furtively beyond the maid at the four ladies, in negligee, about a white-matted table. His gaze alighted on Robbie at the farther end, facing obliquely toward him. As she twisted, half-rising, uttering sound, the dark eyes in his stiff face flickered, lowered to the fire on the hearth. His neck had reddened, he had not spoken, when his eyes came back, eager yet fearful, to meet hers.

Ratliff saw only astonishment on Robbie's face. There was no dead stare! There was no reproof, no question, no consent, no welcome—scarcely recognition. This all in an instant, and in the next the sense of her reality, her nearness had overwhelmed him, and he was striding across the room, his arms outstretched.

'Why didn't you let us know?' she said, with face uplifted. But as he embraced her, she hastily lowered it and received his kiss on her forehead. She stood away and he felt a sudden ebbing of his blood, a chill.

He turned, smiling, murmuring apologies for his intrusion, shook hands with Robbie's mother and Aunt Miriam, met her Cousin Ruth. They had risen to go, but Robbie held them: asked her aunt to ring for the butler, flung her mother an appealing glance. He stood silent, openly awaiting their departure, confused at what had happened, what was happening.

But he found himself at the table and Robbie having him served breakfast over his protest. He tried to catch her glance, but she avoided him, kept talking. She had changed, but how? Her look had told him nothing of which he could be sure. She had been stiff, perfunctory in his arms. How much of this was for him and how much for the outsiders? How much because of three months' separation? He could not swallow food, the coffee was bitter in his mouth. Too long! Too long! he thought. Could he account for it to her? What had happened? She was almost like a stranger in my arms, he told himself, feeling sweat break out about his lips and his forehead. Wiping his face, he pushed his chair back and looked at her. He could not go on with this.

But Robbie did not see him in private after breakfast. She said collectedly that she had an appointment to keep, that he would be wanting to transact the business he had mentioned in his letter. He went on to the banking district of the city to visit his men, was unable to return for the mid-afternoon meal, and, when he did, Robbie was out.

It was after supper in the stiff-backed, Simonton parlor when they were finally alone together—alone on either side of the indolent fire, the black marble mantel, the white alabaster bust, staring off into space.

Robbie's face looked at once bloated and thin, her mouth was drawn and her olive skin had a sickly cast. She looked away from the mantel and figeted with her handkerchief, then she gripped the polished arms of her chair and spoke. 'Why did you come, Ratliff?' Her voice was almost harsh.

He had been recrossing his knees. 'Come?' he said, setting both feet on the floor heavily.

She gazed at him with uncertainty. His face somehow did not seem quite familiar. His bold, male figure seemed strange to her. 'Yes, of course you had business here. But, I mean us—it would have been all right, easier, maybe, if you had just written me—I mean.'

He jerked forward in his seat, reddening dully, but he spoke with restraint. 'If it's the long time you mean, Robbie—I know, God knows—but think a little how long it's been for me!' He paused, looking at her for reassurance. Her grave eyes did not change. 'I thought you needed time,' he said, 'time to get well. And I have been in the grip of things—every living minute since the storm.'

'No, Ratliff, not that—you don't need to save my feelings—it's too serious. I can't have any vanity about it. I'm not bitter. Your letters made it clear—mostly what you didn't say.'

'Letters?' he said, lifting his head, feeling his half-conscious impatience snatched from him.

She went on. 'I have already prepared myself. In fact, I had already seen our—our great mistake, before you found it out.' She glanced at the fire, then she lied a little. 'I have only been waiting for you to bring it out in the open.'

He went pale. 'Don't talk like that!' He was out of his chair, coming toward her. He halted, his eyes squinting, then widening, as he stood staring. 'Don't trifle!' he said, in a violent whisper.

A flush tinged her cheekbones and she glanced down at her hands on the chair. She knew that she had been mistaken in part: Ratliff still loved her—at least he thought he did. And this would only make it harder, she told herself, but she felt a satisfaction still. She lifted her face resolutely and went on, her voice quiet, prepared for what it said.

'I'm not blaming you. The fault was mine. I don't know how I could have been so blind to everything—so ungrateful to my own father and mother—so cruel. The realization didn't come till after—afterward.' She paused, swallowing, glancing at him with eyes now feverish.

Ratliff swallowed, too, feeling the floor sway beneath him.

'I have had some time,' she said. 'I did need time and I have had enough to see. It was an awful thing! I didn't believe it could happen, happen to me—a deadly, willful'—she broke off, glancing away—'sinful love.' Her eyes came again to his dazed, bloodless face, then lowered to the floor. 'I can't bring my father back.' Her voice shook and she strengthened it. 'But I can still do something to soften her blow. And that is my mission now—I have no other justification for living on. I can't leave mother, Ratliff.'

He made his way toward the fire, taking a great breath, shaking himself, rubbing his hand over his long face. No, she was not yet well, he thought. He turned back suddenly and was speaking hoarsely, fast. 'The hurricane brought my chance to break the ring—to be a buyer—to get on top—to make a place for you where everyone will

403

show respect, hold their tongues. It meant watching, working, driving every minute. I could not stop—I could not pause till now—to get my breath to tell you. Darien will be a fit place for you to live in now, I promise—you and your mother.' He lowered his head and walked back to the marble mantel. 'That's why I'm late.'

He stood staring at the blaze. 'Sinful love!' he said aloud. Then he was confronting her again, moving toward her with measured steps, his neck corked, his face restrained. 'Listen, Robbie, now listen close!' He spoke with grim softness. 'You don't know what sinful love is— you can't. The preacher, the wedding didn't make our marriage right: God did—that morning, in that back room of the church. I know your father's death was a shock, an awful thing. But you don't know why he died—I don't—we can't: that was between him and his Maker.'

Robbie was shaking her head. 'No, Ratliff,' she said. 'Not for me— that's too easy—my conscience—'

'You're not well yet.'

'I'm well enough. No. I've thought and prayed about it, too long. Our love was not sinful in the way you mean. I believe even that it was not a sin for you. But it was different with me and I let it possess me above everything.'

'It was the surest thing you'd ever known, you said.'

'Yes.' She glanced up at him quickly, her eyes focusing for a moment, then they grew absent and she lowered her head. 'I was too sure—and not sure enough of other things. But I have come to see it clearly, now. I am only thankful that I can still do something to deserve my mother—maybe earn the forgiveness of my father some day, the forgiveness of my Aunt Mag.'

After the one moment, she had withdrawn again, the strange veil, the sickness lay between them. His shoulders sagged. 'But you're my wife,' he said huskily.

'I killed my father!'

'But you're my wife.'

404

'Our baby, too.'

'You're still my wife.'

She remained gazing at the floor. 'Ratliff, I don't know—it can't seem right—She got up slowly and steadied herself against the back of her chair. 'I'm very tired now—I can't say any more tonight.'

But his mind did not leave off. When Robbie had sent him to bed in a room across the hall from hers, he lay with his hands gripped together beneath his head on the pillow, staring up at the invisible ceiling. He wondered if he could be wrong. He had been so sure. The storm had come: he had not dreamed it, planned it—it was greater than his plans.

It had brought death and suffering to some—some who did not seem to deserve it. But who was he to question the way of the hurricanes? He had not helped those who suffered, drowned—he had not been there. That had disturbed him, but could he help, when he had been given to see his chance, the way that had been set for him? It had been hard, maybe cruel, but can a man shirk his course, his destiny?

Sinful love! Robbie was lost, confused in her grief—it was her mother's doing. He had been too long away. Too long! The feel of her neck—the tender, sensitive turn at the shoulder—was suddenly on his cheek. His temples beat, blood pressed hard against his skin, his body tingled. He came out of the bed and stood barefoot in the darkness. Her blood had been made his: their blood: their body. They had been joined, not to be sundered. He strode toward the door, his nightshirt whipping his knees. This damned fog of Bible talk had shrouded Robbie's mind, her feeling. But it was there. She was still a woman—his woman—not to be put away. He was across the hall, at the entrance to her room. His body burned. Yes, one! She'd see—she'd know again. All this talk would fade like mist.

He opened the door, took a step into the room. Then he stood there peering through the darkness toward her bed. The covers seemed awry. Their vague whiteness gathered form: a figure kneeling on the floor. He saw the shoulders heave, heard the stifling sound of Robbie's voice.

He was suddenly subdued, cold, weary. He turned noiselessly back and went across the hall.

CHAPTER

38

BUT ROBBIE *did* go back to Darien with Ratliff, went the following day. She had got a surprising answer to her prayer—or so it seemed to him. Though his uncomprehending pleasure—she announced her intentions at breakfast—was tempered later by her explanation that she could not deny, however sure their mistake, however unfit she felt, that she was his wife. Moreover, her mother would soon be wanting to return. After all, it was her home, and she, Robbie, must learn to live in it again. This was duty.

Still Ratliff's confidence, taxed by the night, bore him stoutly in the morning: Robbie's decision—whatever she said, or thought—could not rest utterly on resignation. He and Darien might seem bad medicine at the moment—it was so with the sick—but they would cure her. He would make the whole arrogant outfit wear their Sunday-School manners around her before it was over—even her Aunt Mag.

Oddly, Bud True was the first object of Robbie's complaint, after her quiet return to their tall, gray, and now completed house on the Ridge—as her first week home ended, three days before Christmas. It was not the incivility of his scowling and turning away, when she had spoken to him on the street, she said: she had found that he was acting the drunkard at home, mistreating his wife.

Ratliff set his thin coffee-cup down carefully in its saucer on the walnut breakfast table and meditated. Bud had become a problem, in spite of the brilliant use he had put him to. Since the pre-Christmas log *freshet* began (within a week after he got his office open), Ratliff had used Bud as a persuader, an evangelist of trade, at the Boom, manifesting to the timber-runners that the new house was of their kind and for them, organized to give upriver men a break—and enjoining them to let Sutton and True have the last crack at their timber, the refusal. Ratliff had put the True in his firm name for that purpose—and to keep the other buyers guessing.

The *break* had been no fake: he had actually paid high prices, run up the market, had bought—to the astonishment of the buyers—the bulk of the timber bought so far, before they began to understand they would get no timber at the price they wanted and could afford to pay. But Bud had been effective in making the drift to him into a practical corner on the market. Ratliff had thought to bear with Bud's drinking—he had kept pretty full most of the time—but now it was clear he was growing worse and the day before he had (against express orders) bought two rafts, bought them with a drunken sweep of his big arm—at fabulous prices.

'I'll have to hide Bud's bottle,' Ratliff said, getting up from the table. But he spoke more seriously when Robbie did not smile.

That day he transferred Bud to one of the firm's private booms, as an inspector: after a hot outburst over his drunken spending. Downcast, Bud took off his store-bought coat and turned his liquor bottle over to Ratliff. He did not even protest Ratliff's demand that he 'shave' the high prices they were *having to pay* in his reinspection of the timber, he was so crestfallen.

But Robbie knew that she had spoken only for Bud's good—and that of his poor wife, for whom she felt a responsibility. Complaint was far from her thoughts: they were now filled with the sense of Darien's absolution. From the first afternoon that she drove down from the Ridge, dressed in deep mourning, she felt a renewed cordiality in the town. Mrs. Atkins, whose respectability had never suffered from the rumors about her husband, and Mrs. Drew, the wife of the cashier of the Bank of Darien, had asked warmly after her health and her mother's, had condoled with her over her father's death, going out of their way to say that apoplexy was such a dread disease: it seemed always to strike vigorous people, was always fatal—they had known so many cases.

Before the week was out, Mrs. St. Johns, the wife of the bank's president, had led a group of graciously sympathetic ladies—Mrs. Birdsong and Mamie Day, of rice-planter families; and Mrs. George the elder, of the timber firm—into her parlor. And on the afternoon of her breakfast-table mention of Bud's behavior, most of the Christmas-tree committee of her church called to seek her help with the gifts.

Ratliff thought admiringly, when she told him about it at supper, that she had used a proper balance of her Christian charity and family pride: she had given handsomely toward the fund, had asked to be allowed to help wrap the presents, but declined to go on the festive excursions to the camps and islands to leave them. Not that she was submitting her behavior for his approval, or thought of it, he knew: she had spoken with reserve, as if casually, of her plans, smiling a little. But he noted a change in her face, even her skin: it seemed clearer, more alive.

He made no comment on this revived cordiality in her church and circle, but he could not suppress a smile, a slow smile that spread in spite of him, that would not leave his face. And there would be more to come around, to be feelingly polite: every damned buyer and his crowd, before he, Ratliff was through. Already old man George had sent him word to 'drop by.' This was the first move and Ratliff would wait: the anxiety was theirs, they must admit it, unanimously. They were suffering from the break in the price of lumber he had forced, from the rise he had effected in the timber market. He had just begun to squeeze.

During Christmas week Mrs. Simon George the younger, Mrs. Clare, Mrs. Schardt, and Mrs. Stuyvesant and her daughter, Marie, had called on Robbie—and a number of lesser people. The Stuyvesants asked them to dinner—Marie had been an intimate friend of Robbie's. Ratliff could glean only casual news of these visits during his broken evening hours at home (the demands of his task always grew, they never let up), but from what he learned, he felt sure they must be, that they were, having their effect on Robbie—especially sure when Cashier Drew, the Sunday-School superintendent, called and asked her to take her old class back. Robbie declined. Ratliff was warmly approving in this when she told him, until she explained that she did not now feel worthy of the trust. Still he took comfort in the submission on her face: it was better than the dead look. Even on New Year's Eve, when he said he had to make a business trip to Philadelphia and she responded, with quick interest, that she would go to Charleston to stay with her mother—even in the face of this he remained confident: the cure was working, beginning to have effect.

Ratliff returned a week later. With the aid of his broker he had been able to establish the line of credit he sought, had chartered twenty schooners, closed new timber contracts; he had done well in Philadelphia, but on the Monday morning of his arrival he was little cheered. His Sunday's pause in Charleston had failed on its mission: Robbie was staying on: she wanted to bring her mother back with her and Mrs. Macgregor was not quite well, and (the controlling factor, he discovered finally) she still awaited a response from Aunt Mag— the reaction of her dead husband's sister to her plan to come to live with her daughter and son-in-law.

The day did nothing to lighten his temper, limber his hard-set face. He had found a note from China on his desk, saying that she wanted to arrange to borrow money and needed the stock in his timber company she had been promised.

China was impatient; he was sorry, but he could do nothing: he'd not incorporated yet; he could not—his creditors wouldn't hear of it, and he could not sacrifice a drop of credit, of life blood. But it was awkward, and more awkward still, he had had to demote Bud again.

The superintendent of his Mayhall Creek mill complained of the timber that Bud had let get by—instead of helping in this tight fight, where they needed to cut corners, find new corners to cut, he had been drunker than ever and, the miller insisted, had sent on stuff that the public scalers would only have dared to pass with Bud's connivance. Ratliff had shifted Bud to a night watchman's job, where he could do less harm. It all had brought a bitter taste into his throat, put a cramp in his stomach, but he forgot it in work.

He thanked God he had no time to stop and worry. He had, could have only one worry: to remain strong enough to keep squeezing the Darien ring, to keep squeezing till he made little ones out of big ones, till the Dales hollered *calf rope*.

And Ratliff was still half-conscious of this thankfulness, as he rapidly made out lumber schedules, before beginning with his cablegrams and letters, at nine o'clock that night in his office on Market Street, when he looked up to find Bud standing beside his desk.

Bud wobbled on his crutches, finally bracing an elbow against the desk's roller-top to steady himself. Gray stubble stood out on his down-slanting face, which had a thinning, pallid look. He hawked and spat heavily on the floor, then raised his eye to Ratliff's. 'Hunh, so you're too busy to come kick my butt yourself. You send a man!'

Ratliff leaned back in his chair and sighed. 'Ain't you ever going to get sober, Bud?'

'Hell, naw—not in Darien—but not sober—to hell with that!' He spat again. 'I come heah to tell you to hell with you! You think I'm drunk and don't know nuthin'.'

Ratliff laughed dryly. 'Naw, Bud, you're not drunk!'

Bud squinted laboriously and his eyes focused. 'Snake Sutton, I found you out—I seen it happen to you and tried to stop you, but naw, you 'uz done tail-tangled with these damn Darien dogasses. I quit.'

'You can't quit me, Bud.' Ratliff's face softened. 'Damn, you *are* loaded!'

'You done son-of-a-bitched me,' Bud went on, ignoring Ratliff's words—'all your friends; gittin' ready to, them you ain't already. I know what you aim to do, done heard: quick as you weed out some of these heah companies, get holt o' the thing, you aim to take all us ragged-assed rafthands' timber for nuthin'—give us ration money— weevily ration money!'

'As soon as!' Ratliff smiled. 'Who's been talking to you, Bud?'

Bud brought his big hand unsteadily up from a crutch handle and, after a second try, wiped his mustaches. 'Think you can make a whashman out'n Bud True! Well, you kin just take your Goddamn whashman job and you know what you kin do with it!' He wheeled with a giant swing of his crutches to leave, lost his balance, and went down on the floor.

Ratliff helped Bud to his feet, got him out to his buggy and drove him home. At the gate he said, 'Now, get sober, Bud, and get ready to go to work tomorrow night—I need you.' He grinned wryly as he turned the buggy around. The horse walked on slowly and he drew the animal to a halt to listen.

A long halloo sounded in the distance to his right, from the river. Timber coming in tonight, he thought. The swinging cry had been round and full-throated and mellow. About the mouth of Cathead Creek, he told himself, looking off at the soft blackness of the moss-hung oaks, then up at the star-frost in the heavens. A second halloo answered, mellow, but smaller and more remote: it must have been close to Rifle Cut. Then a third, thin, far away, swallowed up in its echo. Raftsmen called to each other as they had always called, in the night—coming to Darien! The last river yell must have been almost at Reaphook Bend—but not there: he saw again in wavering firelight the giant shadow, bending back from the oar handle, the solid chest sending up its deep, echoing crescendo. Only the mighty Bud could ever be heard at the Boom from Reaphook Bend!

Suddenly the night was still and he was cold. He clapped the reins over the horse's back—God, he hadn't touched his letters yet!

Before the week was out—it was the day after Robbie came home from Charleston—Atkins's timber house folded, went into the hands of the bank. In his office, Ratliff laughed—the old gar had got what was coming to him—laughed more than once, though bitterly. Robbie had arrived alone (Aunt Mag relentlessly opposed her mother's plan), alone, in the solitary sickness of a dumb creature. The memory of her look dried up his smile and he stared out of the window, his neck swelling, blood mounting to his face. Atkins was a little fish: he wanted shark!

Still his squeeze was telling on the ring. On Monday of the following week old man George and August Schardt came to his office. They came as friends, they said, and brought the proxies of the other firms. His wild plunging could only ruin him in the end. It was costing everybody money. Darien houses had always done business on a friendly plane, to everybody's profit. When they had spoken, they sat there, the one bald and domed, the other gray and squat—like two uneasy 'possums, Ratliff thought. He rose, strode to the window beyond his desk and stood staring out of it for a time, seeing nothing, but giving rein to the deep, sweet throbbing of his pulses. Then he gripped himself, turned with tilted head and said, 'Friends of *mine* don't' come by proxy.'

413

He still could squeeze, though it was hard and growing harder. He was thankful that he had the income, the whole income, from his tavern on which to live, for Robbie must not feel the strain. He even had had to milk the business some: the boy, Eddie, could not draw the trade and he was now too busy to give it time. But he was breaking even on his timber house and the rest were not.

He wondered at the Dales: they had been hardest hit by the storm, he had picked off eleven of their accounts in England, Italy. They were buying nothing at the Boom. Of course they had great leaseholds, but the open market affected contracting, too, and they had to meet his prices to sell lumber. Still they did not show the strain.

On the first of February, he leased the Atkins mill and other properties from the bank, with an option to buy. Near the middle of the month Marcus came to him to forewarn him that he must have his money when the loan fell due, on March first: at least ten thousand of it. Ratliff was forewarned, he said, frowning a little at first, then leaning back in his swivel chair and smiling, but he never answered Marcus. Hell! He wanted to borrow more, not pay back—he could not pay. Marcus held a good mortgage: he could sell the tavern—when the court decreed it his. If Marcus couldn't make the tavern bring fifteen thousand when he got it, that was his business. Christ, it wouldn't hurt the old Jew to lose a little once in his life! Not when the ring was choking!

Ratliff was sure he heard a gurgle, saw a darkening flush. There was strain in the Darien air: the tugboat men nodded to him with hushed respect when they visited his office, the idle clerks in the stores came out to the doors to watch him pass; the rumors (he had planted some) ran at the cable office in the saloons and whorehouses; raftsmen were growing dubious of the checks of Stuyvesant-George and Schardt and Schiewitz; even the pontifical Presbyterian preacher had eyed him with grim piety, in passing on the street.

Then, on the first afternoon in March, Henry Stuyvesant stood in his office doorway, smiling awkwardly, saying, 'A few of us are having an oyster bake at my fishing camp. Can you come?'

Ratliff got up, holding to the edge of his desk, forgetting to invite the man in.

"Just us timbermen, you know,' Stuyvesant added.

Yes, Ratliff thought he knew, and he gripped the wooden ledge harshly. 'Just us?' he said, and nodded. He could not trust his voice to say more: a striction clamped his chest. An oyster bake—but there'd be shark meat, too!

Still Ratliff was disappointed: the Dales did not attend. Duke Pitt was there for Dawson and Clare, and old man George, a little shakily, had given his word that the Dales were 'all right' and had pointed out the legal difficulties in 'a general meeting.' 'If the Dales are afraid, so am I,' Ratliff told them bitterly. He still could squeeze, by God!

It came so casually, so oddly—in an English way, Ratliff supposed, as he thought it over before his parlor fire that evening (on Wednesday, following the oyster bake). It left him still uncertain—uncertain of its import, as he had been uncertain of his senses when he had opened the envelope, taken from a runner's hand, while he stood on the bluff at Cathead Creek, watching the loading of his schooners.

He had stared at the brief, formal letter with the lumber schedule attached, stared through the coming dusk at the slight, crisp words: 'Could you gentlemen handle items X and XIII with us?' His eyes still blinking, he had become suddenly conscious of the negro loaders: the sound of heavy timbers in the ships' hulls, the measured chant of voices—'Whiskey, whiskey, oh whiskey is the life of man!'—the sweating swing of black arms: the beat of it. *Could you gentlemen . . . with us!* The beat of it was suddenly the beat of his pulses—his sweating, timber-swinging, nigger pulses—and this had had the slight, trifling, harmless look of a foil.

415

But it was the handle of the foil extended. Yes. Ratliff rocked his chair and looked up at the clock. He could see it no other way. In the past the buyers had sometimes called on each other to share some part of a big contract. Usually the element of time was the reason, though never with him. But this was a general contract, running for the remainder of the year.

Hell, the prices are subject to market revision, he told himself, halting his chair. They are trying to buy off your competition. But he'd gone over that before: he couldn't' take the contract away from them—and they had offered him their own terms.

By God, they're against the wall! He was rocking again, sharply. They know they can't live to fill that contract if they don't make peace with you!

Still he wondered: the great house of Dale and Coventry? And should he take it, or stand and keep slugging? God, what are you after? You've brought 'em 'round—got 'em askin' you to quit—that letter's *calf rope,* in English!

But was it? He stood up, searching the room with his glance and walked toward the mantel. Could it be some smooth English trick— was it, indeed, the *handle* of a foil that he saw?

He heard the front door shut and glanced at the clock again. A moment later Robbie appeared in the doorway and he lifted his face from the firelight, smiling. Her eyes bore their usual withdrawn look, and her lips the sleeping smile. He shifted his gaze.

But, as she approached the hearth, there showed in her cheeks a tinge of color he had not seen. The prayer service had been strange and very moving for her, she said. Very moving: Aunt Mag was there. But the strangeness of it came back to her now, as she thought upon it. Old Doctor Maclin, their preacher, had prayed that Darien business men might not forget God in their dealings, that the innocent and helpless might not suffer, if it were His will—about madness in the heart.

416

Ratliff's nostrils had flared at her mention of Aunt Mag, and he had turned to the fire, as she went on. Now she paused, moving her hands at her sides hesitantly, looking at his grim profile. 'She came to me after the services—she wants us to have a talk together.'

'Who?' he said, his gaze still on the blaze.

'Aunt Mag.'

He gripped the mantel. Aunt Mag! Her image—the cold mouth crumpling, the stiff neck bent—flashed before him. His face slowly flushed, as if with drink, and suddenly he was laughing—quietly, evenly at first, as a hen cackles, then harsh and high.

'Ratliff!' Robbie cried out.

He looked up, his jaw caught back, and saw her staring at him. She had recoiled: her lips were parted, the gathering flesh at her cheekbones trembled, her eyes were wide and dark. Quickly, she turned and hurried from the room.

Ratliff!—the sound echoed back from the shut door, like a whip-lash—*Ratliff!* The first passion he had seen on her face since her father's death —and it was fear, cold fear! What in God's name had he done? He grew weak and sick. It was as if he'd struck her! 'You clumsy fool!' he said aloud. But why was she so frightened? they'd licked the Dales—brought Aunt Mag around. But he could not dismiss the memory of her eyes. They stared at him, as if they were seeing him for the first time, as if he were hideous!

He winced and shifted his stance. Was he so lowdown, so mean? He had brought all this about: Darien's welcome, Aunt Mag. So harsh? So lunatic! Suddenly he was moving through the door, down the hallway to her room.

It was the first time that he had sat on a hassock, sat at a woman's knees, since he was a little boy, and he was dumb—his stomach burned and quivered and he could not control the shaking of his shoulders.

Then he found that he was talking—not knowing what he said, or why. His ugliness, his cruelty came of hard licks, beginning here—his own mother's—when he was a boy. She had betrayed him, after his father's death, with another man—had borne a bastard child. That shame had been his first lesson in cruelty—had shaped his first curses, sent him off to the swamp to live with negroes.

He paused and felt the strain of Robbie's swallowing. She bent over him and laid a cheek upon his head. 'Oh, Ratliff!' she whispered. And the whisper passed into his sense like sleep.

'I was too little to defend our name,' he said, 'to pick out the man.' His voice suddenly hardened. 'And I don't know till yet.' He felt her stir. There was a smell of perfume and her breasts brushed his cheek. His blood leaped and his arms went about her waist. God, he thought, she is here! He raised his head.

Her gaze wavered and went past him. 'Oh, Ratliff—hate, all these years!' But he did not loose her waist and she relented, saying sadly, 'I'll pray for you.'

CHAPTER

39

BUD TRUE ROUNDED the sandy street corner and swung onward for a dozen strides before he paused on his crutches to look up. He shifted his props quickly to catch his balance and his bushy gray eyebrows swept down in a scowl. He shifted again in the loose footing and stood staring—staring at a glossy, black, bright-wheeled carriage at his ramshackle gate, before his small shabby house.

'Goddamn!' he said, swinging forward again, grinding the rest of his mutterings in his teeth. But he took only one stride and halted: a purplish flush had mounted to his face, and he rubbed his brow, now beginning to throb, with a trembling hand. That infernal woman of Snake Sutton's again!

A tincture of ill-ordered and fragmentary impressions of the past winter flooded his consciousness, twisting his face with pain: the lonesome feeling when he finally had to admit to himself that Snake had gone rotten; the sickening realization that he, Bud, was just a joke to him; headaches and shakes (he never used to have them); the black moment in the poker game when the shakes came on him and clouded his judgment; the morning feeling of being alone in Darien without a job and unable to get away. And, mixed through it all—at every turning-around in his own house—the sickly, pious-eyed, nosey face of that woman!

He moved on slowly. If you just hadn't lost your nerve in that game, he told himself, in dogged insistence against the contrary collusion of circumstances. It was the game in which he was going to treble his stake to buy back his farm and quit Darien for good and all. After the night he had broken up the partnership—that wasn't any sort of partnership and they both knew it, though Snake didn't think he'd quit—he had drawn out his five hundred dollars. This had been his stake and he had felt lucky when the game opened. But when he had lost four hundred of it, a blinding headache and shakes came over him and he had gone out for a drink—that had ruined him. The bad run had kept up. Before February started, he was flat broke.

He glanced up at the team ahead. He could remember back before she had that show-off outfit. But, God, she was just as bad in a buggy—the day she'd knocked at meal-time and he had sung out to come in. He was still at the table and Ibby was behind his chair, where she always stood when she wasn't handing him something, where she belonged to be. He had asked the woman to sit down and eat (for manners' sake). 'No, thank you,' she had said, making out to laugh, but with her pious look. 'If your wife isn't good enough to sit and eat with you, I guess I'm not either.' She had set out to ruin Ibby, to come betwixt them, from the first.

He halted before the carriage and, as he lifted his gaze, he was sure that the coachman had just looked away. Now the negro sat face forward, lumped down in the front seat with his feet on the dashboard, a brown derby resting on the front of his head. Bud gazed at him for a moment in slight surprise, but as the negro continued to ease the hat-brim over his face, Bud's eyebrows twitched irritably. All of a piece: this Goddamned nigger and carriage and the woman, he thought. He drew himself up, filling his chest, and cleared his throat hugely.

The coachman jumped to life, twisting his head around and pulling off his derby. 'Howdy, Mister True! Lawd Gawd, you scared me!' He grinned and held the hat in his hand. 'I 'uz dozin'.'

But Bud did not speak: he had noticed a white dusting, as of meal or flour, on the driver's coat-sleeve. He nodded and turned stiffly toward the gate. The whited sleeve had made his eyes smart. It was not the first suspicion he'd had : there had been times during the past month that it had come to him that he had not bought the groceries on his own table—come to him when he was sober enough to think of it. He had asked Ibby about it once, and she had laughed and said, "Law', I didn't know you 'uz that full when you toted in that sack!'

He *had* been keeping pretty full and the thought then he might have brought the groceries. Though when he got around to studying about it, he knew that the tavern, where he got his liquor on the credit, didn't handle groceries, and he'd picked up only three days' night-watching. He'd known better: still he kept denying it to himself—till now. His fattened cheeks trembled.

He had halted at he steps and he stood staring up at the front door, but he did not see the *door*. His stomach drew up, shook, turned over. No, by God, he couldn't stand the sight of *her!* He started to turn aside, when he suddenly became conscious of the coachman: the negro's eyes on his back. He hesitated, feeling a stringhalt he'd never known before. But for a moment only: he snorted and swung to the left. Hell of a high come-off when I start payin' mind to a nigger driver! he thought, moving on around the side of the dwelling to its rear.

When the carriage had driven off, he entered his house through the kitchen. Beyond the open doorway, he saw his wife hastily gathering scraps together from their counter-pane-covered bed. Her rounded back and long-fingered hands gave her the look of a praying mantis.

Bud thumped to the middle of the room and stood frowning. Ibby raised her wrinkled face, with its wisps of gray hair—escaped from the hard-drawn knot at the back—hovering at her forehead.

'What's *she* up to now?' he said.

Ibby smiled. 'Just a quilt we're makin'.'

'She don't want no quilt out'n you. She's got enough to cover a barn, I reckon.'

'I know, Bud'—Ibby's voice was flatter than usual and slightly accusing—'but you know we need the money, need it bad—and it's good pay!'

Bud dropped his gaze. 'That's what I thought,' he said, moving on his crutches, his wincing face to the floor. It was like that dress he'd come home to find on Ibby's back: it hadn't been worn, Ibby mouthed. It was one *she* had bought for when she had her baby she never had. But he'd made Ibby give that back. He reckoned she did! He looked up quickly. 'Did that woman bring groceries heah?'

Ibby clasped her hands together under her faded, checked apron and drew in her breath. 'Bud, I tell ye, she means all right. She don't know no better'n she does, but she means the best.'

He halted beyond the foot of the bed and suddenly towered upright. 'She just wants to have somewhere to ride with her nigger and carriage, to hand out her Jesus bread and look down on us—and you'd be *beholden* to her!'

'Bud, I wish you could git used to bein' a cripple. 'Tain't none of your fault you can't work no more.'

He had lowered his eyes at her mention of his incapacity, but now he squinted them fiercely. 'Cripple aer no, I don't have to eat her bread—aer put up with her around this house—not another time!' He wheeled toward the door. 'By the Eternals, I'm goin' down and tell Snake to keep his woman away from heah!'

The slender, fair-cheeked young man at the counter in the outer room of the Sutton and True Market-Street offices responded to Bud's inquiry for Ratliff with cold brevity. Mr. Sutton was away.

Bud hunched back on his crutches and gazed at the thin trace of a blond mustache on the clerk's upper lip. 'When'll he be back?'

'We don't know.'

'Where's he gone?'

'Do you have business with Mr. Sutton?' The clerk turned half-way with an air of forbearance.

Bud swallowed and frowned. 'Now look-a heah, young man, if I hadn't, I wouldn't-a come heah.' He paused, then suddenly his eyes burned and his voice quivered. 'My name's still in this firm—and I reckon I got some rights heah—at least enough to know where Snake Sutton's gone!'

The clerk dropped the pen he was taking from behind his ear and flushed pink. 'Oh, sir! Are you Mr. True? . . . I didn't know sir!'

Bud felt better, vastly better. The clerk went on to say that Mr. Sutton had left instructions if Mr. True called to satisfy his wishes, whatever they might be. Bud swung back and forth before the counter, feeling suddenly excited and shaky. He grinned, trying to cover it with a frown. His throat felt very dry.

'He didn't leave any refreshmint around heah, did 'e?'

'Refreshment?'

'Whiskey—it's the only refreshmint theah is.'

'Why, I don't know, sir—I'll see, sir—'The clerk moved off, leaving his pen on the floor.

Bud drummed on the counter with his fingers until the clerk came back and led him into the inner office, where a brown quart bottle and a glass of water stood in the center of a long table. He uncorked the bottle without a word and took two stout pulls at it, before he set it down. 'Now, where'd you say Snake went?'

Glancing at the bottle, which was now only two-thirds full, and swallowing first, the clerk said Mr. Sutton had gone to Charleston and would go on to Philadelphia. It was about the consolidation.

Bud didn't know about the consolidation and the young man showed surprise. The timber firms were all joining up into two big groups. Stuyvesant-George and Schardt and Schiewitz had already announced plans for union with Dawson and Clare. Sutton and True were going to join with Dale and Coventry—though, really, it might be put the other way around, he believed. Mr. Sutton had gone to see his bankers and was not expected back for a week or more—possibly not before the end of the month.

Bud had picked up the bottle again, as the clerk talked, and had uncorked it. 'What! You mean he's gittin' in the bed with one of this heah Darien crowd?' He rammed the cork back into the bottle, staring at the man.

Bud's anger, his chagrin at Snake's absence, were swallowed up in disgust. As he got out on the street again, he recalled that during the past month he had thought several times of going to him to borrow the money to buy back his farm. Now he was thankful he hadn't. He was finally through with Snake: and Snake had better keep his woman away from his place! Bud looked down: Christ, he'd brought away the liquor bottle in his hand. He frowned. How'd he come to do it? And why did he have to show off in front of that peewillie! He paused for a moment and stared at the bottle, then moved away with it still in his grasp.

Before the week was out, Ibby came down with her stomach trouble. Bud had told her she'd never get shed of it as long as she dipped as much snuff as she did. And on the following day, when he came home for supper he could tell that Snake's woman had been on the place again. Ibby tried to dodge at first, but she had to admit it. There were cooked victuals, for one thing, but hell, he could tell *her* smell! All around—like ten foot behind a coffin. It hurt him the way

Ibby took up for the woman—hurt like a fishhook in his gullet: it was hard to believe!

On the next afternoon, as Bud rounded the sandy corner, the doctor was driving away from his gate. It gave him the shakes. Ibby wasn't in the habit of having the doctor for her stomach. Bud knew who had sent him! And he damn sure didn't aim to let *her* hand out her glitter-gold for it, even though he didn't have a copper in his pocket.

He was not prepared, however, for what he found inside, when he pulled up at the bed. He saw it as soon as he handed Ibby the glass of water: a frilly, lace nightdress. He almost dropped the tumbler.

'Where'd you git that thing?'

'I didn't have a garment fittin' to wear, Bud,' Ibby said, holding in both hands the shaking water glass—'not to see no doctor in.'

Bud stood up, his face working. He thumped back and forth across the room, then halted abruptly at the foot of the bed. 'If you don't take off that damn nightshirt of her'n, I'll tear it off'n you!'

Ibby got along poorly that night and his dosing didn't seem to do her much good. By morning he had decided to go get the doctor's prescription filled. He'd get hold of the money somewhere, somewhere—he damn sure didn't' aim to let Snake's woman fill it. When he got ready to leave, he told Ibby he would be back as quick as the druggist could fix the medicine, but if *she* came while he was gone, not to let her in—tell her that he didn't want her in the house again.

Bud had the opportunity to deliver his message himself, before he had got out of the neighborhood, out of McIntosh-town. The be-derbied coachman drew the dappled horses to a halt under a roadside oak as Bud approached and Robbie leaned from the carriage and hailed him. 'How's Mrs. True this morning?'

Bud had not seen them until she called out—called out in that chirrupy voice, holding to the carriage-top with her long-gloved arm. He shunted about on his crutches in the sand to get his balance, to

425

get hold of himself, to make up his mind whether and how he should answer her.

'Oh, is she bad off?'

His face reddened and he felt his good leg go weak beneath him. 'She's tol-able!' he blurted to give himself time, not looking up.

'Well, you shouldn't take *her* word for it, Mr. True. The doctor told me last night that her condition was serious.' Robbie's voice paused (the voice with its trained ups-and-downs to show a concern that it never did for him. Bud knew her pious eyes were on him, awaiting his reply. His head hung heavy and he kept swallowing). She went on. 'Mrs. True's so afraid she'll be a bother—I'm afraid she hasn't let you know—'

His hands on the crutch-holds gripped white, though they still trembled. He stared at the little conic hollows that belittered the sand at his feet. Finally he lifted a squinted face and looked at her, met the gray, blurred eyes, withdrawn yet gazing into his with assurance— with the assurance that he was booze-broken and jobless, that she had put victuals on his table, that his wife had taken them humbly, that he was beholden to her! Bud's face grew purple. His mouth opened, but he did not speak. He dropped his gaze and turned away.

When he entered the taproom at China's, he thumped up and down the floor for a time, still burning with his bafflement. His voice had come to him after he moved on, as quick as the carriage wheels sounded behind him. Why had the headache, the palsy taken him again—just at that moment? What had stringhalted him? What was it about the holy hussy? Those sickly eyes? Words had come to him hot and heavy, like light'ood knots and liquor bottles—the right words to put her down—when she had gone—all the way here to China's. He slowed his stride. His dry throat had bethought him well: he could borrow the money for the medicine from China, too.

China was beside him, her loose-sleeved arms holding out a tray with two small glasses of whiskey on it. As Bud tossed his off, she said, 'Sit down: you'll wear out those crutches.'

He let himself into a chair. 'I tell you, China, that woman of Snake Sutton's is a ha'nt—a holy hellcat!'

'I ain't surprised.'

'If she keeps comin' 'round my house botherin' Ibby—I went down to 'is place to tell Snake he had to keep her away, but he waun't in town.'

'Yeah, I know—I've just had cause to find that out.' China got up with the tray and refilled the glasses.

Bud blinked when he saw her wrappered figure move rapidly toward the bar and his eyes brightened. He waited to down his whiskey before he spoke. 'How you mean?'

China sat down at the table beside him and sipped at the raw whiskey before she spoke. The years of her profession were telling on her. Her face was taking on the pallid fat common to house prostitution, her lips were thinning. She now drew them in dryly. 'I went down to see 'im myself, the first of the week—after he wouldn't answer my letters.'

'What's he done to you?'

She finished her drink and her nostrils hardened, showing tiny red veins at the base. 'I reckon he's beat me out of my share of the tavern.'

'The hell you say!'

'Beat me out of the stock he promised me for it—the stock in the company he was going to organize so big!'

Bud batted his eyes, frowning, and China told him of the secret contract Ratliff had drawn and put into a lock box of his safe. Each had had a key to the box, but when finally she had tried hers out yesterday, it didn't fit. And Eddie at the tavern had seen him go into the lock box.

China noticed Bud's glancing toward the bar. She came up from her seat abruptly and got the whiskey bottle. She spoke with it in her hand, her black brows lowering and her yellow eyes flaring up. 'The son-of-a-bitch *did* me, all right!' She moved on to the table and sat down. 'I reckon every woman gets done by at least one man—but it's hard for me to take from Snake!'

Bud's red-rimmed eyes suffused and he poured himself another drink. 'I know—God knows, I know, China—he's a rotten fish! He's ruint!' He swallowed the whiskey. 'And it's that Goddamned woman done it—I tell you, China, she's a ha'nt—she's a brimstone bitch! Yes-suh.' His eyes glistened. That was the name he'd called her: it came back to him. He recollected, could recollect now how the words flew out of his mouth at her—there at the oak. He wiped his mustache and nodded weightily. 'I reckon she won't be trackin' 'round my house ag'in! By God, I got her told! Got her told this mornin'.'

China looked at him quickly, then down at her whiskey glass, as he went on. His big voice thickened. If she didn't leave his wife alone, he told her, if she darkened the door again, he'd wring her neck.

China grinned, but her eyes glittered. Delia, the maid, was standing at the swinging door, motioning to her. 'What is it, Delia?'

The old negress jerked her head toward the front of the house.

'Is it Cap'n Henry?'

'Yessum.'

'Tell 'im to come on back.'

Seborn Henry's blunt red face—now sided with gray—appeared in the doorway after a moment. Bud had got upon his crutches and nodded to him. 'Don't go, Bud!' China said. Henry was depositing a second bottle on the table. Bud came back and poured himself another drink. They talked, both at once, of Snake's perfidy. China repeated her story. Bud got up, as if to leave, but China caught him by the arm. Her eyes brightened. 'Tell Sebe how you cussed out Snake's wife awhile ago.'

Bud stood blinking, swaying a little on his crutches. He belched, then his purply cheeks flattened and his brows drew down fiercely. 'I told that Christ-cryin', Jesus-jumpin', brimstone bitch . . .' His voice rose harshly, his breath whistled through his red-tipped nose, he thumped back and forth across the room as his tongue and obscenity thickened.

China broke into heavy laughter. Henry's face spread and he called out, 'That's tellin' 'er, Bud!'

Bud turned wild, staring eyes in their direction. Abruptly, he halted before them. His bellowing had ceased. He spoke now in a hoarse, low voice, trembling with restraint. 'Oh, so y'don't b'lieve me? So ole Bud's a joke!' He whirled, brushing past the table, and thumped out of the room.

China and Henry sat, looking after him for several moments, their mirthful faces set in stiff lines. 'God, he was drunk!' said China finally.

Henry turned to the table and made a sound of surprise. He examined the almost empty bottle on it. 'I'll be damned,' he said. 'Not too drunk to tote off that quart of special stuff I brought you!' He poured the contents of the remaining bottle into their glasses. Apparently he had been drinking before he came, for the signs of intoxication were marked already. He sat now slumped down in his chair so that his paunchy front touched the table-edge, a heavy, secretive smile on his face. 'So you finally got a bellyful of this Sutton?'

She grimaced and drank off her liquor, setting down the glass unsteadily.

He swallowed his slowly, asking her questions about the foolishly irregular transaction with Ratliff, and she replied with unrestrained bitterness. After a meditative pause in which he still wore his drunken smile of mystery, he said: 'So you've come to see the light! I knew him before anybody—I know the lowdown on him—I know what his real name is and how he came to change it—better'n anybody, I reckon!'

She blinked and focused her eyes harshly on the blunt red face. 'All right, Sebe—don't get full of liquor riddles, now!'

No, he said, he had known Snake when he was still a shirt-tail brat, twenty years ago, up on the Ocmulgee River, in the little one-horse town of Nine-and-a-Quarter. Sutton wasn't his name: his name was Flournoy—Bob Flournoy's boy—if Nellie did Bob right that time. He wouldn't know: she had served Bob's memory too well: *he* had laid Nellie many a time after Bob died. Her last kid—born too late to get under the Flournoy cover—she claimed was his.

China leaned over the table toward Henry, her lips loose, her eyes glistening. 'And Sutton ain't his name!' It was a fine story for her to circulate, she thought. 'The Honorable R.P. Sutton, big timber merchant, married to Major Macgregor's daughter!' She laughed, her voice guttural, then rising high. 'You sure he ain't your kid, Sebe?'

He grunted. 'No, by God! He's one I wouldn't admit to if he was.'

They both gave way and roared. They had another tumblerful on that.

She set her glass down, still smiling, but suddenly the smile dried up. The last drink had been too much: she turned pale and hurried from the room.

When China came back an hour later, she was even paler, but she was soberer, far soberer. She approached the table where Henry now lay with his head and arms sprawled out, dead drunk. She gazed at him for a time, listened to him snore. Then her nostrils curved in disgust. 'No, by God—you were right—he's not *your* kid,' she said aloud—'not yours!' She turned away.

There was a soreness in her vitals, not from retching. She had never entirely given Snake up, she knew, till now. 'Hell!' she broke out angrily. 'He never gave a damn about you!' He had been like all the rest: after her body; he took her money—money! That was what

430

everybody wanted. She appreciated hers, too: it had come the hard, the mean way and she meant to hold on to it—what was left. And, by God, she still had some, enough to enjoy, to comfort her.

China poured herself a small drink, but when the odor struck her nostrils she set it down again. She walked to a window, pausing for a moment, then moving on restlessly. She should never have talked Snake into coming to Darien in the first place—it was part her fault. Damn it—damn it to hell! She stood staring at the table where Henry's form lay slumped, but she no longer saw Henry, or heard him snore. Right there beside that table! After Snake had killed her brother, Bob. The memory caught her up. She felt again the singing sureness in her chest, the exaltation. . .saying, *All I know is, I'm on your side!* And he had put his hand on her shoulder.

She blinked and turned away. Well, the son-of-a-bitch can't take that away from me! she thought. . . .

As Bud moved homeward he lurched. The brim of his black wool hat shoveled up in front and his fierce red features sagged. At each step he appeared to be falling, but the swing of his stride caught him up. He muttered in a throaty monotone, yet there was fury in it. They think Bud True's a joke, he said.

He had forgotten to borrow the money for the doctor's prescription from China. But he damned China now and her money. Even more, he damned the frog-eyed druggist, who refused to let him have the medicine on credit. He damned Darien that harbored them: China and her bladder-faced Sebe Henry, the pill-roller and all his hoggish kind, Snake Sutton—and most of all Snake's hateful woman, who'd witched him, made Ibby sick!

By God, he'd sell his gun and get that medicine—no high-snouted, nubbin slut was going to hand it out to him. They think Bud True's a joke. He had told Ibby he'd make haste; he wondered how long he'd been—and he still didn't have the doctor's pills. He'd have to make another trip, another trip. He couldn't remember where his shotgun was—or had he sold the thing? Goddamnit, then he'd take his pistol—his Smith and Wesson was under the mattress still.

When he had rounded the sand corner and gone on a pace, he finally remembered to look up—a little furtively at first. He steadied himself on his crutches and squinted. The nigger and carriage wasn't there. No, by God, he'd got her told—just like he said. They think Bud True's a joke!

Inside the gate, he paused to draw the liquor bottle from his pocket and suck its *dreenings*. Then he thumped up the steps and in his door. He kicked it shut behind him, moving swiftly toward the bed. Then he jerked to a halt. A black skirt. A woman was rising, turning from the bedside.

Robbie faced him, her eyes widening, her lips parting in surprise. She brought her hand other throat quickly and said, 'Mr. True, your wife is a very sick woman!'

What did she say? It didn't matter! He stood staring. The sinews in his face tightened like ribs, his eyes burned slowly into focus. His huge body came forward, toward her, towered above. Just scared mouth-workings—the sneak!

Robbie stepped back against the bed. Her eyes darkened, her face paled. Bud loosed a crutch and gripped her shoulder. She quailed in fright. The action set his brain ablaze: he was unbound. He knew, knew with a sense of inevitability, of final settlement. His arm flashed upward, down. There was a small, flat pop, swallowed by the sound of splintering glass. Robbie crumpled to the floor.

CHAPTER

40

RATLIFF REACHED Darien in the afternoon of the day after Robbie's violent death. The wire he had received in Philadelphia had said she was *seriously injured*—had only said that. It had not prepared him for the hideous news he had found in the Savannah paper, when he chanced to buy one out of Charleston. The black type, the words, had exploded under his eyes like gunpowder. He had read it to the end, with a slowly whitening face. Relentlessly, and still a little hopefully, he had read it through again. Then he had merely stared at it. For the last three hours of his journey he had sat with the black print before him on his knees—sitting on after the train had reached Darien, until the porter shook him by the shoulder.

Now he stood on the station platform, holding the paper yet in his hand. He had the still, bloodless face of an unconscious man. He turned his head slowly about. His eyes were like fish eyes: big-pupiled, ringed with clear green, staring. His brows and lashes splayed, stood stiff. Below the platform at the railroad crossing, the sheriff and one of his men gazed mistily in his direction. Beyond the crossing were a carriage and a buggy with hovering ladies in them. They glanced at him, sidelong, then looked away. Across the tracks, in front of the stores, were vague furtive faces beneath hat-brims. To Ratliff they appeared but faintly animated, like people in a dream. He shook himself.

From the left, the Dales, father and son, and his lawyer were hurrying toward him with lowered eyes. As he reached Ratliff, Edward Dale extended his hand.

But Ratliff ignored the hand. He grasped Dale's coat-lapel abruptly and stared searchingly into his face. 'It's true?' he said. The voice was toneless: it sounded like the crunching of cardboard.

Dale started back and winced, but he met Ratliff's gaze and nodded.

Then, still holding on, Ratliff looked into the faces of Geoffrey and McDeeds, the lawyer, and finally into the face of the sheriff, who had come up. His eyes were still vacant, but a dogged incredulity flickered in them. 'And Bud did it?' He looked again at McDeeds.

The long-jawed, impassive lawyer flinched and nodded his head. 'In a drunken craze,' he said.

Ratliff's dead lower lip twitched with returning life. He loosed Dale's coat and picked up his Gladstone bag. The men blinked. He was walking away. He walked fast, at a rocking gait, as a sailor goes, or a drunken man. His shoulders were hunched, his head drawn down against them.

He had moved several yards before the men recovered from their surprise. The sheriff and McDeeds took long running strides to catch up with him. They grabbed him by the arms, but he shook them off, 'No,' he said. 'I want *Bud* to tell me that.' And he would have turned again, but the two of them restrained him. Bud was in jail, the lawyer said, heaving heavily, and he made no denial of his act, as the paper reported: he had a copy of Bud's confession.

'Let's not make a public spectacle,' the elder Dale breathed, coming up, looking sharply at the sheriff—'it's bad enough!'

They loosed Ratliff and he looked about, as if he were seeing the surrounding people for the first time: the ladies in the vehicles, now staring at him with faintly shocked yet curious faces: the men under the covered sidewalk across the tracks, standing still, with lifted heads.

'Son, you can't do that now.' Dale spoke to Ratliff gently. 'You must go home—Robbie's body is there.'

'Yes.' Ratliff said. He kept shaking his long head, as if to clear it. He glanced about again, then lowered his gaze and followed them to the carriage.

Edward Dale talked in a low voice, intermittently, as they drove homeward. Darien was staggered, too. Ratliff had everyone's sympathy. Though only religion could sustain a man in such a trial.

Ratliff spoke but once. 'In a drunken craze,' he said.

Along the sandy street from the station, through the outskirts toward the Ridge, women appeared at their windows, on their porches, children climbed picket fences to stare. The faces were like bottle flies; the looks became a remote, irritating drone, through the slanting sunlight. Then he was ushered up the steps of his tall house and in through the doorway past other flies—vaguely familiar faces, glancing curiously toward him as they retreated—and, with tread suddenly muted, on down the hallway to the gaping door. Edward Dale loosed his arm at the threshold and he stepped into the room.

There was a hush of voices and he lifted his eyes to the semicircle of women near him. Their rocking-chairs had halted and their pale hands and handkerchiefs fluttered. Two of them nodded, but they met no recognition in his gaze. He merely shook his head slightly and moved past them toward the bed—the dark frame encompassing a shadowy white plain. His eyes fastened on the bedstead, moved guardedly to the counterpane, pointed sharply beneath it, then along the smooth white slope to the pillow. His turning head halted with a jerk.

Within the hollow of the pillow, within the dark wreath of hair, Robbie's face was *still, still*—absolutely, infinitely, irrevocably still! His back gave in and he shuddered, as if he had been stabbed. Slowly, as he stared, his neck and face swelled tight and grew a purply gray. Death's common cadaver was masked in Robbie's features—death, distinguished only by brutal violence!

Suddenly he turned upon the retreating women. His eyes were slices in his face and shone malignantly. He brushed past them and from the room.

Edward Dale and McDeeds overtook Ratliff at the barn and with the aid of James Simonton, Aunt Miriam's husband, restrained him. He must not try to kill True, Dale told him. The man would be hanged: let the law take its course. Such behavior was indecent toward his dead wife, not yet buried—toward her family and his position. Ratliff only stared at them with hostile eyes and struggled on.

They pinned his arms and held him. Dale was not sure from his hoarse mad words whether it were True or some of them he wanted to kill—or only that he cursed his God. But they got him to an upstairs room and locked him in—unwillingly, though less through their restraint, Dale thought, than his confusion.

It was after midnight when he appeared again in the room where Robbie's body lay. His silent entrance startled the group holding wake: three young women and a man. They were quick to suggest that they leave him there in privacy, and he nodded his head. Aunt Mag was standing by the bedside, bending over it, and she raised up with a grim frown on her face, but when she recognized him she turned and walked out behind the group.

He had stood impulsively by the center table, by the lamp, until she left. Now he strode to the door and shut it on her back and on the drone of voices from the hall. He turned the key. 'I'll lock the buzzards out,' he said. 'They don't really love you, Robbie.' His eyes stared feverishly past the lamp. 'They despise you on my account, despise us both!' His voice was a violent half-whisper. 'It may *have been* crazy Bud, but they are glad you lie here so—they want to see me suffering!'

His shadow from the lamp fell across the bed and he slowed his movement, gazing hesitantly at the vague mound of cover, and for a time he was silent, his face working. 'God knows, I *am!*' he said shakily and broke off. He looked down at the head on the pillow. 'But that's for you, Robbie—you alone—to see, to know about.' The pallid features, he discerned, were touched by a smile—a familiar smile: the same sleeping smile they had worn since her father's death. 'For you to laugh at if you will,' he said. 'If it can do you any good now!'

He turned quickly and strode to the far window. He grasped the frame on either side and clung to it, staring out into the night. Finally he came back and sat on the edge of the bed, sat by the slender form beneath the cover. He touched the folded hands upon the counterpane, but drew back. No: they were warmer even then, he'd rather keep them so. The oval of her face seemed small, beneath the pointed nose, below the dark, closed eyelashes. A little thing and frail—too frail, he thought, and you never brought her anything but harm!

'I know, Robbie,' he murmured, 'sickness, pain, grief—I pulled you into my thorn patch—brought you the scorn of your friends and kin, your father's death. And now it's you!' he stared at the closed eyelids, the still smile, muscles working in his jaws. 'I put you in the way of death—with my blind hands, I laid you here!' He gripped them now between his knees and his voice tightened with insistence. 'But before God, Robbie, I never had it in my heart to hurt you!'

The eyes seemed suddenly open in the shadow—dark, staring at him with the look that had dried his laughter that night before the parlor fire, the look of fear. Pain brought him to his feet, exquisite pain that cut him through—his belly, chest, his forehead. He walked the room. 'Hell, you'd struck her down long before she lay there!' he

437

said, through clamped jaws, after a time. 'You struck her down before she knew—before you laughed—and she came finally to *see* you.'

His walking slowed. But the laugh had been forgiven! He paused, staring at the table lamp, as the memory, the feeling of Robbie's cheek upon his head while he had sat on the hassock, touched him. The slack, yellowish flame of the lamp sputtered, seemed to rise. He'd almost won her back to live, there that night in her bedroom—to his life. The flame sunk back. Though it had ended with her praying. He turned away. Still she was getting well.

He sat again at the bed. For a moment his glance paused on her forehead, above the temple, at the edge of the hair, where discoloration showed, then he looked quickly down. It fastened on a the small, shadowy mole at the soft turning of her neck and he bent forward a little, but checked himself, his eyes suffusing.

He turned away and sat twisting his hands between his knees, while tears, his first, slid down his face. 'I loved you the best I knew how—I gave it everything I had,' he said. 'I sweated, I worked, I stole, I throttled them for you, Robbie. I built you a house against their hate—I scared, I choked them out of their scorn—I did my damnedest.' He got up from the bed and walked loose-footedly away. 'But it wasn't enough!'

He looked at the low flame in the lamp, the marble base beneath, at the gaping fireplace. He turned to his window that framed the night, now grown gray. 'Where did I fail?' He gazed out through the mist at the plain of the marsh.

The marsh had been a gun-metal color that New Year's Day and they had stood on the *Hessie's* deck and smiled at it—it seemed a lifetime gone, those two weeks spent away from Darien—beyond its curse! They had been laughing at the captain's story. Ratliff felt again the light pull of Robbie's arm through his, the sway of her body, the bracing air. He had sought out Darien Bluff: she turned away. And

438

she had been gazing backward over the way they came, when he laughed and looked down.

Yes, she'd sensed it, too—it was upon them even then—this doom. Why did we come back? he asked. Why? He shook his head. She didn't speak her fears, nor me, mine. We held our peace: I don't know why. And all that's come since had to be, perhaps. God did not will it otherwise—hers, nor mine!

He frowned. Somehow, they'd left so much unsaid—he never could be frank. It did look like, with Robbie—Robbie, the one living human that was his—he could have toted fair, full fair. He shook his head, still frowning. 'I guess you know now,' he said in his barely audible voice, half-turning toward the bed,' That I held back, kept secrets, told you lies? It hurt, hurts me now, but somehow it didn't come right to tell you. You couldn't be told where the dirty roots to your Sunday-School flowers led; you couldn't know why your scornful crowd made out they forgave you, took you back—I couldn't tell you that!'

He gazed off at the softly brightening mist. Suddenly it burned red before his eyes. And she forgave them! Robbie had crawled back to them, scorn and all! He felt heat in his neck and face. God, it hurt him still to think of it! The damned hypocrites!

But his feeling spent itself quickly and weariness returned, a greater weariness. Maybe she forgave their hypocrisy, too. He could not know. They were her kind, her kin—they understood, perhaps—perhaps, they *did* forgive. After all, it wasn't Robbie they despised: it was her taint of you, he told himself. And after all, she was their blood, their kind—not yours. Blood and kind that never could be yours!

The knob rattled in the locked door. 'Yes,' he said, from the window.

'That you, Ratliff?' the voice was Edward Dale's.

Ratliff turned round. The lamp flame looked white and spent and the room was light now from the windows. 'Yes,' he said.

'The undertaker's here with the casket.'

Ratliff looked toward the bed. The window beside it that he'd left in darkness now cast a clear, cold light upon the counterpane: it was rumpled where he'd sat. He hastened over and straightened it, averting his eyes from the stiff corpse face.

CHAPTER

41

TWO DAYS AFTER Robbie's funeral, Ratliff, in an office in the courthouse, read depositions of the murder case against Bud True. He sat at a dark varnished table, gray-fretted with dust, at either end of which were his attorney and the district solicitor. His heavy, purple eyelids paused from time to time as they lowered his gaze along a page of foolscap. The sockets about them were hollow and his cheekbones stood out starkly. Below, the yellowish flesh sunk away and had a flaccid look, except for ropy muscles about his mouth. The dark lids paused, but they never lifted. And, at the end of China's statement, the eyes stared long.

The other depositions had been those of witnesses who only saw Bud drunk. China said he had called Robbie's name and cursed her. China, too! he thought, pain stirring his limp frame. Yes, he could no more depend on her oath in this than any of the rest. He felt a hollow loneliness.

Then Bud's muddled words, if they were his words: with an empty whiskey bottle!—he didn't know why, except that he was drunk—that she, Robbie, kept coming to his house—would not leave his wife alone. *And Robbie had been at Ibby's sick-bed, nursing her!* It made no sense.

Ratliff shook his head. There was something weird, fishy about it all. Could it be a hellish conspiracy? He raised his eyes briefly, but returned them to the blue-bound papers and kept his silence. He felt, he knew, without the need to think: if conspiracy it were, he had no friend, no one here to counsel with. He lowered his hands to the table and his shoulders sagged.

But a conspiracy: that made no sense, either. Who in Darien would plot Robbie's death? His, Snake Sutton's—aye, many hands and with good will! But Robbie—unless it was that his enemies could not be appeased to take his *life*—must exact torture! His head began to ache. He propped his chin wearily on a palm and glanced at the round pinkish face of the solicitor. You couldn't confide in that dolt, he thought, with a sharp feeling of repugnance. His eyes lowered to the dusty table-top, and the scene about it of the hour before passed through his mind.

'The defendant had some real, or fancied, cause for animosity toward your wife, or you? the fellow had said in his brisk, professional voice. He was from another county and knew little about the case. Ratliff felt the cold relentlessness of the words again, his own throat tighten.

Edward Dale had glanced at Ratliff, extending a hand toward the solicitor in polite agitation, but McDeeds had beaten him to the rescue: 'Yes, yes—former employee—discharged for drunkenness—I'll go into all that later.'

The table had rustled with solicitude, but Ratliff had caught the glint in Aunt Mag's glancing eyes—he knew that glint underlay all the solicitude—though he was too weary, too sick now to care.

'All right, sure,' the unchastened voice had gone on. 'With intent clarified, I think we can and should ask the gallows in this case—it's first-degree murder—such a brutal crime—I suppose that meets with no dissent?' And the pink fat face had confronted him—as if it said: *Step lively there—here's the rope to hang Bud True.*

It had cut his wind and the solicitous McDeeds had only made it worse: 'I think I can assure you, my client is in no wise included to shirk his duty to the state, or to society?' Then all around the table they had sat silently and looked at him with the question on their faces.

The blind, dogged feeling that the whole thing was a conspiracy returned to Ratliff. He must get to the bottom of it somehow, he told himself, straightening up in his chair. And so little time. 'Wednesday—Wednesday'—the voices sounded in his ears gain, like a sentence. Only two days until the grand jury would be called into session—only two days to find out, to accept or reject, to make up his mind—his weary, his bewildered mind.

At nine o'clock that evening, he appeared in the lobby of the jail. Since he quit the solicitor's office, he had questioned his coachman, talked to the deputy sheriff who arrested Bud, pondered the facts, the evidence he knew. It made strange sense; still it gave no clue, revealed no loophole for Bud. Intent came stranger still. He had demoted Bud and Bud got mad, drunken mad, but even in his wildest wrath Bud had not thought of striking him. There was a time when Bud could kill a man, if he had to, but a *man*, not Robbie!—drunken, fractious, joking Bud! Ratliff could not make up his mind, could not go on, without hearing it from Bud's mouth.

The heavy-jowled, squint-eyed jailer screwed up his face and canted it to look at him when Ratliff made his request. Then the man's vacant half-grin subsided and he gazed down at his desk. He'd have to talk to the sheriff about a thing like that—True had hardly got good and sober yet.

As the man made his way toward the sheriff's quarters in the front of the building, Ratliff mused. Sober yet! It was hard to believe: the way booze had broken Bud—Bud, who could carry a barrelful; Bud,

443

who had practiced strict temperance on the river. He thought of the April trip long ago, soon after he had returned to rafting, when he'd stayed drunk in spite of Bud's remonstrance and had broken his oar. But Bud had seen to it that he got sober when the jug ran dry—and the river had furnished its grisly moral lesson—the river and the rivermen!

The iron door behind Ratliff clanged open and he turned about to face the sheriff: a short man who advanced, yanking at his gun belt fretfully. He was not of a mind to give his consent to such a visit—he hemmed and hawed. Finally he said he would go back and talk to the prisoner and if he consented—Ratliff had grown impatient, frowned at him, as he retreated with the keys.

And while he waited, the mouth of the jailer caused his frown to thicken. This True wasn't so dumb as they made out he was, the jailer said, his squinting face canted knowingly. *He* knew his game: True was trying to play crazy, shaking the bars in his door and calling out all sorts of gibberish. He had said once that Captain Sutton's poor wife had witched him—called her a bad name, she-devil was what it was—once said he might as well hang: 'She'd done ruint me anyhow,' was the way he put it. 'Ruint us both, and Ibby, too.' The jailer didn't know who all he could be talking about.

Ratliff wheeled and walked away, met the sheriff at the inner gate. The prisoner wouldn't answer him, the sheriff said. But Ratliff overran official reluctance, was led back into the iron-grilled corridor and to the door.

He blinked his eyes. In the dim light of the cell, he could barely make out Bud's hulk, in long drawers and undershirt, squatting on the edge of a quilt-covered bunk, facing the wall opposite. He had not stirred when the sheriff announced Ratliff, and he did not lift his head now that Ratliff spoke. Ratliff sensed that the sheriff was at his elbow still, and turned irritably and stared him into a hesitant retreat, then stepped into the cell.

444

He saw, as his eyes grew used to the light, that Bud's great head sagged between thin shoulders and that the arm on his knee had a wasted look. His jaw hung loose, like a shoe last in a sack. The sack was his pallid, sunken cheeks, stubbled with dead-white beard. A numbed inertness overspread the brow, the lowered gaze, though Ratliff could perceive that he was aware of him from the corner of his eye.

Like an old, wind-broken ox, stalled at the yoke, Ratliff thought incredulously, and gooseflesh hardened on his neck and spine. Was it Bud, was it really Bud? He felt inclined to weep, then a suffocating tension gripped him. Could this dumb, broken old man have killed his wife? He took a step nearer, putting his hand on the chain that suspended a corner of the bunk, and cleared his throat. 'Did you do it, Bud?' His voice had the sound of crushing cardboard.

Bud's eyes blinked, shifted, but there was no answer. After a long, staring moment, Ratliff began to tremble. He stepped quickly to the door to see where the sheriff stood and returned. There was a feverish excitement in his face. 'Is this thing a frameup, Bud?' he whispered hoarsely. 'Have they put you into this?'

Bud shook his head, as if at the buzzing of a fly. He frowned slowly and lifted his face. He spoke in a harsh, dry voice. 'Kain't yuh leave me alone now, Sutton? I done admitted to it—ain't that enough?'

Ratliff flinched, then his neck swelled and his arm shook the chain it held, but after a moment he turned away. Bud's crazy, he thought; he has surely lost his mind. He moved to the cell door and lifted his foot to step out, yet he turned again and went back. 'I can't believe it, Bud—why in God's name did you do it?' he said huskily. Bud only frowned and shook his head. 'You, of all men in the world! Robbie, of all people!'

Shaking his head still, Bud spoke gruffly. 'Whiskey don't pick, nor choose.'

Ratliff held on to the chain. 'But it ain't like you, Bud—sober, or drunk—me, the oldest friend you got!'

Bud's numb face winced, began to work. He made a throaty, growling sound, and suddenly he was upright, on his feet, holding to the lattice of the cell. 'Friend!' he said, and his bleared eyes shone. 'Not since you quit the river, not! And she always was ag'in me.' His head, as he stood bracing himself, shook with palsy and his dry voice cracked when he spoke again. 'I done it, Snake, and I'm man enough to take the consequences. 'Tain't nuthin' to be gained a-mouthin' 'bout it!' He stood straight now on his one good leg, his head thrown back, its shaking stilled, his brows drawn down with their old fierceness, and he stared on at Ratliff, stared accusingly.

Ratliff's anger had flared in Bud's cell. Passion had shaken him violently and the hand gripping the bunk support had been hard to restrain. It may have been well that the sheriff had moved back to the door and spoken to him. Bud seemed no longer harmless and pitiful, he *should* be hanged! Ratliff had left the jail with a hard face and eyes that glittered. His wrath had burned bitterly through the night—till sleep released him.

And in the morning, as he sat in his armchair in his library, he blew upon the coals again: Bud was not crazy—he was a drunken beast! But somehow the coals did not blaze up: his anger did not immerse him. He gazed out of the window toward the marsh and felt alone, strangely, utterly alone. It was as if he lay surrounded by an empty, forceless stillness—as if he had been cast there by a horse now fled, at the end of a mad, precipitous ride.

'What the hell has happened to me?' he asked, turning to stare at the wall. *Why did it happen? Why is Robbie dead? Why did Bud, of all men, kill her? Why am I here alone, without a friend—without anything—without a God, I guess—Why?* He gripped the chair-arms and stared on.

446

Yes, Robbie. Robbie, he had somehow failed. He relaxed a moment and leaned back. But surely he had been right there: if he'd ever known, felt dead sure of anything, it was that God had willed their marriage? His gaze was on the ceiling, and fleetingly, thinly, her face passed before it: the eyes, dark, staring, with the look of fear, before the parlor fire. He winced, and half-rose from his chair, but sat slowly back again. Yes, you got so hard, so ruthless, he told himself, that even she was scared of you!

But it could not have started there: that had betokened the end. He leaned his elbow on the chair and rubbed a sweaty, shaky palm over his forehead, through his hair. And the beginning: the morning in the church, in the little back room, where he'd been so sure—'Yes, by God! And we'll ask your father, too'—What of that? But he *had* asked him! Ratliff was not now convinced.

It would take too long to get his consent, you thought, and you hated the old man Macgregor so, he told himself. Oh, you persuaded Robbie, but were you really thinking of Robbie then, and of your God? He rose and paced the floor.

'And He gave you a second chance,' Ratliff murmured, letting himself into the chair again, the eyes in his yellowish face, fever-blurred. The hurricane. And it wasn't *your hurricane,* but God's, for his own inscrutable purposes. Yet you had your opportunity and read it wrong. You failed your chance to be there, help tote in the drowned, the distressed, restore the wreckage—to win your way to Darien's better, warmer side, and a place for both of you. Thinking only of Robbie, you said. But you were thinking of yourself and your hard feelings against them!

Near noon, however, Ratliff was brought back to the present moment, to the Darien he had made for himself. In a note apologizing for his intrusion, Edward Dale asked an urgent business meeting, and Ratliff felt wearily annoyed as he read. But one sentence stirred his anger: a sympathetic suggestion that a long, recuperative journey, a European trip might be arranged for him. European trip! Yes, Dale would like to get him out of the way now and quickly, to get his hands on things! By God, you are no more selfish, no more grasping, no harder than Dale, or the rest of these damned buyers, he told himself. He'd be there to a dead certainty, he'd be in Darien right on with satisfaction of knowing they were not enjoying it.

'Tell 'im I'll be ready after the meeting at the courthouse in the morning,' Ratliff barked at Dale's coachman through the door.

But the wine of his power did not warm his blood through the afternoon. It grew stale, feeble, in the face of his unremitting consciousness of the courthouse meeting. Dale had arranged that, too, taken over the case—and even old man George had dug up a witness, McDeeds had told him: a steamboat captain who had heard Bud defame Robbie. Ratliff was pacing the shell walk in his garden and his face flushed. George knows Bud was your old river-mate: he wants to see him hanged, he told himself with sudden vehemence. They all do: to torture you! He turned and strode into the house.

But in the library, at his window again, his loneliness returned—a sense of solitude that spread beyond the marsh's sweep, beyond the hairline horizon. It seemed unbearable. God, it won't bring Robbie back, he thought, a flat copperish taste rising in his throat—none of this—even hanging Bud! He dropped into his chair. 'Even hanging me and Bud both won't bring her back!'

He stared on painfully at the wall, as the phrase echoed in his head: *me and Bud both.* He had used it many times, over many years—though not so much of late. 'It ain't fightin' be it 'gaitors aer men, that makes a raftsman: it's a-puttin' your timber to this Boom!' The words shook out of the mist of his memory: he had thought them over often in those days—river days. That was the raftman's First Commandment: put your timber to the Boom. And it was right! He sat up, a sudden stirring of certainty, of discovery within him.

448

He got up nervously and moved away from the chair. Me and Bud both, he repeated. It brought him now a lift: a memory of triumph: the afternoon he had sat on the capstan of the *Hessie*, beside Bud, among his fellow raftsmen, after he had duped Pitt with hollow logs. He paused at the heavy, book-littered table, tasting the emotion over again. It was more than triumph, than applause, that you felt when you sat there, he told himself finally. You felt a solid sort of security— and something more: a hard-earned ease of conscience—yes, conscience was the word. The conscience of a riverman!

But you're still a riverman, he told himself, holding on to the table; you've never thought of yourself as anything else. He gripped the edge for a long, a dreadful moment, then turned away, his mouth open, his lank face twisted. There had been no flash, no image, no panorama of his struggle here—for his tavern, for the inspectorship, for his present high position—but its cumulative, till-now-unrecognized residue of disgust, had welled up in him, like bitter undigested food. He walked the floor. 'A riverman!' he said aloud. You quit the river, quit rivermen. You had washed the mud off your feet, you said. And since, you've beaten them and betrayed them, when and where it served your ends. No. You deserted the river. You came to Darien to make her *your son-of-a-bitch*—to hang Bud True!

It was late the next morning when Ratliff mounted his bay mare to ride over the old shell road to Darien, to the courthouse. It was later, and he swung his leg over the saddle in haste and clucked the horse on, as his foot fumbled to get the stirrup. He bent forward and urged his mount into a gallop, through the open gate, along the sandy lane under an arch of moss and bough, to the hoof-ringing highway. The meeting was less than an hour away, and he hurried.

But it was more than time he fled. He had been harried throughout the night by questions still unanswered, by bitter, weighting choice, by dreams. Restful sleep had not come till daybreak, till complete exhaustion, and he had overslept. His dressing, his cup of coffee, had been done in a numb, half-waking, shrinking dread.

And now he rode in haste to escape the thoughts, the dreams whose shadows lay upon him. And he glanced about, as he swung with his saddle, diverting his attention to bush, to tree, to limb along the way: the familiar way, passed in season and out—and once in the angry grip of a hurricane—and he in Destiny's grasp! It was useless: to wake, to look, was to return to his bitter world. Subconsciously his hand reined in the mare: his thoughts had caught up with him.

He leaned over his horse's neck as he rode, actually, physically bowed, but the bowing, the bending he felt within him was lower far. The numbness of shock had partly gone and feeling had returned to his emotional being—and with its pain a pervading, an awesome sense of punishment. Fever hardened. From time to time he glanced quickly, half-consciously over his shoulder, as if he heard a footstep, felt a shadow. He muttered aloud, 'Dreams! Just dreams!' And once he turned his mare about, toward home, though he brought her around again. The question hammered in his head, like a horse's hoofs: *What has happened to me, and why?*

He loosed his reins, gripped the saddle pommel and sat up. 'Power is not enough!' he said finally and aloud, 'here, or anywhere.' The horse moved slowly on. You called them blind, butt-headed bastards there on Clayhole Bluff, he told himself. You quit the river and came to town. But you never did join up—to anything. Yes, you thought you'd joined with Robbie, but you never did accept her—what she stood for. You tried to make her yours: what you stood for.

And what was that? Nothing. Nothing, but your selfishness! It had been something once, but you kicked it off behind you. You had no crowd. You had no rules—you dropped them, too, after you got here; you broke your bonds with everyone—and self, blind self, swallowed you.

Selfishness becomes greed and hate, when turned loose. And greed and hate have no heart, no shame—they keep no faith with man, or God. They eat up a man's integrity!'

'Blind, butt-headed bastards?' he muttered, as he pulled the rein. They may not have known how to handle the buyers, but they knew who their friends were! Suddenly, his knees gripped the horse's sides and he caught hold of the pommel with his hands. The skin on his neck grew rigid and his hair set itself, stood out. The dream, the vision of his fitful sleep, had swept down upon him.

There on Clayhole Bluff, with the darkness coming on, and it had seemed that he, Ratliff, stood watching the raftsmen turn one by one to leave him, their faces strange, livid, sightless. Then suddenly, with great, soundless detonation, a light came up the slope from the creek and he looked and saw that it was Bud—not broken, or crippled, but towering high—billows of smoke whirling from his short-stemmed pipe and over his shoulders. And Bud came on, with giant strides, and the sun was at his back. Nearer, nearer he came. And Ratliff had awakened in cold sweat and shaking.

Then sleep returned, and Bud was coming toward him again, luminous in heavy fog that lay upon a dark, swollen river with which Ratliff found that he was struggling, on a raft, a bow oar in his hands. And again Bud moved in giant strides, and again smoke—now fiery red—whorled over his shoulders from his pipe. He spoke no word, but he grew bigger as he came, at him, at Ratliff, until he was gargantuan. And Ratliff saw his face, the great cheeks flattened and the brows drawn down, and then his eyes—they were the hard, accusing eyes of Bud standing in his cell in the jail. And Ratliff, quailing, cried out and dropped to his knees. Then between Bud's giant limbs, beyond, in the amorphous, the disintegrating mist, he saw a thin, a fading steamboat, and he recognized the shadowy texas and the green blinds.

451

The mare had stopped and Ratliff found, as the remembered vision faded, that he had drawn the rein in chokingly. He loosed it with fumbling hands and slowly relaxed. Robbie went, as Poss had gone, he mused. The horse began to move. 'It was Bud's hand,' he said aloud, 'but not Bud's will!' Suddenly, he kicked the mare's sides, yanked her rein, put her into a gallop.

The others all were waiting when he and McDeeds finally entered the solicitor's office: the Dales, their lawyer, the round-faced state's attorney. And they sat about the same dark varnished table with its smears of dust.

McDeeds held back to let Ratliff move ahead, and his usually impassive features showed uneasiness. But Ratliff's face, still thin and pale, wore a solemn, a tranquil look, and his level eyes were clear and green. He advanced deliberately. He was sorry to have kept them waiting, he said, but he had a decision to make.

He stood at the table-end and slowly tilted his long head, looked goat-wise down his cheeks. 'It is this,' he said: 'I think the defendant, Bud True, is plainly insane and was insane when he killed my wife. I will not agree to prosecute him.'

He turned, putting his black hat on his head, and spoke to McDeeds as he passed him. 'You can reach me in the future at Longpond: I'll be up on the Oconee.' He walked out of the room, from the courthouse into the sunlight.

THE END

An Afterword:
Brainard Cheney and *River Rogue*
by Stephen Whigham

Brainard Cheney published his first novel, *Lightwood*, in 1939. The novel covered a period from circa 1870 through 1890, retelling in fiction the story of the Dodge Land Wars. Local landowners ("squatters") battled northern investors who came to harvest the vast timber forests in south Georgia along the Ocmulgee and Oconee Rivers. The book received favorable reviews and sold modestly.

A fifth-generation native of the area, Cheney grew up in Lumber City on the Ocmulgee River. He knew of the long, colorful history of rafting timber down the river to sell at Darien on the Georgia coast. He wanted to re-create that lost world in a 'picaresque' novel of the era. As a boy of sixteen, he experienced the waning days of the river-rafting culture, once working as a bowhand on a timber raft.

Cheney applied for and received a Guggenheim Fellowship to begin as of April 1, 1941. The funds enabled his return to south Georgia to research and write his second novel, *River Rogue*. The Guggenheim Foundation's Report for 1941-42 notes that Cheney was: "Appointed for creative writing; tenure, twelve months from April 1, 1941."

Newspaperman Cheney used his investigative skills in preparing the novel. Interviewing local raftsmen and assorted river men and once again traveling as a raft hand downriver, he alternated living between Lumber City and Darien during the latter part of 1941.

The Cheney archives at Vanderbilt University contain numerous small notebooks used in his information gathering. Written in pencil, the notes reveal extensive research and interviewing. Assisted by his friend, Robin Bess, he located many elderly denizens of the once-booming timber trade. Their stories inform the narrative of Ratliff "Snake" Sutton, timber rafter and protagonist of *River Rogue*.

Robin Bess, born into slavery eighty years earlier, once rafted timber on the rivers. Still strong and vital in 1941, he traveled with Cheney through the area's backcountry helping to reimagine the lost world of the Ocmulgee and Altamaha timber rafting era. Cheney's third novel, *This is Adam*, tells Robin's inspiring story.

In a 1942 newspaper article, Brainard Cheney recounts spending several weeks in Darien while working on the novel. He rented a room in a local home, taking his meals at a restaurant nearby. He later speculated that his shadowy presence piqued the interest and even the suspicion of the local citizens of the small town.

Towards the end of his research, he rose early one Sunday morning to take a long drive from Darien to Savannah. He drove along, his thoughts enmeshed in the late 1800's and the river rafting culture portrayed in his book. The scenery along the way evoked strong images of that now-vanished era. Returning to Darien, he visited the local café for a late lunch. Cheney commented to the proprietor that people on the streets appeared worried and distracted.

"You haven't heard?" the man responded. "Japan attacked us at a Navy base in Hawaii and we are now in a war."

For months, by his own description, Cheney had resided in the world of old-time Darien and rivers of days gone by. Current events brought him back into the present with a thunderbolt. He remained in Darien for most of December and finished the new novel soon after.

River Rogue appeared in 1942. Once again he received good reviews and modest sales. MGM optioned the film rights. Wartime budgetary restrictions later prevented its production.

Brainard Cheney published two more novels, *This is Adam* (1958) and *Devil's Elbow* (1969). He died in 1990 at the age of 89.

CPSIA information can be obtained
at www.ICGtesting.com
Printed in the USA
LVHW081150170520
655852LV00016B/739/J